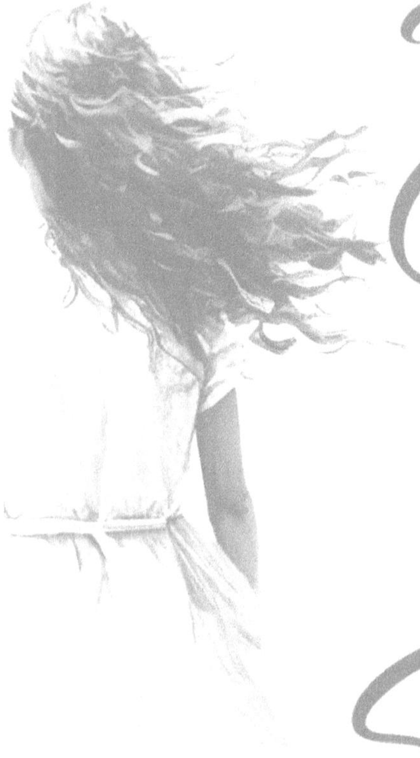

The Other Side of the Season

Jenn J McLeod

The Other Side of the Season. (International)

Second edition January, 2025 (01/2025) by Wild Myrtle Press.

First published in 2016 by Simon & Schuster (Australia) Pty Ltd

Copyright ©Jenn J. McLeod 2025

National Library of Australia Cataloguing-in-Publication entry

Creator: McLeod, Jenn J., author

Title: The Other Side of the Season/Jenn J. McLeod

ISBN: Paperback 978-0-6459976-3-7 and ISBN: eBook 978-0-6459976-2-0 (epub)

Subjects: Modern & Contemporary Fiction, Family Relationships, Australia

Dewey Number: A823.

Cover design by Annie Seaton

Photo credit: © scaliger / Adobe Stock

Font: Alpine by Charles Borges de Oliveira / Adobe Fonts

Printed and bound in Australia.

Wild Myrtle Press does not mass produce and store books in warehouses. We print as required with Ingram Spark Publishing because POD (print on demand) books are more economically viable and environmentally friendly. The author has not used AI to create the characters, nor to bring them and their stories to life. Also, as we are proudly Australian, we use Aussie spelling and language (edited by humans). :)

As always, to Jeannette (The J) McAnderson, who supports me no matter the season - and no matter my stormy writer moods!!

I prefer winter when you feel the bone structure of the landscape, the loneliness of it, the dead feeling of winter.
Something waits beneath it; the whole story doesn't show.

Andrew Wyeth, 1917–2009

PROLOGUE

THE BLUE MOUNTAINS, 2015

Sorry was all he wrote, each shaking stroke of his pen scratching against the sheet of fancy paper. Unspoken, the solitary written word seemed hollow and meaningless. There were so many things to be sorry about. Sometimes he was sorry he'd been born at all. But how does one explain that in a letter? Besides, who would care to know all he'd done— and all they had done *to* him?

Outside the guest room, winter-grey mountains sat against a dawn sky brushed purple and gold. Soon enough, the familiar mist would tinge the world outside his window blue. The haze was oil particles emitted by eucalypt trees, fusing with chimney smoke from nearby houses—homes warm and welcoming of family and of friends. That's what life was meant to be like.

Not like this.

Not alone.

Not sad, not scared, and not sorry.

And yet there was that single, unsaid word staring back at him from the page.

Sorry.

And he was so very, very sorry, penning a brief message and

addressing it: *To anyone who cares.* Three short sentences over three lines. The writing of them a defining moment for Albie.

But this second note—this apology—was more complicated. This would be his last chance to explain what he was sorry about.

If only he could find the right words so she could understand and know the truth.

His version of the truth, at least, because there's two sides to every person and another side to every story.

WATERCOLOUR COVE, 2015

'Get that clodhopper of a foot off my dashboard, Jake.' Sidney thumped the lump of solid shoulder muscle sculpted from his years of hauling heavy tubs of ice and freshly caught fish.

'Huh?' Her brother mumbled himself awake. 'What's up, sis?' A flick of his finger nudged the brim of his peak cap higher, letting Jake peer over the top of his metal-rimmed sunglasses. 'And what have you done with Byron Bay?'

'Sit up,' Sidney replied, noting the signpost. 'Two kilometres and we're there.'

'There where, exactly? Didn't we not long ago cross over Mooney Mooney Creek Bridge?'

'About four hours. You've been great company.'

'Four hours from Mooney and we're in Byron? Really?' Jake sat straight. 'The place looks different from what I remember.'

'Very funny. This isn't Byron Bay, and you know it.'

'Then I take it your "we're there" is premature. Wake me when we arrive, will ya? And do you think we can turn the heat down? A bloke could bake in this car.'

Her brother burrowed back into the seat, rested his chin on his chest and pretended to nod off again.

'I made an executive decision while you were sleeping,' Sid announced, glimpsing her travel-weary face in the rear-view mirror and wishing Jake hadn't got all the good looks.

He peeked sideways from under his cap. 'My big sister is making decisions on the fly? Since when?'

Jake was right. While he'd inherited the impulsive gene from some distant relative, Sid, older by ten years, was usually more prudent—a mix of her mother's cautiousness and her father's need for order and routine. But with the recent overdose of motherly advice, and with life about to flip on its head in a matter of months—her routine out the window—a little spontaneity seemed like the perfect panacea.

But the detour wasn't entirely spur of the moment.

'Sidney? Out with it.' Jake sat up again, taking an interest in the change of scenery. Where thick unwieldy trees and shrubs had lined the roadside earlier, vegetation was now sparse and pruned to accommodate traffic signs, advertising billboards, and local tourist information. 'Where are we and what are you up to?'

'Nothing!' Even Sid thought she sounded like a guilty ten-year-old. 'I saw the name of the town and I liked it. Watercolour Cove sounds special, don't you think? And I needed a break from the highway driving.' Sid also silently enjoyed the feel of her new car wending its way along the narrow ribbon of bitumen that traced a wide river, on which an occasional deep-sea fishing boat floated at anchor, bows pointed into the breeze. 'Isn't this view beautiful?' she asked. 'Besides, Byron Bay is overrated, overcrowded, and overpriced—even in winter. We *are* both out of work.'

'And lying never has been your strong suit, sis. What gives? The idea of this road trip was to check out the employment scene. There'll be jobs in Byron. Besides, the further north we go, the warmer the winter for cold frogs, like you.' Jake attempted to adjust the temperature control again.

She slapped his hand away. 'I agree there are probably more job opportunities, but also more people vying for them. The odds might be better in a small, out-of-the-way place.'

Jake eyeballed his sister. 'How out of the way are we talking?'

'Oh, a few kilometres from the Pacific Highway.'

'There's that face again, Sid. I've known when you're fibbing, ever since you told me the tooth fairy forgot to leave money under my pillow. How many is a few kilometres?'

'Ooh, about twenty-five—give or take a kilometre. Besides, I needed to refuel.'

'And a twenty-five-kilometre detour from the country's busiest highway was your best re-fuelling option?' Jake checked the time as Sid pulled into a small garage in the heart of the Watercolour Cove township.

'Too late to hit the highway now. It'll be beer o'clock soon enough. This town better have a pub.'

'No pub!' Her brother repeated the petrol station attendant's answer while the bloke robbed Sidney of an exorbitant amount of money for one night's villa accommodation in the caravan park behind the garage. 'I've heard of the pub with no beer, mate, but what kind of small Aussie town doesn't have a watering hole for thirsty travellers?'

The attendant shrugged. 'Renovations. Closed till July.'

'July? That's an entire month away.'

Another shrug. 'Today is the first day of winter. Few people come here at this time of year. Most head further north. Byron's warmer, with better swells.'

'Told you so, sis.'

Sid slipped the credit card back into her wallet. This trip was going to cost more than she'd first thought. Money that would've been better off earning interest until the end of next month when she planned to be back home, in time for the July sales. She'd be needing new furniture and stuff to set up her own place because she wasn't staying at her mother's any longer than necessary. Mid-October was her absolute deadline. *If* she survived her mother that long.

'Fish co-op only operates till two pm.' The attendant handed Sidney a giant key tag, the words *Gumnut Cabin* burned into a varnished piece of wood. 'The Fisho's Club on the other side of the cove is good for a beer, and it's walking distance. Follow the path from the seawall, head along the beach and up the other side. You'll see it past the jetties and before the co-op. Bistro's open and not bad, *if* Cook's having a good day.' The mechanic with the winter tan flicked his wild mane of surfer-boy bleached hair.

'I like my seafood,' Jake said.

'In that case, take the car and follow the river back along the bottom of the mountain behind us. A few kilometres along you'll find Moonlight Oysters.'

Jake took the villa key and his sister's elbow, guiding her out of the small shop. 'Oysters! Okay, now we're talking. Come on, sis, your shout.'

'Maybe tomorrow, Jake. I don't want to get back in the car. Let's walk the main street and check out the Fisho's Club for dinner tonight.'

'Don't get excited about the main street,' he said, having surveyed the same short length of divided road with its median-strip garden bed bursting with brightly coloured pigface plants.

A row of shops, each one painted a different colour, lined one side of the road, and opposite was a beachside reserve, but with a poorly placed public amenities building that blocked what would otherwise be breathtakingly beautiful estuary views. While a painter of considerable talent had attempted to re-imagine the scenery, the artwork was no substitute for real life. Further along the street, the footpath detoured into a paved courtyard ringed by more small businesses: a café with wooden tables and chairs fixed in place—market umbrellas folded away and stacked in one corner—a tattoo parlour called Squid's Ink, and a hairdressing salon called Salt Spray that advertised fifty percent off foils. Sid needed a spruce up. She might feel like crap most days, but—to use her mother's expression—there was no need to look like she had given up caring completely. Not one to mince her words, their mum's critical business eye and expectations flowed over to her family, often resulting in criticisms—like her daughter's increasingly frequent fashion faux pas. Natalie, on the other hand, looked immaculate day and night, her make-up faultless from breakfast to bedtime, with not a single strand of bottle-blonde hair ever out of place.

Standing outside the only unoccupied shop in the small courtyard, and staring at the section of window glass not obliterated with political posters and community notices, Sid caught her reflection: the comfortable track pants pulling a little too tight, the shapeless hoodie hanging a little too loose, and more hair *out* than *in* the elastic band. Mourning her job loss, and the seven years of her life given to building Zeus Design Studio, Sid had ceremoniously ditched business suits months ago for comfortable pants and oversized jumpers. She'd also given up complexion-enhancing makeup, expensive foils to enliven her mousey-brown hair, and styling products that added no style because, according to a magazine article, all cosmetics and dyes were potential poisons. Instead, Sid was rediscovering a love of face freckles, no longer bothering to cover the sprinkling that had speckled her nose and cheeks since childhood. And, much to her mother's chagrin, no longer did she wrestle with the round brush and hair dryer to coerce the waves into a more corporate look, instead convincing herself that unemployment was a liberating experience to be embraced. And so far, so good. With the odd bit of freelance work to keep money coming in, she was eating three healthy meals a day and thinking positive—most of the time—about herself and her future.

But on those days when it appeared her mother was right about Sid giving up on everything, including her appearance, she struggled emotionally and looked for ways to occupy her mind. Recently, while sorting the recycle—just because—she'd found a letter. And not just any letter. A scrunched letter in the bin.

'Are you listening, sis?' Jake said, tugging at the ponytail Sid favoured these days.

'Sorry, Jake, I'm more tired than I thought. What were you saying?'

'I told Mum we'd ring when we got to Byron,' he repeated. 'Better call and fill her in.'

'No!' Sidney snapped. 'I mean, yes, we can call, but maybe we shouldn't tell her where we are *exactly*. It's not as if a small detour matters and she might worry. Besides, it's only been a couple of days. Let her settle into Melbourne. We know how full-on a visit to Aunty Tasha's can be.'

'Sidney? What are you up to?'

'Nothing, Jake.'

'Nuh-ah! This is not your *nothing* face. This is your *uh-oh flippin' fish-cakes* face. And I *will* tell Mum, you know. I'm not too old to dob if my big sister leads me astray.' The conspiratorial squint suggested he was kidding, easing her concerns.

'Mum's upset enough with the B & B shutting, and that terrible business. She doesn't need to know about our change of plans.'

Jake stepped in front, blocking Sid's path. 'Then tell me, or I'll—'

'Okay, okay. I found something.'

'Like what? Gold in them big ol' hills up there? What about sunken treasure in the little cove, me hearty?'

'A letter, Jake. I found a letter. Can we keep walking, please? This wind is cold.' She darted around her brother, forcing him to follow and catch up.

'Keep talking,' he said. 'Where did you find this letter?'

'At home. In the bin. I assumed Mum threw it away.'

The pair crossed the road, heading for the crescent-shaped stretch of sand the bloke at the bowser had said would lead them to the Fishermen's Club.

'You owe me an explanation. I'll have a draught beer at the same time. Come on. Get a move on. A man could die of thirst at this pace.'

'Well, flip me a fishcake!' Jake looked up from the letter in his hand as Sidney returned with a glass of pale ale for him and a lemon squash for her, hoping the sugar would hold back the headache.

'Now *you* know as much as I do.'

'And this is why you've dumped me in a town with no pub,' Jake said. 'Hmm! Might it not have been better to ask Mum? Or are the two of you still playing no talkies since the last spat?'

'Ask her what? Why she's never told us we have a grandfather living only a seven-hour drive north of Sydney? And why, when he's asking to reconnect with his son, she chucks the letter in the bin. Did she even answer? And why not share the news?'

'All reasonable questions,' Jake said. 'Do you have any answers? Did you ask?'

Ice cubes bobbed in Sid's glass as she poked at them with the drinking straw. 'I sort of fished around two weeks ago when I found it.'

Jake snorted. 'Sis, you fish like you drive.' He folded his arms on the table and shook his head. 'I knew something was going on with you two. The atmosphere at home has been colder than a Tibetan tin toilet seat.'

'Try living there day in and day out.'

'No thanks.' Jake sculled his beer. 'One visit a week is more than enough. So, what resulted from your fishing expedition?'

'At first, Mum said she was respecting our father's wishes. Then she reminded me, in true Natalie fashion, how he'd been estranged from his parents since marrying, and that he'd wanted nothing to do with them.'

'And then you what?' Jake asked.

'Well, then we kind of argued—again—about something I can't remember. You know how Mum changes the subject when it suits her.'

Their mother had been furious. In hindsight, confronting Natalie about the letter over dinner had been a bad idea, especially with mother and daughter not seeing eye to eye on much over the years, including their recent disagreement.

'And then?' Jake stared harder.

'I suggested she was wrong to keep something like that from us. Dad was the one with the family issues. Surely you and I can choose to reconnect with our relatives.'

'And so, Sid, you planned this little detour from the get-go.' Jake sounded miffed. 'And you figured you'd let me in on the secret when, exactly?'

'Look, Jake, we'll get to Byron, okay? In the meantime, you might like to know our grandfather's letter mentions a beach house in Watercolour

Cove. Naturally, I was curious to see the place. A couple of days here won't hurt.'

'And the fact that this grandfather of ours is in prison doesn't add a degree of difficulty, Sid?'

'I'm kind of working things out on the run. Sorry I didn't tell you sooner.' Sid's gaze followed her brother's to the cluster of shacks set back along the beach, their front yards wild with dune vegetation.

'No worries, sis. Maybe this detour is not such a loony idea. After all, I didn't see too many houses as we drove through town, and if this grandfather of ours has a property in Watercolour Cove … Well, just check out those little beauties lining the beach. Pretty awesome if he owns one of those joints. Visiting him may put us in his good books *and his* will.' Jake winked.

'Be serious, would you?'

'I am, sis. A cheap reno, rustic tables, a small menu featuring the day's freshest seafood straight from the trawlers. Welcome to *Jake's Beach Shack Café. Ta-dum!*'

'Dream on, little brother. Firstly, we need to decide what to do about the information in the letter.'

Sid had found it while transferring paper from the kitchen tidy to the recycling bin, muttering as she'd sorted, 'How hard can it be to put paper in the recycling, Mum?'

While separating the collection of cardboard cartons and discarded tissue boxes from the rest, the envelope had landed on the floor. Seeing her father's name and a handwritten forwarding address had piqued Sid's curiosity. More than a decade had passed since his death. Why, or importantly how, would someone know to forward a letter to his wife in the Blue Mountains?

'And I assume, sis, you know where the Mid North Coast Correctional Centre is in relation to where we are now?' Jake asked.

'About an hour's drive inland.'

'I see, and the solicitor addressed the letter to Dad, so they assume he's still around.'

'Yes, and whatever happened between Dad and his parents must've been more serious than—as Mum tells it—disagreeing with his choice of a wife. So, Jake, we should take this matter one step at a time to avoid treading on anyone's toes.'

'We?' Jake sat straight, launching into his all-too-common meerkat pose.

'Or not,' Sid said. 'You don't *have* to stay or get involved. I'm more than happy to get in our grandfather's good books on my own. I'll let you know how things go.'

'Yeah, right, like the tooth fairy all over again.'

'I'm serious, Jake. Give me a few days to arrange a visit to the jail. If I choose to stay longer, you can take my car and head off.'

'You want to stay here so much you'll let *me* take your new car?'

Sid grinned. 'And that's why I insisted on bringing my pushy. I'll get by on a bike.'

'Are you planning to cycle that thing all the way back to the Blue Mountains when you're done?' Jake chuckled. Then his head cocked to one side. 'Come to think of it, sis, you're getting a bit beefy on the back-side. Exercising might keep that middle-aged spread at bay.'

'Thirty-five is hardly middle-aged. You'll know yourself in ten years. And nothing's spreading, thanks very much.'

'Yeah, but something's different about you. I mean, what's with the soft drink? Unless … Hey, are you preggers? That might account for the humungous arse you're cultivating.'

'You're hilarious, Jake.' Sid fiddled with the loose-fitting top. 'Wondered when you'd notice.'

'Seriously? My big sis is going to be a mum? Woo hoo!'

'Shush, Jake,' she said, a finger pressed against her lips. Sid wasn't announcing her pregnancy to all and sundry yet. At her recent appointment, the doctor had expressed concern about the baby's small size. He was monitoring both Sid and her little bump carefully, but Jake didn't need to know the detail, in case he told their mother, who would surely have something to say about Sidney not taking care of herself. 'I figured I'd break the news to you if you hadn't worked it out by the time the kid turned one.'

'Oh, so funny, Sid. Cheers, big ears!' Jake raised his glass and Sid realised how lucky she was to have him as a brother.

'So, like I was saying … I can take the train back from here, or if the timing's right, you can collect me on your way south.'

'Hmm.' Jake seemed to contemplate his options before grinning. 'I'm your brother and you're preggers. There'll be no getting a train alone and lugging a bike.'

'Pregnant ladies catch trains all the time, Jake.'

'Yeah, well, not my sister. In fact, stay off the bike.'

Sid smiled. 'Pregnant women also ride bikes.'

'Not in this town they don't. Look at those hills.'

Sidney squinted into the sienna-coloured fireball of sun now scorching the hilltops gold. The mountainous terrain sure was steep. Perhaps she should've expected as much when her quick web search described Watercolour Cove not as a town but as a tourist attraction. Those hills were the Great Dividing Range's most eastern point, and the only place where the north/south escarpment that stretched along the eastern side of the continent connected with the ocean.

'One for the road,' Jake said, already en route to the bar.

With a slice of sun barely hanging on, the hills were now a dark backdrop to the small seaside town nestled at their base. From the closed-in deck of the club with its smeared plastic awning, Sid stared through the sea mist at the fuzzy yellow lights of the village. One by one lamps flicked on, lighting the seawall walk but leaving the crescent-shaped cove in darkness. Only the white crests of small waves were visible where they rolled onto the shore.

'Starry night,' she said as her brother returned with his second beer. 'It'll be cold.'

'Not in Byron!' Jake's grin was so wide it spread to her own face.

She poked out her tongue and wrapped her jacket around her body before pointing at the glow atop the tallest mountain. At first, she'd thought the spot was a star.

'See the tiny light, Jake? At the highest peak?'

'Sure. What about it?'

'I wonder what sort of person would live up there?'

'Easy answer,' he said. 'Someone who doesn't ride a bike!'

2

THE GREENHILL BANANA PLANTATION, 1979

'Get off those bikes, you two, and help Albie and Matthew. These bananas won't pack themselves. And put your jumper on, David, or you'll catch your death.'

'Yeah, moron, what Dad said. It's winter now. Or maybe you're planning on painting yourself some sunshine.'

Tilly wished she could defend David by delivering the mouthful of expletives Matthew's wisecrack deserved. She didn't.

'Hey, Dad,' David said, ignoring his brother. 'You'll never guess what Tilly and me did today.'

'I'm sure I can, boy.' He looked at his teenage son with a mix of love and tolerance.

'Let's show him, Tilly.' David was already flipping open the satchel hanging by her side—the one she always purposely draped between her breasts to make them look bigger.

'It's here somewhere.' David fossicked for his sketchpad, displaying the drawing on an upturned box where his father's knife skills swiftly and expertly de-handed bananas from thick stems. 'I was teaching Tilly about the rule of reflection—how everything has one.'

'One what, son?'

'A reflection, Dad.'

'Is that so?'

David nodded, stepping back as if critically appraising the artwork. 'I'm planning on a study in reflection for my final year assessment work at school. See this?' He pointed to the paper. 'If an object leans to the left, its reflection will also lean to the left.'

Tilly wished David wouldn't show her drawings to anyone, especially with his brother close by. Without even looking, she knew Matthew and the other workers in the packing shed would be grinning and rolling their eyes at each other.

'Reckon she learns quick, Dad?'

'If you say so, son. Now, I want you cleaned up, and be quick about it. Oh, and wash the charcoal off your face and hands before you touch the bananas.'

'Yeah, no *Marhkt* bananas at Greenhill. Right, Albie?' Matthew and his packer mates grinned like the idiots they were, shoving each other in a silent show of solidarity.

More like stupidity, Tilly mused.

Morons! She poked out her tongue, first at the boys, and then at Albie Marhkt for letting them make fun of his surname.

'Back to work, you lot. And Tilly?'

She turned, and in a voice sweeter than the scent on Mrs Hill's favourite roses, said, 'Yes, sir?'

'You should go home. And I'd be giving *your* hands a good scrub before your mother sees you.'

'Yes, Mr Hill.'

Tilly rammed her hands in the pockets of her pants and looked across at David, already doing what he'd been told, his hands in a lather of soap over the washbasin at the rear of the shed. There was no need to tell David anything twice. At seventeen, two years her junior, he was a good and obedient son—and smart. She'd figured as much the first time she saw him, in 1974. She'd been fourteen years old when Ulf had introduced them on the steep trip up the Greenhill plantation road. For five long years, she'd stuck it out on this mountain. David made the days bearable.

She turned toward his older brother, Matthew, and then looked at Albie, David's best friend, who lived with her on the Marhkt's plantation next door. With a quick flick of her middle finger, she spun around and strutted up the hill to the fork in the road that would take her home. Once there, Tilly would tiptoe down the hall, keen to see her face in the bathroom mirror before Hilda.

⁎

'I'm a zebra!' Tilly giggled at her reflection.

Having unsuccessfully scrubbed the charcoal stains from her cheeks, forehead and nose, she focused on the charcoal dust on her pants and in the pockets. She'd be in terrible trouble for getting dirty, but trouble and Tilly usually went hand in hand, and it wasn't unusual for her and David to lose track of the time. Today, the pair had spent too long at the cove—too caught up in leaving their mark on the most out-of-the-way rock on the seawall.

They'd begun their pastel drawing escapades years before, climbing down at low tide to the rocks closest to the waterline. Once there, they could stay out of sight, and the daily high tide would wash away any evidence of wrong doing. While some locals called David and Tilly vandals, and their work graffiti, such claims only encouraged the pair. Today, realising they'd spent too much time generally mucking about, David had packed up in a panic, tossing pens, paper, paints and pastels into their satchels before racing to collect their bikes at the start of the seawall.

'Last one is a rotten egg,' Tilly had yelled. Being lighter, nimbler, and faster, she'd easily taken the lead. But as laughter slowed her, and David closed in, she staged a stumble and dropped to the ground.

'Tilly! Oh no! Where are you hurt?' David asked, his eyes and hands surveying her limbs for visible injuries. 'Can you get up?'

Though tempted to ask that he carry her, David wasn't tall and athletic like his brother. Besides, she'd faked the fall to beat him. Tilly like winning. Also, she knew David would worry and put his hands on her to check for injuries. She liked him touching her, even encouraging him with tickling games when some hand grazes lingered longer in certain places.

'I can walk, but you'll have to hold me. Like this,' she said, wrapping his arm across the curve of her back.

'You know what, Til?' David said as they walked. 'One day, I'll choose the biggest rock above the high tide line and paint you a forever message that can't be washed away. And I won't care if everyone sees it.'

'What will the message say?' Tilly asked.

David winked. 'You'll have to wait and see.'

3

WATERCOLOUR COVE, 2015

'We wait?' Jake's outburst caused curious glances from other club patrons at the bar. 'For how long, sis?'

Sidney shrugged and slid her phone back into her pocket. 'How should I know? I asked for him by name and enquired about the jail's visiting times. The woman on the other end of the telephone said someone would call back during business hours.'

'They have business hours?'

'A prison isn't like a hotel. No twenty-four-hour concierge and no transferring calls to cells. Ringing them at this time of night was dumb. Besides, they probably verify the legitimacy of callers, and you and I are unlikely to be on a visitor list.'

'You didn't ask about him?'

'Not over the phone, Jake, and I can't cross-examine the woman.'

'Why not? You're an interrogation expert, sis.'

'And you, brother, are hilarious.' Sid's smile faded as she stared over his shoulder at the now pitch-black cove. 'Here I was thinking the hard part was deciding what to say to the man.'

'We could rob a bank, I suppose. That'll get us inside the joint.'

Sid didn't laugh. She lost her sense of humour around the same time she lost her job, her partner of seven years, and most of their shared friends.

'Why do you want to see the guy so badly, Sid? I never thought you cared about not having grandparents and all the messy stuff comes with extended families.'

'I did at school. The girls would talk about their huge family events, and how they'd borrow their sister's clothes. You?'

'Nah, not really into borrowing girly clothes, but big family feasts would've been cool. All of us sitting at a huge table picking at platters. We also might've had more people at Dad's funeral,' Jake added, serious now. 'Having no one from his side of the family made the whole thing sadder.'

'Members of his family died young. Isn't that what we were told growing up?'

'Yeah, and once upon a time I believe what I was told, including how tooth fairies forget.'

Sid didn't respond to her brother's joking, instead reminding him, 'None of this is remotely funny.'

'Neither is upsetting Mum, sis, and this caper of yours will, for sure. Maybe let it go.'

'But we're here now. The jail's not far away. I could take a drive there tomorrow. Fronting up and making enquiries in person, and with ID, might help the process, or even clear us for visiting on the spot. But if we must wait around here—all joking about inheritances aside—I seriously am happy to stay in town on my own.'

'Nah! I'll hang around Watercolour Cove, too,' Jake said. 'This could get interesting. Hey, love!' Jake nabbed the attention of the female bar attendant collecting glasses from an adjacent table. 'Know of any temporary work opportunities for a big, burly bloke like me?'

The girl raised a well-shaped eyebrow and shrugged, jerking her head towards the bar. 'Noticeboard has the odd thing, or you can ask at the co-op tomorrow.'

'What about a place to bunk down on a semi-regular basis?' When the girl glanced in Sidney's direction, Jake was quick to clarify. 'With my *sister*. So a couple of rooms.'

'Try the caravan park. They have two-room villas with a sofa bed. Nice, but not cheap. Entrance is behind the petrol station, over the road from the seawall.'

'Yeah, we know it. Thanks. Maybe I'll see you around.' Jake winked at the barmaid and gulped the last of his beer before burping a short tune.

'Oh, Jake!' Sid laughed, grateful to have a brother like him. 'I love you, you big ape. Come on. Let's go find a room for the night. And you'd better not snore.'

'*Brrr*! Shut the door, quick,' Sid demanded before the wintery sea breeze could seep into her bones. It was way too early to be facing the morning.

'Problem solved,' Jake announced.

'And which problem would that be?'

'As of now, we have a place to live—for free—and a paying job.' He plonked onto the chair opposite to Sid at the small table positioned under the villa's air conditioner, now rattling hot air into the room.

'Seriously?' she asked while scooping another spoonful of the healthy, homemade muesli she'd cooked and packed before leaving home: no salt, no sweeteners, no surprises. 'Where is this too-good-to-be-true opportunity?'

'I went running while you slept.' Jake was busy polishing the skin of an apple with his shirttail. 'By the way, Sid, your snoring would wake the dead.'

'Yeah, yeah, get on with your explanation.'

'Okay, well, I figured I'd check out if there was work going on a local trawler.'

'And?'

'Nothing on the boats, so I was checking out the fish co-op—at the same time checking out the blonde behind the counter. Her and I got talking and there's work on a local property—perfect for you *and* me.'

'Both?' Sid queried. 'Doing what?'

'Chuck some of that horse chaff in a bowl for me and I'll tell you.'

Sidney complied, but she worried. Jake had the worst employment record of anyone on the planet. Their mother was constantly on at him about being more responsible, while spoiling him rotten and doing his weekly laundry. Never short on ideas, the rambunctious, rebellious, and restless Jake had been a wild teen and a big dreamer. He'd failed to get good grades at school and also missed out on their mother's creative genes—and her ambition. Instead, he flitted from one seasonal hospitality job to another because the pay rates generally allowed six months working and six months skylarking.

Still with his boyish crop of dark curls, Jake had grown into their father, but that was where the resemblance ended. Both good looking, their dad had been a hardworking man who prioritised financial security, often to the point of penny-pinching. Frugal was probably the first word Sid had learned as a child. Reliable, loyal and a high achiever, she liked to think she took after him in that way. Father and daughter were also trusting, which meant disappointment came easily and too often. On the contrary, her mother trusted no one. Fiercely protective, Natalie took no prisoners. And no fight was too big when it came to family, which often meant arguing with her husband about not spending enough on the children, especially when they finally had the funds.

While Sid cared less than her mother about the material things money could buy, she shared both Natalie's creativity and drive to succeed. Sid hadn't realised how fiercely protective she could be, and how much like her mother she really was, until standing in front of Damien all those months ago. And what a moment of absolute clarity. The look on his face remained etched into her brain.

'You should've told me before, Sid,' he'd said that day.

—⊹—

'I'm telling you now. I've only just found out. It's not like I have a crystal ball or saw it coming.'

'No, Sid, but you have a thing called contraception. You told me you had it covered.'

'I did. It … It just happened.'

'Really? So, you didn't do this to make me marry you?'

Sid gasped. '*Make* you marry me?'

'Sorry, Sid, that sounds harsh. It's just …' Damien paced back and forth between the breakfast counter and the window of their tenth-floor apartment with its view of Melbourne's Yarra River. 'We never discussed kids.'

'But we did, Damien, before Lloyd and Justine's baby christening. When Lloyd asked you to be godfather, you told me you loved the idea of raising a child.'

'Yeah! Sure! Lloyd's child—and on a weekend, or every now and then. Shower the kid with gifts and hand it back. That kind of kid, Sid. Besides, my best mate asked. Was I supposed to say, "Thanks, but no thanks"? I thought you knew I was being polite.' When Damien reached out for her hands, Sid desperately searched for something to keep them busy, like tucking her shirt in the top of her trousers. She couldn't even look at him. 'You know I don't have what it takes to be a father full time. I'm busy growing a business. Our business is our baby.'

'I see,' Sid managed to say. 'And what do you expect me to do now?'

His shoulders jerked. 'I don't know. I thought we wanted the same thing. Now I'm kind of stumped.' The shaking head thing reminded Sid of a disappointed mother. 'Are you sure? Do we need another test?'

'If you're asking am I pregnant with *your* child, then the answer is yes.'

'Right,' was all he muttered into his coffee cup.

'Say something, Damien,' she demanded.

'I don't want to say the wrong thing and unduly influence your decision. This isn't my call.'

'Mmm, I see.' Sid knew then just how strong she had to be. 'So, I'll be making the biggest decision of my life on my own. Fine. I know what needs doing. Thanks for helping me see what's best.'

'Good girl,' Damien said before kissing her cheek, snatching up his car keys, and heading to work.

Jake shovelled a spoonful of muesli into his mouth and chewed it down before giving Sid a cocky grin. 'Did you hear me, sis? I said I'd like this recipe. It's good.'

'Sure, whatever.'

'Ooh, someone got out of the grumpy side of the bed this morning. Hearing about the job might put a smile on your dial.'

'Sure, Jake, when you're ready. I have all day to watch you eat breakfast.'

Washing the last mouthful of cereal down with a slurp of tea, Jake slid his cereal bowl to the centre of the table as though the dish might pick up the spoon and run away to the kitchen sink all on its own.

'Cushy caretaking job, only a few days a week,' he announced. 'And with perks you'll love.'

'Perks?' she queried while walking to the kitchenette. 'What sort?'

'For a start, it's a tourist operation with accommodation *and* a gallery —and pretentious prancing around an art gallery is right up your alley, sis. I, however, get to do the hard yakka and keep the property maintained.'

'And we get to live in?' Sid called back over the clatter of cutlery and running water. 'Sounds too good to be true. Who's offering the job?'

'Pearl referred to the place as The Greenhill Plantation, so I'm guessing it's the Greenhill's place.'

'And where exactly do we find these Greenhills?'

Jake wiped the back of his hand across the milk droplet on his chin. 'Last night, sitting at the club, you were curious about who lived in the house on top of the highest hill. Well …' Another grin, even more smug. 'If we pass muster, sis, you and *me* will live there—that's who.'

'Seriously?' Sidney bent over to peer out the villa's rear window and up through the tall palm trees. In the early morning light, the distant mountain was a patchwork of green and gold, with a narrow, winding ribbon of roadway leading to the dwelling perched at the very tip. 'And you're sure the job is for the two of us? Who told you?'

'Grab your coat, Madam Sceptic. I'll take you to the fish co-op and you can hear it all yourself from Pearl's lovely lips. Then you can tell me how smart I am.' Jake took the tea towel from Sid's shoulder. 'But be sure to pile on the praise so I make a good impression on Pearl.'

'Pearl?' Sidney pictured a little old lady with mauve hair and a matching twinset busily wrapping smelly fish in paper.

'Yeah, now get a move on, sis. She wants to meet you.'

As Jake blustered into the shop, Sidney close behind, the woman behind the counter waved.

'Hey, Pearl, this is my sister.'

Sid might have raised a hand in a hello had her arms not been tightly wrapped across her chest for warmth. Pearl, on the other side of the fish counter however, wore not very much at all. She was tiny, young and pretty—unusually so—with her skin colourless and her hair bleached as white as the shaved ice she spread across the fresh fish display that reeked of seafood and saltwater. The place ponged a lot like Jake when he'd worked at Sydney Fish Markets, coming home to Natalie's on a Monday, and always with a week's worth of laundry sealed in a plastic garbage bag. Jake's weekly cook-up night had been the one positive thing about Sid's move into her mother's house. But when her brother brought his smelly clothes home, she had wanted to hold her nose. She wished she could do so now.

'Hey-ya, Jake.' Plump lips painted bright red, smiled. 'And you're Sidney.' The girl extended the palest of arms, a purple climbing rose tattooed from her shoulder to her elbow. Her hair, currently in a pony-tail with the fringe held back by a pair of dark sunglasses resting on top of her head, was pure white, not simply over-bleached, as Sid had first thought. One thing was for sure—Pearl wore her complexion beau-tifully.

'Nice meeting you, too.' Forced to shake hands, Sid immediately regretted the cold, wet contact. 'Jake said you know about the Greenhill place offering work and accommodation.'

'Sure do. I head up the mountain a few times a week. I do remedial therapy—like massages and stuff,' Pearl clarified.

'You mean like a masseuse?' Jake's eager enquiry received the same eyebrow-raising reaction from both women. Sidney knew how his cheeky pea-sized brain worked.

Pearl grinned and stepped out from behind the counter. 'Not quite, Jake. There'd be even less call for *that* line of work in this town. My customers need healing hands, and most come to my place. I have a room set up. Others I visit, like the bloke who runs the gallery. I enjoy the work, plus he pays me to mind the shop, so to speak. It's a pleasant change.'

'From working with seafood?' Sid asked.

Pearl's snicker suggested fishy comments were right up there with her brother's masseuse remark. Sid wasn't sure either of them had impressed Pearl.

With the toe of her red gumboots, Pearl kicked a crate of fresh milk across the floor, lowered her sunglasses to her face and began stocking the self-serve fridge, at the same time talking over her shoulder. 'After all these years, the smell no longer bothers me. But about the job … Green-hill was one of the earliest banana plantations in the district, and for years the most productive—a third-generation family business. But things changed in the 1990s slump—about the time I was born. Twenty-five years on, the main house is an overpriced B & B throughout summer for snobs, and a gallery for artistic snobs all year round. Because the place provides an outlet for local artists to display and sell their work, I tolerate the arty-farty folk—if they bring their money with them.'

Jake butted in. 'Sid's keen to know about the accommodation.'

'There are two worker cottages, while the main house has six guest bedrooms with two share bathrooms. The two of you will occupy the smaller, self-contained caretaker cottage.' She grinned—probably at Sid's expression—and kicked the empty milk crate so it skated over wet tiles to the far end of the counter. 'If it helps, there's a pull-out sofa bed. Past managers have been husband and wife.' She shrugged. 'Maybe play it by ear for a few days. You could make your own accommodation arrange-ments in town, of course. But take it from me, a villa will send you broke.'

'Don't we know it,' Jake said, examining the icy display.

'Besides, I can tell you from experience, having helped out on the hill since the last workers bolted, travelling up that road every day gets tire-some, which makes me thrilled you're interested in the job.'

'Have there been many past managers?' Sidney queried. Maybe this offer was too good to be true.

'There's nothing sinister about the place or the job, if that's what you're thinking. Mostly people are travellers passing through. Like you, they come, stay a while, and go. Although …' Pearl scanned the shop before leaning over the counter, a finger beckoning Sid closer as she slid the sunnies to the top of her head. Pearl's eyes, blue and framed by strikingly white lashes were the most dazzling Sid had ever seen. 'The owner can be stroppy. He dislikes art snobs and elitists equally. As the gallery gets a few of them, he mostly keeps to himself, and he *never* mixes with the guests when they're staying.'

Or the help, Sidney figured. That was fine with her.

'And when do we meet him to talk about the job?' she asked Pearl.

'He leaves the hiring up to me, and as I'm a jill-of-all-trades until the jobs are filled, consider yourselves hired—unofficially.'

Sidney was confused. 'Unofficially?'

'By that I mean don't go telling the taxman. You're paid cash in hand. Easy money at this time of year. Well, for the next few months, anyway.'

'Why the next few months?'

'The B & B is closed until the end of winter, and the gallery only operates Thursday to Sunday. To be honest, I reckon he'd shut the place down if the gallery wasn't on the council's cultural trail. Gets a few day tourists, either coming from Coffs Harbour in small groups by bus, or sightseers in their own cars. Others take the trip up to the gallery simply because the road is there. They see the trek up the mountain as a challenge for their city four-wheel drives. But no matter,' Pearl shrugged. 'As long as they buy something at the gallery before they go. That's where you come in. You're basically minding the shop and being paid isolation money, given the isolation.'

'Hmm, I see.' Sid mused. *Isolation money or danger money?*

4

WATERCOLOUR COVE, 2015

Sid parked and waited, as arranged, on one side of the closed gate at the bottom of the mountain, car rumbling at an idle to blow warm air while Jake grumbled about the temperature. But her brother perked right up when Pearl, on a recumbent tricycle, rode past them, stopping to unlock the chain, and to shove the gate with all her might before riding the metal frame open, like a child. Coming to a stop against a ramshackle shed and an askew sign with faded lettering—FARM GATE HONESTY BOX—Pearl secured the gate, then slid a GALLERY OPEN sign in place. The lower B & B section of the sign remained unchanged: CLOSED FOR WINTER.

As Sid shifted gear, preparing to drive, Pearl raised a hold-on hand and disappeared into the shed. A moment later, she reappeared riding a small quad bike.

'Now we're talking,' Jake quipped. 'Let's go, sis.'

Even Sid felt a small thrill as the tyres of her car clawed the winding roadway. While recently graded, the higher they climbed, the skinnier the track, and the sharper the bends.

'You glad I bought a four-wheel drive now, Jakey?' Sid asked, remembering how he'd teased her when discovering she'd bought a Jeep.

'Yeah, now you only have to learn to drive. Look at Pearl go.'

'Well, Jake, feel free to get your own wheels and drive them any way you want. Until then, shut up in the passenger seat and get your foot off my dashboard, or you can walk the rest of the way.'

'You and whose army will make me?'

She took a swipe at his knee. 'Oh, *when* will you grow up?'

'Forever young, that's me.' He cast a cheeky grin her way. 'And forever your family. Too bad you can't pick your relatives, eh?'

Did little brothers, even twenty-five-year-old ones, ever stop being so annoying?

5

THE GREENHILL BANANA PLANTATION, 1979

Matthew shoved another empty banana carton into David's chest. 'You can ask me all you like how much longer this will take. My answer will be the same. Until the bloody job's done. I'm sick of you skiving off with that girl.'

'You're jealous. You wish Tilly liked you and Dad was sending *you* to university.' Goading his brother about Tilly was wrong, especially as Matthew sucked when it came to keeping a girlfriend. 'Once I have my arts degree, I'm going to come home and marry Tilly.'

'Over Dad's dead body. He doesn't like you hanging around her—and for good reason.'

'What reason?'

'For starters, she's older than you. And don't get him going on where she comes from. And for your information, Davo, if I *was* keen on Tilly, you wouldn't stand a chance.'

'Yeah, right!' David squinted up at his brother stacking heavy cartons on a pallet. 'Like any of that stuff matters. Dad can't control me once I turn eighteen. That'll be next year.'

'And by then she'll be twenty.'

'So?'

'*So*, Davo, she'll have worked out you're an immature twerp and a dreamer who does nothing but tell everyone how clever he is and how famous he'll be. She'll also be long gone. There's no pinning down a wild spirit on a cruddy banana plantation. While you and me don't have a choice—bananas are our family business—she's got a life to live and no good reason to stay. As for you, Dad might support you in Sydney, but only if the business is profitable. Uni or not, there's no getting away from the fact you're part of this family, which means doing your share so he can retire one day.'

'You're wrong about Tilly,' David said. 'We have plans. And Dad has you to take over the business. And you can have it—money and all. I'm not a banana farmer. I'm an artist who'll be famous enough to make my own money. You wait and see.'

'You can't paint a profit, Davo,' Matthew said. 'And these bananas don't pick and pack themselves. You also can't have too many workers on a place like Greenhill. If nothing else, you'll be back here on your uni breaks to help in the packing shed. And when I *am* running this place, you won't get off so easy.'

David studied his brother, older by ten years and still living at home. 'Matthew, did you never want to get away from here and study something —*anything?*'

'Education hasn't always been free like it is now. Besides, some of us are smart enough without all that higher education crap.'

Something in his brother's shrug—the way he changed subjects whenever David started spouting about his arts degree and his future with Tilly —suggested Matthew did care. And Matthew *was* smart, his business acumen and natural ability with numbers leaving David for dead. And whenever Dad had a barrow to push with the council, Matthew did the writing. He was especially clever and super-precise when composing letters. Why their father had never seen the benefit in furthering his eldest son's education, David didn't know. Maybe Dad didn't think Matthew needed to be any smarter. But then he'd berate his eldest son, calling him a lost cause.

'Do you see yourself still carting forty-kilo bunches of bananas until you're old, Matthew?'

'Sure! Dad's done it all his life, and his dad did the same into his seventies. Physical labour keeps a body and a brain young and healthy. So do bananas.'

'Yeah, yeah, I've heard as many times as you about how good bananas are. I get it.'

'I'm just sayin', I plan on living a very long time, right here on this mountain.'

Not David. He planned on making every minute count.

'I want to paint and draw and create. I want to experiment, do the impossible, show people—'

'Davo, you're dreamin'. You're a banana boy from country New South Wales. You'll never be famous.'

'Pro Hart was a miner from Broken Hill.'

'Who?'

'*Pfft!* Typical.' He waved a dismissive hand in his brother's direction, wishing Matthew could be excited about his and Tilly's dream, their shared passion for new art, and plans to exhibit their works jointly. People would travel long distances to *oooh* and *ahhh* and buy their pieces. He wanted to tell Matthew dreams were also hard work—dreams worth chasing, that is.

Tilly got so excited whenever they talked about the future, like on the last day of summer school break, while hiding out in their secret cave to escape the insufferable January heat. The underground chamber, halfway up the Greenhill mountain, was a huge hole in the side of the cliff-like ridge and with a view all the way to the ocean.

That day, inside the cave, Tilly had strutted around all hoity-toity, mimicking artistic types with their fancy cocktails and flamboyant fashions. With a beach towel as a turban and her shirt flung around her neck as a makeshift scarf, she'd pranced about in her bikini, waving a pretend cigarette and crying out, '*Darrrrr*-link!'. Welcoming imaginary guests, she would plant air kisses on imaginary cheeks and usher potential buyers towards David's latest drawing. 'Isn't my lover's latest masterpiece absolutely *marrrr*-vellous? *Aw*fully glad you could join us at the grand opening of our very *grand* gallery called—'

Tilly stopped and spun around to face David.

'What's the matter?' he asked.

'What on earth will we call our very grand gallery? How will the invitations read?'

Watching from the sidelines, David smiled and sashayed over to Tilly. 'Well, *darrrrr*-link!,' he said, taking both her hands in his. 'I believe the invitations will read: David and Tilly request the pleasure of your company at the grand opening of—'

'No, no, no, *darrrrr*-link,' Tilly interrupted. 'You obviously mean Tilly and David. A lady always goes first.'

'Perhaps we'll be Mr and Mrs by then.' He dropped to one knee like he'd seen in the movies, drew the back of her hand to his lips and kissed it. 'You *will* marry me one day, won't you?'

Tilly's hand cupped her mouth, slapping her speechless.

'Well?' David asked. The place was strangely silent without the echo of her constant chatter. 'Say something.'

'Of course I'll marry you.' Tilly launched herself at him with such abandon he lost balance. David fell backwards onto his bottom, while Tilly landed so hard on top of him that the beach towel turban she'd fashioned unravelled to cover David's face.

'That's if you don't suffocate me first, Tills.' He tried laughing as he knocked the towel away, but the weight of her hands on his chest was crushing, while the tips of her hair—still smelling of saltwater from their earlier swim—tickled his nose.

'Let anyone try to stop me becoming Mrs David Hill.'

'I adore that face you pull.'

Tilly stiffened, pushing herself into a seated position and sliding onto the ground next to him. 'What face?' she demanded.

David sat up and hugged his knees to his chest. 'I'm teasing you.'

'Well, don't. Not until you've told me you love me and want to be with me.'

'I do.'

'Honestly?' She played with the ends of her hair, twirling a strand tight around her finger before letting it spring back.

'I really, really love you, Tilly.'

'How much?'

'More than there are rocks on the seawall.'

'Oh, David! You're my rock and I need you.' Tilly tugged at his arms, draping them around her neck. 'I can never be alone. I can never become my mother. You can't ever leave me. Promise?'

'Why would I leave? We share the same dreams.'

They kissed and David desperately wanted to go all the way, but each time they came close to making out, eagerness was his undoing. He'd wanted it so badly that he tried too hard and felt too much too early. His brother, on the other hand, seemed to bonk girls without any emotional attachment. But David wasn't his brother. He needed to connect physically, emotionally, and creatively, and he wanted the first time to be good for them both. David didn't simply want sex with Tilly. Their first time together would not only be meaningful, but David wanted to go off like a firecracker.

Firecracker! A thought crossed his mind. *The new year! That's it!* Somehow, if he could arrange a rendezvous with Tilly at midnight, fireworks would be a certainty, even if David turned out to be a fizzer. But with December almost a year away, could he wait that long?

. . .

'Davo!' Matthew was yelling. 'Quit daydreaming or we'll be here till bloody Christmas. Dad needs these boxes loaded on the truck today.'

'Okay, okay.'

Little did David know, with Tilly making her own secret seduction plans, Christmas was about to come early.

'What kept you?' Tilly called from where she huddled at the back of their cave. The corner was the best place to escape the winter winds that blew straight off the ocean, then whipped through the Greenhill plantation, swirling around the mouth of the cave before scooting up the hill. 'Look, I'm almost done. Last one.' She'd been working on the knitted rug for weeks, sewing dozens of small, colourful squares together. 'Wanna try it with me?' She raised a corner of the blanket, inviting David in. 'I'm *so* cold.'

David had barely let his art satchel slide off his shoulder when Tilly tugged his arm hard. He dropped onto his knees before her. 'I love it, Tills.'

'As much as you love me?' She covered both their bodies with the rug before propping on one elbow over him to peer into his eyes. 'Prove you love me.'

'But, Tilly, we shouldn't—'

'Shh!' She was straddling him now and leaning forward, her lips teasing his. 'Together forever, remember? Now kiss me back.'

Afterwards, as she rested her head on his chest, David struggled to stay still. He'd imagined sex, but never expected going all the way would feel so awesome—and he had gone off like a firecracker. Now every nerve in his body twitched, making him want to jump up, run from the cave and crow like Tarzan. *TILLY LOVES ME!*

If only Tilly wasn't anchoring him to the spot, her head on his chest, a finger slowly circling that place where his heart pounded.

'I feel so special right now, David.'

'Yeah, well, I'm feeling something, alright, Tilly,' he quipped, making another play at her nipple.

Tilly slapped his hand into submission. 'Stop that. I'm talking about our future. Imagine a life together away from here.' She sighed and squeezed him tighter. 'Somewhere out there is the perfect place for our gallery. Maybe a funky inner-city warehouse. Do you think Sydney or Melbourne?'

David's mind stuck on the words inner-city warehouse. 'What are you talking about, Tills? If you want funky, then the old slipway by the seawall will be perfect.'

'Be serious, David.'

'I am. Why not the slipway? Matthew is writing a letter on the matter for Dad. You know he occasionally gets on his high horse with Mayor Brady. Dad's telling the council that Dinghy Bay needs a working slipway to support the fishing boats. He's suggesting a grant application to get a new facility built, among other things.'

Tilly lifted her head from his chest, her face inches above his own. 'What are you going on about?'

'By the time I'm done with uni, the new slipway will be finished, leaving the old one up for lease. The historical society won't let them demolish the adjoining buildings. Dad might even help us buy the place. Rustic is a great backdrop for contemporary art, and the natural light is amazing. There'll be room to hold workshops, as well as spaces we can hire out. A kind of country retreat for artists who need a creative space to recharge.'

'You're not serious.' Tilly shuffled into a seated position on top of him to stare David down, her hands hard against his chest. 'You *are* serious! When were you going to tell me about your slipway plans?'

'Dad said the new facility is a good two years away at least, that's if there's not a change of government and—'

'David, David, stop talking.'

'What's the matter. Tills?' He wished he hadn't mentioned the slipway at all.

'Weren't you always going on about Sydney this or Melbourne that?'

'Yes, to attend university. The plan was to come back here to paint and to be with you. That way I'm on hand to help Dad during harvest.'

'Nup, no way! Staying here was never the plan. We never agreed, and I always thought ...' Tilly lowered her face into cupped hands, her limp body a dead weight on David.

'Don't cry,' he urged. 'As long as we're together, it won't matter where we have our gallery. Together forever, right?'

'But how would our work get any notice out here?'

'Just look at Pro Hart,' David replied, upbeat. 'They discovered him in—'

'Oh, you and bloody Pro Hart!' Disentangling herself from the blanket, too angry to bother about the bra twisted under her arm, she dragged the skivvy back over her breasts. 'Pro Hart's success is a once in a generation thing. You'll never be him. Never. And our dream will *never* come true if we stay in this crappy town, on this crappy hilltop, with crappy parents. I won't stay on this mountain with the Marhkts. I won't,' she pouted. 'Tell me you'll come with me. Tell me I'm more important than a bloody banana farm and a dilapidated boat shed. Tell me we're family forever, David. Tell me you'll take me away. Tell me now—or else.'

David could not understand where this sudden anger had come from. Tilly wasn't faking. He'd never seen her so mad. 'Or else what, Tilly?' he asked, finally able to sit up. 'Come back here and we can kiss and make up.'

'I'm too cross. When you've stopped being a mummy's boy and you've decided to get away from here, you'll know where to find me.'

6

THE GREENHILL BANANA PLANTATION, 1979

'I found you.' Moonfaced Albie Marhkt stopped in the open doorway to Tilly's bedroom and peeled a banana. 'You've been hiding away and angry for days. What's up?'

'Nothing.'

'Doesn't look like nothing. You look kinda different.'

Tilly zipped her mean mouth shut. Albie was the odd-looking one. Upon first meeting him, his appearance had reminded her of a walking caricature with a head too big for his body. Five years on, and with the same pimply forehead, premature balding, a broad nose and googly eyes, he was a gangly version of odd.

'Nick off and leave me alone,' Tilly said, slumping further into the sagging mattress with its worn-out springs.

She'd shared the same room with her *"new brother"* when she'd first arrived at the Marhkt's plantation. Albie had not long turned sixteen and, being tall for his age and oafish, the schoolyard bullies had already nick-named him Mr Potato Head.

Tilly, the tough newcomer to town, soon ended the bullying, only to see the Marhkts pull Albie out of school to work full time in what they called 'the family business'. The couple had been unable to have their own children, so a shrewd Ulf and Hilda had fostered a son, knowing a male would keep the banana plantation and market garden viable for longer. With Albie taller and stronger than most boys his age, he was suited to the demands of a plantation, yet young enough to ensure many more years' productivity.

It was six years after Albie's placement that Ulf and Hilda fostered fourteen-year-old Tilly, and straightaway she understood her role. Having a daughter meant Mrs Marhkt could spend less time looking after the house and cooking the meals. In the beginning, Tilly and Albie shared a room, until she told the Marhkts that he interfered with her while sleeping. It wasn't a total lie. Albie's constant crying out and the creepy, unnerving groans and moans had interfered very much with Tilly's ability to sleep soundly. Consequently, he received a clip over the ear from Ulf, and from then on slept on a stretcher bed in the sleep-out section of the veranda that doubled as Hilda's pantry for excess dry goods. Still, the night-time noises and sobbing continued. Albie cried a lot when he thought no one could hear him.

Much to Tilly's surprise, and despite the punishment and uncomfortable quarters, Albie never said another word about her accusations to the Marhkts. He could have got her back every time she told tales—or for every house rule she broke—but instead, Albie protected Tilly. In return for his loyalty, she made him her confidant, keeping him onside with attention and kind words—much like a person rewards an enthusiastic puppy.

Only when she was older and he began misinterpreting Tilly's confiding and kindness as something more—and his hands got all octopus-like—did she have to remind him they were as good as brother and sister.

'We have the same parents—sort of—and we get to call the Marhkts Mum and Dad. That makes you my brother,' she'd say.

'But we're family forever,' he'd reply. 'That's what you tell me. Family forever.'

'Sure we're family.' Tilly always fed back what he needed to hear. 'But that's all, Albie. I just don't see you the way you want.'

'You might, soon. When I'm twenty-one I'll be a real man and you'll see I'm the right one for you. It'll happen one day.'

'Oh, okay, well, I'll let you know. Oh, and Albie?'

'Yes, Tilly?'

'That day—the day I see you're the right man for me? That night the moon will turn blue.'

Tilly wished Albie would nick off now.

'I told you to leave me alone, Albie.' But he remained in the doorway to Tilly's room, chewing banana like a cow chews chaff. He'd since outgrown his puppy-like eagerness, his pimples were now pockmarks, and he had a stilted gait, hunched shoulders and a shifty look that meant his gaze never lingered too long in any one direction, like he was on the lookout for something. Something that made him afraid. 'I meant what I said. Now bugger off.' With a huff, she kicked out, shoving the door so it slammed in Albie's face. Then, hugging a pillow to her stomach, Tilly cried tears—real ones.

For the last ten days—since she and David had argued and she'd stormed from the cave—Tilly had waited, wished and expected him to come begging. He would for sure, looking for more of what she'd let him have that day. And she had more to give, keen to reward him for finally agreeing she knew what was best for their future together. But when David didn't make the nightly journey from the Greenhill property to her bedroom window at the Marhkt's, when she'd let him climb in and they would stay awake into the early hours of the morning kissing, cuddling, and conspiring, Tilly assumed he was expecting her to crawl back to him, begging to be loved. Clearly David didn't know her at all because pleading was the last thing Tilly would do. Begging to be loved was what her mother had done, and look how that had turned out. If David truly loved Tilly, he would come to her.

But when another week passed, and David treated her no differently to Albie whenever the three of them bumped into each other, Tilly grew angry. Then she grew desperate, wasting hours trudging back and forth between their two favourite places to hang out: the cave and the rocks at the seawall. During one of those beach walks, she bumped into Matthew coming back from a surf, his wetsuit exaggerating his long legs and a fit torso beneath black rubber. He was barefoot, his hair dripping, the morning's wintery wind drying the water trickles on his face into lines of crusty salt.

'Hi-ya, Tilly,' he said.

'Hi-ya, yourself.'

How could siblings be so different? Where David was short and spirited, easily excited and popular around town, his older brother was offhanded and gawky, although athletic. Matthew looked after his body. He had to—lugging banana boxes and enormous bunches of fruit over steep hillsides was not for the weak. Matthew also jogged daily like clockwork—same course, same time, twice a day, every day: rain, hail, or heatwave. Over the years, Tilly had seen him date just about every girl in

Dinghy Bay, including those from the surrounding farming district, but not one relationship lasted beyond a few months. Tilly and David would make jibes about him having bored every one of his girlfriends to death.

'S'pose you're lookin' for David,' a dripping-wet Matthew said, his smile unusually smug.

'Nup.' Tilly stared past him to the white-crested water beyond. 'Is David looking for me?'

Matthew breathed deep, like Ulf did right before Albie got a talking-to for messing up. 'Look, Tilly, let me give you some advice. You know Davo is heading off to uni next year, but he'll be back home in the holidays to work. Dad is adamant Davo pays his way. So, if my little bro wants this fancy arts degree, he'll do what he's told. Always does.'

'And I suppose you don't?'

Matthew's flinching at the nasty retort looked like a child preparing for a slap. 'I'm older. I can do what I want, when I want.'

'Oh really? You know what I see,' Tilly retorted. 'I see someone so stuck in their ways that you'll grow old and die in this place.'

'That's not true. If I wanted to go, I'd go—anytime.'

'Oh yeah? Just like that.' Tilly snapped her fingers. 'You'd leave?'

'If I had a good reason.'

'Well, I hope you find one and bugger off. *I'll* wait for David.'

'Good luck with that.' Matthew made to walk away, but faltered, turning back. 'Tilly, I really shouldn't say anything, but …'

'But what?'

'Mum and Dad—especially Mum—expect Dave to make something of himself and his art. I heard her telling him one day to be the artist she never had the chance to become.'

'What's that even mean?' Tilly snapped, her frustration growing.

'Davo gets his talent from our mum. Marrying Dad meant she gave up the chance to travel and study under some famous American painter.'

'But your mum and dad are so lovey dovey. Always smooching and holding hands. Kind of embarrassing at their age, don't you think?'

'It's not like Mum regrets her decision to marry Dad. Times were different in their day. She was expected to marry and raise a family, not go traipsing around the world. Instead, she settled for family life, hoping her child would get the experiences she missed out on. Davo got the artistic genes. He wins. We lose, Tilly.'

'What are you talking about? We lose what?'

'There are winners and losers in life. You and me are the losers. We don't get handed the same chances. We're left behind to find our own opportunities. But winners, like Davo, have goals to reach, and Mum sure won't allow him to do anything rash that might curtail his creativity. I'm real sorry, Tilly, but … The truth is, they don't want him to settle down yet, and certainly not with a girl Dad says comes from "the wrong side of the tracks". You don't understand families. You never had one. But Davo does know about family expectations and responsibilities. Now, I'm not sure what's going on between the two of you right now, but whatever it is, Davo is at home more often and helping Dad, putting him very much back in the good books. In fact, a university in Melbourne is offering a placement that includes a place to stay, and Dad's contemplating the option.'

'How do you know all this?'

'I know coz Davo likes to rub that kind of news in my face. Anyway, Tilly, I think enough of you to let you know that for the next four years, or more, that's where he'll be. See ya.'

Four years! Melbourne! No, no, no! Tilly couldn't let herself believe Matthew's version, not for a second. But no way would she go crawling to David and apologise. If David was not going to tell her or come to her and apologise, Tilly needed to do something else, and fast. The thought of living in this place for four years or, worse still, dying here, having never lived her own dream made her want to puke.

Tilly lurched towards the public toilets in the grassy reserve at the end of the seawall, her urge to throw up stronger than her need to avoid the putrid combination of stale septic waste inside and fish guts from the cleaning table outside. She stumbled into a cubical and slammed the door, sending a flurry of pigeons from their perch under the eaves. After gagging and producing nothing more than a long string of spittle, a pain jabbing her stomach. Tugging her underpants down, Tilly straddled the seatless toilet bowl, kangaroo-style, but when the pain made the awkward position unbearable, she dropped her butt to the cold, hard rim.

She didn't care that the toilet felt like ice.

She didn't care about catching a disease.

And she didn't cry when a terrifying series of spasms shook her body.

Tilly was too focused on figuring out when her period was due, and on the pale pink knickers stretched between both her knees now spotted red.

7

THE GREENHILL BANANA PLANTATION, 1979

Tilly caught Albie's refection in the bathroom mirror, his eyes—big and dark and kind—staring back from the door.

'Not now, Albie,' she said as the urge to vomit returned.

'I'm sick of you telling me what to do, and I'm not going away until you tell me what's wrong. You've been sulking for ages.'

Tilly needed kind eyes right now. She needed someone to want her and care for her and tell her everything will be okay. Even more, she needed an explanation, and not a Hilda-type commentary, like when Tilly's very first period had come on.

It happened not long after arriving at the Marhkts' property, with Hilda telling Tilly straight up: 'Every month the body gets very sad and cries red tears because there's no baby. And that's the way it should be each month until you're married and have your own house. Make sure that's the case.'

Tilly had always been crystal clear about the challenges unwed mothers faced, but less certain about what her body was currently going through. With the spotting unusual and unnerving, Matthew's news added to the desperate nature of her situation—likely pregnant with David's baby.

She'd run home from the seawall and fallen onto her bed to silently but vehemently curse her mother, because it *was* her mother's fault that Tilly was trapped at the Marhkt's, with the only way out being Hilda's medicine supply in the bathroom cabinet. Immediately after swallowing the six blue tablets from the yellow pill container—the one with the white screw-top lid and impossible to pronounce name on the label—Tilly had stuck her fingers down her throat and vomited the lot up.

Now, as she crouched next to the toilet bowl, Albie dangled a warm washcloth in front of her face.

'Gosh, what did you eat? You chuck up like that again and we might need the priest from *The Exorcist*. I thought your head was about to do a three-sixty-degree spin.'

Fear manifested in more tears and wobbled her voice. 'Shut up, Albie.'

'Hey, don't cry. I'm sorry.'

'I'm not *crying*. I don't *cry*. Only babies cry—babies and you.' She swiped his hand away and stood—too fast judging by the spinning sensation in her head.

'No need to be mean, Tilly. I was joking. Give me that washer.' He snatched the face cloth and held it under the running tap. 'Come to bed and lie down.'

'Wait!' The taste in her mouth was so vile, she almost threw up again. She felt disgusting—full stop—her mind constantly wandering back to that day in the cave with David. She'd said things—harsh and unthinking—that Tilly wished she could take back. But David would say words are like toothpaste. Once out, there is no putting them back again.

'Here.' Albie put a toothbrush in Tilly's hand and curled her fingers tight. 'Brush. I'll be back.'

'Wait.' Albie hovered obediently, allowing Tilly to study both their faces side by side in the mirror. She tried picturing his face instead of David's every morning for the rest of her life. Then she asked, 'Do you want to stay in this place forever, Albie?'

'I guess, but only coz the place will be mine one day.'

Studying their reflections, she recalled Matthew saying there were winners and losers, and that she and him were both losers. But what did that make Albie? A loser, like them?

Whatever he was, Albie remained her confidant. She could tell him how David had confessed his love and tricked her into believing him, and how he'd taken her virginity, then stolen her hopes and dreams and the chance of a future away from this mountain. A desperate Tilly could tell Albie anything. He'd believe her, of course.

'Come on, Tilly. Rinse and spit and off to bed before Mum and Dad get back from Bingo.'

After wiping her face, she let Albie take her hand and lead her to the bedroom and to her bed. Pulling back the bedcovers, he guided her down and lifted her legs onto the mattress.

'You really don't care if you die here, Albie?' she asked as he placed the folded face cloth on her throbbing forehead. 'You'd let them dig a hole and bury you under a banana tree, never having experienced life?'

Albie shrugged.

'You and me never asked to live in this place,' Tilly continued. 'Who's to say, if the Marhkts hadn't picked us when they did, the next couple to come along might have been city people. We might be living in a mansion with servants and stuff. Imagine that!'

'But the Marhkts ... They saved me, Tilly. They saved us. They're good to us. They're family.'

'Not mine. My mother's dead and my father ... Well, I have no idea who he is and no desire to know. But you, Albie ... What you told me about that stuff that happened to you ... before the Marhkts.'

Albie did that shifty eye thing. 'What about it?'

'You told me people knew what was happening to you, but they did nothing. You said the Marhkts knew all about it too. It's those perverts at the boys' home that make you cry in your sleep. Am I right?'

Albie's chin dropped to his chest, as if his colossal head was suddenly too heavy to hold up. 'I don't want to remember.'

'Shouldn't those who knew got you help?'

'I didn't need help then and I don't need help now. I've got what I need —a family—and like you say, family is forever. The other stuff before no longer matters.'

The *other* stuff Albie refused to speak of included an unmarried mother who had loved him so much that when life got too hard, she surrendered her six-year-old son and let the authorities in Malta fly him to the other side of the world. The first orphanage in Australia had been horrible. Then, when Albie was nine and with only broken English, fast-talking strangers had made him sign forms he couldn't read. Within days, the tall-for-his-age boy had found himself in another home—a Catholic boys' home in the West Australian desert, on the other side of the country, where him and other boys did manual labour in forty-degree temperatures.

'You know I don't think about that place anymore, Tilly. Don't make me.'

Albie rarely spoke of his past, but a street-smart Tilly could fill in the blanks. Both abandoned as kids, she and Albie were everything alike and nothing alike. Maybe that made them perfect for each other. Soon he'd be twenty-one. He could drive a car—so could she, only not legally—and he wasn't afraid of hard work. He'd protect her. They'd look out for each other.

'Albie?' Tilly raised herself up on the bed, both elbows digging into the mattress. 'Would you go with me if I had to leave here?'

'Why would you have to leave?'

Tilly huffed. 'Just answer, Albie Would you go with me?'

'Maybe, but what's making you leave and where would we go? How would we survive?'

'You and me, Albie, we're the same. We've lived rough—on the streets, in fleapits, with strangers. We don't need the Marhkts. We have each other. We're not losers. We're survivors.'

Albie's over-sized eyes blinked their confusion. 'You and me? As in the two of us *together*? As in a family forever?'

When he smiled, one corner of his mouth turned up as if caught by an invisible fishing line. Tilly had hooked him.

'That's right, Albie, a family forever. We'll make our own. Only not here. Ulf and Hilda will never allow you and me to be together in that way, or have a family of our own.' Tilly pressed Albie's hand on her belly. 'Imagine your baby in here. Would you like that, Albie?'

Clasping the back of his neck, she drew her top high over her breast, exposed one nipple, and guided his mouth. But, not trusting that she wouldn't puke up again should she see his sweaty, pockmarked face against her skin, Tilly turned her face to the window and said, 'I believe there's a blue moon tonight, Albie.'

Tilly woke alone, having banished Albie to his own bed. The last thing she wanted was to have the Marhkts return early from bingo and find him in her room.

He'd come sneaking back once already, whining on the other side of her closed door. 'Can't we do it again? I can do it better.'

'No! Go away,' she'd yelled back, burying her head under the pillow to muffle her loud cursing.

What was sleeping with Albie meant to achieve? Was she making sure she was really pregnant to force David into following her? What if David's baby was still in her and the blood-spotted knickers had been perfectly normal? The article she'd read in *Dolly* magazine suggested bleeding happened and was no cause for panic. Tilly sure wasn't used to feeling so out of control, but she also wasn't stupid and she feared being single and with a child. The concept brought back terrible memories of her mother's constant battles: to find work, to find housing, to find a husband—to stay sober. Some struggles were won, but mostly her mother had failed, eventually losing her battle with booze and drugs.

But Tilly wasn't her mother, and to prove it, she made a commitment on the spot. *No more pills, no more panicking, and no more dumb decisions.* If nothing else, Tilly's experiences on the street and in the home had taught her about strength and determination. Alone, she would survive the streets—no problem. But with a baby? No, she couldn't do *that* on her own. Nor should she have to, except that David's absence and total disregard for her feelings suggested education and pleasing his parents were more important to him than Tilly. He'd made it known in the cave that day. He didn't want the same things. Maybe he didn't really want Tilly—until he found out Albie did. So, Tilly would work with what she had. She could wrap Albie around her finger—no problem. Albie would do. Albie loved her. Albie had, and would always, protect her. He'd protect her baby, too. But Albie would need a reason to leave the Marhkts, and Tilly crossed her fingers that what they'd done tonight would give him one.

'Go away, Albie,' she growled, hearing the gravel crunch outside her window. 'Stop peeping.'

'It's not Albie,' came the whispered reply. 'It's me, and I'm not peeping.'

'David?' She sprung out of bed, straightening her shirt.

'Of course it's me. Why would Albie be sneaking around your bedroom window? Is he bothering you again? You should've told me. I'll—'

'Shh, no, of course not. Nothing like that.' Tilly grunted as she nudged the old sash window higher, cold air smacking her in the face. David looked small standing below her window looking up, his hands tucked in the pockets of pants pulled tight over stocky thighs, while his feet did a little jig to keep him warm. 'What time is it?'

'Don't worry. Your folks aren't home yet. I just couldn't stay away any longer. I don't care what Matthew says. I had to see you, Tills.' He put his hands to his mouth and blew into them. 'It's kinda freezing out here in the dark and I can't see you. Can I come in?'

'No, I'll come out. Stay there.' Fearing she'd see evidence of what had transpired, Tilly didn't turn on her bedside lamp. Instead, with only the moon's glow, she scrambled into her jeans, stopping to tug a brush through the matted hair at the back of her head and shuddering at the memory of Albie's eagerness to please. With her limited experience—all knowledge gleaned from *Dolly* magazines, romance novels, and girl-talk at school—Tilly guessed he'd tried too hard. From Albie, there'd been grunting and groaning, and declarations of forever love but with little else, while Tilly had feigned rapture with an Oscar-worthy performance. But rather than lying all lovey-dovey in Albie's arms afterwards, she'd dashed to the toilet to scrub herself clean.

Having wrapped a blue chenille dressing gown around her body, Tilly tiptoed down the hallway, pushed open the creaking front door, and slipped her freezing feet into a pair of gumboots. When she turned around, she slammed smack-bang into David.

'I've missed you, Tilly.' He wrapped her in his arms so tight the breath squeezed out of her lungs. 'I've been stupid and I'm sorry.' His kisses peppered her face and neck, clumsy hands clawing at her boobs. 'Can we start over? Nothing's the same without you.' He pulled back and grinned. 'I thought maybe we can make up. If you know what I mean.'

'Oh, David, why now?'

'Why now?' he repeated, his amusement clear. 'Because we're here and it's cold, and I kinda liked the last time we were together.'

'No, I mean, why did you wait so long to come over and tell me how you felt?'

'Because Matthew said if I played things cool, you'd come to me. But you never. So, here I am. Just don't tell him or he'll give me a hard time.'

She took a step away, trying to see David's face in the dark. 'Your brother told you to stay away?'

'I know what you're thinking, Tilly. Like, since when do I listen to him? Dumb, eh?'

Rendered limp, like a rag doll, David pulled her back into him, his voice reverberating in her ear, the tone low but urgent.

'I had to see you, Tills. To tell you before talking to Dad and Mum tomorrow. They need to know we have our own lives to live, our own plans away from here.'

'Oh, David—'

'Shh! Say you forgive me for being so pig-headed about us leaving. If a big city gallery is your dream, then it's my dream. I do love you, Tilly.'

A flash of light cut through the darkness, along with the sound of the Marhkt's old ute groaning its way up the hillside.

'Quickly, I have to go back inside.' She kissed David hard on the mouth before shoving him along the path. 'Tomorrow, first light, down by the seawall. We'll talk. Now go.'

David didn't budge. 'Not before you tell me.'

'Tell you what?' she asked, feeling both flustered and euphoric.

'That you forgive me, and you'll live with me and be my family forever.'

'Yes, I forgive you and I'll love you forever.' She shoved his chest again and giggled. 'Now go.'

With a final peck, he slipped into the darkness. There was no danger of him getting lost. David was well-acquainted with the garden pathway that snaked through the vegie garden and linked their two houses. In fact, both she and David could walk it blindfolded.

Barely containing her silly grin, a sound like twigs snapping underfoot nearby, startled her. As she tuned towards the banana plantation, stumbling on a loose stone and cussing, she knew he was peeping.

Albie.

8

WATERCOLOUR COVE, 2015

'Watch where you put your feet along here,' Pearl warned as Sid meandered over the rocky and overgrown track. 'The burrows up here are real ankle turners.'

'What sort of animal makes them?'

'Could be any number of creatures. Banana country has spiders as big as your hand, rats as big as cats, and venomous snakes longer than this path. Although not so many snakes out and about in winter.'

Well, that's a plus! Since moving back into her mother's house in the Blue Mountains Sid had encountered all the above, but something about Pearl's plurals—rats, spiders, snakes—made her squeamish. Size was less of a concern for Sid. Big spiders and long snakes were easier to see and avoid. It was the small, sneaky, silent pest that Sid watched out for these days. *Like rats named Damien!*

Sid cursed under her breath. So much for getting away so she could stop thinking about Damien, in particular his parting words. Having watched her lug her own suitcase to the door of their Melbourne apartment, he said, 'This wouldn't be happening if you'd only been more careful and not let yourself get pregnant.'

As partners in life and in business, leaving Damien had meant losing her job. But their breakup also added an awkwardness among shared acquaintances—personal and professional. Basically, Sid was starting out all over again. At least moving in with her mother saved on rent, and she'd secured freelance design work so she could pay her way. It wasn't constant work and enough to afford her own place—yet. Some jobs were freebies, in the hope more work followed, and some jobs, like this one, were a means to an end.

Despite the potential threat of venomous bites, she had a paying job and—*bonus!*—free accommodation. Their new digs, perched atop the highest hill in the area, afforded spectacular vistas in every direction. To the east, the sparkling blue Pacific Ocean stretched as far north and south as the eye could see, the winter winds whipping up white caps. Behind the main house, looking westward, was a swell of emerald-green hills tipped white.

'The white you can see covering those hills is some sort of netting?' she asked Pearl.

'Blueberry farms. They took off about the same time as the banana slump in the nineties. Locals refer to the new industry as *The Blue Revolution*. Great for the region's economy, Dad says, but I reckon the bird netting is a blight on a once beautiful landscape. These hills and valleys used to be lush with green from all the banana plantations and avocado trees, but towns that survive need to grow,' she said. 'If you and Jake want more paid work, the money from fruit picking isn't bad. When the blueberry seasons peaks, caravan parks fill with workers.'

'Does this mean we expect to see the Big Banana make way for the Big Blueberry?'

'Egad! Don't let anyone hear you suggest that, not even in jest. If The Big Prawn, The Big Mango, The Big Bush Turkey, and the Big Guitar aren't big enough. Oh, and I heard Nyngan, in country New South Wales, is erecting a Big Bogan this spring. So, no, Sidney, this country does not need another *big* anything.' Pearl laughed, then waved an enthusiastic hand at Jake, who was trailing a little behind them. 'Hey, Jake,' she called. 'If you want to unpack the car, put everything in the first cottage. Back along that path a bit. The bigger one on the left. Not the second one. Okay? I'll show Sidney the gallery and the office.'

Sid followed dutifully and silently, surprised at both her brother's acquiescence and the sight of another pathway weaving around flowerbeds and pruned shrubbery. It was too early for spring blooms, but a few impatient jonquils seemed eager to show their beauty, while two rosellas, resplendent in pale hues of red, green, yellow, and blue, sat on the edge of a birdbath. They flew high into a nearby flowering gum as Sid and Pearl approached.

The gallery's exterior was surprisingly modern but simple. A Colourbond roof in forest green blended with the surrounding hills, with cedar wall panels and supporting beams the colour of ripe peach. Hanging under the veranda's shade-giving roof was a jungle of kinetic artworks in glass, metal, paper, and driftwood, while a ramp provided access to a gallery—a building quite unlike the red brick facade on the principal residence they'd passed by. The last of Sidney's doubts about the job vanished as Pearl led her into the gallery with its highly polished timber floors and two walls of windows flooding the room with sunlight.

'I can tell from your expression you'll fit in here just fine. Not everyone appreciates the architectural detail.' Pearl walked from window to window to lower each shade with the press of a button. 'The boss likes natural light, but the blind system is clever tech that will self-adjust with the sun. We use LED lighting. Much cheaper, and a safer option for fragile works, especially those on paper. The boss loves his watercolours!'

'The boss, yes, I haven't asked his name.'

Pearl shrugged. 'I've always called him "Boss" and so has every other worker. And Greenhills has had plenty come and go.'

'I see, okay. Boss it is.' *Don't let good manners break with tradition!* 'This place seems very exposed to the elements.'

'That's true! The banana plantation has a prime position on the hillside, protecting the trees from the savage southerly and westerly winds. That make the gallery a sitting duck—hence the outside shutters you'll need to close every afternoon. The red button by the door, there, is all you need to press when leaving,' Pearl added. 'And from personal experience, if you see bad weather coming across, go quick. You don't want to be up here in an electrical storm—or any storm. And we get our share of them come storm season—October onwards and right through summer. The one time I got caught up here totally freaked me out.'

'Thanks for the warning.' Sid didn't mention she and Jake would be long gone by October and this trip would have been one big adventure—a successful one if only she could get through to someone at the correctional facility.

'Give me a sec,' Pearl said before disappearing into a back room.

With Sid's eyeballs aching from trying to take everything in, she rested her gaze on a display of Aboriginal art and recalled a discussion between her mum and Aunty Tasha when Sid had been about twelve.

Natalie had insisted—in a way only Natalie could—that an Indigenous art exhibition featuring local artists was a good idea for Tasha's gallery.

'There are some clever and prominent artists in this very neighbourhood,' her mother had told Tash. 'You invited me to join your gallery because you saw how I'd lifted Raphael's reputation. You thought I'd make a difference here. So let me. I'll introduce you to a couple of artists, show you some of their works, and you'll see in them what I do. I'm talking serious contemporary and commercial paintings and sculptures by super-talented artists, Tasha. Agree to holding an Indigenous art exhibition, then leave me to make the arrangements and you'll see the interest: from those looking to decorate a wall at home, to the interior designer wanting something contemporary for a client—not to mention the savvy investor.'

'Investors?' Aunty Tasha fingered the long headscarf dangling over her shoulder, twisting it in a way that reminded Sid of the pretty girls at school who'd twisted their locks when flirting with boys. 'You do know the 1990 winner of the John McCaughey Prize was an Indigenous artist? And one of two Aboriginal Australians to exhibit in the Venice Biennale that same year.'

'I didn't know,' Tasha admitted.

'*And*, I hear the National Gallery is in talks over the paintings for a Rover Thomas exhibition. Get in on the ground floor and watch the gallery grow.'

For every objection, Natalie had an answer, leaving Tasha to either admit to a prejudice or agree to the idea. Natalie's enthusiasm—her husband called it badgering—always worked, but she wasn't yet done.

'I'll show you some stunning Aboriginal art in many forms: on canvas and linen, in textile, and jewellery design. Yes, there are sculptures in wood and weavings, but also this incredibly talented young woman who works in watercolours. Her stuff will blow your mind, Tash.'

'Hello? Earth to Sid!' Pearl was staring. 'I asked if you liked the Aboriginal pieces.'

'Oh, yes, sorry. I was miles away.'

'You looked it. Jake said you'd get all gooey once you saw the gallery.'

'He did, did he?' Sid smiled. 'I was just reminded of something, but you were going to show me ...?'

'The cash register.' Pearl pointed. 'Assuming you know your way around a computer, the gallery has a basic website that needs updating with new pieces. A revamp is on the boss's list of things to do, just nowhere near the top. I don't think he knows how to go about arranging a website redesign. Not that it matters. We get plenty of online enquiries from both the public and art organisations. Take contact details. The boss deals with those, and also any government or gallery buyers. Oh, and he responds to the emails, so ignore them. And, like I said, I'm here a few days a week, usually raiding the herb garden and fruit trees out back.

You're free to do the same, and if you need time off, or if there's anything you need to know, ask me.'

'Or ask the boss?' Sid queried.

Pearl shrugged. 'Sure, if you see him, you can ask.'

Was there a protective tone in Pearl's voice? The woman's next words confirmed as much.

'I don't like to bother the boss unless something makes it absolutely necessary. He's more creative than administrative and this place more therapeutic—part labour of love, part penance.'

Penance? Keen to know more and about to ask, Pearl added, 'Speaking of therapy, I'd best get over to his cottage and let my hands work their magic.'

'He doesn't live in the main house?'

'Nope! You'll see him in the gallery sometimes, but rarely in the main house. Like I said, he keeps to himself. He's also finishing a commissioned piece in town, so he can be away a lot. I'll go see him now and call back to check with you on my way out. Enjoy!'

Sidney was alone and yet not lonesome among myriad artworks, with the gallery's scent a reminder of the pots of putty she'd played with as a child, moulding coloured goo into shapes while in her mother's studio. Incredibly, the familiar smell of art—a blend of baked clay and linseed oil—was a panacea, soothing Sidney and making her wish she'd studied painting or sculpture, rather than the clean, clinical world of graphic design.

Her phone beeped with a message from Kurt, the head of Windsong ad agency. He was offering her a freelance job. An urgent one. *A paying one, hopefully!* Packing her laptop at the last minute had been a good decision. She'd take the job, of course, even if meeting the deadline meant staying up past midnight. If this gallery job remained as quiet as it was now, she could make a start on the Windsong project sooner rather than later. After replying to Kurt, Sidney googled the Mid North Coast Correctional Centre, hoping a politely worded email might get her further than calling out of the blue again.

'Great! No email address listed.' She put her phone away, deciding to do as her brother had suggested and not rush. 'It's not as if you're going anywhere, Granddad.'

'Whoa!'

Jake's high-pitched whistle made Sid smile. Her brother, not at all artistic—or so he claimed—was easily impressed by those who were.

Sidney thought he sold himself short. The way he plated his signature seafood creations showed real flair. He understood the important elements, like colour placement and texture. And, clearly, he appreciated the gallery.

Their family home had been like a gallery—the one their mother had dreamed of owning outright but never did; not even when she had the chance after their father died. Codicils to his will had detailed the money from his life insurance policy was to be set aside to establish the city gallery his wife had always wanted. There was more than enough to buy a commercial property outright, or something with more character and rustic charm. Whatever she'd wanted. Only, without her husband, Natalie became her own still life—inanimate, inert and uninspired. Even her partnership with Tasha suffered. Natalie lost all feeling, all desire, all ambition.

One day, Aunty Tasha had tried to explain the changes to Sidney.

'It's hard to lose someone you love. But when you *are* at your lowest—when anger and self-pity dominate every thought—you sometimes need to be the only person in the world experiencing such debilitating grief. You don't want to know someone is going through what you are. But because your father isn't the only one who died when the towers came down, your mother's grief is, well, diluted by the thousands of strangers all over the world mourning the loss of their loved ones. She's struggling to come to terms with her feelings.'

My mother is struggling at not being the centre of the universe? Sid remembered thinking at the time.

There was insurance money and compensation payouts, including a substantial lump sum from their father's company, as he'd been in New York on business. Their mother could finally afford her own gallery, but her enthusiasm for life had died. It wasn't until several years later, with the city having lost its appeal, and with Jake moving into a share flat, that Natalie packed up the family home, which no longer housed a family, and moved herself to the Blue Mountains. With extensive grounds, a vegetable garden to keep her busy, and a huge house, the property offered the perfect hideaway and ample project opportunities. Inspired and rejuvenated, Natalie planned to turn what had been a rundown B & B into an accessible artist retreat.

If her mother had needed a new project—a different fight to win—she found one with the Blue Mountains council and the man next door who was, in Natalie's words, 'an ignorant, uncooperative and idiotic nuisance'. Disapproving of his new neighbour and her plans, the man did everything possible to stop the business going ahead.

'Gotta feel sorry for the guy,' Jake had told Sid during a visit from Melbourne. 'Poor bloke doesn't know who he's up against.'

Sid never stayed with her mother for long, and she didn't make the trek often, partly due to the train trip from Sydney airport to the Blue Mountains taking longer than the inter-city flight time. Had distance and location motivated Natalie's move? Sid often wondered, especially given mother and daughter clashed more often than not.

Natalie's battle with her neighbour, including meetings, mediation and many, many letters, eventually ended peacefully, with the council approving Natalie's plans to add a guesthouse with a loft room, and an external studio and exhibition space. Naming the place *Brushstrokes in the Bush*, word quickly spread around the art scene. Most artists paid for the pleasure, and business boomed, until she started letting the small loft studio out for free to struggling artists with limited resources and nowhere to paint. That's when her least favourite neighbour, fed up with "drifters and derelicts living next door", erupted, putting his house on the market as a final thumbs up on the matter.

So what did Natalie do? Represented anonymously by a lawyer friend of Tasha's, their mother secured the smaller property at a very good price. She named the B & B extension *Dharug House*, after the original indigenous inhabitants of the area, and promptly let it out to more artists in need of somewhere peaceful to find their muse. The indomitable and unstoppable Natalie was back to her old self.

***

Jake whistled his stamp of approval for the life-sized nude on the gallery wall.

'Very Rubenesque,' Sid stated.

Shooting his sister a devilish grin, Jake replied, 'My thoughts exactly.'

'What do you think Mum would make of this place?' Sid asked.

'She'd go ape and you know it. Sure is a bit of everything. Spotted a favourite yet?'

'Not really, although for some reason I'm drawn to the big canvas behind the desk. I think I want to be that young girl with the flowing hair and walking barefoot on a windswept beach. But I want to know if she's walking to someone or away from them.'

'What do you think, Jake?'

'I reckon I'll leave the arty-farty stuff to you.'

Back at the cottage that night, while Sidney worked on the design job for Kurt, Jake cooked a seafood dinner.

'Nothing fancy,' he announced, sliding the bowl of fettuccini under his sister's nose. *'Voilà!* Behold my foody version of a nude. A voluptuous feast for the eye that is simple, with undressed and unadulterated seafood fresh from the co-op today.'

'Oh, you are so predictable, Jake! And a superb cook.'

After dinner, Sid stayed up working, grateful Kurt's deadline was keeping her mind off the prison visit.

Waking early to a cloudy sky and light morning drizzle, the temptation to stay tucked up in bed was strong, but so was the thought of meeting her grandfather. If she hurried, she could be on the road and then be back at the gallery in time to open. If she ran late—because by some miracle she got to see her grandfather on the spot—she'd ring Pearl and hope she could hold the fort.

First, she needed to haul her brother out of bed and remind him not to worry their mother about the prison visit. They'd find the right time to relay the news.

Like, maybe in another decade—and from a distance!

9

THE GREENHILL BANANA PLANTATION, 1979

How Tilly might break the news about Albie to David had kept her awake for hours. But by the time the sun's first light squeezed through the small rip in the roller blind, she'd decided. David had to hear everything from her first, and she'd start by telling him how he'd hurt her, leaving her scared and confused. She'd then say it was Albie who came on to Tilly while she was vulnerable. David might get angry and threaten Albie, like he'd done before when Tilly had implied Albie was up to his old ways, but she'd quickly calm and distract him in her usual way. First, she had to get to David before Albie did.

Having dressed hurriedly, she raced her bike down the hill, knowing David would be at the seawall, his beloved paintbrushes and pastels close at hand.

'I couldn't sleep either,' he said when seeing Tilly. 'But I would've missed this. Nature's own magnificent watercolour.' When he raised his arm to create a sweeping arc, his hand connected with the brolly protecting both his easel with the half-done drawing of a misty, mauve-tinged seascape. 'Look at the reflections on the water. And those colours. Moments ago, the sky was Prussian blue and burnt sienna. Both go together perfectly,' David said. 'Like we go together, Tilly.'

'Speaking of going together …' Tilly prepared herself to confess every-thing. She'd practiced what to say on the ride down the hill. But now the truth tangled with the possibility David might hate her.

'Here's my earlier watercolour.' He slid the paper out of his satchel. 'What do you think?'

'Put it away, David. It'll be ruined. The air is too wet this early.'

'I was mucking around and playing with colour. I love colour.'

Ordinarily, Tilly would have embraced his enthusiasm, but she was too cold, too edgy, and too impatient to listen this morning. She wished he'd shut up and let her talk.

'See here, Tills.' David was saying. 'See where two complementary colours meet and merge? See how new colours are born when they blend? We're creating something unique and wonderful. Like us,' he said. 'We are also complementary. We go together.' He jumped onto a seawall boulder to perform a clumsy pirouette.

'David, quit mucking around.' She held out a hand. 'If you fall I'll …'

Grabbing the hand she was waving at him, David yahooed and broke into a gangly groove, and for a second, she wondered if he'd been smoking the *wacky tobaccy* old Merv grew in the forest behind the beach shacks.

'First, I want to show you something,' he said, leaping from one rock to another until he was back on solid ground, landing inches from Tilly and tugging her arm. 'Come with me.'

'Where to?' With her patience wearing thin, so was her voice as doubt festered. Telling David was possibly the dumbest idea ever.

'Just come with me, Tills. It's a surprise. Up here a bit.' He tugged on a reluctant Tilly, urging her forward. '*Ta-dum*! What do you think?'

Tilly + David = family 4 ever

He'd painted the words on the flat face of the biggest rock, where everyone who wandered the seawall would see it. A rock so high and dry that no tide would ever wash away his message.

'This is the only rock I can afford to give you for now, but let it be my vow to you. And see?' He pointed to the heart-shaped border—a mosaic of broken china, shells, and turquoise-coloured sea glass—painstakingly pieced together and glued. 'I used complementary colours.'

'David, I thought—'

'Yeah, you thought I was avoiding you. I was, sort of, but I've put our time apart to good use. And being down here has helped me think about what I want.'

Tilly silently cursed her stupidity. This was all Matthew's doing. He'd made her doubt David *and* herself. *He'd* made her look to Albie. Now Albie could ruin everything.

'You mean you haven't been angry with me? You really love me, David? Forever and no matter what?'

'Forever and no matter what,' he repeated. 'We're meant to be together. I've known it since the first day we met.'

'But your dad and your mum … They have plans for you.'

'I don't need their plans,' David told her. 'You once said I was your rock, Tilly. Well, you're mine. Yes, they're my family and I love them, but we can start our own family.'

Tilly's heart smashed so hard against her ribs. These last weeks had given her heart a battering, and like the growing swell now buffeting the seawall—supposedly impervious and built to last—she knew even the strongest of things can wear down, weaken, and break.

'So, you *do* want children, David?'

'Sure, one day,' he said. 'First, I'd need to sell a few paintings and get us a place of our own. But we're young. We've got our whole lives. I'm thinking babies can wait until we're famous artists with our own gallery —one wherever you want. I don't care, as long as I'm with you. My parents will need to lock me up and throw away the key to keep me from you. And even then, I'll break out. I won't be a prisoner. No big walls with barbed wire will keep me from being with you, Tilly.'

10

MID NORTH COAST CORRECTIONAL
CENTRE, 2015

'So much for big walls and barbed wire,' Jake quipped, as he hoisted himself back into the four-wheel drive and slammed the door. 'And so much for finding our felonious grandfather and getting the lowdown.'

'Two weeks!' Sidney could only shake her head. 'That's why they wouldn't speak to me over the phone. I guess, when an inmate dies, they notify next of kin first. Perhaps, by now, another letter is sitting in the letterbox at Brushstrokes. Thankfully, with Mum in Melbourne, we can check on the way home.'

'We know more than we did, at least,' Jake said.

'Yes, thanks to you and your Prince Charming act in there.'

'Women find me naturally charming, Sid. I can charm anything out of anyone, including that Joan 'The Freak' Ferguson lookalike.'

Her brother prattled on about the Prisoner TV show he loved. Meanwhile Sid mulled over the little information provided by the prison official. Sure, manslaughter was a serious offence and demanded suitable punishment, but imposing a significant sentence on an elderly man over a car accident seemed severe. Was there more to the story?

When pressed for detail, the prison administrator had referred Sid to Sly Taylor. The name sounded familiar. The letter Sid had found, asking their father to come home and claim the family property, had been signed by a lawyer named Taylor, from a firm called Taylor & Brumsteer.

'Hey, sis.' Jake prodded the soft part of Sidney's shoulder. 'Do you plan to look up the legal eagle, like The Freak suggested?'

'What sort of name is Sly for a solicitor?' Sidney responded vaguely.

'More importantly, sis, what do we do now?'

'With my whole purpose to meet our grandfather, we might as well head off. We've got no reason to stay.'

Disappointment flashed over Jake's face. 'Or maybe we check out if one of those little beach houses has our family name on the door. The letter mentions property in town.'

'If that is the case, we'll have to involve Mum. She must know something, and she might see things differently now our grandfather is dead.'

'You have a point, sis, but in the meantime … I know I gave you a hard time for detouring here without a heads-up, but we both have paid work and I'm warming to the place.'

'Oh, I know what's warming you in the middle of winter, and it's not the job.' Sidney smiled.

At twenty-five, Jake still hadn't had a grown-up relationship. Her brother's cockiness and occasional lack of tact didn't attract women to him, even though the bravado was to cover his shyness. In his late teens he'd fallen hard for Cindy Cooper, who soon dumped him after her parents suggested Jake might turn out to be a bit of a no-hoper and restless, like his father. Sidney remembered her outrage, even growing defensive. It was true, their dad might have seemed difficult and a little detached, but people were wrong about him, and Cindy's parents had been mistaken about Jake. He simply needed a partner who got him.

'Let's take our time, sis. Mum's not expecting us. In fact, going back early might bring her home from Melbourne prematurely.'

Her brother had a point. 'I guess there's no urgency, apart from a burning curiosity that's best doused until Aunty Tasha can calm Mum. I can maybe dig deeper then.'

'If anyone can soothe the savage Natalie beast, our Aunty Tash can,' Jake said. 'In the meantime, sis, you could ask Pearl if she knows about a fatal crash. Then again,' he added, 'if asking means we discover our grandfather really was a crook and the town bad guy, or if you turn a simple question into one of your interrogations and stuff up what I might get going with Pearl, then—'

'I don't *interrogate*,' Sid snapped. 'And you don't need to worry about me taking the polish off your Pearl. You might be the guy for her.' Her brother looked so chuffed Sid almost regretted the joke she was about to make. *Almost!* 'Because what I know for sure is this, Jake. A small irritant, like a grain of sand, makes a pearl. And you, little brother, can be *really* irritating.'

'Very funny, sis, but you might watch and pick up a few pointers, because you really need to get back out there and shake off that moron you ditched.'

Rather than dismiss her brother's relationship advice, she wondered if Jake had been a better judge of men all along. The few times he'd caught up with her and Damien—usually during a fleeting visit to the Blue Mountains for the obligatory birthday or Christmas catch up—Jake's behaviour towards Damien lacked the brotherly bond she'd hoped both men would share. Rather, Jake was more wary dog, protective hackles bristling. Was the ability to sniff and detect a creep at ten paces a male psyche thing?

Sid turned the key in the ignition. 'Get your feet off my dashboard and we'll get back to work.'

Jake sat bolt upright like an expectant puppy eyeing a treat. 'We're sticking around?'

'Sure! If we've got a room and a job that pays, we'll stay. Better to spend the winter here than in the Blue Mountains. It's not like I have anyone waiting for me.'

11

WATERCOLOUR COVE, 2015

Pearl dropped by the next day for morning tea, dumping her dillybag on a chair in the garden before walking to the gallery door and calling to Sid, 'I've brought tea for two.'

They sat together at a small table, Sid enjoying the semi sun, while Pearl sat in the shade and donned an over-sized straw hat with a floppy brim. First twirling the teapot in a circle three times, Pearl slow-poured into the cups.

'Smells amazing,' Sid commented. 'What blend is it?'

'Lemon, sage, and honey—all harvested fresh from the garden, including the honey. The boss keeps bees.'

'Ooh, I love bees—and honey.'

'Then you're in luck,' Pearl smiled. 'There's plenty in the main pantry. You do know to help yourself to whatever you need from the kitchen, right?'

'No, actually. I figured, what with the B & B closed, the main residence would be locked up.'

Pearl hooted. 'Locked? Up here? Nothing gets locked, except the gallery. Oh, and the boss doesn't tolerate pussyfoots, so don't wait for permission, or to be invited. If you want tea or biscuits, or whatever, help yourself. If cooking up a storm is your thing, the main kitchen has all the mod cons. And if you have questions, ask.'

'I, ah, do have one question,' Sid ventured as a black and white butterfly stopped to rest on the teapot's handle. If only the ones flapping about in her tummy would settle. 'I gather there's been a few car crashes on the road leading into town.'

'A lot less since the highway upgrade,' Pearl answered. 'But our turnoff still has a reputation for being a black spot, especially during holiday periods and with drivers who don't know the road. I guess you're asking because you saw the roadside memorial on the way into town. That one was the worst of the worst, with the fatalities all from one family. Devastating for everyone.'

Sid somehow swallowed her mouthful of tea without gagging, but her stomach roiled, and she felt herself grow pale and clammy. 'The driver killed an entire family?'

'Worse,' Pearl whispered as she eyed the immediate vicinity. 'The father survived. He not only woke up in hospital, in a critical condition and with long-term leg injuries, he had to accept his wife and two kids didn't survive. None of us can understand that kind of grief until faced with something so unfathomable.'

Sidney topped up the tea she no longer wanted, also topping up Pearl's cup in the hope she kept talking. She did.

'I was away at the time, living in the city where road crashes generally lead the nightly news. I guess I developed a certain detachment to such events involving strangers. It's very different in a small town. It's the numbers thing.'

'What do you mean—numbers?' Sid asked.

'The smaller the population, the stronger the connection. In a place like Watercolour Cove, everyone knows someone who knows someone, so when tragedy shocks our little community, we all feel the loss. But what's sadder still is when tragedy divides a small community and, despite the years, some grudges never fade. What I'm saying is this, Sid.' Pearl's voice fell to a whisper as if the plants had ears. 'Yes, a few dreadful accidents have impacted our community, and people here have long memories. Many were pretty pissed off that a bloke who killed a local family, leaving the father lame, got such leniency. Dad reckons the sentence was likely because he was old. All that said, it's best you steer clear of such topics.'

'Yes, I understand,' Sid stuttered while wanting to ask, "how old?".

'Are you okay, Sidney? Your face is almost as pale as mine, and that's saying something.'

Sid was nodding when a noise startled her *and* the family of lorikeets nearby. The sound—a loud *buzz buzz*—seemed to have emanated from the base of the nearby grevillea bush.

'Oops!' Pearl smiled. 'Did I forget to mention the sound of customers? That noise is the entry gate alarm when a car passes through the gate at the bottom of the hill. There are several rock speakers around the property.' Pearl pointed at a lifelike brown stone concealed beneath the shrubbery.

'I should've realised,' Sid said. 'We have a similar alert system at our B & B—Brushstrokes.'

'You own a B & B? You never said. Kind of makes you too qualified for this gig.'

Pearl laughed as Sid waved a dismissive hand. 'Not at all. It's Mum's thing, and the business is closed temporarily while she visits friends in Melbourne.'

'Well, the system here is simple enough, but wherever you are—main house or cottage—you'll need to prepare for customers. No rush, though,' Pearl explained. 'A local who knows how treacherous that drive can be will take around five minutes to climb. A moron will take less, but there's fewer of them, luckily. I'll hang around long enough to know you aren't inundated,' she said with noticeable sarcasm.

Having assured Pearl she was fine, Sidney went on to sell two paintings to a newly married couple from Brisbane. A second vehicle arrived before lunch and the words painted on the side of the man's truck had made Sid laugh: *Coastal Landscapes: when home is dirt by sea.* He was a large man—certainly no Jamie Durie—but with the same impeccable taste in outdoor art. He'd lumbered around the garden, choosing several pieces, including the table Sid and Pearl had enjoyed tea on that morning.

The Brisbane people stayed chatting to Sid for ages about all things art, disappointed to find the B & B no longer operating, but promising to check again in spring. For a moment Sidney contemplated referring them to Brushstrokes in the Bush before she remembered it was also closed—the blinds drawn, the website offline. Instead, the fate of her mother's dream business remained a big question, which was a shame. Brushstrokes had made the perfect retreat for so many people. Hadn't it been the perfect hideaway after Sidney split with Damien? Well, perhaps not perfect. Running back to her mother was the last thing Sid thought she'd be doing at her age. But Damien had left her no choice. He'd also waited until the morning of an important meeting to break the bad news.

The compact kitchen of their inner-city apartment had, for years, demanded a well-choreographed routine of darting back and forth between the kettle, the toaster, the fridge and the sink, with the pair taking turns to stop and check their respective phones for messages. Occasionally, mid-routine, they'd bump into each other and laugh so hard that their euphoria would lead them to the bedroom for morning sex, missed buses, and late business meetings.

But since breaking her news to Damien, things had changed. Their routine became one of wide berths and polite apologies, until one dreadful morning, somewhere between mouthfuls of toast and muesli, when Damien dropped his bombshell. He'd uttered the devastating words as though referring to the second slice of toast Sid handed him—buttered to the edges, the way he liked it.

'I don't want this,' he told her.

'The toast?' Sid asked, confused.

'Any of it. There's not supposed to be a baby.' Then, as if he'd merely bumped into her, he added, 'Sorry.'

Strangely, Sid's first instinct was to laugh. Damien was being Damien. She'd seen this reaction before. When forced into a corner, he resembled a pouting toddler refusing to eat their peas. Only he didn't thump a chubby fist and shout, 'No, and you can't make me' on this occasion. His face said it all.

'Damien, I understand the baby news is a surprise—for us both.' Sid tried a smile. At least it felt like something similar to a smile. Then she tried for a laugh. 'In fact, honey, when the doctor broke the news, I almost fell off the examination table.'

Damien remained statue-like, his stare as cold as the untouched toast on the plate, his words colder still. 'But you agreed marriage is a state of mind. You didn't care for a piece of paper.'

'Well, yes, but that piece of paper gets a whole lot more important when there's a baby,' Sid retorted. 'It's no longer just about us. But I agree we shouldn't rush. Although, I'd hardly call getting married after seven years together a rush. We have time.' When Damien didn't react, she looked down at the cereal spoon she gripped tight. 'Geez, Damien, I don't see the issue. We'd be formalising our living together. Married or not, your name goes on the baby's birth certificate.'

'It does?'

'Naturally. You're the father!'

'Mmm, right, yeah,' he hummed, setting his Adam's apple into a little up and down dance. 'You see, Sid, that's the thing.'

'What thing?'

'Me and fatherhood,' he replied. 'We can't. I'm not ready.'

'Well, hon, you have a few months to *get* ready. You're going to be a dad and I'm going to be a mum. Ready or not, that's the truth of the matter.'

'Well, if we're being truthful, hon, there's something—'

Both exasperation and fear laced her next question with sarcasm. 'Something like what? You better not say there's another woman.'

'I wouldn't cheat on you, Sid.'

'Phew!' Sid sighed and moved in for a hug, only to have Damien step back.

'I'm just not sure I'm ready for one person forever, let alone two. Can you understand?'

The metallic taste of blood let Sid know she'd bitten her bottom lip a little too hard, but as Damien tugged a tissue from the box on the bench and reached towards her mouth, she snapped.

'Don't you dare show me you care.'

How could she have gone to bed in love and woken up to a crazy conversation like the one she was having right now?

'Sid, please, we already have the perfect partnership. Me with my business acumen. You with the creative nous. And with a studio on the cusp of being exactly what we'd planned. If only—'

'You're talking about the *business*?' She was shouting now, no longer caring if the neighbours in the next apartment heard.

'Yes, because we agreed the business was our baby, and well, to be honest, I'm feeling a little … conned.'

'Conned?' she spat the word back. 'Are you serious?'

'Look, Sid, I'm sorry. I didn't mean—'

'Stop, Damien, you're not doing this to me now. Not this morning. We have the Welshman presentation in an hour. I need to focus.'

'See, babe, you love our business and you're putting it first.'

'Yes, I love it, Damien. I've put seven bloody years of my life into it.'

'Yes, and in a few years, Zeus Designs will reward us both for our dedication and sacrifices. You understand what I'm saying?'

'Ah huh, yep. I do.' She studied Damien, shrugged and picked up her bowl of milk-soaked muesli. 'I guess I need to make a doctor's appointment. Come along if you like—or not. The choice is yours.'

'You're doing the best thing by getting rid of it,' he said. 'And I'll be there for you.'

For days afterwards, as Sidney picked dried specks of homemade muesli off the floor and the glossy white kitchen cupboards, she wondered ... How was it possible that those tiny specks could be so obvious to her and yet she'd failed to see what sort of man she was living with?

Reminding Sid of those kitchen cupboards was a colourful oil-on-canvas titled *Confetti*. Standing there, in awe of the artist's obvious patience and dedication, only the melodic sound of wind chimes moving in trees broke the eerie late-afternoon silence on top of the mountain. Earlier, her brother had whizzed past the gallery and tooted the quad bike's horn. Hitched to the bike was a trailer loaded with fallen garden debris—the result of a wet and windy evening. Happy to see her brother in his element, Sid had smiled and waved. But with the chill of a retreating winter sun rattling Sidney's bones, tea with honey beckoned—if only to settle her tummy after her depressing reminiscences about Damien. After tea, she'd find Jake and brag about selling so many pieces in one day.

Locking the cash register and popping the keys in the pocket of her jeans, she rubbed her still small belly, smoothing the loose-fitting top.

'Tea might help you grow, Little Bump.'

The residence was unlocked, as Pearl had stated. Still, walking into a stranger's house felt weird.

'*Helloooo?*' Sid called. When no one answered, she stepped inside and immediately felt at home. 'Wow!'

As a child, she'd asked her mother one day, 'Can one house have too many paintings?' Small at the time, she'd thought her mother's paintings enormous.

'Never,' Natalie had replied. 'It's all in the way they're displayed. One should never overcrowd walls, though.'

Her never-overcrowd-the-walls rule had failed to reach this rambling old house atop the mountain, with pictures of every shape, size and medium spread across multiple walls. Although the frames were made of various materials—ornate metal, timber, and polished resin—the collection somehow worked together. The room's decor in general—the colour coordination and scattered ornaments—spoke of a feminine touch, with elaborate mirrors artfully positioned to reflect the light. While the house seemed the type one could happily poke around for hours, what Sid needed was to find the kitchen and make tea to calm her belly, before returning to the gallery.

Who knows, Sid? You might just have another customer before day's end.

Heading to the rear of the house, passing several closed and numbered guest rooms, Sid was passing a darkish hall branching off to the right when a whimper sounded. The noise came again, louder and more frantic.

'Hello?' Edging cautiously along the unlit passageway, she passed three more numbered guest rooms before stopping outside the fourth and furthest door. A sign, handwritten in black marker pen, read: *No Entry.*

About to turn away, the whimper changed to loud snorts, and shadows flickered in the crack of sunlight under the door. Sid tried the handle but, rather than closed, the door seemed wedged, as if it had blown shut. No doubt swollen with age, releasing it required a nudge only, but an invisible force reefed the door wide open, and an unidentified ball of brown fur pushed frantically between her feet before scampering down the hallway.

Sid clutched at her chest, fright riveting her to the spot. *A possum? A giant rat perhaps? Or worse, one of those big hairy spiders Pearl had said lurked in the banana trees.* Standing deathly still, letting her heart rate calm, Sid found herself teetering on the precipice of curiosity. While the unlit room was not so dark that she couldn't make out the contents, she should have ignored the temptation to enter. She should have backed out, closed the door, walked away.

She didn't.

She couldn't.

Not after spying the canvases and feeling an inexplicable pull.

The room was musty, with all but one of its sun-blocking shutters closed. Sidney flicked the light switch, to no avail. *No bulb.* Adjusting the louvres helped a little, the slanted beams of sunlight adding shadow and depth to the sketches. The room's contents were breathtaking, with drawings covering every spare space, even pinned higgledy-piggledy to the old plasterboard walls. Other canvases and boards sat stacked like cards on the floor, with the largest propped against walls. Several were of the same woman, with some full-length drawings and others focused on aspects of her face and body: a mouth pursed and puckered; eyes closed, open, smiling; the graceful angle of her neck; the fall of her hair; the turn of her wrist. In a bizarre and obsessive way, the artist had broken the woman's body down into a series of sketches, pulling her apart piece by piece, every emotion captured on canvas: the sombre, the wistful, the vivacious.

One piece stood out. The detailed semi-nude had the subject kneeling and surrounded by magnificently textured rocks. She was young—not much more than a girl—and wore only a paint-splattered skivvy raised to expose breasts in a tangle with her bra. The almost life-size piece showed the model's head thrown back in rapturous laughter. Or had the artist captured her at the height of sexual pleasure? Elation licked the skin on the back of Sidney's neck when she realised she wanted to laugh with the woman, share in the thrill and in her uninhibited joy. Was the model a real person, Sid wondered, or perhaps the artist's carefully crafted composite? The woman of his dreams, perhaps? Other nudes were confronting, and Sidney tried to imagine what it would be like to bare everything—to have her body and emotions dissected, to expose herself so completely.

While there was something beautiful about a woman's form portrayed on canvas, Sidney knew she could never be *that* reckless, nor as brave because Damien had knocked any sense of self-worth out of her with his parting words: 'You're making the wrong choice, Sid. You're not the type to go it alone. Do you know what a baby will do to your body? Babies change *everything*. Ask my brother and his wife what happened to their sex life.'

Sid squinted at the louvered sunlight now painting its own picture over the walls and floor, highlighting a table festooned with old palettes, dried tubes of paint, and paintbrushes stiff with neglect. A tower of art books listed precariously in one corner, and as her finger traced the spines—Pro Hart, Nolan, Lindsay, Namatjira—she caught sight of a slender notebook tucked between several ring binders. With its pages bunched, and with Sid's compulsion to smooth them, she admired the linen feel of paper tinted the palest of pinks and featuring a rose watermark.

Unlikely to belong to a man, and with the urge to flick open the cover stronger than the fear of discovery, Sid paused to listen for sounds down the hallway, or for the buzz of the gallery alert system. Then she smoothed the crumpled pages caused by the cramped confines and read the inscription scrawled over the inside cover:

For my Rose among roses.
So you can write to me every day—always and forever.

Sid thumbed the pages, expecting to see the unruly and unreadable scribblings of an artist. Instead, the neat handwriting of a letter writer with a distinctly feminine style filled every page. The salutation was simple enough, but Sid read on, her guilt battling with temptation.

Guilt lost.

Biting down on her bottom lip, and with a final furtive look at the door with its *No Entry* sign, Sid sank down in the old leather office chair and read to herself:

My darling husband,

The property is so quiet. I miss you and your big, booming voice. I remember when the children were young, how you would sing your favourite Slim Dusty songs in the shed where you thought no one could hear. Now I sit here in your favourite chair, writing to you, hiding from a world turned angry. I close my eyes to imagine the chair's arms as your arms, coming to life and wrapping around me, holding me, supporting me, comforting me.

Without you, we remain lost but somehow managing. I think you heard about young Tony Sheaves leaving just as the tourist season was upon us. Thank goodness we can rely on the ignorance of newcomers to town to ensure we have the help we need. That is until they, too, hear the gossip. It is as you predicted. So many of the people we once called our friends are deserting us, blind to anything other than their own pain. Do they not think we also feel pain? Do they not see our tears or remorse and remember the struggles we endured? With the house never so isolating, I pray we are reunited soon.

David keeps me company, of course, and does his best to fill the property with colour and beauty. The gallery is getting more and more interest, and Ernie Watts has recommended council secure a grant for a sculpture down by the foreshore to mark the town's centenary in 2015. Of course, these things take years to come to fruition—three or more, we're told—but we can be very proud of David. He could have let what happened destroy him. Instead, he has your strength for pulling through the tough times. Be assured of our undying belief and faith that one day the plantation will again be filled with love.

I do so look forward to every letter from you. Hearing your voice, too, is wonderful, but it is our letters that bring back such fond memories of our courtship. These young things with their computers and silly smiley faces will never know the joy of words, or of simple pen on paper hugs and kisses.

Oh, I almost forgot. Your last letter mentioned Albie Marhkt tried contacting you. I dare not ask, and yet I am curious about his purpose. Not to mention the hide of the man. Perhaps in your next letter you might tell me more.

One other thing I must—

A sound somewhere in the house pulled Sid from the letter. Footsteps. Someone was coming. Panicking, she slid the notepad back between the books and jumped up, keen to slip out of the room undetected.

Too late.

A man stood in the doorway, glaring at her, forcing Sid to adopt her it-wasn't-me-Mum stance: hands behind her back, shoulders pulled taut, innocent eyes wide and blinking.

'What are you doing?'

'Pearl said I could make tea,' she replied weakly, a shiver of sheepish guilt snaking its way along her spine. 'She said to let myself into the house.'

'Tea?' His gaze did another sweep of the room.

'I didn't mean to be rude.' Rude sounded better than snoopy. 'I'm Sidney. My mother named me after Sidney Nolan.' Was useless trivia a reasonable defence? She coughed to clear the croak in her throat. 'There was a noise in this room. A possum, I think. Either that or the rats up here truly are enormous.' Her attempted humour failed, the man's silence making the moment more awkward. 'Okay, you've got me. I was snooping. Sorry. But I saw the works in here and couldn't help myself.'

His stare darted from her to the paintings and back to Sidney again. 'You're the new girl in the gallery.'

'That's right.' Even though it had been a while since anyone had referred to Sid as a girl. 'Nice to meet you.'

When the man said nothing, not even acknowledging her apology, Sidney was suddenly just plain cranky. She lifted a defiant chin. 'If you'll excuse me. I'll go make that tea.'

Because the man didn't shift quickly enough, she ducked under his arm that braced the doorway and strode down the long hall, her need for tea stronger than ever.

12

WATERCOLOUR COVE, 2015

Everything Sid needed was on the kitchen bench, pushed back and lined up along the tiled wall, but within reach—no hunting through cupboards required—which was just as well. Hadn't she snooped enough for one day?

'Great first impression, Sid,' she muttered while inspecting the hand-written labels on wooden canisters.

'I thought so,' came a deep voice from behind. 'And I'm not the only one.'

Startled, Sid spun too quickly, almost knocking a cup to the floor. In the doorway was the same man—her boss—but for the first time she noticed the two forearm-style crutches.

'This is for you.' Without extending his arm—because he couldn't while supporting himself—he wiggled the envelope pinched between his thumb and index finger. 'Take it, please.'

Hesitating, Sid stepping forward, asking, 'What is it?'

'I thought cash in advance appropriate.'

'I don't understand.'

'A short time ago I received an email from a customer praising your performance this morning. Most of the people I hire are backpackers passing through town. As the gallery rarely benefits from such an intimate knowledge of art, I thought a cash advance might be an incentive to … stay.'

'Oh, I'd be happy to wait till payday. No incentive necessary,' she added. 'This job is exactly what I need. I'm Sidney, by the way.' Without thinking, she extended a hand, promptly snapping it back to her side and picturing the red rush of embarrassment painting her neck and cheeks.

'So you said.'

'Morning all!' Pearl blustered into the kitchen, her timing perfect. 'Tea for two, or tea for three, boss? Join us?'

'Not for me. I'll let you ladies get on with it,' he said and retreated, leaving Sid stumped.

'That was awkward,' she whispered to Pearl. 'I didn't see the crutches straight away.'

'Is that the first time you've met?'

'Yes.' *If I don't include the episode up the hallway, Sid* added for her own amusement. 'You never mentioned he was … you know?'

'After a while you don't notice,' Pearl said. 'I guess that's why I didn't mention the crutches. He gets around on those things better than I get around on two good legs.'

Sid doubted that. Jake, her fitness-freak brother, had already gate-crashed Pearl's five-kilometre dawn run, followed by the warm-down workout on the sea wall.

'The boss has done well—physically. A more determined man I've never met.' Pearl took over the tea making from a still-stunned Sidney. 'And especially given the devastating chain of events. Name your poison.' Pearl was pointing to the array of tea flavours on the bench, some loose leaf, some store-bought bags. 'Still, it's not a person's physical capability that allows them to bounce back from a tragic accident. A person needs courage and bucket loads of self-belief. The whole affair was an absolute shocker for the family.'

Devastation? Tragic? Absolute shocker? The shudder that ran all the way through Sid to the tip of her fingers made the tea decision—a calming brew—easy. Pearl had talked about a shocking car accident the other day. Was her boss and the survivor—the father of two left maimed by a reck-less driver—one and the same? And what if Sid's grandfather was the elderly male driver responsible?

'Earth to Sid?' Pearl nudged as she dropped two chamomile bags into a pink teapot patterned with a gum leaf design. 'I was saying, from what I hear he's lucky to have come as far as he has. While he gets around fine on the crutches, it wasn't always the case.'

'How do you mean?'

'This property isn't exactly easy to get around in a wheelchair, but I reckon that's what drove him. He never gave up, instead training his body over time with short bursts of activity, but always with a place to rest.'

'I'm not following you.'

'You haven't noticed how many seats there are around the garden?' Pearl pointed beyond the kitchen window. 'They're scattered everywhere —around the grounds, on the porch, inside the house. He started with small physical challenges, forcing himself to stand. Then he built strength by making himself walk from chair to chair where he'd rest before continuing. Rarely is he in a wheelchair, in public anyway. Honey, Sid? In your tea,' Pearl clarified.

'Oh, sure, thanks.'

Sid had noticed some wheelchairs: one in the main house and another on a veranda. With both chairs covered in paint, she'd assumed they were someone's idea of art. Thank goodness she hadn't tried selling one earlier. *Talk about the ultimate gaffe!* Then again, she'd seen crazier exhibits when her mother had been curator of a fringe art gallery in Melbourne. Sidney had spent her formative years in a special penned-off area in the store-room, her days spent playing with paint and clay—smelling art, touching art, listening to critics talking about art. She'd lost count of how many gallery openings and exhibitions she'd attended with her mum. No wonder Sid related to the scent of art now.

'The body responds in ways we can't understand,' Pearl was saying as she drizzled honey. 'Muscle manipulation, stimulation, touch. They all help. Anything's possible, and people will respond to different therapies.'

'Art as well,' Sidney added. 'Any creative endeavour, music included, can be therapeutic. For a while I considered heading back to university to study art therapy.'

'Not anymore?'

'No, I, um, have different priorities. The timing isn't right.'

'Well, I reckon you could be onto something. Throwing himself into developing the seawall art project over the last twelve months has been therapeutic for the boss.'

'Are you talking about the statues, or whatever, down by the fore-shore? I wondered what was under the tarps. Why does closing up or covering something tempt us to peek?' *Or to ignore no-entry signs!*

'You're looking a little pale again, Sidney.'

'I was feeling a little queasy earlier.'

'Why don't you finish your tea and go for the day? The gallery closes in an hour. I'll stay. Then I'm meeting Jake to go riding together.'

'I heard. Jake asked to borrow my bicycle. What have you done to my brother, Pearl?' The pair giggled. 'And thanks. I sure won't say no to an early mark. I'd like to drop by the seawall, get some fresh air and check out the rock art before dark.' Sid pulled the phone from her pocket. 'I should call Jake and tell him where I'll be.'

'I'll tell him for you.'

'Oh, okay, great. And Pearl? You should know something. My brother can be a bit of a daredevil. He's young and into extreme everything. Just sayin' …'

Pearl smiled. 'I don't mind extreme. Albinism often holds me back, so when I can, I do. Speaking of extreme. Be sure to take a jacket when you go. Those winter winds coming off the ocean late in the afternoon will rip your skin off.'

As Pearl had predicted, the bitter sea breeze stung, until Sid became too immersed in the hundreds of hand-painted messages on rocks along the seawall walk. With a scarf tucked around her neck and chin, head down and hands snug in the pockets of her puffy parka, she pushed through the on-coming wind until reaching the furthest point where the river estuary met white-capped open water. A silver-haired couple—the only other people silly enough to be out—had themselves draped across a boulder, spindrift slapping them in the face as they awkwardly attempted a selfie.

Assuming the faded artwork meant the rock was *theirs*, Sid asked, 'Can I take that photo for you?'

Having smiled for the camera, the couple, whose love had clearly not faded as much as the paint, thanked Sid and she turned to head home.

Probably close to half-a-kilometre each way, if not more, Sid assumed a nice day would see the breakwater the ideal destination for anglers, cyclists, or those walking to keep fit. Daily exercise was definitely on Sid's must-do list, but not in this weather, even though anglers happily battled the elements, which included a potentially dangerous swell that forced them to dodge the odd rogue wave. One tiny artist was at work and Sid stopped to admire his progress. The industrious young boy had paint-stamped a smooth-faced rock with his handprint in green, yellow, and blue and was instructing his mother to write the word FAMILY.

Sid's mood might have plummeted, if not for the boy's excited squeals of, 'Red! Red!' while tugging on the red kelpie's collar.

As if the mother intuitively knew Sid was expecting—probably by the way Sid was hugging her belly—she grinned, rolled her eyes, and said,

'Another day, sweetie. Time to go.' No doubt the little artist was planning to complete his family with a red paw print.

With the wind now pushing against her back, Sid positioned the jacket's hood and strolled on, stopping to ask a bearded gentleman battling the wind to bait his hook if he was catching much.

'Nothin' legal.' The man straightened and shielded his eyes with a hand. 'Not these days. Used to catch whatever we wanted and no one would care. Different place back then. Idiots running the show now. You need a licence to catch a fish and yet they let hooligans paint over the rocks.'

'Hooligans?' The word slipped out before Sid could stop it.

'Outrageous and dangerous, if you ask me. Paint makes the rocks slippery. Not sure which council idiot allowed such shenanigans in this town. Obviously the same one who agreed to change a perfectly sensible town name to Watercolour bloody Cove.'

'What was it called before?'

'Dinghy Bay, on account of the number of rowboats that once lined the sand.' He nodded towards the crest-shaped beach with fewer than six beach shacks and less upturned tin boats. 'Had a few boats meself back when we's was allowed to catch fish. Nowadays, the ol' knees and back are no good for bobbing around the ocean. Instead, I'm out here like a bloody barnacle trying to keep a grip on this bloody seawall with all its bloody graffiti. In my day, defacing public property was illegal.'

'Some designs are clever, don't you think? Makes me wonder about the people behind the art.'

'Art *schmart*! You young ones think all this rubbish is romantic.'

'But some artists have gone to a lot of effort. What about that one?' She pointed to the man's left. Though faded, the predominantly blue and orange design was framed with small shells and sea glass, making the heart shape both masterful and purposeful—and not just lazy repetition. How many times had Sid heard her mother say, *"Complementary colours are king and colour blocking requires an artist confident with the colour wheel"*. Within the border, almost lost in its intricacy, were two names, one faded: *David and ...* was it *Lilly*? 'That one, there, is romantic.' She pointed. 'I wonder if these two lovers are still together?'

The fisherman snorted. 'Not likely. She pissed off out of town before the paint on that rock was dry. Never seen again. Not so romantic now, is it? The girl couldn't have broken more hearts if she tried.'

Broken hearts? Sid wanted to tell the old man she knew all about those. One of Damien's last questions had crushed hers. 'Is the baby *really* mine?'

he'd asked. A stoic Sid had stayed silent as she left the room, refusing to cry because her mother would say tears were a sign of the weak and helpless. Sidney couldn't afford to be either—not then and not in the future. She'd be a mother herself soon enough.

'Have you lived here a long time then?' Sid asked the old man.

'All me life and not planning to go nowhere else. Five beach shacks, three old codgers left, and all hanging on to our little piece of local history. We might have one foot in the grave and grandkids nipping at our heels, desperate to get their hands on prime beachside real estate, but my lot will wait till I get carted out in a box.'

A thought sparked. Might this angler know her grandfather? While tempted to ask, Sid instead heeded Pearl's earlier advice and kept her curiosity in check. The old man wasn't shy about speaking his mind.

'Okay, well, thanks for chatting. After tolerating this wind, I sure hope you catch *something* you can keep.'

'Most likely a bloody cold. But this sea breeze is nothing. Wait until we get a decent southerly buster. Them winds will likely blow an apple through a tennis racket.'

Leaving him to mutter into the wind, Sid resumed her walk back to the carpark, seeing a stretch limo nearby, the driver safely cocooned inside. On the beach to her left, a blissful and barefoot bride and groom posed for photos and laughed as the wind played havoc with layers of lace and chiffon. Behind them, children in jumpers and swimsuit bottoms busily built sandcastles, while others ran out of the water, shrieking with the cold but skipping back in again. Feeling colder still just watching the antics, Sidney was contemplating the warmth of her car when she observed the three wrapped sculptures on the nearby green space, and a man struggling to tie down the blue tarp on one sculpture.

It's him!

In place of track pants and a shirt, her boss wore baggy jeans torn at both knees, a chequered wool coat in navy and red that hung to his thighs, and fingerless gloves in black—the same colour as the scarf around his neck. Even under the black hat, the brim shadowing his face, Sidney recognised the ratty ponytail of grey whipping about. She could say hello, give him a hand, but a third encounter today might only result in a full trifecta of faux pas. Thankfully, another man stepped up to help. *Good!* Sid needed to get up that mountain road before dark. But with the winter solstice not far away, the sun was already pulling a blanket of mountain under its chin, the eastern side of the hill in full shadow. Before long, a darkness would fall over the tiny town.

Leaving her boss to his work, she could return another day to explore the seawall's rock messages in more detail. Maybe she'd do her own handprints and write her own promise for the future.

Yes! As soon as she figured her future out, that's exactly what she would do. And maybe, not too many months from now, she'd come back and add Little Bump.

13

WATERCOLOUR COVE, 2015

The unusually warm winter's morning Sidney awoke to was a welcome relief after yesterday's wintery winds. After finishing her muesli, she decided against the more direct sandstone pathway to the gallery, preferring the rough trail that skirted the edge of the mountain-top. Although aware one misplaced step might wake a hibernating snake or send her skidding down the steep slope, a lazy walk to commune with nature would be good for her mental health. She took it slow, occasionally staring down the hillside through the rows of perfectly aligned banana plants. With so many trees, a person falling would likely resemble a marble in a pinball machine being bounced from obstacle to obstacle and ending up who knows where.

The morning view from the ridge was worth the risk, with its vista of mountain and simmering sea quite spectacular. Sid could almost understand the thrill an extreme sport lover experiences when throwing themselves over a cliff, or out of a perfectly good aeroplane. Sid's wildest adventure to date was a road trip with her younger brother.

Having focused on the view rather than where she was going, Sid missed fork in the road that would have taken her to the gallery. Taking a stab, she wound her way through a field of avocado and pecan trees, only to find herself looking at the small cottage. Nearby, standing at an easel, was a familiar figure in a black hat. The man wore no shoes and no shirt, only baggy white pants flapping about his ankles and covered in more paint than his current canvas. Half-dressed and without the bulky coat he'd been wearing on the seawall, he appeared smaller and less intimidating. Suddenly, her curiosity—an invisible but insistent force—was drawing Sid from the shadows.

'Good morning!'

Nothing. No response. No recognition at all. Not from him, anyway. Her approach did raise the ears of a small dog lazing on a wooden bench —an ugly, plain brown dog that could, for all intents and purposes, double as a possum. *And that's being polite!* It then occurred to Sid that she might have insulted her boss by mistaking his best friend for a pesky possum. *You may have even said rat, Sid.*

'It's a beautiful day,' she tried again, that wilful curiosity her mother was always carrying on about kicking in. But it seemed her boss was having one of those crotchety days Pearl had warned Sid about.

Being rude might make some people give up and go away. Not Sid. Being ignored bolstered her resolve. Moving close enough to see the detail in his painting, the colours on his palette, the fine moth holes in the old felt fedora pulled low over his eyes, Sid spoke again, adding a touch of steel to her voice. 'May I see your work?'

Without stopping or offering her a cursory glance, he huffed and puffed cigarette smoke, looking like a grumpy old dragon. 'You don't have enough pieces to critique in the gallery?'

'No, um, yes. Ah, that's not what I meant.' She heard the tremor in her voice. 'I'm not wanting to critique—'

'Then why be curious about my work? Does your inquisitiveness have no bounds?'

'I like *art* and enjoy watching artists work,' she said, refusing to acknowledge his barb. 'I grew up surrounded by some great ones.'

'Artists or their art?'

Despite the whoosh of humiliation heating her cheeks, Sid's stare locked on as if challenged by a schoolyard bully to fight. She could drop her mother's name, impress him with the galleries Natalie has managed over the years, *and* the artists she's discovered, but before Sid could speak, she saw it: a movement, a tiny curve of the mouth. *A smile?* Okay, so, it was small, short-lived, and most likely sarcastic, but it was a smile.

With one crutch supporting his left arm, he used the other hand to retrieve a packet of breath mints from the back pocket of his pants. 'Trying to give up the smokes—again. Seems two crutches aren't enough for me when times get tough.' Shaking out the tiny pellet of candy into a palm already occupied with a walking aid looked awkward, but he managed and, as an afterthought, offered the packet to Sid.

'No, thanks,' she said.

Presuming the mint offer was an invitation to stay, she stepped closer. The work was unexpectedly luminescent and brilliant for a watercolour. The subject also took Sid by surprise. Had she expected a painting of the same woman to confirm her boss was the epitome of the arrogant and obsessed artist?

'Oh, it's a landscape!' she said.

'Well done,' he rejoined as his hand delved into another pocket. He tossed something, setting the brown dog's tongue in motion on the ground around a bench seat. 'But not quite Hans Heysen or Arthur Streeton.'

'I don't know about that,' Sid responded. 'It's different, yes. The colours are vivid and the style smooth and loose. It certainly draws in. I like it.'

'Thank *you* very much.' With a slightly theatrically bow, he popped another small, white mint. 'I consider my job done.'

Sid wanted to laugh. Was the guy using rudeness to drive her away? *Ha!* He had a lot to learn.

'Do *you* like it?' she probed.

Choking on the mint, he coughed up the words, 'D-do *I* like it?' Then he laughed—a big, genuine guffaw from deep within his belly. 'You're a perceptive woman. Or should I say persistent? You remind me of someone I knew a long, long time ago.'

'Who was she?' Sid asked, going for broke.

'Hardly matters. I'm sure you're not the least bit interested in long-time-ago tales. I tell a story in much the same way I paint landscapes. Not well.'

But the claws of curiosity had dug deep, hooking Sid. 'What if I said I *was* interested in your old stories?' When his shoulders fell and he looked away, something made Sid want to reach out, to connect emotionally and physically. 'Are you all right?'

'This weather is too warm for winter. Pablo thinks so. Don't you, boy?' He scooted the dog along the bench seat, lowered his body down, and leaned his crutches.

'I suppose it is warm when away from the water and out of that icy wind.'

The man donned his shirt and was buttoning it when he squinted up at Sid. 'Forgive my bad mood. Today has me feeling the effects of too many losses, too close together. It's the same every winter.'

'Mmm,' was all Sid dared, though tempted to tell him she understood loss. But before uttering a word, he positioned his crutches to stand. Was that the extent of their conversing?

'Come on inside,' he said, startling Sid straight where she stood. 'I'll show you I can be hospitable when I want to be. I can probably manage tea. You like your tea, as I recall.'

'What about your work?' Sid queried, concerned. 'You can't leave it out here.'

'You asked me before if I liked it.' He picked up his cigarettes, hesitated, and returned them to the easel. 'I don't. Not at all. Come on, Pablo.' He whistled, then turned to Sid. 'You coming?'

'I'll fix the tea, Boss,' she said, wondering if he'd expected she would. Not that he wasn't capable, even while juggling two cumbersome crutches, but the kitchen seemed rather, um, chaotic.

'Thanks. And the name is David,' he said as Sid set to work.

'Oh, okay, well, *David*, can you point me to the tea bags?'

'Tea*pot* and leaves,' he said, training his finger on the counter. 'And if you insist on getting intimate with my kitchen while I watch, you can tell me what you're doing here on my mountain.'

'You mean "what's a nice girl like me doing in a place like this"?' Sid laughed at the old gag. David did not. 'Okay, well, I'm on *your mountain* because *you* gave me a job at the gallery. And in your kitchen because you offered tea.' To her relief, the cheeky response didn't make him mad. On the contrary, David's grin said he'd met his match.

'I meant, what brought you to Watercolour Cove, especially given Byron Bay is the young-person's mecca and not far away?'

'Someone broke my heart a little while ago and I had to move home.' Sidney stepped around Pablo's wagging tail. The dog seemed to have forgiven her for mistaking him for a rat. 'Sadly, Mum and I, well ...' Unsure how much to share, she said, 'As we don't agree on much at present, I hit the road.'

'With your brother?' David cocked his head. 'Siblings who get on are rare, in my experience. You're lucky.'

'You don't know my brother,' she quipped before noticing David's expression shift.

The man had just gone some place very dark.

14

THE GREENHILL BANANA PLANTATION, 1979

The cave grew unexpectantly dark, forcing Tilly and David apart. Blocking the entrance, almost obliterating the view of a sparkling Pacific Ocean, was Albie, hands on hips.

'What are you doing here?' Tilly asked, busily tucking her shirt into her jeans.

'What are *you* doing here—with *him* and like *that?*' Albie responded angrily. 'Oh, wait, I know the answer, don't I, Tilly? Must be another blue moon.'

David stiffened. 'What's got up your nose, mate?' When Albie's hand instinctively went to his very pronounced proboscis, David laughed. Not to be mean. Sometimes Albie's reactions were just so funny. 'Don't be a dickhead. I didn't mean you had a booger flapping in the breeze. You sound pissed off. What's up?'

'You're what's up?' Albie said. 'Does David know, Tilly?'

As David's smile switched from wry to wary, Tilly panicked and stared hard at Albie, pleading for loyalty. 'I'm not sure what you're talking about, Albie?'

David walked over to his long-time friend and neighbour, Tilly hovering behind him. 'Listen, mate, I know how many times Tilly has told you she's not interested in you like that.'

Please, please, please, Tilly mouthed at Albie.

'Trying to break us up makes no sense, mate. Tilly's with me. Always has been. Always will be. Wherever we end up—here or somewhere else—

it'll be together. Forever family, right, Tills? Listen.' Albie looked uncomfortable when David stepped forward and hooked an arm around Albie's neck. Before being rivals, the two boys had been good friends. 'Don't take what I'm about to say the wrong way, mate, but … It would be good if you buggered off while me and Tilly … You know? Nudge, nudge! Wink, wink! We're kind of getting into something. Reckon you can make yourself scarce?'

For a second Albie looked crushed. Then he looked furious.

'Wait.' Tilly stepped between the boys. 'Don't be mean, David. He's family.' She took Albie's hand to lead him away. 'Let's go and talk in private. You can tell me what you want.'

Leaving David grumbling to himself in their hideaway, she ushered Albie back along the rough path to the fork in the plantation road. Once there, she pulled him into the shady grove at the start of the Marhkt's banana plantation and lunged at him so hard, the force of her hands slamming against his sizeable chest knocking him onto his butt.

'Good grief, Albie! What are you thinking? I thought we were friends. What's wrong with you?' After momentarily contemplating his lap, the boy—she had trouble thinking of him as a man—looked up. 'Spit it out.'

'You don't want me anymore,' he mumbled.

'Aw, geez. Seriously? Are you still on about that night? What we did meant nothing, Albie. It was a favour, and it was one time.'

A blink tipped tears over his ruddy cheeks. 'But you and me—'

'There is no you and me. I gave you what you wanted. That's all.' Tilly's voice grew impatient. She never knew what to do when Albie got all emotional and needy. 'You *did* want it, didn't you? You wanted me.'

'Yes, but—'

'No buts, Albie. You agreed it was our secret and no one would ever know, right?' Tilly folded her arms.

'I did?'

'We're mates, Albie, and mates don't dob on mates.'

'Mates?' He slumped, as if that single word somehow sucked the tantrum out of him.

'Look. I don't want to hurt you, but I need to make sure you understand a secret is forever. Tell me you do.'

His nod reminded Tilly of the faded dog figurine glued to the dashboard of Ulf's car. 'I do. I understand you're just like everyone else. No one has ever wanted me for keeps.'

'That's not true,' Tilly insisted, her anger subsiding. 'The Marhkts wanted you.'

Albie scoffed. 'They wanted a worker. My own mother didn't want me enough to keep me.'

Tilly closed her eyes, groaning on the inside. She never knew what to say or do when Albie got morbid about his mum.

'You said you loved me, Tilly.'

'I do. We have a special bond, for sure. You're my brother. You've always protected me.'

'That's not what I meant. You said you wanted to be with me and we could go away together. I've got money. I've been saving up and making plans. I went looking for you to tell you, but … I guess I'll go on my own.'

Tilly was immediately curious. How much money had he saved? But she couldn't ask, not now.

'Look, Albie.' She sighed. 'The right girl will come along one day—I promise.'

He got to his feet, dusted his pants, and wiped his shirtsleeve over both his cheeks, leaving behind a dirt smudge. 'There'll only ever be one girl for me. "Together forever", were your words,' Albie said as he turned to walk away. 'I'll never forgive you, Tilly,' he called back. 'You won't hurt me again.'

15

WATERCOLOUR COVE, 2015

'You *will* hurt yourself if you don't take it easy on that thing,' Sidney called from the gallery veranda where she inspected the colourful perimeter of ceramic planter pots. The last few days had delivered ample life-giving rain. 'I know that expression of yours, little brother, so I remind you it's not a toy. A quad bike can kill an experienced rider. Do not even think about hooning around.'

'Relax, sis, I've ridden a million times. They have these babies at the Sydney Fish Market.'

'You haven't ridden *that* bike, and you haven't ridden one on winding dirt tracks.'

'The boss wants fresh supplies of bananas and avocados down at the gate, and I need to check the honesty box before the tourist group arrives around noon. If you prefer, I could take one of those cables and swing through the trees like Tarzan.'

'Tarzan? More like big, bumbling ape.' Sid knew Jake was goading her. Her brother enjoyed extreme adventures, but he wasn't silly about safety, and Pearl had already warned him to stay clear of the disused flying fox cables that crisscrossed the hillsides. In times gone by, the system of wires would've played a vital role in conveying back-breaking bunches of bananas to the roadside packing shed.

Jake would've loved those early days. Her brother thrived on manual labour and enjoyed seasonal work that offered him a new employer, a different challenge, and something to learn and to inspire him. *Maybe Jake was the smart one after all.* Far from the no-hoper Cindy Cooper's parents had labelled their daughter's high school crush, Jake was actually teaching Sid about starting over, adjusting, and being brave.

'Change can be scary,' he'd told her. 'But you can do it, sis. Just gotta improvise, adapt, overcome.'

What might Jake think of his big sister if she admitted to having had second thoughts about leaving the familiarity of her life with Damien and Zeus Design Studio, even though she knew what staying with Damien would've meant for her baby?

'Hey, sis!' Jake's voice cut through her thoughts. 'You okay? What's with the belly rubbing?'

'Gas, if you must know. What were you saying?'

'That I'm in a hurry to get done and get out of here. Me and Pearl have a date.'

'A date, eh? Hope she's a woman of simple tastes.'

'Very funny!' Jake checked the trailer hitch was tight, mounted the bike, and double-checked his pocket, drawing out a key, probably for the honesty box. 'I like her, sis.'

Sidney bit back a smart alec retort. She'd never seen her brother so serious while talking about a woman. Ordinarily, while waiting for his laundry to dry—every Monday without fail—he'd update Natalie, and Sid if she was there, on his latest conquest. While Jake and his fish-market mates might manage to hook up most weekends, the women were, in their words, "the catch, kiss, and release type". And no wonder, Sid would say to herself. What hope was there for malodorous mates who exuded a fish-market fragrance as the night wore on? One day, their mother—taking matters into her own hands—added a good dose of lavender oil to the machine's rinse cycle. The next day at work, the blokes had ribbed Jake about smelling like the ladies' loo. But Pearl seemed indifferent, or perhaps impervious to the scent *and* to her brother's annoying habits. As the daughter of an oyster farmer, maybe she was used to fishy smells. From what Sid had seen these past couple of weeks, the girl seemed nearly as keen on her brother as he was on her.

'I like Pearl, too, so I'm asking you to take it easy on that thing so you make that date.'

'In the wrong hands they might be dangerous, but only idiots fall off four wheels.'

'Just. Be. Careful,' she called over the roar of engine noise as he accelerated away.

Tugging the puffy vest across her chest—the zipper no longer met over her belly—Sid settled into a chair, closing her eyes to allow the winter sun to warm her face. Though tiring easily these days, she felt surprisingly calm—and happy—for the first time in months. Getting away was smart—and necessary, given the Blue Mountains gallery was most likely still roped off with crime scene tape. Initially, Natalie had asked Sid to accompany her to Aunt Tasha's, but Sid wasn't keen on going back to Melbourne. Then Natalie, the master manipulator, demanded she go, probably hoping Damien would wake up and Sid would make up because, according to the law of Natalie, a baby needs a father. But Sid had set her mother straight.

'Mum, this is the twenty-first century. Single mothers are no longer shunned by society, and the authorities don't take babies away from a woman who's failed to snare a husband.'

'I'm not suggesting you *snare* a husband.'

'And you're surely not suggesting I beg Damien to take me back.'

'Beg? No. But often a man doesn't know what he wants until a woman reminds him. You're beautiful and talented, Sidney. You can make a man do what you want.'

Sid could hardly believe her ears. 'Are you *kidding*, Mum? That's *exactly* what snaring a husband is. And in case you haven't noticed, those heady decades of women batting their eyelashes to get ahead or have guys swooning at their feet are no more.'

'Don't you be facetious.'

Sid reared up. 'Don't *you* be ridiculous, Mum. I'm not making a man do anything he doesn't want. That includes being involved in his child's upbringing. Damien's made his choice. If he has a change of heart in five or ten years from now he can be involved, but he'll fit in with *my* life— wherever I am and whatever I'm doing at the time.'

'In that case, Sidney, cut all ties now and move on. That option is better and less confusing for the child.'

'I will not, Mum. Nothing that's happened between me and Damien should stop his child from knowing him. I can't think of anything sadder. If a dad is still around, father and child deserve the opportunity to know each other. But *I* will be the parent who decides for this child until he or she is old enough to choose.'

The conversation ended there with her mother up and walking away, leaving Sid seething.

·   ·   ·

Thankfully, Sid could not be further away from her mother's manipulation and angst. Warm in the sun, Sid stared blithely at two yellow masked plovers—a breed notorious for fiercely defending their patch, but also for the shared responsibility of choosing, preparing and protecting the nest location.

'You're a lucky lady to have such a devoted mate,' she said, having identified the bird with the smaller yellow wattle on its face.

But at the buzz of the gate alarm, the pair squawked and flapped about, ready to defend their patch. For Sid, the imminent arrival of customers would be a nice distraction, even though it meant leaving her spot in the sun. Crossing the polished floor of the gallery, Sid caught sight of herself in the highly polished steel sculpture at the centre of the room. Finally, her bump was getting bigger. Turning sideways to inspect her profile in the reflection, she was rubbing her palm in small, soothing circles when a voice startled her.

'Stunning piece,' David said. 'What do you like about it?'

'Oh, ahh, I, um …'

He grinned. 'Hopefully you'll be slightly more articulate when a customer asks.' Outside, five elderly ladies of varying size burst from the confines of a tiny hatchback. 'Come on, Pablo, that's our cue to disappear.'

And he did, skedaddling through the side door faster than any man in history—not counting Damien after hearing her baby news, of course. Sid straightened her loose-fitting shirt and welcomed the ladies, allowing them an opportunity to browse while she stood on the sidelines, enjoying their antics and comments over a male nude collection.

An hour later, having sold four small artworks, she was on the veranda, waving back at the four cardigan-covered arms flapping out each window of the car, and calling, 'Thank you, ladies. Take it slow and be careful.'

16

THE GREENHILL BANANA PLANTATION, 1979

'I said *be careful*, David. And your father wants you home before dark. It's a study night.'

Tilly often heard his mother calling across the neat front garden she sweated over in summer, all the while lamenting the harsh winter winds that stopped her growing her treasured roses and daphne. She instead settled for more rugged, salt-resistant plant varieties like coastal rosemary, colourful pigface, and flax plants. Rose also had her husband keep the Indian hawthorn shrubs hedged because she insisted the dense shrubbery offered a little extra protection from the winds that pummelled the mountain from August until October, when the ocean brought warmer north-easterlies in time for summer holidays.

But Rose's repeated safety warnings were uncalled for. David was always careful. The closest thing to a risk he took was waiting until his parents were in bed before climbing out his bedroom window and negotiating the dark and unkempt track to reach Tilly's house. The journey was dangerous because, unlike Greenhill, the area surrounding Ulf and Hilda's house was more junkyard than garden. Rubbishy items—like discarded tyres, obsolete machinery parts, splintered wooden crates and pallets—had lain in the same spot for so long that weeds and grasses had wrapped themselves tight, rooting the ugly clutter to the spot. Whenever Tilly suggested the Marhkts make Albie tidy up, Ulf would make wisecracks about the clutter being Albie's unique artistic expression, and Hilda would laugh. In the wet, David would sometimes have to skirt around the edges of the plantation slopes where it was less boggy. Precarious at the best of times, but more so after rain, one misplaced foot could be the difference between making Tilly's house or sliding, bum first, down the steep sides of the plantation and banging into a tree or two—or four—along the way. With the trunk of a banana plant being ninety percent water, hitting one hurt like hell.

'I know that firsthand,' David had told Tilly one day. 'I've lost count of how many times I've head-butted a banana stump. But seeing you is worth a million tumbles.'

This morning, Tilly was extra worried because David hadn't shown up at her bedroom window last night, as expected. On top of little sleep, and desperate to see him, she now had to spend the day weeding the vegetable patch with Hilda. Albie was expected to help in the garden, but he'd feigned some pain and now lay crying on his bed. Tilly didn't believe in crying. Manufactured tears were okay, though, and crying on demand could be useful. This morning, Albie sobbed like a baby and didn't seem to care who heard him.

As Tilly and Hilda picked at the soil with hoes to loosen the choking vine weed and recover the last of their pumpkin crop, they heard Albie's occasional moans. Hilda would look over at Tilly, give her a curt smile and nod of reassurance, and return to her task.

There had been a cold snap overnight that wasn't going away, even with the sun beating down. After a while Tilly stopped to chafe her arms, rubbing both hands back and forth to wipe away a sudden rush of goose-bumps. Except for birds chirping in the big poinciana tree, Tilly's world otherwise quiet. Where was the noise that normally floated up from the packing sheds? Today, David's dad was breaking in new workers. Tilly had been looking forward to them starting because more men on hand meant more free time for David to concentrate on his final assessment piece and end-of-year exams. Also, when he didn't have to juggle the banana business with his studies, Tilly got more of his time. Sometimes she wished he'd just leave school early, like her, and focus on his art.

'But I need a good result to get into uni,' he'd tell her.

'Why?' she'd argue. 'You don't need a degree to paint. And you don't need a degree to teach art, because you're going to be too busy being a famous artist.'

And a father, Tilly mused while bending to scoop a handful of weeds Hilda had pulled.

'Aww, crap!' She gasped and dropped the hoe, desperate to hug her tummy and ward off more sharp pains.

'Mind your mouth, young lady,' Hilda chastised over the phone ringing in the house. 'And there'll be no faking illness from you. We have more to do.' With her reproachful look trained in Tilly, Hilda ripped off both garden gloves and slammed them into the dirt before making a dash for the back door.

In agony, Tilly dropped to the ground, not caring the damp brown dirt would stain her jeans. What was happening? Was she losing the baby? Was she even pregnant, or were the pains due to one of those sexually transmitted diseases she'd read about in the latest Dolly mag. How could she know for sure?

'Tilly?' Hilda called with unusual urgency in her voice. 'Tilly!' The screen door whacked the house cladding, sounding like a gunshot. 'Where's David this morning?'

Forcing herself to stand and to shout, she replied, 'How should I know where he is? I'm here working. Why?'

'He's missing, his bed wasn't even slept in. What do you know? And don't give that innocent little shrug of yours. I know about your night-time rendezvous. Now, get yourself over to the Greenhill property and tell his parents what you know.'

'But I—'

'Now!'

Without thought for her own safety, Tilly hurdled fences and Albie's junk, twice skidding and landing hard in the boggy mud. When halfway through the barbed wire boundary fence, a horrible caterwauling erupted. The sound, like nothing she'd ever heard before, came from David's mother, Rose.

An ambulance transported David to hospital—firstly the local facility, and then onto a specialist spinal unit in Sydney. For three days, Tilly could do nothing but wait on the mountain for news, or for David to come home and hold her. On the fourth day, Ted and Rose returned to Greenhill. They came alone, with down-turned mouths and sad eyes.

Ted immediately summoned Ulf and Hilda to the house, asking them to bring Albie and Tilly. Gathered in the living room, Ted was standing over Matthew and shouting, while Rose fluttered between them, helpless to protect her son.

'Are you stupid?' When Ted's backhanded slap across Matthew's head knocked him to the ground, Tilly instinctively touched her own cheek—the memory of her mother's cruel discipline never forgotten.

Rose screamed, begging her husband to stop, but Ted couldn't hear over his thundering voice. 'Do you know what you've done?'

The older man, his brawny body honed from carting bananas, was a giant in a dangerous mood and poised to strike again had Rose not clung to her husband's forearm as fiercely as a mother can, while her eldest son huddled on the ground, arms wrapped to protect his head.

'I'm sorry, Dad, I didn't think—'

'No, you didn't think at all. Why not call for help?'

Frantically buzzing back and forth, Rose tried comforting both husband and son. She liked to make everything right in the world. Tilly always thought her to be the best kind of mother a girl could want, but as god-fearing as the family was, their all-embracing tolerance and acceptance never truly extended to the likes of Tilly.

'You might as well have strung him to a rafter in the packing sheds with your own hands,' Ted hollered. 'You broke his neck.'

Tilly couldn't believe Matthew would harm David. She'd witnessed the brothers' half-hearted fisticuffs, usually over something insignificant, but Matthew knew he was the stronger and the fitter of the two. He didn't have anything to prove.

'I swear we weren't fighting. I saw the slip marks in the mud. I followed them and found him,' Matthew said. 'I wouldn't hurt David. He's my brother.'

Rose clung to her husband's arm—for all the good that would do. The tiny woman looked like a bird holding back a bear.

'You should've told us he wasn't in his bed, Matthew. We might have gone looking and got to him earlier. For God's sake, why didn't you tell us?'

'I didn't wanna say because …' Matthew shot Tilly a sorry look. She held her breath. 'Because I thought I knew where he was. I guess I didn't think—'

'No, you'd need a brain for that,' Ted berated, shaking Rose's hand off his arm.

'But I found him, didn't I?' Matthew said defensively.

'And you should've fetched me before moving him, you stupid boy. *If he comes out of the coma, he'll likely be paralysed, his life ruined. And you'll be reminded every day it was all your fault.*'

Tiny thorns of terror needled Tilly, like a swarm of paper wasps prickling her skin. She wanted to scream. *STOP! This isn't real. This is a night-*

mare. She wasn't standing here in David's house hearing the saddest news and staring a wide-eyed warning at Matthew as his palms cupped both ears. Tilly also wanted to block Ted's shouting and the sobs, but she dared not move for fear of drawing attention to herself.

Ted's focus shifted to Albie. 'What about you, boy?' Like a pitchfork had poked his bottom, Albie startled to attention. 'I saw you pair when I was coming up from the packing shed. You were near the boundary fence. What were you arguing about? What do *you* know? Speak up, boy.' Ulf faced off with Albie and yanked his wrist. 'If I find out you had something to do with this …'

Did he know something? He'd had that falling-out with David. The boys had argued over her, and she'd listened, hidden from their view. While she hadn't made out every word, she'd heard David laughing and goading Albie, teasing him, almost daring him to take his best shot. Tilly had left them to it, laughing all the way home over the boyish antics. But she wasn't laughing now. Albie, with his bulging googly eyes darting back and forth, his face white, and his pinched lips quivering like a five-year-old, looked ready to blurt out everything, including how he'd got upset over David and Tilly's plans, and how Tilly had slept with Albie before dumping him for David.

Desperate to stop Ted and Ulf bullying him into confessing, Tilly stepped into the centre of the room, steeled herself and asked, 'Can I see him? Can I see David, please?'

When everyone turned to look at her, Rose stepped up, her voice aquiver with concern. 'Don't you think you've done enough, Tilly? In fact, you're just as much to blame. All that provocative strutting around the property, tempting the boys so they fight over you. Had David not been sneaking out at night to see you he would not have been on the pathway in the dark and he wouldn't have fallen. If not for you I'd still have my boy. I'd have my David.' Helped by Hilda, Rose crumbled into a seat to wail in a way Tilly had never heard.

In the corner of the living room, Ted stiffed, his stare intensifying as though he was hearing about his son's night-time adventures for the first time. Rose probably only knew because she was a mother, and mothers know there's no keeping a fledging in the nest once they've tasted flight.

Tilly had wanted to like Rose. She was like a magpie—nest building, feeding, protecting her young, and happy to have them hang around well after other bird breeds have kicked their kids out of home. Right now, though, she looked stunned and frail, like the poor rosella that had struck Hilda's kitchen window and plummeted to the porch. By the time Tilly had rushed outside with an old shoebox—because she'd heard a secure, dark space gave birds time to recover—the rosella was upright but stunned. Carefully scooping the fragile, feathered body into her hands, Tilly had begged the creature to live and fly away. But the bird fell limp on her palm.

'Oh, no, wake up,' she'd pleaded. 'Wake up. I need you to be free and fly away for me.'

Tilly had cried and cried. She'd cried even more over the lone rosella perched in the tree outside her bedroom window. For days it had patiently waited, while its mate-for-life lay still in a box on Tilly's dresser.

'Did I kill it?' she'd asked Hilda.

'No, dear. Some things are not in our power to save. What's important is you stayed till the end.'

'It's mate did, too,' Tilly had said, glancing out her window at the lone rosella.

Tilly turned to Rose. The woman had stopped wailing, and Ted no longer lorded over everyone. Rather than yelling, he was kneeling before Rose, his words comforting.

'Please, Mrs Hill, I have to be with David. I have to tell him—'

'Please, stop!' Mr Hill said, his voice hoarse. 'What don't you get, Tilly? There is no telling David anything ever again. David isn't there. Our beautiful, spirited boy is gone.' Rose whimpered and fell limp against her husband's body. 'His mother will go back tonight. She'll be with him until the end. It's a mother's place to stay with her son. The rest of you— Matthew, Tilly, Albie—I can't even look at you. Leave us.'

With Ulf the first to leave, Hilda Marhkt was left to herd Albie and a reluctant Tilly to the front door.

Alone outside the cave, numbness shielded Tilly from the full force of winter winds whipping up the mountainside. How could she feel anything without David? He had to be okay. He had to live and fly away with her—mates for life. They had plans. They had dreams. They had a baby. At least she'd thought they did. Tilly was still so confused by the horrible pains she'd experienced, and the blood still spotting her underwear. To be sure, she needed to see a doctor—only not the creepy old codger from the dingy surgery in the main street who'd tell everyone at the Fisho's Club about the young girl who got herself in trouble. A city doctor was best. If allowed to visit David, she could see a doctor there. Or maybe, Tilly thought as she dragged her knees to her chest and rocked back and forth, maybe losing the baby was best. She couldn't raise a child alone and trust herself to not end up like her mother—single and on the street, and desperate to do whatever she could to make ends meet. But how did she make a baby disappear? No Dolly magazine article or Dear Dolly letter ever said.

For now, with confusion clouding her brain and the cramping in her stomach no match for the ache in her heart, Tilly made a promise.

When the time comes and I can finally get away from this place, David, I'll live the life we planned. And if I'm a mum, I'll be the best ever. I promise.

17

WATERCOLOUR COVE, 2015

'Do you promise me?' Sid heard Pearl ask.

Her brother replied, complete with school-yard hand gestures, 'Cross my heart and hope to die.'

'Don't say dumb things,' Pearl berated. 'And do up the straps on your helmet. You think the designers put them there as decorations?'

'You tell him, Pearl,' Sid said, joining the pair at the front of the gallery. 'Jake, we need to talk.'

'Uh-oh, sounds like family biz.' Pearl picked up the colourful dillybag, her constant companion. 'But before I go, Jake, and speaking of family, do you want to come down to my place tomorrow? You can check out the oyster leases. There's always a cold beer at my dad's.'

'Cool.'

'You, too, Sid,' she said as an afterthought.

'I'll pass. But thanks.'

'Okay. See ya.'

Jake waited until Pearl was out of earshot. 'This better be important, sis.'

'It is. Something's been on my mind since chatting with a guy fishing off the seawall. I need to ask you about that.'

'You choose *now* to quiz my fish brain?'

Sid chuckled. 'Those are your words, not mine. And no, I do not want to quiz you about fish. Do you remember wondering if our grandfather owned one of those old fishing shacks on the beach?'

'Could explain my love of fish,' he quipped.

'I was thinking more in terms of when someone dies. There's usually family or next of kin, right? And our grandfather died weeks ago. Prison administrators would have family or next of kin details.'

'Spit it out, sis. I've got places to be.'

'Well, I can understand the prison people not giving out inmate information to any Tom, Dick or Harry who waltzes in off the street looking for their long-lost relative. There'd be a process when a prisoner dies in custody, right?'

'You wanna just tell me, rather than quiz me?' Jake said while Sid's mind tuned over with possibilities.

'Okay, so say the solicitor acting on his behalf got that first letter to his son at Brushstrokes, then presumably they sent another letter to notify of his death.'

Jake tried to scratch his head, his fingers instead hitting the safety helmet. 'We've talked about this already, sis. We agreed there might be a letter sitting in the letterbox at home.'

'*Ooooor …*' Sid said, her voice going on a little rollercoaster ride.

'Or what? And would you stop with the pacing thing? You're making me dizzy.'

Sid rammed her hands onto her hips. 'What if there's no letter at home because another family member is listed as next of kin, and they were notified of his death instead?'

'You mean a relative? Like Dad had a brother or a sister? Wouldn't we know if there was a sibling?'

'We can't know the truth about anything anymore. Who's to say there's not a blood relative out there? An uncle or an aunty. A real one— not like Aunty Tash. Maybe even a grandmother.'

'Well, flip me a fishcake, sis! You could be onto something. But like I said, I've got prettier fish to fry, *if* I can get these jobs done. Let's catch up later.'

The urge to interrogate her mother—yes, interrogate was the right word on this occasion—was suddenly so strong, but Sid remembered the unusually fragile woman who'd looked back from the taxi window as the cab drove away from her beloved Brushstrokes in the Bush. Sid had never seen her mother shut down so completely until that horrible incident. Beautiful Brushstrokes was no longer the retreat responsible for bringing Natalie back to life after her husband's death. In the beginning, the small B & B with a gallery for local artists was the perfect therapy. Not even the occasional drama—like the thieving weirdo artist who'd broken into the main house, last year's firestorm that had seen the neighbourhood evacuated, or the septic system that had overflowed during the Christmas holiday season—seemed to have ruffled Natalie's feathers. What *had* been her undoing—what had sent her mother into a rare downward spiral—was finding a man hanging from the rafters in the loft, and the drawn-out police investigation that followed.

Mother and daughter might've been at odds often, but seeing the indomitable matriarch falling to bits had made Sidney want to be there for her, even offering to hold her mother's hand each time the police arrived. But the Natalie of old—the one who occasionally shut down to everyone—had shaken her daughter's hand away and berated her for being clingy. So, with a lot of help from Tasha, Sid had made Natalie see a stay with her best friend in Melbourne made sense. Aunty Tasha knew the right thing to do.

18

THE GREENHILL BANANA PLANTATION, 1979

'It's my fault.' Matthew sobbed. 'I keep telling Dad I'm sorry, but what I need to do is to tell David.'

Tilly climbed over the seawall to sit beside Matthew on the same boulder. 'Your dad shouldn't blame you.' Edging closer, she rubbed a hand over his back. 'It was an accident. Your brother took the wrong path on a wet night, then slipped and fell. But he'll be home soon and you can ask for forgiveness. David will understand.'

Matthew's head shook so oddly, Tilly feared he was seizing. 'But I did stupidly move him—because he asked,' he added. 'David was whingeing about the pain in his head and trying to sit. I asked him what else hurt. He said, "Nothing, just my head". So, I propped him against a tree trunk before going for help. When I tried explaining to Dad, he went ballistic. Do you know how many times he's said, "You might as well have killed your brother"? How do I live with what I did, Tilly?'

'Shush, Matthew,' she soothed. 'David's not dead. He's injured. He'll recover. He's strong. He has a reason to live.'

Matthew sobered and stared at Tilly, his head cocked to one side. 'How much do you actually know about David's condition? Are they telling you anything?'

'Just that we must wait for him to wake up.'

Silence settled around the pair like the sea mist closing in.

'If only it was that simple, Tilly. *If* he wakes—and that's a big if—he'll be stuck here on this mountain and needing a wheelchair and machines to help him breathe.'

Tilly was about to hit out at Matthew for telling fibs about his brother, as usual, but what she saw in his face scared her.

'He'll rely on our parents for everything. There'll be no leaving, no art school, no fame. Dad says it'll be no life for a man, which is why he's meeting Mum at the hospital. I think they're discussing what's best for David, but Dad won't let me go so I can say sorry and goodbye. I-I figured you knew the score, Tilly.'

Tilly hadn't heard anything after the words *stuck here.* Suddenly, her stomach fluttered. Baby or colly wobbles? She didn't know. She'd never been pregnant before. She'd also never had all-the-way sex before that day in the cave when she and David had planned their escape from Greenhill.

Oh, David, David, what do I do? If she was pregnant, Ulf would kick her out. She'd be alone and desperate, just like her mother.

A thousand questions fought for space in Tilly's head, but with only one answer. No way could she be stuck in this town forever. If David can't walk or talk or breathe by himself, then he can't be a father. Ted and Rose will force Tilly to give the baby away and then ban her from Greenhill forever.

'Are you hearing me, Tilly?' Matthew was asking. 'I have a right to see my brother, but Dad's never taken me seriously. David was his favourite.' He sniffed hard several times before wiping his face with the sleeve of his jacket. 'I might as well disappear. He keeps telling me to get out. Maybe I'll bloody go and let him look after this place without me and David to boss around.'

'But David will be home. He *will.* He's going to be the next Pro Hart.' If Tilly stayed positive and said the same words over and over, like a wish or a prayer, her David would come back. But what if the unthinkable was to happened? What if … 'Matthew?' she said softly. 'If you're serious about leaving Greenhill, where would you go?'

'Anywhere I can get a job,' he replied, his mien more upbeat. 'And maybe even find a girl who'll like me enough to marry me so I can be a better husband and father than my old man.'

A father? Tilly's baby will need a father. Herding the million thoughts racing around her head, there were two ways she could fall right now— into a heap and on her own, or into the thing closest to David. His brother.

Switching her tone to sweet and needy, she looped an arm through his and snuggled closer. 'In telling you this, Matthew, I'm thinking about what David would want.' She had his attention. 'He'd hate us to be sad or dwell on what ifs, and he sure wouldn't want us to stay lonely. And we won't be alone if we stick together, and you don't need to hear your father remind you every day how useless you are.'

'Why would you want me around? I'm not David. You and him had such big dreams. I've ruined everything, Tilly,' he sniffled. 'I'm so sorry.'

Inside, Tilly groaned. She couldn't say what she needed to say with the man blubbering like a child. 'Look at me.' She moved to squat in front of Matthew's bent over body and rattled his shoulders. 'It's you and me, Matthew.' She wrapped her fingers around his. 'We need to grow up and you need to listen to me. You're right. You did rob your brother of his dream, and staying here will remind you and me every day. That's why we have to go.'

A quick swipe of a sleeve cleared his eyes of tears, but not of questions. 'What? Where?'

She took a big breath in and exhaled the words before she could change her mind. 'Together we can live the life your brother won't. *You* can make David's dreams come true.'

'How? I-I don't … I don't paint.'

'You'll support me while *I* paint. We can save up and establish the David Hill gallery. We can live his dream *for* him. And when we're famous, and we have money, we can invest in Greenhill to prove you worthy of your dad's praise.' She didn't allow Matthew time to object. 'If you stay in this place, you'll forever be David Hill's useless brother. You're almost thirty. Have you ever been with a girl long enough to … You know?' When Matthew didn't reply, Tilly said, 'Figured as much. It's time to grow up and make your own decisions. Be with me,' she said, 'because I can't risk staying here and I can't be alone.'

Wide eyes, bloodshot from his tears, stared in disbelief. 'Be *with* you?'

'You said you want to marry and have a family. Let's do it—for David.'

'But Tilly, you once told me you'd never be a mother. Has something changed your mind?'

'Maybe.' She turned her back to him, nestling her body between his legs and her head on his chest to watch the distant horizon.

'I'm not like my brother.'

'I know,' was all Tilly said.

'You and him … You have your paintbrushes. The closest I come to being creative is picking up a pen to write letters for Dad. Davo and I couldn't be any more different.'

'Matthew, David would be the first to tell you both paintbrushes and pens can tell a story. You'll thrive away from this place. You only need to decide what you want. If your brother can't live his dream, don't you owe it to David to live yours?'

'You can help me make David's dream come true?'

'Of course, Matthew! We can pack and be on the road to Sydney in no time.'

'What would I tell Mum and Dad?'

Tilly twisted around to stare him down. 'Do you think they care? To them you'll always be the cause of grief they'll never get over. You don't deserve to be Ted's whipping boy. Just leave. Say you'll come with me, and I promise you a forever family.'

Matthew's nod stayed small, so did his smile, but it was enough. If she couldn't have David, she and her baby would be safe with Matthew.

'We'll go tonight. Winter solstice is the longest night of the year. By daylight, we'll be starting fresh.'

19

WATERCOLOUR COVE, 2015

'The winter solstice *what*, Jake?' Sid asked while she adjusted the fancy window louvers to allow the morning sun to warm the gallery.

'The winter solstice picnic,' he replied from outside where he hung a new piece—a woven hammock—between two uprights on the veranda. 'There's this picnic thing Pearl does down by the seawall to celebrate the longest night of the year. I gatecrashed, and it was *sooo* cool.'

'Last night? On the seawall? I imagine it was freezing.'

'No, I meant Pearl is cool. Like *really* cool. We kinda have nothing and yet everything in common.'

'How is that possible, Jake?' Sid asked as she re-positioned three artfully woven cushions on the hammock, standing back to eye the placement.

'Well, we both love our food.' He chuckled. 'But while I grew up worshipping the sun, Pearl had no choice but to worship the moon, which is obvious if you compare our complexions. When her and I stand side by side she reckons we're the human equivalent of a neenish tart.'

'Pearl worships the moon?'

'Well, maybe worship isn't the word she used. That makes her sound a bit, you know, zombie apocalypse, when she really is a regular girl. Not only that, but the woman can cook! Seriously, Sid, she's been cooking forever. When they were kids, her five brothers had played outside, leaving Pearl stuck indoors to help her nonna in the kitchen. She's cooked family feasts all her life. Last night's winter solstice picnic was for one, but … Whoa, if that's what she cooks for one … I won't eat for a month.' Jake forced his gut out, turned to the side and rubbed his stomach. 'Hey, who do I look like right now?'

Sid smiled when she realised, while Jake had raved on, she'd been rubbing her belly. This trip was turning out to be the best decision. While her purpose for coming no longer existed, Sid was seeing another side to a brother who she'd only ever seen as an annoyance. She liked the grown-up version, and if Sid couldn't have her happy ever after, maybe she could live vicariously through her brother's blossoming romance with Pearl.

'I like her a lot.'

'I'd have never guessed.' Sid chuckled. 'You go for it, Jake. At least one of us is getting laid.'

'Oh, I reckon you got laid all right!'

'Who got laid?' Pearl asked, appearing around the corner and walking straight up to Jake, planting a kiss on his mouth, sound effects included. 'Not you, I hope.'

Sid shot a warning look at Jake. She didn't want her pregnancy disclosed to casual acquaintances. Then again, her bump was not so little, and Pearl's relationship with her brother had shifted from the *casual* to the *close friend* category. Best that she owned it.

'Morning, Pearl. Jake's giving me a hard time about getting pregnant.'

'I figured it wasn't bloat, but I also avoid making assumptions, especially after making the ultimate gaff with a client a few years ago.' Pearl laughed, walking over to hug Sid. 'Congratulations!'

'Thanks.'

'Mmm,' her brother hummed, still licking his lips. 'You've been snacking on the leftover smoked fish bits from last night. They were my favourite.'

Pearl heaved herself into the hammock and hugged one cushion to her body. 'My nonna had an old Estonian saying: *Better a salty morsel than a square meal of sweet.*'

'I am loving your nonna.' Jake planted another kiss on Pearl's mouth. 'And Sid, I'll whip some up for you to try. As soon as Pearl shares the recipe.'

'Sorry, family secret.'

'Oh, yeah? Bet I can get it out of you.'

With Sid deciding three was a crowd, she left the love birds giggling, the hammock in full swing, and Pearl trying to squirm out of Jake's grip.

20

THE GREENHILL BANANA PLANTATION, 1979

'Quit with all the squirming, Matthew, and leave me to drive,' Tilly demand.

'But you don't have a licence, Tilly. You can't just do whatever you like.'

'Not having a licence doesn't mean I can't drive.' Tilly could feel Matthew's stare. Three hours ago she'd felt his apprehension as they'd packed the car under the cover of night. She'd also smelled the beer on his breath while he'd written a note to his parents. Tilly never asked what the note said because the detail didn't matter. Nothing mattered except getting away so they could forget and start over. 'Besides, Matthew, if we're going to marry, there's something you should know about me.'

'What? And why are you turning off the main drag?'

Tilly steered the Torana away into a rest area, pulling the car into a heavily wooded area before turning off the ignition. She would have climbed into the back seat had the suitcases and banana boxes bursting with their belongings not been in the way.

'Tilly?' Matthew's voice shook. 'I asked you—what should I know?'

She leaned across, drew his face to hers and kissed him deliberately hard on the mouth. 'That I can do whatever I like when I like. And right now, I really *like* you.'

21

WATERCOLOUR COVE, 2015

'He likes you, Sid,' Pearl announced from what was now her favourite place—the colourful hammock.

'Who likes me?' Sid asked, sweeping again after the small gecko foraging among the crunchy mound of leaf matter decided to scurry away.

'The boss does. He's not used to having someone around to comment on his work, let alone someone who knows the stuff you do. My snazzy spectacles hardly do justice to the colours and textures in a fine work of art.' She nudged her dark glasses and made a face. 'But you really know your stuff. You *see* his work.'

'About the glasses,' Sid queried, changing subjects. 'Does albinism make you sensitive to light?'

'Among other things. The worst part is not being able to drive, but most of my out-of-town clients come to me. What's annoying is that me and Marilyn won't get a chance to hit the highway together.'

Sid stopped sweeping. 'Marilyn?'

'My Kombi van.' Pearl sighed and dropped one leg over the side of the hammock. 'I love Marilyn. If only the authorities would let me have a licence to drive. It's not that I can't,' she explained. 'Just not legally, not on public streets, and not with these peepers.' Pearl lifted her sunnies above her eyes and let them drop again. 'The tricycle gets me most places around town *and* keeps me fit.'

'Yet you have a car you call Marilyn?'

Pearl had rolled off the hammock, her focus on two hanging mobiles in a knotted mess—more evidence of overnight wind gusts. 'I wanted a Kombi van, and my parents have always been, like, "Don't let albinism stop you from doing whatever you want, Pearl". Then Dad heard they were stopping production a couple of years back, only to find one at the wreckers. We've been restoring Marilyn to her former beauty. The boss did the panel artwork.'

'Oh, I know the one. It has the Marilyn Monroe graphic!' Sid said over the clanging sound as Pearl worked on releasing the tangle of hollow bamboo tubes from the ceramic shards of a second mobile. 'Yes, I saw it parked near the mechanical workshop.'

'Hard to miss and a real beauty, like her namesake. Once she passes rego inspection, the legend will be back on the road.'

'Why a Kombi?'

'My dad had one when he was young, and according to him hippy vans symbolised all the important things in life: freedom, independence, peace, love. I relate to all those. So, with the family's restoration help, I'll soon be handing over the keys to my niece, having done my job of preserving the legend that is Kombi—and Marilyn Monroe—for the next generation. I'll also have someone else to bribe into driving me around to my massage clients.'

'Clever!' Sid said, surrendering the broom to help Pearl make more progress disentangling the two mobiles. 'And can I ask why remedial therapy?' she enquired, taking the weight of the bamboo tubes as Pearl poked and pulled.

'Initially I contemplated beauty therapy. I had a pretty rough time in my early teens when I thought the key to feeling good about myself was how I looked. I used to change my appearance by painting on eyebrows and lashes. I once added a Marilyn beauty spot. Then I realised beauticians do a lot more. I'd be waxing and bleaching and zapping clients with lasers. Not only do I not consider such treatments therapeutic, with my eyesight I might've waxed or zapped goodness knows what on some unsuspecting client.' Pearl laughed and peered closer still at the knotted mess of strings. 'My early decisions were all about wanting to fit in by looking like my friends. But most albino girls struggle to look like a regular person. I had to learn who I am is not what people see—or what I let them see. It's what's inside. While my parents are awesome, being around David made me realise I'm capable of being more *and* doing more with my life. He's also let me see it's inner strength that's important, and by accepting, rather than rejecting life's challenges, we learn to adapt and overcome our self consciousness.'

'Improvise, adapt, overcome,' Sid said. 'Jake taught me that not very long ago.'

'That information about your brother doesn't surprise me at all.'

Really? Sid said to herself. This trip with Jake was doing everything *to* surprise her.

'I would've preferred a full-on personal trainer gig,' Pearl continued, 'except I'm restricted in what I can do outdoors, and working in sweaty gyms nine to five is not my idea of fun. Remedial therapy, however, involves working muscle and tissue in dark rooms with soothing music playing. Thinking my hands can help heal, or ease someone's pain and make them feel better, is rewarding.'

'You've obviously helped David.'

'Me? Nah, I can't take any credit. He took control of his situation years ago. But he's not young and tires more easily these days, so my job is to kick butt and pick him up—psychologically speaking—when he's down. I simply remind him how far he's come. We get on well because we both deplore self-pity. Ha! I did it,' she declared while taking a swipe at the now freed artworks. 'Never give up.'

'You referred earlier to David's *situation* and mentioned the wheelchairs.'

Pearl climbed back into the hammock and set it into a swing. 'Like I said, he rarely uses a chair these days. Lucky for him his family could afford the right rehab. If he'd had to rely on what small towns like this provided at the time—travelling to and from the hospital in Coffs Harbour—I don't think he'd have made such incredible progress. His parents also really pushed. According to my dad, David's old man didn't tolerate weakness, and his mum encouraged David to take up art again when all he could do was mope. Her passing devastated him.'

When? Sid wanted to ask. The man had mentioned too many losses, too close together. Had Sid known before now, she might have understood why he kept to himself. 'What happened to his mum?'

'Not sure exactly. She went to the hospital for a minor procedure but never came back home. I didn't ask for the detail. I know the family has suffered more than their fair share of tragedy. Mum reckons David's accident splintered his mum's heart, and what broke it was her eldest son disappearing soon after, and without a word. Some around town blamed him for David's accident.' Pearl shrugged. 'I guess nothing says guilty like running away.'

'And that was how long ago?'

'Decades. David wasn't even twenty.'

Sid stopped short of expressing her relief. There *was* no connection to her grandfather's incarceration and David's injuries. *Thank goodness!*

'That's sad for the boss, but I, too, know all about fractured families.'

'David's dad was the problem. Ted was a hard man, but they got on. No choice. He *was* a savvy businessman and lucky, buying the neighbouring plantation for a song, unaware a massive cyclone would soon wipe out Queensland's banana plantations. Overnight, New South Wales bananas went from six dollars a box to one-hundred and twenty dollars. Demand soared and the Greenhill plantation hit the jackpot, but it was a one-season wonder. Afterwards, old Ted shifted focus to other money-making ventures. Some locals thought he was greedy, but my dad reckons he wasn't bad. He was a family man constantly on the lookout for opportunities to make a buck. He actually established the B & B as an interest for his son. Shame a lot of folks forget that he also did plenty of good things for this town.'

'What sort of things?' Sid asked.

'For a start, he was the one behind the town's name change. This place used to be called Dinghy Bay.'

'Yes, I heard that. I was chatting to a local fisherman who was none too happy about it.'

Pearl chuckled. 'I can guess who. Most people said the new name made sense. Tourists, especially overseas people, would pronounce it *Dingy Bay*, as in dull and gloomy. The name Watercolour Cove is more appealing and more fitting, especially given the focus on art.'

'Why didn't the father and son see eye to eye?' Sid asked.

'They clashed creatively. Ted envisaged a fancy B & B, whereas his son wanted something less formal to hold workshops or school camps for disadvantaged kids from regional areas.'

'Let me guess. Ted won?'

'Ted *always* won. Another reason he eventually got local noses out of joint.'

'If you don't mind me saying, the boss hardly comes across as kid-friendly—disadvantaged or otherwise.'

Pearl smiled. 'He's not as grouchy as he seems. He has bad days, but he can just as easily be a softy—and like I said, he's really taken to you.'

'He wasn't that impressed at first.'

'You took him by surprise.' The sun shifted, catching Pearl's face in its rays. She sat up and hung both legs over the side of the hammock to face

Sid. 'And I'm not referring to your rendezvous with him in the art room. You, Sidney, are a long way from the caretakers he's had in the past— everything from happy hippies to grey nomads. Ordinarily, he'd have little to do with the help.'

'Really? And yet he trusts anyone with his gallery?'

'CCTV and good accounting technology,' Pearl said. 'Cameras every- where. He's not terribly trusting—and for good reason—until he gets to know you.'

'I see. Well, I must remember to smile for the cameras. Speaking of smiling. I can't seem to wipe the silly grin off my brother's face.'

'Oh yeah?' Pearl picked at the frayed hole in the knee of her jeans. 'That's good then.'

22

WATERCOLOUR COVE, 2015

A loud *vroom, vroom, vroooooom* split the normally peaceful mountain air, the roar loud enough to stop Sidney mid sales pitch on the giant dragonfly garden feature made from recycled metal. The potential buyer was another landscape gardener, and Sid was determined to seal the deal today.

'Will you excuse me a minute?' she asked, before treading purposefully back through the garden to the gallery.

The same sound must have disturbed David, who was making his way as hastily as he could down the path from the cottages.

'That noise didn't sound good. What do you reckon?' Sid called to him, questioning arms wide, palms turned towards the sky. The engine noise had faded, and the mountain fell silent again. Too silent.

'Likely a bike-riding daredevil testing the road up,' David yelled back. 'We get the occasional thrill seeker who attempts the plantation road too fast. Did you hear the buzzer?'

'No,' Sid said absent-mindedly as the word 'daredevil' hit home. *Oh, no!* 'Jake was on the quaddy earlier,' she called to David. 'He'd loaded the trailer with chopped wood. I told him to take it easy.' Sid was now in a full sprint, turning towards the plantation and the rough track that skirted the edge—a recognised shortcut to the road down the hill.

David called out a warning—something about rain … wet … slippery —but she couldn't slow down. Sid had a bad feeling.

'Jake?' she screamed down the densely planted slope. Every two steps she stopped on the precipice of the plantation and shouted again. 'Jake, are you down there? Answer me.' What would she tell their mother if something were to happen to him? 'Jake, can you hear me?'

'Sid!' Her brother's voice floated up from somewhere amid the maze of banana trees.

Following the voice, she followed the fresh ruts, stopping where they tipped over the edge to become slick tyre tracks over several metres. There, she glimpsed the up-tuned quad bike. The terrain looked terrifyingly dangerous, and reaching Jake would require clambering down twenty-or-so metres on her bottom. It was that or risk falling. But what could she do once she reached him?

'Jake! Don't move. I'm trying to think.'

David called her name, his gait hurried but awkward. 'Pearl's phoning for help.'

'I'm sure I can get to him,' she called back.

'No, Sidney, don't risk it,' Jake yelled back. 'I can wait for help if you can maybe get me something to stem the bleeding on my leg.'

'Bleeding? How bad is it?'

'Bad enough. Take off your shirt and … I don't know. Maybe wrap it around a rock and chuck down.'

'No way, Jake. I've never heard such a stupid suggestion. I'll bring it down.'

He yelled some more, but Sid tuned out as she took her first slide. Sticking to the same ruts, she scooted on her bottom until catching sight of Jake. The quad bike was off to the side, the trailer, separated from its hitch, hard against her brother.

'I wish you hadn't risked it, sis, but it's bloody good to see you. I'm not feeling so good.'

'Please, stay with me, Jake,' Sid begged while ripping her over shirt into strips. 'Help is coming. Where are you bleeding? Is it bad?'

Jake nodded as the landscape customer from the gallery slid into her peripheral vision. *Good!* She'd need his muscle to shift the trailer if she was to reach Jake's wound.

'Stand back and have a tourniquet ready, in case,' he said.

'How's it look?' Jake asked after the hero of the hour manoeuvred the trailer the away.

'Oozing is good. No major vessels,' Sid replied—*if* she recalled correctly from the first aid session she'd arranged for Zeus Design employees. 'What happened?'

'I promise I was being careful, Sid. The trailer load shifted and skidded in the mud. Took the lot over the edge, including me. It happened so quick.'

'Did any part of the bike or the trailer hit you?' She prayed not.

'Nup! I came off before it rolled, but I hit my head on a trunk. Nothing to damage in there.'

Her brother was trying to make jokes, but his normally suntanned face was fast losing colour and she feared he would lose consciousness. She couldn't wait.

'Do you want me to get him up the hill for you?' the customer asked.

Sid looked from the man to the bleeding leg, and to her brother, who seemed increasingly disoriented.

'Jake? Jake?' she shouted. 'Can you hear me? Stay with me and tell me where it hurts.'

'My head hurts.'

'What about your legs? Can you feel pain?' He seemed to think for a moment. 'No. Nothing. Should I?'

'Don't, whatever you do, move him,' David called down. 'The local SES crew is en route, and an ambulance is coming from Coffs Harbour. Tell Jake to hold on. Tell him to wait. He'll be fine.'

Sid only realised then that she was crying.

23

WATERCOLOUR COVE, 2015

'Is that you, Sidney? It's about time I heard from you and Jake, but the phone reception is terrible.'

'I said, how's the Melbourne weather?'

'The weather? In Melbourne? Right now it's freezing and blowing a gale, so Tasha is making us a hot tea. Perhaps I should've gone north. How's Byron Bay?'

'The weather here is, um, good. Say hi to Tasha for me,' Sid said, stalling.

'Hello from Sidney,' Natalie repeated to her best friend of over twenty years. Sid could picture Tasha blowing her signature kiss at the telephone receiver.

'Now, how's the trip going? Had enough of your bar-hopping brother already?' A scratching sound suggested her mother was covering the phone with her palm. 'What did I tell you, Tash? Sid is far too serious to be the Byron Bay type.'

'Mum, listen to me.' Sid needed her mother to focus. 'We didn't get to Byron Bay. And before you have a fit, I can explain. But first I need to tell you about Jake.'

'What about Jake? I knew you two wouldn't last five minutes. Tasha, darling, sounds like Jake's up to his old tricks. What's my boy done this time, Sidney? Is he near the phone? Pop him on if I need to deliver a Jake chat.'

Sid understood the term 'Jake chat'. Growing up, the mother and son sit down behind closed doors had been a common occurrence. When he wasn't on detention after school, Jake was being sidelined in sports for being too boisterous. Exuberance, Natalie would say in his defence. Then there were the numerous phone calls from the local hospital as doctors set another limb in plaster. While as a boy he'd tended to bounce, rarely suffering serious damage, such calls would make any mother anxious. And Natalie, for all her faults, was a good mother—some of the time.

'I can't hear you, Sidney. Hello? Tasha I think I've lost her.'

'No, Mum, I'm here. It's, um—'

'Spit it out, Sid. What's he done?'

'It was an accident. I'm so, so sorry.'

After a beat of silence, Natalie kind of moaned. 'Oh, my God! You crashed your car? Oh, Tash, Sid's crashed the car.'

'No, no, not a car accident, Mum. A Jake accident. He's okay,' she hurriedly added.

Anxiety quickly gave way to annoyance. 'Oh, for goodness' sake. What this time?'

'He came off a bike. He was riding on the property where we're staying and—'

'A bicycle?' Natalie sounded relieved. 'Oh, will that boy ever grow up? Jake fell off a bike, is all.' Natalie updated Tasha on the conversation. 'And I thought we were finally over him falling off things—except for last Christmas and his drunken skateboard party trick.'

As a youngster, Jake had been typical of boys: competitive, into all kinds of sports, indestructible and invincible. There hadn't been a weekend that their mother didn't sanitise skin scrapes and bandage broken blisters. Those early family holidays usually involved father and son off bushwalking, kayaking, or fishing, while mother and daughter discovered the sights and smells of the national park, putting their experiences on paper with pastels—little to no conversation required.

'It's more serious, Mum. He came off a quad bike. The track was steep and slippery. There'd been rain overnight and—'

'Put Jake on the phone,' Natalie ordered.

'What?'

'Put your brother on the phone—now.' Silence. 'Sidney? I want to talk to your brother.'

'Mum, he ... He's okay. He's talking—make that complaining. You know Jake!'

Natalie's angst seemed to lessen. 'So, you'll be heading home from Byron soon? Oh, hang on, Sidney. Tasha, what was that you said?'

'There's a loudspeaker, Nat,' Tasha was saying in the background. 'Give me the phone.'

'Mum? Mum, what's going on? I'm trying to tell you—'

'Yes, Sidney, I'm here. Tasha is putting the phone on speaker so she can hear.'

'Hello, Sidney darling.' Tasha's earsplitting voice forced the phone away from Sid's ear, the loudspeaker clearly working.

'Sidney, I want to talk to Jake for myself,' Natalie said.

'I'm not with him right now. Hello, Aunty Tasha,' Sid added, finding the dual conversation distracting.

'Tell me when you'll be coming home. I'll have Tash arrange my flight back to Sydney. Tash, see what's the earliest, would you?'

'We can't come home yet,' Sid said quickly. 'They've admitted him. The doctors are doing tests.'

'Tests? What sort of tests? Which hospital? Byron? Ballina? Lismore? I'm coming straight away.'

'We're kind of south and closer to Coffs—the Pacific Coast Hospital. But, Mum, no need to—'

'Tasha? Change of plans. I need a flight to Coffs Harbour. Sidney, Tasha's looking for flights now. I'll be there as soon as I can.'

'Mum, please don't worry. I can let you know when they tell me more. Maybe wait until the scans of his spine are done and the doctors have—'

'Sidney!' Natalie snapped. 'When you have children of your own, you'll realise how futile it is to tell a mother to not worry, especially when she hears any combination of the words son, spine, scan. Go ahead, Tasha, book the next available flight. I'm going to Coffs Harbour.'

24

PACIFIC COAST HOSPITAL, 2015

Her daughter rushed through the sliding doors of the hospital and straight into Natalie's arms, reminding her of the many times Sidney had greeted her father with the same eagerness when he returned from a work trip every fortnight. But this was not one of those happy-to-see-you greetings. Sidney promptly burst into tears and Natalie stiffened, fearing bad news.

'Oh, Mum, I really am glad you came.'

'Of course, Sid, now dry your eyes and take me to your brother. Come on,' Natalie urged. 'What's the latest?'

They walked and Sidney talked, filling her mother in on the examinations and procedures Jake had undergone so far—mostly precautionary.

'Jake's been amazing. He's got such a positive attitude. Pearl said that's often all it takes for a person to get back on their feet and walking.'

'Who is Pearl?' Natalie paused allowing an orderly pushing a bed to pass. 'And what do you mean by get back to walking? You said he fell off a bike and hit his head. I thought the CAT scan was a precaution. Please, tell me he was wearing a helmet.' They hurried on towards Jake's room, Sidney leading the way. 'Answer me, Sid?'

'He had a helmet on, Mum, but the fall from the bike wasn't the problem. It was the trailer and a steep hillside crowded with banana plants.'

Natalie desperately wanted her daughter to stop speaking. So many questions in her head clamoured for attention and answers, but she had no ability to utter a single word.

'A serious cut to one leg has the doctor worried about infection.' Sid stopped at the intersection of two corridors as if trying to get her bearings. 'Down here,' she confirmed, toting Natalie's suitcase behind her. 'The bike's trailer flipped and rolled before hitting the trunk of a tree. While Jake went down the hill with it, the doctors are confident the lack of feeling in one leg is due to swelling on the spine. He landed heavily against a tree trunk. He never lost consciousness. In fact, he was joking up until medical help arrived. Thankfully, they didn't take long, despite the distance and difficulty reaching him on that mountain. By then I'd checked him over, stemmed the bleeding, and helped him sit.'

'You what?' Grabbing her daughter's arm, Natalie jerked Sidney to a stop. 'Are you telling me he was injured after falling down some out-of-the-way mountain and you moved him rather than wait for proper help?' The frustration of being drip-fed information, not to mention the never-ending hospital corridor, was testing Natalie's patience. 'What mountain, Sidney? Where?' she demanded. 'Where is my precious boy?'

'In the room at the end. On the right.'

'Sidney, you'll have some explaining to do after I … Oh, Jake! Jake, darling.' Natalie let her handbag drop to the floor as she rushed forward, planting multiple kisses on her son's forehead and cheek. 'You've given me such a terrible scare.'

'Sorry, Mum.'

A nurse appeared, jerking the privacy curtains closed behind her. 'Can you both leave while Doctor checks Jake's wound?'

Outraged, Natalie glared, ready to insist a mother's place is by her injured son's side for as long as he needs her. She wanted to tell the nurse she'd just flown hundreds of miles, and walked as many blasted steps in this blasted hospital, to see her precious son. But before uttering a word, Sidney piped up, tugging at Natalie's elbow.

'We understand. Come on, Mum. I'll buy you a coffee. Pink Ladies' Café does a good one.'

'Great idea,' Jake called as they left the room. 'Come back with a flat white, no sugar. I'm sweet enough.'

⚊⚊

At a café table for two, tucked away under the foyer's sweeping staircase, Natalie looked at her daughter. 'I'm very disappointed in you.'

'Me? Why? What did I do?'

'What's this Coffs Harbour detour about? Or was Byron never your

116

intended destination? And tell me why you chose to lie to me over the phone when I asked about Byron Bay's weather.'

'I'll explain, Mum, I promise, but I thought we'd focus on Jake before I fill you in on the rest.'

'The rest?' Natalie studied her daughter's face. Now all grown-up, she was a reflection of her father—a man forever missed and never forgotten. 'You know I dislike secrets as much as I do lies.' Natalie recognised the hypocrisy in the statement. Her daughter's expression suggested she had too. 'How much more is there to tell?'

'Not much, Mum. A couple of things. Just one. But I'm not keeping *secrets*. In fact, you probably know more than I do. I just didn't want to say anything until after we'd seen him.'

'Seen Jake?'

'No,' Sid said, sounding cagey. 'Until we'd seen the man in the letter. I didn't want you doing your "The matter is closed" thing and shutting me down.'

'What man in what letter? Please, Sid, I've hardly had a wink of sleep. Not only was I up before sunrise, but I also spent forty-five terrifying minutes hurtling down a highway in an open convertible being driven by a soon-to-be-senile septuagenarian. My hair will never be the same again, Jake is lying in a hospital bed upstairs, and I am at my wits' end. Forgive me if I'm not keeping up.'

'The letter is why we came here,' Sid said. 'I saw an opportunity to know our grandfather—Dad's dad—and for him to know Little Bump when he or she comes out.'

'Oh, Sidney!' Natalie didn't know whether to feel angry, shocked, or terrified. What she desperately needed was to regroup and deflect. She *needed* her nothing-to-see-here face. Reaching nonchalantly into her bag, she pulled out the small purse holding a tube of lip colour and a mirror. 'To be honest, Sidney ...' she said through lips pulled taut. 'I'm disappointed that a letter is your focus while Jake is upstairs in a hospital bed. But since you raised the subject ...' With the smack of newly painted lips, Natalie dropped the lippy back into the bag on her lap. 'I'll tell you the same thing I told you when you first asked about family. Your father wanted to leave his past behind. He made a choice many years ago, and we honour his memory by respecting that choice today. End of story.'

'But Dad's been dead for over ten years.'

'I think I know how long your father's been dead, Sidney.'

'I didn't mean ... Mum, I'm sorry. I-I didn't think there'd be any harm in visiting the guy in prison.'

Natalie flinched. 'You actually went to the prison? Oh, Sid! And you roped Jake into this conspiracy?'

'No one's conspiring, Mum. The fact the letter was sent in the first place implies our grandfather didn't know Dad was dead. The man needed to know, and I figured that if he saw he had grandchildren who cared, the news of Dad's death might be easier.'

'And now, because of your wilful curiosity, your brother is in hospital.' Natalie pushed the cup of watery grey coffee to one side. 'While the doctors are with Jake, you can take me to your accommodation. I'll freshen up before coming back. I assume you're somewhere nearby? Then, you and I will continue this conversation. But, Sidney, you *will* respect your father's wishes. Promise me you'll have no contact with that grandfather of yours.'

'That won't be hard,' Sidney said in a beaten-down voice. 'He's dead. He died a week before we arrived.'

'Oh, I see. Well, probably for the best. Now, can we go?'

'One more thing, Mum. I don't have anywhere "nearby" for you to freshen up. The nurses have been turning a blind eye to me bunking down in a chair by Jake's bed, saving me a long drive in the dark. The place we've been staying is down the coast. A short trip. Pearl lives there —in a beach house.'

'Pearl? What is this pearl you keep referring to?'

'Pearl is a girl. You'll like her. She got us a job, and the place is amazing. I get to sell gorgeous arts and crafts, and down the road a bit, in town, there's this *amazing* seawall filled with painted messages and … Mum? Mum, are you okay?'

⸻

Hospital staff had been swift to find Natalie a bed in emergency, despite her insisting too little sleep and food, combined with anxiety, had caused the racing heart and light-headedness.

'Rest, a sandwich, and monitoring will see your mother right,' the nurse told Sid while floating across to the patient in the next bed, leaving Natalie to wonder if the woman was still referring to her. 'Nothing to worry about,' she added perfunctorily.

Nothing to worry about? If only that was the case.

'Bye, Mum.' Clutching her handbag and ready to leave, Sid bent down to peck Natalie's cheek. 'I'll be back as soon as they discharge you.'

'In the meantime, make sure your brother has company, Sidney. Hospitals these days expect family to be on hand and do the job for them.'

A look passed between her daughter and a different nurse pushing the meds trolley, but Natalie didn't care. She had more dire things to worry about.

'This will make you feel better, Natalie. Hold out your hand.'

Usually particular about the drugs doctors prescribed, Natalie readily accepted the tiny pink pill delivered into her open palm from a giant paper cup. Not that Natalie wanted or needed a sedative. What she craved was a magic pill to turn back time and wipe away all her worries. But how far back would she need to go?

To before she'd discovered that poor man hanging in the loft?

Back further to when her husband died, or her children were born?

Or way back to the night she'd made the biggest mistake of her life?

Even better ... What a wonderful panacea this tiny pink pill would be if it could wipe those earliest memories when, as a five-year-old child scared and living rough, she'd watched her mother administer that final, fatal drug overdose.

25

'One needle won't kill you, Jake,' Sid said. 'Don't be a wuss.'

'That's not a needle.' Jake squeezed both eyes shut, mouth set in a grimace, ready for the sting. 'That's Luke Skywalker's lightsaber.'

'And we're done,' the nurse announced.

'Really?' He lifted his shoulder to see. 'You're gorgeous *and* very good.'

'Thanks. I'll be back.'

Sid drop her bag on the visitor chair. 'The news is all good, little brother.'

'Then why are there still giant daggers regularly thrust into my arm and arse, and why do *you* look like crap? You've been crying. Fighting with Mum already?'

'I told her about us trying to visit you-know-who.' Sid lowered her voice to a whisper as the same nurse returned, this time pushing a small trolley with bandages and gauze. 'Mum freaked out,' Sid added, but refrained from disclosing the dizzy spell keeping Natalie in emergency overnight.

'You have another visitor,' the nurse announced.

Jake beamed. 'Morning, Pearl my girl.'

'Hey, yourself, hunk.' In the flowing, flowery pink skirt, hand-knitted yellow and blue striped jumper and wearing an orange scarf and beanie, Pearl swept into the room looking a lot like an enchanted fairy—the kooky kind who might turn up to birthday parties with a sparkly wand

and magic dust to sprinkle. The kind who promises every child's wishes would come true, and they believed her.

No glitter wands or fairy dust needed to charm Jake today. Seeing her little brother fall under Pearl's spell was magic, and just the tonic Sid needed to mend her own broken heart.

'Glad you could get here, Pearl,' Sidney said as the girl bent over the bed, entangling her hands with Jake's on his chest, eyes locked on each other. '*Soooo*, it seems my cheer squad of one is no longer required. I'll go find Mum.'

Part way down the long hospital hallway, Sid noticed the glass door to a courtyard ajar. And after a night propped in an uncomfortable chair in the waiting area, the sunny seat looked dangerously inviting to a stressed and sleepy Sid. Settling on one of several bench seats, she restarted her phone. A message alert buzzed.

Mum!

One message reminded Sid to secure a nearby motel room. The other read:

Discharged, finally. En route to see Jake.

At that very moment, as Natalie passed the sunny courtyard, every muscle in Sid's body stiffened as though trying to make herself small enough to hide behind the giant grey-green agave plant.

Too late!

Last night, Natalie had duly dismissed her daughter, insisting she needed no company. Her brother had needed Sid more, and she was to make sure Jake was never without a family member for support.

'Ah, hi, Mum.' Sid sprung out of the sunny seat to greet Natalie with a hug. 'I saw your message just now. How are you feeling?'

'Why aren't you with Jake?' Natalie snapped, her over-protectiveness back in full working order.

'Jake's fine. Pearl arrived. I'm giving them space. Wait until you meet her. She's a local girl and Jake's totally smitten.'

'I cannot believe you would be so careless, Sidney.'

'By leaving Jake alone with Pearl, you mean?'

'Don't be facetious. You know very well I'm talking about gallivanting all over the countryside and trying to contact that man against your father's wishes.'

'*That* man is—*was*—my grandfather, and I'm not gallivanting.'

'And I suppose you're not responsible for Jake being in a hospital bed, either?'

Sid gasped. 'I wasn't even there. The accident wasn't my fault. It wasn't anyone's fault, Mum. It was an accident, and I was so scared when I found Jake.'

'You were *scared*?'

The mocking tone shook Sid. 'Of course. Quad bikes can kill, and he'd landed hard up against the trunk of a tree.'

'And yet you moved him?'

'Why do you keep on at me about moving him? I'd never hurt Jake.'

'You used to make up stories to get your brother into trouble. You were jealous about Jake being the favourite.'

The accusation sucked the oxygen out of Sid. 'Oh, Mum, why bring up such a trivial thing? I was a kid.'

'And his big sister. He's always looked up to you. Jake is young, and with his whole future ahead of him—marriage, children, and in the correct order, I hope,' she added. 'If by sneaking behind my back you've placed him in danger and put his future at risk, I will hold you responsible.'

'Mum, why are you being so mean? I told you I wasn't there. I found him *after* the fall. I went looking for him.'

'And you moved him. Oh, the damage you could have done!'

'No, Mum, I didn't move *him*. I moved the bloody bike trailer. And I didn't do the actual moving or strain anything in process, in case you were about to ask if *I'm* okay. I had to get in to stem the blood flow on Jake's leg wound. Anyone would have done the same. I've told you this, but you seem intent on not believing me.'

'The fact remains that you put Jake on that quad bike because you refused to listen to me and respect your father's wishes. He'd never have been anywhere near that quad bike if you'd gone to Byron Bay.'

Sid fired back, hands on her hips. 'Even for you, Mum, this is a total overreaction. I won't let you stress me and my baby out. No more.'

'What are you talking about?'

'It's what you do. Rather than admit you're wrong, or you made a mistake, you find ways to turn whatever it is around to lay the blame on someone else.'

'Don't exaggerate.'

'Exaggerate?' Sid snorted. 'Geez, Mum, you bloody do.'

'Stop with the blasphemy. Who taught you to speak like that?'

'*Geez* and *bloody* are not blasphemy. And stop trying to change the subject. You do that all the time, too. When an argument's not going your way, you move on, and we're all expected to forget whatever it was we were arguing about. Well, newsflash, nothing that hurts ever goes away completely. Every harsh criticism, every statement of blame, every dressing-down over the years … They're all a tiny scar in here.' Sid prodded her chest where her heart beat wildly.

Her mother didn't move. She didn't blink. Natalie might have been a stone statue set in the pebbled garden. Sid paced to the other side of the courtyard. Unfortunately, not far enough that she couldn't feel her mother's stare. She looked everywhere but at Natalie.

'Don't you walk away from me, Sidney.'

Sid turned sharply, hands on her hips again, her defiant chin pushed out. 'Don't you talk to me like I'm five years old.'

'You're acting like a child.' Natalie tut-tutted. 'When I was five years old I …'

'You what, Mum?' Sid no longer cared who heard them. 'When you were five years old *what*? You've *never* talked about your childhood, and you clammed up whenever I asked about the past. If you won't give me answers, then of course I'm going to go looking for information anywhere I can.'

'Oh, so you want answers? You want to know where I was when I was five years old?'

'I do.'

'Well, Sidney dear, I can tell you where I was *thirty-five* years ago. In labour for two days. Clearly, you were stubborn and refused to do what I wanted even then.'

'Oh, Mum.' Sid dropped resignedly onto a seat. Natalie had done it again, masterfully switching subjects and the blame to make her daughter feel bad. Sid had two choices. She could act like a five-year-old sulking at another of her mother's hurtful throwaway lines about what a struggle her first-born had been, or push her mother to talk about the past. 'Will you *please* tell me something, Mum?' *Anything*, Sid said to herself. *Anything to prove you're a human being with a heart—and not an alien hatchling delivered to Earth.* 'Please, Mum. Dad used to talk about stuff with me all the time, like how you met. But that was his version. I've always wanted to know the other side of the story. Your story, before you and Dad met.'

Natalie sighed long and loud—obviously in case Sid was missing the trillion other signs of her growing impatience. 'With Jake in hospital, it's hardly the right time, and I honestly do not know what I can tell you.'

'Anything, Mum. One story. One thing about your childhood.' Sid cried tears, no longer caring if it resulted in another lecture about strength being an admirable quality for a woman. She wasn't feeling strong. Sid was struggling. Mostly she struggled to see she would ever be a good mother, happy, or trusting of another man again. 'Mum, I was so desperate to stop thinking about Damien that I took a road trip with my brother to find a stranger. So, tell me anything, Mum.'

'Sid, putting the past behind us often requires we cut all ties and agree to never look back. You made your choice about Damien. There's no use wanting something you'll never have.'

'This isn't about me wanting Damien back, and I *am* thinking about my future. But if I can't make a go of a relationship when we both had so much in common, will I ever find a partner? Is there such a thing as a soulmate? If not, if my baby doesn't get to have a father figure—my choice or not—at the very least there was a great-grandfather out there.' Sid dropped to the garden seat and buried her face in her hands. 'The letter was a catalyst. I had to get away. I had to. And I need to hold tight to someone or something—anything.'

A passing cloud momentarily dulled the sun, adding a chill—other than the one surrounding mother and daughter. But as the sun peeped through, Sid witnessed the slow thawing of her mother's mien, the sharp edges melting. Again, Sid was hopeful of ending whatever this angry mother-daughter moment was about.

'I'm sorry about your grandfather, Sid. And you can do much better than Damien. Not that you asked for my opinion. As for my childhood,' Natalie continued, 'there was nothing particularly interesting.' While not the answer Sid hoped to hear, it was a start. 'I've told you a million times. My life began when I met and married your father.'

Sid lifted her face to her mother's. 'Your marriage worked, even though you and Dad were so different. Maybe Damien and I were too alike. Here's me thinking our issues were because of the baby.'

Natalie put a hand to her heart. 'Never, ever blame the baby for the choices *you* make.'

Sid hesitated. Was there a veil of early tears in her mother's eyes?

'Mum, I didn't mean to lay blame. I was simply suggesting it wasn't the baby news that broke us. I'm not sure we were meant to be together, but we were too busy being business partners to stop and realise.'

'Mmm, people thought your father and me an odd couple. I can only say for every brush there's a stroke and for every painting there's a frame.

You'll find your perfect match, Sid darling. In the meantime, you'll have your hands full with a child.'

'I want my hands full. I know that for certain. I truly believe things happen for a reason, and I'm glad Damien didn't *do the right thing* and marry me. I can't imagine living my life with the wrong person, or someone who felt they'd been tricked.'

'Tricked?' An obscure expression played on her mother's face.

'Yes, Mum, tricked. I'm certain Damien used the word more than once in relation to the pregnancy. That's why I needed to get away and pull myself together. Soon enough, I'll be someone's mother.' Sid smiled through a sniff and dabbed the corner of both eyes. 'I want to be a good one.'

'You will be. Not only that …' Natalie clutched the edges of her jacket with one hand and hooked her handbag over the other arm. She walked to where Sid sat, stopping to stroke her hair. 'Before you know it, that baby who relied on you for everything will have grown strong enough to fly away and not need you anymore.'

'I do need you, Mum.'

Natalie scoffed, smiled. 'Darling, I remember you on the first day of school. Every child clung to their mother's legs, except you—too curious about the day ahead. Whether or not you felt it at the time, you knew to show strength. I was the same at five.'

'Really? I can't recall something from so long ago. I'm surprised you can.'

'Oh, I remember all about being five, Sid. Question is, did *you* remember to find me a motel room?'

26

BRAIDENFIELD HOME FOR GIRLS, PARRAMATTA

At five years of age, Tilly—as Natalie was called—knew more than most kids starting school. In fact, she'd learned to count to five well before, because five was the number of times in one night her mother would answer the door of their inner-city flat, but always after dishing up Vegemite toast for dinner. Afterwards, she'd tuck Tilly into the stretcher bed—the one behind the magical curtain capable of turning little girls silent and invisible.

Five was also the number of foster homes Tilly was shunted between after her mum died, with each *new mother* finding a reason to return her soon after: too timid, too sooky, too withdrawn. Whatever *withdrawn* meant, Tilly didn't know.

Uncontrollable by ten, Tilly's next stop was the Braidenfield Home for Girls, an institution in western Sydney that quickly put an end to any sooky stuff. With Braidenfield no place for the weak, it only took a couple of months for Tilly to be branded too loud, too pushy, too vulgar. Whatever *vulgar* meant, Tilly didn't know.

Those years at Braidenfield taught Tilly to survive, to control, and to win, eventually winning the hearts of Ulf and Hilda Marhkt, a couple from the country in need of a daughter. 'A kind girl,' was the request. 'One in need of domesticating.' Someone young and malleable to be a sibling for their sixteen-year-old foster son.

'We live in the country on a magic hill. The highest around,' the lady called Hilda had told Tilly, painted lips smiling down.

'High enough to see the ocean?' Tilly asked.

'All the way to the sea's horizon.'

Whatever the sea's horizon was, Tilly didn't know.

Tilly didn't know lots of things. She'd never seen the sea, she'd never had a big brother, and she'd never had a family home. To Tilly and her mother, the word *home had* meant a couch in a stranger's lounge room, or a spare bit of space on someone's back porch. When things were at their worst, home for them both was the inner-city streets of Sydney and the back seat of a draughty car.

Tilly had been five when they moved into the station wagon with a busted door lock and broken windows that wound down all on their own. At night, she'd lay awake listening to angry shouts that sounded far too close, and police sirens that sounded too far away. For hours, or so it seemed, she'd stare wide-eyed at the dark shapes creeping across the car's bonnet and windows. And only when they slipped over the boot and merged with the darkness behind the car would Tilly breathe again and wish for morning. Then, only when the first rays of sun swallowed the last scary shadow, would she try waking her mother.

Five was also the number of girls an envious teenage Tilly—one morning shy of her fourteenth birthday—had watched being prepared for visitors to Braidenfield. That day, five became her lucky number. Lucky because only four of the chosen girls had turned up at the special visitor's room in time. Poor pretty Penny—the fifth girl—had unfortunately run into a door, hit her nose and sent blood gushing all over her lovely blue dress with the white bunny rabbit border above the hem.

Tilly had immediately rushed to the special room—the one with the comfortable chairs where the visitors sat before leaving with a little boy or girl—sometimes one of each. Waiting that day, in a red dress, was the lady called Hilda and her husband, Ulf. Tilly blurted the news about Penny picking a fight with another girl, and how Tilly had found her crying and taken care of her bloody nose before tucking her into bed.

'I told Penny I'd come tell you she was too sick.'

'You seem like a sweet and caring girl. What's your name?' the lady in the red dress asked.

'Tilly.'

'I believe Tilly is exactly what we're looking for, Hilda, darling,' commented the nice man in the corduroy jacket. 'Do you agree?'

For a moment, his wife stared, like a right-into-the-soul type stare. But Tilly had played the whoever-blinks-first-loses game, and she was no loser. So intense her return stare, so determined to not blink first as she waited for the woman in the red dress to answer her husband's question, Tilly's eyes welled up and she had to poke at the corners to soak up the wet.

'Don't cry, dear.' The woman took Tilly's hand to pull her into her bosom. 'Your friend will be fine, and you'll be perfect. Right, Ulf?'

'She's older, but yes, my love. And such an unusual name. Lovely. Just lovely.'

Tilly could have told Mrs and Mr Marhkt the truth. That her name had come about during her mother's arrest several years ago. When asked her daughter's name, the slurred response had sloshed around in her mother's mouth until, like stockings in a washing machine, the name Natalie came out all limp and tangled and sounding more like Tilly. Right after that, her mother puked on the police station floor.

'Thank you, Mrs Marhkt.' Tilly might have added a Von Trapp curtsey for effect. She wondered if that's what the other four younger girls—her competitors—would do. But Tilly was smart. Too smart to give her game away with such corny fakery. Hilda would have seen through her act for sure, and Tilly was not spending another day at Braidenfield.

No way! She had a new life waiting. High on a magical green hill, in the town called Dinghy Bay, and with the Marhkts and a big brother to protect her, life was going to be perfect, and Tilly would be the perfect daughter and the perfect sister to Albie. She'd make sure of that.

For a long time, Tilly would think about poor, pretty Penny, and if maybe the next visitors had picked her and given her a forever family. Memories of those years at Braidenfield were especially strong at Christmas time when the Marhkts put a tree up. Tilly had never seen an actual tree inside a house. And she'd never seen so many wrapped packages with her name on them—maybe even more than those boys next door. The hoity-toity Hill boys were always acting like they were better than everyone else. Albie got on okay with the younger one, David. Tilly liked him too, but his older brother, Matthew, was a rude moron and plain weird—in Tilly's opinion, anyway.

Some of the Marhkt's Christmas presents—mostly practical—she kept, shoving the good ones under her bed, out of Albie's sight. The art of hiding things, including feelings, was a lesson she'd learned at Braidenfield, and one not easily forgotten. The gifts she didn't want she sold for a few dollars, hiding the money away in a tin kept in the hollow stump of a dead tree at the farthest point of the property. When the Marhkts asked about the missing gifts, she'd confessed to giving them away to the Aboriginal kids who lived out of town.

'The ones who aren't as lucky as me and Albie,' she'd explain to Hilda.

'Didn't I say so that first day, Hil, honey?' Ulf would tell his wife. 'Tilly's a very *loving* girl. A very, very special girl indeed.'

Tilly had won over Ulf—no problem. Hilda not so much. She ran the household like a dormitory supervisor, ripping the bedroom curtains aside each morning to roust Tilly, the clatter frightening her awake.

Tilly had hated mornings and sleeping in ever since.

27

COFFS HARBOUR, 2015

The clatter of wooden curtain rings startled Natalie. Her daughter was attempting to darken the motel room by drawing the drapes. If only the gaudy fabric could mute the constant drone of passing traffic outside the matchbox-sized accommodation.

'Can I get you anything before I go back to Jake, Mum?'

'Some peace and quiet would be nice,' Natalie said while inspecting the bathroom's mouldy shower. 'But that's unlikely with the Pacific Highway at my door.'

'At least you can freshen up, and the bed looks comfier than the chair in Jake's hospital room. I'll see if I can get this air conditioner working properly.'

They'd been fortunate to secure a hotel room close to town at all, given every other option—from motel to caravan park cabin—was booked by car enthusiasts attending an international car rally. Not bothering to unpack a bag, or even change out of her travel clothes, Natalie lay down, wishing she had more of those tiny pink pills to send her off to sleep. Simply being back in this town was hauling all kinds of uncomfortable recollections to the surface, and Natalie didn't want reminders of the past. She'd spent years trying to drown memories of Braidenfield, her time on the mountain with the Marhkts, and the worst mistake of her young life.

One day, somewhere short of celebrating a year in business with Tash

—now her partner in their trendy Sydney gallery—that terrible mistake had popped to the surface. The voice that had drifted over the phone that day was the last thing she'd expected or wanted to hear.

'Hello, Tilly.'

'Albie?'

'I see you in the newspaper going by the name Natalie these days.'

She glanced over at the single gallery customer, then spoke warily, her voice low. 'Where are you calling from?'

'I'm in town and hoping you'll meet with me. It's been a long time. A meal or a coffee?'

Natalie swallowed hard. 'Today?' She looked over her shoulder to the back office and glimpsed her daughter through the gap in the partially open door. Sick and unable to attend school, Sid was asleep on a makeshift bed on the floor. Even with cheeks ruddy with temperature, and greasy hair in need of a wash, her daughter was beautiful. The sight—perhaps more the current situation—triggered an urge to hold her daughter, to stroke her hair, to tell her everything will be all right. But would it if Albie was back in her life?

'When you're free,' Albie urged. 'Today, tomorrow, or whenever. We need to talk.'

Natalie bit into her lip, her mind awhirl with questions. *Why? What about? Should she ask him outright? Yes! Get it over with, Natalie. Then tell him, ever so briefly, about the pact you made with Matthew—to never look back, to never begin a sentence with what-if, to never think about the past or mention certain names again.* Maybe she could imply Matthew's jealousy would make it impossible for them to meet. Or tell him if they *were* to meet, Matthew would be joining them. *Would that be good or not?*

Natalie couldn't think straight, not with the gallery customer having stopped in front of a Richard Claremont oil on canvas. Claremont was a young, up-and-coming artist whose impulsive brushwork and vibrant palette drew lots of interest from gallery visitors. The customer obviously had good taste, and he looked well-off—perhaps even ready to buy. Natalie offered a won't-be-a-moment smile and wave before turning her back and cupping a hand around her mouth and the receiver.

'I have customers,' she told Albie. 'Leave me your number and I'll call back. Hold on. Let me write it down.' Her hand shook as she scrawled the numbers on a Post-it note and then stuck it in her diary, out of sight. 'I've gotta go. I'll call you, Albie.'

Natalie hung up and slumped into the office chair, only then remembering about the customer. But he'd already slipped out the door.

Damn!

Over the next few days, Natalie's thoughts constantly returned to the phone number in her diary. She didn't like that Albie had found her, or the way the conversation had made her feel. Married to a good man, mother to two wonderful children, and with a house in the suburbs with all mod cons, she had no need for regrets, no cause to dwell on the past, and certainly no desire to invite the past into their lives. Natalie wasn't a bad person. She'd done what she had to all those years ago because there'd been no choice. So young, so desperate, so afraid, she'd needed a way off that mountain, but not with Albie.

Having written a brief note to the Marhkts, basically saying *thanks* and explaining her need for adventure, Tilly made her way to the Hill house in the dark, and into Matthew's room to implement Plan B.

Earlier that fateful day, while sitting on the seawall together, Matthew had taken little convincing to leave with her, or so it had seemed. Having endured his father's wrath, grief and blame, he was more than ready to rebel. But Matthew, unlike his young brother, didn't cope well with spur-of-the-moment decisions. He worked differently to David. Matthew liked to weigh up the pros and cons, including, Tilly feared, the merits of waiting rather than running, especially given his mother was absent. But Rose was in Sydney and keeping a vigil by her youngest son's hospital bed until he no longer needed her.

'Until the hardest job a mother can face has been done with devotion and dignity.' Ted had told Hilda while Tilly hid in the hallway. 'There is no going back and wishing things were different, my love, and no matter our decision—and we must choose what's best—neither will give us our David back.'

Time, Tilly thought, unable to stop herself sliding down the wall, stopping when she hit the floor, her face awash with her tears. Time was not something Tilly had on her side. Nor was there any going back—for her or Matthew.

While on the seawall, she and Matthew had made plans together—at least she made it seem like he'd contributed. Only when talking about waiting to hug his mother goodbye had Tilly taken charge, knowing the longer the pair delayed their departure, the more chance Matthew might change his mind—or have it changed for him—and every day meant Tilly was further along in her pregnancy. So, to meet Matthew's need for motherly hugs, Tilly had made him want *her* hugs more—and to want to be a father to the child they would soon make—*his* child. A child that would tie Tilly and Matthew until death they do part.

'Matthew,' she said, emptying her hand of small pebbles by tossing them into the water beyond the seawall. 'You don't want to upset your mum, and you definitely don't want to see David. I know because I sat with my mother for days, begging her to wake up—to *please* wake up.' Tilly realised then she was stroking her palm, imagining the dying bird from Hilda's porch that she'd desperately wanted to live. 'I grew hungrier and more scared with every sunset, until a lady and her husband broke into the car and called an ambulance. But it was too late for Mum. She was dead, and I never want to see a dead person again. Matthew? Are you hearing me? There's no saving some things. Hilda told me that. And I can tell you, the death of a loved-one is a horrible memory that never goes away. Lifeless and cold is not what you want the last memory of your brother to be.'

'But, Tilly—'

'Don't, Matthew. Let your mum be there with David, the way it should be. You can't do anything, and you get a say, so be a man and start making your own decisions.' Tilly clasped his chin between her fingers. She needed him to see her. 'I know you're hurting, but the way your dad treats you … It breaks my heart. That's not what fathers do, is it, Matthew?' Tilly answered his question with one of her own. 'Family should be forever. Let *me* be your family. We'll live *for* David and let David live within us.'

'*Shh*,' she whispered, having climbed ever so silently through Matthew's bedroom window. Then, slipping into his bed, she pressed a finger to his mouth. 'Take me. Now.'

'But I am taking you,' Matthew replied matter-of-factly. 'In the morning, like we said.'

Tilly giggled. 'You say funny things, Matthew. I meant, make me yours.'

'I've always wanted you to be mine. I've been so jealous of how you and— Oh gosh!' He moaned and grunted, eyes wide and staring. 'Tilly, what are you doing?'

'Shush! I said stop talking.' And with that, Tilly drew him into her.

Early the next day, before anyone rose, including the sun, the pair drove away from the mountain, Matthew's old Torana G-Pak—green, like an unripe banana—bulging with belongings. Once at the bottom of the road, as they passed through the Greenhill gates, a new life ahead, they made a pact. The gate was a symbol of closure—no looking back, no reflecting on the past. Never again would she or Matthew speak of Greenhill—of David, of Albie, of parents. And there would also be no more Tilly. It was time to grow up, and Natalie was a very grown-up name.

They erased their childhood.

They started again.

They had a baby.

They named her Sidney.

Natalie sat up in the bed, muttering her discontent. 'So much for rest.'

The motel room was claustrophobic with its heavy curtains closed. But looking out at a busy highway was not conducive to relaxation either, especially with the sun bouncing off windscreens, reminding Natalie of blinding headlights. The proximity of traffic was too strong a reminder of the times she and Matthew had lived out of their car. For close to a month, after being kicked out of the crowded terrace in which they'd squatted after arriving in Sydney, the Torana had been home. At least she'd found them both work with the local supermarket—Natalie behind the cash register and Matthew stocking shelves at night, which meant both jobs came with 'five-finger' benefits.

They scrimped and saved and eventually had enough money coming in to afford a small flat above a mechanic's workshop. With her art supplies initially restricted to the ballpoint and felt pens she routinely pinched from work, she started a series of four-by-six-inch sketches in black and white that depicted the melting pot that was Marrickville, finding the charm in old buildings and in the quirky and colourful locals. But she could only achieve so much without the proper paper and pens. A little more shoplifting helped her acquire the brushes needed to execute the pen-and-wash effect she was after. Each mini masterpiece was then pasted on a card, married with a white envelope, and sold at various weekend markets. The board on which she glued her creations, and the clear cellophane and curling ribbon she used to make bundles of five and ten cards—justifying the price tag—came courtesy of the inattentive art store cashier. A little older than Natalie, mid-twenties probably, the boy who worked every Wednesday was not wise enough to notice that, despite the newborn she toted, Natalie's belly still had quite a bump. It was amazing how many supplies one could secrete under a maternity top.

While Natalie's larger pieces sold well, she mostly stuck to water-colours, because when urgent baby cries demanded her immediate atten-tion, a watercolour was less messy and easier to walk away from than oil and acrylic paint. The growing stash of art supplies allowed her to add other creations to her market stall. Some required she pinch stuff from op shops, like the discarded music box in need of a re-vamp. She would spend her days painting new designs on old wares and selling them for a good price. Meanwhile, Matthew worked part-time painting road mark-ings and filling potholes on local roads. But rather than card-playing and smoking through morning tea, Matthew kept busy calculating how to reduce hot mix wastage to save the company money. His workmates made fun of him, but Matthew had the last laugh when the boss, impressed by his analytical ability, offered a logistics role in the office.

With Natalie's art and Matthew's bigger pay packet, the pair was finding their rhythm as a couple and as a family, making plans together and slipping into a routine that satisfied her husband's need for calm, constancy, and order—as much as a baby allowed. When Natalie secured work four nights a week as a cleaner at an inner-city art gallery, Matthew flew solo with baby Sidney, somehow learning to cope with the chaos only a toddler can cause. Natalie assumed love had something to do with that particular miracle, and the bond between father and daughter deep-ened with each birthday.

The years passed, their bank balance grew, and somewhere along the way, totally unexpectedly, Natalie fell in love with Matthew. After ten contented years together, and another baby—this time a boy they named Jake—they were a happy family. Natalie had found her place in the world —first as a mother, then a wife and a working woman. But their story might have been very different if not for Natalie's determination to ensure David's daughter had everything.

It was that single-mindedness that had driven Natalie to be whatever else was needed—*when* it was needed.

And it was a certain gallery owner, back in the early nineties, who'd taught her to improvise, adapt, and overcome.

<h1 style="text-align:center">28</h1>

SYDNEY, 1990

After less than a year, the night-time cleaning job at Raphael's Gallery had merged into a kind of girl Friday role by day, which saw Natalie assigned general admin duties. With Matthew studying, and her precious girl growing far too quickly, there were still financial struggles, but Natalie's dream of owning her own gallery never faded. Often left alone in the gallery, she would swan around and chat to customers as if she owned the place. And she learned lots of new things, too, like the word *philanthropist*. She'd had a terrible time pronouncing it at first, practising both the word and her smile in the bathroom mirror. She also figured out fairly quickly that people paid a lot of money for things she was more than capable of painting with her eyes shut.

Having the support of some heavyweights in the Sydney art world, the gallery owner—a man in his mid-forties whose photograph often featured in the social pages above the words *seen here with philanthropist and art critic, Raphael*—was, in real life, Ralph Snodgrass. Natalie first saw the name on an electricity bill and a council rates notice when she'd accepted Ralph's offer of a full-time office job assisting the manager.

By twenty-six, thanks to Ralph's generosity and belief in her, she knew all about spreadsheets. Initially fluking her way through the office job, sneaking files home on floppy disks and insisting Matthew teach her, she learned how to use a computer. Lucky for them both, she was a fast learner. The years flew by, with Ralph—who referred to himself as her mentor whenever he introduced Natalie—teaching her about government art grants, even helping her apply for creative development opportunities in her own name. One successful application secured her a spot in a seven-day artists' workshop. The other self-development grant was an actual cash payment, and she saw nothing wrong with putting the money towards a new pram when baby Jake came along. Throughout her pregnancy, Ralph remained supportive, generous, and inspiring, while the starchy gallery manager with the humungous hump on her honker treated Natalie like some sort of low-life grub. Whenever she'd looked down that nose of hers at Natalie, someone came to mind.

Someone from the past.

Someone who had stood in young Tilly's way.

Someone called Pretty Penny. Pretty Penny with the lovely blue dress and bloody nose.

When Natalie returned from maternity leave to work full time, and the gallery manager went back to enjoying her extra-long lunches when Ralph was away, an inexplicable oversight—a spreadsheet anomaly and an unaccountable shortfall in the accounts—saw Miss Look-Down-Her-Nose Gallery Manager summarily dismissed, and Natalie graciously accepting the promotion.

Once both children were in school and Natalie was free of parental responsibilities—Monday to Friday at least—her metamorphosis from low-life grub to butterfly was complete. Natalie was now Raphael's 'plus 1', influential and glamorous and infiltrating the city's arts and cultural scene. Her dream of a big and colourful life suddenly seemed possible, except for Matthew who, already socially awkward, withdrew further into his introspective shell. On the rare occasions Natalie took him to art functions, she would later berate him for hijacking conversations, for spouting too many facts and figures, or for expounding unwanted and inappropriate political opinions. Matthew didn't *get* other people, and often they didn't get him. At home, Natalie sometimes had to scream to make her husband understand she was hurt or angry or frustrated. After which he'd retreat to a room on his own where he would cut out newspaper articles for no apparent reason, or hunch over his computer to problem-solve something for work. Thankfully, her husband's management role with the construction company was growing and changing, which meant more business trips. But he often seemed distant when he returned home. At first Natalie assumed his moodiness to be the result of disruptions to his routine. Then she wondered if there might be something else going on and perhaps the so-called business trips were a cover.

One night, stopped in the doorway to the study, she'd asked a sullen

Matthew outright. 'Are you having an affair? I'd understand if you were, or if you'd contemplated one.'

Matthew's head jerked up. 'What makes you think I would?'

Natalie shrugged. 'Things between us are somewhat strained. And let's be honest. It's not like our marriage was based on love.'

Matthew stared, face stony. 'It was for me.'

'Oh dear, that came out wrong. Forgive me. I guess I was steeling myself in case …'

'In case what, Natalie?'

'I'm simply trying to explain how I've grown to love you so much. With each baby you gave me I loved you more.'

'Don't!' Matthew slammed the lid of his laptop.

'Don't what, darling?'

'Don't treat me like an idiot,' he said, standing. 'I'm reserved, not stupid.'

'Of course, my darling. I wasn't implying—' Natalie made another move to hold him, to let her body reassure him of her commitment. Instead, Matthew stalked from the room, but not before she saw the glimmer of tears in his eyes.

That conversation changed everything. Matthew worked all day and studied at night, often until midnight, after which he would bunk down in the spare room to avoid disturbing Natalie. The pensive man grew quieter and even more reflective. Sidney, old enough to be curious, seemed accepting, while Jake was still too young to care. But Natalie cared. Her husband was becoming increasingly difficult and emotionally and physically distant.

Then, out of the blue, Ralph offered to include Natalie's watercolour pieces in an emerging artists' exhibition.

'It's good exposure,' he said. 'And I enjoy giving to you, lovely Natalie, because always give back to me, and in special ways that show how much you appreciate our friendship.'

That afternoon, in his back office, she let Ralph screw her on the magnificent mahogany desk—her legs spread wide, and her breasts squashed flat under the weight of his hand pressing on her back. There was something honest about the transaction. Her boss was one of the few people who saw through Natalie's lies. The pair of them saw through each other's facade. Together, in the back office, he was Ralph Snodgrass—not Raphael, esteemed critic and dealer—and she was little Tilly nobody from the wrong side of the tracks.

When finished with her, Ralph would tug the zipper on his trousers closed and say, 'I'll leave you to lock up.'

That day, he'd stopped long enough to say, 'The punters will love what you do as much as I love what you do—for me.' Then he dropped the two fifty-dollar notes, as usual. 'Make sure you buy yourself something pretty.'

Pulling on her knickers and tossing the shredded stockings in the bin, Natalie cursed. 'What's wrong with me?' *Why let him? Why betray Matthew?* As she tugged her pencil skirt down over her thighs, smoothing the crushed khaki-coloured corduroy over her hips, Natalie felt nothing but contempt. *Never again. Never!* And if Ralph didn't like it, she'd leave—after her exhibition, of course.

After all this time she knew enough people in the industry to find a new job. Hopefully, one with a bigger gallery and salary so she could keep paying for Matthew's engineering degree, while keeping her children in all the things she never had.

From now on, Natalie would set the terms of her employment. Then, when she had grandchildren bouncing on her knees, and she'd sold her own successful little gallery to fund their retirement, Natalie would have lived her dream—or as close to the dream as she deserved.

And she would have her own gallery. *One day.*

29

SYDNEY, 2000

Tash raised her glass. 'I love the name. *Natalie and Tasha* was too much of a mouthful.'

'Agreed,' Natalie replied. 'And we *are* paying the sign maker per letter. *Nat and Tash* is also less pretentious than some gallery names, which is what we're aiming for.'

'Here's to the four effs.' They clinked glasses. 'Fun, funky and effing fabulous!'

Natalie smiled at someone of Tasha's age and eminence using words like *funky*, let alone *effing*. 'Is it too late to change our name to *The Four F's*? These days one can get away with just about anything.'

Tash chuckled. 'Ha! I love the idea of being different. The last thing this city needs is another ostentatious art gallery run by pompous prima donnas.'

'Absolutely, *darrrrr*-link!' Natalie crooned, and for a short, heart-stopping moment she was back in the cave with David, kissing imaginary strangers and sloshing an invisible cocktail in the air.

'You okay, Nat? Your face just now ... It was all—'

'Oh, God, yes, I'm fine.' She swigged the much-needed bubbly. 'I was thinking you and I couldn't be further from pompous prima donnas.'

'Speak for yourself, *darling*!' Tash chortled into her champers. 'Cheers, partner. Who would have thought my stealing you away from that blasted Raphael character all those years ago that we'd end up together like this? I'm ecstatic.'

'As am I.' Turning a cheek to her long-time friend, now business partner, Natalie reined in her flamboyant signature scarf to air kiss her friend. 'Nope, nothing pompous about us.'

'Don't forget to circulate tonight, partner. Rubbing shoulders until our arms are raw is the job. Watch and learn.' As Tash winked and strode to the far side of the room to greet a new guest, Natalie hoped, years from now, she would be every bit as wonderful as that woman.

Matthew sidled up to his wife—a rare but appreciated appearance at a social gathering. 'I see Tasha's in her element. You need to get out there and do your thing. And for what it's worth, I agree *Nat and Tash* is a great name for the gallery. I am surprised you got first billing.'

'It may also surprise you to know *Tash and Nat* was my original suggestion. Tasha is the best thing to happen to me. After you, of course.' She smiled and leaned in to kiss her husband's cheek, surprised when Matthew's arm wrapped around her waist, and he squeezed softly. His reluctance to show affection in public was another of those little quirks she'd learned to live with.

'Speaking of friendship. As firm as yours seems to be, I can't help but wonder.'

'Wonder what?'

'I know *managing* a gallery isn't the same as owning your own. That was always the dream.'

Natalie waved away his concerns. 'Stepping stones, Matthew. And I'm not simply the manager. I'm the face of the gallery while Tash takes a step back to travel. Being her business partner is close enough, and with Tash happy playing the investor and overseas buyer, the place will seem like mine. I'll be making the decisions here at home. We may not have a fifty-fifty financial arrangement, but I know Tasha values my contribution. And after all is said and done, having this gallery with her is still an achievement—and having you here in town for the opening makes everything sweeter.'

'Leo hardly had a choice about letting me fly back early. You did corner him at the Christmas party,' Matthew said with mild amusement. 'He asked me at work the next day if you were always so convincing.'

'I hope you answered appropriately.'

'A wink and a smile conveys so much, my sweet. You taught me that.' Matthew waved away the waiter offering champagne from a bottle. 'You did bully Leo into giving me the time off. I would've made it back from Perth in time without you coaxing him. Nothing could've made me miss your big night, although I can understand why you might doubt me sometimes.'

'I never doubt you, Matthew. You've never once let me down. Even after—'

'Shame about the kids,' he interrupted. 'I was looking forward to seeing Jake in a shirt and tie.'

'Ha! Now that *would* be a dream come true. Maybe one day. Maybe his wedding.'

For reasons she couldn't explain, Natalie and Matthew had reconnected that year. Perhaps it was because Natalie was so happy working with Tash. Perhaps it was that her husband had worked on a fly-in, fly-out basis for the last few years, giving credence to the idea that absence makes the heart grow fonder. Or perhaps it was discovering there might be a legitimate condition to explain her husband's sometimes-exasperating behaviour. Whatever the answer, she and Matthew had fallen into a relaxed and familiar place. Natalie even missed him around the house, which had prompted her decision to stop by Leo's office on her way to work one day, on the pretence of collecting something from Matthew's desk—a casual visit only, during which time she would drop a few hints and ask a few questions.

Leo had been delighted to see Natalie, even taking her to the café in the lobby. The coffee had been ordinary, the conversation anything but mundane.

'Nat? Nat! *Natalie!*' Matthew was grinning. 'You really need to get used to the abbreviation. I was just saying it's a shame the kids couldn't make your grand opening tonight.'

'Oh, yes, well, you know Jake.' Just thinking about the bright-eyed and bushy-tailed boy who'd brought such joy to her life warmed Natalie's heart. 'Getting him into an art gallery has always been an effort. He takes after you on that score. Of course, when I asked if he'd come, he said he would, then pulled one of those if-I-have-to expressions. But before I left the house tonight, he gave me a hug and said he was proud of me for "kicking arse". Whatever that means, I don't know.' Natalie laughed lovingly. 'As for Sidney? Getting her to do anything I say is becoming increasingly difficult. I'm sure I wasn't that contrary when I was twenty. She can't possibly take after me. Do you agree?'

When Matthew didn't answer, instead acknowledging a passing stranger with a nod of his head and a forced smile, Natalie silently cursed. *How stupid!* If only it was possible to retract those three little words. The question she'd posed was insensitive—a result of too much champagne, too much euphoria, and too little thought.

The look on her husband's face broke her heart. 'Matthew, I …'

'It's fine.' He drew the flute to his lips. 'Tasha is waving you over. Best do your thing. I'll see you at home.'

Natalie had thrown a pebble into a pond, her question disturbing the tranquil surface. Now other, bigger questions radiated out from it, the ripple effect in action. Natalie could only hope calm will have been restored by morning.

The happy times didn't last, with Natalie and Matthew again finding fault with each other. She even argued about him not being around to argue with. It was true. He was with colleagues—on a remote mining site in Western Australia—more than he was at home with his wife. *Was he purposely avoiding family responsibilities? A midlife crisis maybe?*

A recent argument about his priorities had prompted Natalie to again drop in on his boss. That was when Leo mentioned the company had offered Matthew a choice of roles—two different opportunities in the Sydney headquarters—which he'd declined in favour of the same remote posting.

Needing to understand, she confronted Matthew. 'Why would you do that?'

'I'm in charge of a great team where I am,' he explained. 'We've worked hard, and the rewards are showing. Leaving before the project is completed will look like I'm abandoning them.'

Like you regularly abandon your family every fortnight, Natalie might have commented. 'Leo mentioned your team loves you.'

The reality was, the man had waxed lyrical about his #1 employee, regaling Natalie with tales of her husband's exceptional paintball skills.

'Paintball?' she'd queried.

'Good for team building and strategising,' Leo had told her. 'Gotta keep the lads—and the ladies—amused. With no shortage of space out there I gave Matt the okay to set up a course. Paintball is a harmless enough sport that men and women can compete in equally, at any age. Even old buggers like me have a chance because the activity is less about physical size and strength and more about attitude and strategising, which is why your Matthew is hard to beat. He's a determined bugger.'

'He is?'

Natalie let Leo ramble, happy to glean more insight into her husband, including his apparent ability to not only keep and coach staff, but also his dedication to the mentoring of his 2IC—a woman called Janet Hobbs.

'Really?' was all she managed.

'Yes siree! And the first woman we've recruited for an on-site project role,' Leo announced. 'She's young and eager and their first field trip together brought spectacular results.'

'Field trip?' Every unbelievable tidbit Leo fired in Natalie's direction hit her hard in the chest, exploding like those brittle bags of dye shot out of a paintball gun.

'Yes, together they're a well-oiled machine that gets things done,' Leo continued. 'At the start, the team took the mickey out of poor Matt and his funny ways. Soon enough, they understood him. They even have team time called *Chat with Matt.*'

Natalie almost scoffed aloud. Matthew didn't chat. Her husband was staid and studious and happiest behind a laptop and locked away in his office, not on field trips with women called Janet Hobbs. He also loathed being called Matt.

'Chat with Matt? Seriously!' she mocked.

'Not at all,' Leo said, mistaking her sarcasm for needing clarification. 'It's a casual chat—management and workers alike connecting and having a laugh. Matt has the knack.'

So, her husband was connecting at work, and yet increasingly antisocial and distant at home. Even on those nights when a nightdress-clad Natalie would linger at the door to his study, her shapely body illuminated by the light from the staircase behind, Matthew would pause what he was doing to promise, 'One more email, hon.' But sleep usually arrived before Matthew. She was losing him again.

One day at the gallery, in between serving customers and taking delivery of pieces for an upcoming ceramics exhibition, Natalie confided in Tash, telling her about Matthew's growing obsession with his laptop, and how she'd suspected for some time her husband might be having an affair.

In response, Tash had merely said, 'Something as simple as a secret can seem like an affair.'

Intended to be reassuring, her words unnerved Natalie. In her experience, no secret was ever simple. Thankfully, Leo had promised to clip Matthew's wings.

'Between you and me, I'll be glad to have that husband of yours kicking butt here in the home office. Leave it with me,' Leo had said with a wink after slurping the dregs of his coffee. 'By this time next year, the current project will be over, and Janet Hobbs will have earned her stripes. By that I mean she'll need her own project and team. There'll be one more overseas trip—a conference in New York I'm keen for Matty to attend—but after that, he'll be all yours. If you're sure that's what you want.' Leo raised an inquiring eyebrow. 'Most wives, mine included, are glad to be rid of their men often.'

Natalie had laughed along with Leo, all the while making plans in her head. With Sidney and Jake needing their parents less, and with Matthew at home more, she could work on strengthening their relationship and start a new chapter of their marriage.

This time next year, she thought while checking the date on her watch.

September 11, 2001.

30

THE BLUE MOUNTAINS, 2008

Having acted quickly to secure the Blue Mountains listing, keen to leave the city and its sad memories behind, Natalie told Sid, 'I did say the property isn't perfect. But there's potential and something soothing about the mountain air. I'm so glad you're here. Your dad would be proud and pleased about us working on a project together.'

Her daughter didn't question the 'working together' bit, but the roll of her eyes spoke reams. Sidney had simply taken time out from her busy career—assisting her boyfriend to achieve *his* dream—to help Natalie relocate her life. Now, mother and daughter loitered on the tree-lined street, united in silence and in a common cause—the making of Brushstrokes in the Bush from what was currently a grand old house littered with amber leaves.

The pair had their work cut out for them. The first job was getting everything Natalie owned unpacked and put in places so as to not interfere with the planned renovations. Thankfully, her daughter was a good organiser, an out-of-the-box thinker, and a visionary—traits that had prompted Sid's million-and-one questions growing up, often driving Natalie to distraction. Sadly, mother and daughter drifted apart, and Matthew's death saw Sidney take out much of the hurt and anger on her remaining parent. Then Natalie watched her daughter date half a dozen men trying to replace her father.

Enter a dapper young Damien who, like Matthew—ambitious and hardworking—had big dreams. Natalie had liked him. She related to goal setting, telling herself she should feel reassured her daughter wasn't getting involved with a no-hoper. She could even admire Damien for his indefatigable business spirit. Then again, Natalie knew a lot about the impact dogged determination could have on the people you love. And Damien was intent on having it all: his own design studio, the big house, flashy car and a stylish and charming wife.

Natalie stared across the street at her own dream—a work in progress. Then, glancing down the road, squinting into the setting sun, she silently cursed the late removalist truck.

When Sid had announced a few months ago, after barely two years working with Damien's start-up company, that she was following him to Melbourne to set up a new studio, mother and daughter had fought terribly.

'I thought you'd be happy for me, Mum,' Sidney had said, having enjoyed one of her brother's dinners. 'You've always said Melbourne is *the* place. The creative and cultural hub, you'd tell Dad. Didn't she, Jake?' Sid sought agreement from her brother, who was doing his best to avoid involvement by turning up the TV. 'Look, Mum, it's not the other side of the world.'

'But Sid, I discussed this venture of mine with you both before deciding to buy. I thought you might take time off and come home. I thought you were excited about working together to get Brushstrokes up and running?'

'I am excited—for *you*, Mum. It's *your* venture. You don't need me. You've always been more than capable. In fact, you're better working alone. I'm sorry. I can't put your dreams before mine.'

'Building that business is *Damien's* dream.'

'And his dreams are my dreams, Mum. We're in love.'

For a while, Natalie let silence speak for her. Then she stood and began clearing the table.

'Okay, Mum, look, I'll arrange a flight to help you pack, and we can drive to the mountains together and unpack. I'll also be back and forth between Melbourne and Sydney several times a year.'

Natalie still said nothing.

'I won't fight with you about this. My life is in Melbourne and with Damien. Even if I was single—especially if I was single—the Blue Mountains, while beautiful, is too isolated. I'd go bonkers.'

How could Natalie argue? Hadn't the prospect of a desolate existence on a mountain driven a desperate young Tilly to do desperate things?

Natalie relented. 'Sidney, you speak of dreams. What about yours? What do *you* want? Surely not to stay Damien's offsider.'

Sid pounded the wood tabletop, ejecting Jake from his prostrate position on the sofa and out of the room altogether. 'What right do you have questioning me, Mum? You've never wanted to know what my dreams were before now. Life with you has always been about you and what *you* want.'

Natalie breathed deep, held it, counted, then slowly exhaled. 'Sidney, every decision I made was—'

'It was for you and your dream!' Sid pushed her chair back and stood. At the same time, Jake returned, apple in hand. 'Jump in any time, little brother. Tell Mum how she dragged the rest of us around behind her.' Unsurprisingly, Jake said nothing.

'What on earth does that mean?' Natalie shouted over the increasing TV volume.

'It means I couldn't even be sick and stay in my bed because you never took time off work. Instead, you left me in a back room at the gallery, telling me it was a special place with a secret door where good girls stayed silent and invisible to the customers.'

'I would never, never say that to *my* child.'

'You did, Mum.' Sid paced the floor, holding back tears. 'I know you worked hard. You were determined Jake and I would have it all. The irony is, we had everything *but* you. Then we lost Dad.'

Mother and daughter fell silent, and so did the room as Jake flicked off the TV and walked away.

'Truce, darling?' Natalie asked, waving the tissue she'd drawn from her bra cup to dab Sid's eyes. Her girl had David's eyes. 'How about we wipe everything about tonight away and try again?'

A stoic Sid embraced Natalie—a short, sharp squeeze—and said, 'Just to be clear, Mum. I said I'd help you settle into the Blue Mountains. I won't stay. I'm just not an isolated mountain hideaway kinda girl.' Sid kept her tone light. 'I'm actually a little surprised you are.'

True to her word, Sid turned up for the big move-in day. If only the removalist truck would turn up. Waiting on the footpath in the dark street was testing them both.

'I've a good mind to dock them for every minute we're kept waiting,' Natalie announced, growing more irritable by the second. 'Unloading in the dark isn't ideal.'

'They probably hit peak hour traffic. Relax and enjoy the quiet,' Sid suggested. 'I love the address. Wagtail Lane sounds idyllic, and wait until you see the business cards I've designed.'

'Business cards?'

'And a website,' Sid added. 'Branding *is* part of what Damien and I do for a living, remember? And while Damien suggested I say nothing until the job is done, I'd rather not keep secrets from you.'

'Thank you, darling. I look forward to seeing the finished result. And Sidney?' Natalie gripped her shoulder, turning Sid to look at her. 'When you are ready to return to your own life, just say so. I understand.'

'Being together will be nice—you, Jake, and me. I'm secretly looking forward to some new culinary concoctions, but don't tell him I said so.'

'Speak of the devil,' Natalie nodded. 'There's Jake's car now. I wonder if he saw the removalist?'

Two hours later, having received instruction on how to unload Natalie's vast and eclectic art collection, the entire house was still ablaze with light, buzzing with activity, and smelling of sweaty men, currently in the kitchen and gobbling up Sid's sandwiches and a beer each.

On a clear coffee table in the living room, Sid set down a cheese board with crackers, and popped a bottle of champers.

'This place really is so you, Mum, and you'll make it perfect in no time. As for the old bar the owners left in the corner, it would make a great guest check-in counter in the hallway, next to the staircase. You might need an electrical point put in.'

'Oh, there'll be tradesperson wrangling required for sure.'

Sid chuckled. 'I pity those tradies! You have a way of getting people to do what you want.'

'You make that sound wrong, Sidney. Like I harass and hurt people.'

Sid sighed. 'I wasn't looking to start an argument. I—'

'Ahem!' The removalist with the blue singlet and stubbies stood in the doorway, boxes in hand.

'No, no, not in here. Can't you see the label? This room is *not* the main bedroom.'

Sid shot the sweaty men a sorry glance and beckoned. 'I'll show you. This way. How were the sandwiches?'

Alone for the moment, Natalie dissected her daughter's accusation. Had she hurt people to get what she wanted? She'd worked hard, and fought harder, and maybe she'd manipulated on occasions, even cheated when necessary. To survive and provide for her family she'd also lied and stolen. But never were her actions intended to hurt. Ralph had got what he wanted—the others, too. The glamorous gallery manager might have lost her job, but she'd found a better one. In fact, Natalie still saw Miss Look-Down-Her-Nose several times a month in the social pages, only not so naturally glamorous these days. And perhaps Pretty Penny *didn't* deserve the bloody nose, and for that, Natalie was eternally sorry. As for Albie…

'Mum, are you listening?' Sid was slicing open the glossy tape on the box labelled *KITCHEN*. 'We need glasses to toast Dad for making this happen. Did you know his life policy was so big?'

'Your father wanted to provide for his family. That's the man he was. He would have hated that the payout took so long to come through.'

'Hey, Mum,' Jake called from the doorway, holding a large box. 'Where do you want to put Dad's work stuff from the hall cupboard back home?'

Natalie sighed. 'Oh, yes, that!' The box of Matthew's belongings had arrived, via courier, just before the Christmas of 2001, with a note in an envelope sticky-taped to the top:

Dear Natalie,

Leo Pelakanigos asked me to, once again, convey our sincerest condolences and deepest regrets for your loss. As instructed by Leo, I am returning Matthew's personal items. You will also find I've included Matthew's company laptop. In the process of picking up where Matthew left off, I found personal folders, including emails, photographs, and financial information. We've removed the company files we need and, with the greatest respect for your family's privacy, Leo wanted the computer returned to the family. I've included a sticky note with the password.

Your husband was a valued team member and mentor. Matthew was a very special person to whom I will be forever grateful.

Yours sincerely,

Janet Hobbs, General Manager—Logistics

P.S. Any questions? Please contact me directly.

Natalie recalled at the time how her gaze had lingered on the office extension number she recognised, tears welling when realising Matthew's 2IC, the woman she'd thought would take her husband away, had simply taken his job.

'Ah, sometime today would be good, Mum.' Jake sounded pained. 'This box weighs a tonne.'

'Pop it in the corner, over there, so I'm forced to look at the thing every day until it's dealt with.'

For seven years the box had stayed in the hall cupboard, and only ever noticed when Natalie dragged the doona out, or packed it away again on the other side of the season.

'Actually, Jake, look for your dad's laptop. I'll ask Sid to get me in.'

'Why bother, Mum?' her daughter asked, sailing back into the room waving glasses and a beer for Jake. 'That laptop is obsolete. Out with the old and useless and in with the new.' Sid's expression told Natalie she regretted the choice of words.

'What if we stop for the night? You kids can check out the Blue Mountain nightlife. It is a Friday. I'm going to have a drink and a potter. Tomorrow we'll start afresh.'

After a contrite Sidney nudged her brother into action, Natalie transported the leftover cheese and crackers to her desk, ready to poke around Matthew's company computer. If it was obsolete, her daughter would know how to best dispose of the thing.

And Sid wasn't wrong about the old Apple PowerBook. Both the unfamiliar keyboard and odd trackball thingamabob was immediately problematic, while the convoluted file system made no sense to a devoted Android user.

Feeling tired and frustrated, and with eyes blurry from staring at family photo files, Natalie was clicking dreamily around the little icons on the desktop when a file list popped open. Her eyes stopped on one folder: *Personal Emails*. Two sub-folders were separately labelled *Greenhill* and ...

'*David?*' The name slapped her awake. What was her husband doing with a file in his brother's name—and on a work computer—when all those years ago, she and Matthew had made a promise to look ahead and not back?

At some point, Jake and Sid returned home, whispering and giggling and unaware their mother sat in the dark, with only the glow from the computer illuminating the room. One hand clutched a glass of red. The other was attempting to hold steady the pointer now hovering over the file folder: *David*. A second bottle of red beckoned, begging to be opened, but another wine would quickly tip Natalie from tiddly to total inebriation. Would anyone blame her?

What were you up to, Matthew? What other secrets will I find?

Natalie's next thought was to telephone the only person who would understand the significance of the discovery. Her best friend and business partner *had* once said, *"Sometimes a secret can seem like an affair."*

'Nat, darling, is something wrong? Marcus, switch on the light,' Tash commanded her adorable other half. 'Is it Jake? Is Sid—?'

'No, not the kids.'

'Okay. Good. No, Marcus, the kids are fine. Yes, I know it's late, but Nat needs an ear. Stay in bed, sweetheart. I'll be back soon.'

'Tash, I'm sorry. Calling you at this hour is unforgivable.'

'Don't be silly. What's up? Tell Tasha everything. From the beginning.'

'I-I have Matthew's old work computer set up, finally.'

'Ah-huh! Go on, darling, I'm here. Just slipping into my robe.' There was a moment of static, perhaps the sound of Tasha's receiver slipping through the arm of her dressing gown. 'So, you were saying about Matthew's old work computer?'

'Yes. I'm looking at it now. There are personal emails saved to a folder, Tash.'

'Just one second, darling. I'm in the kitchen putting on the kettle.' Natalie heard clattering and water running. 'Okay, back again. So, you say there are emails on Matthew's old computer?'

Tasha was usually so attentive, but all her pausing and banging and clanging made Natalie anxious. Did Tash not realise what this could mean? Was her friend even listening?

'Okay, Nat, so who are these emails from? Don't tell me! His 2IC—the ambitious one. What was her name?'

'No, Tash, these emails … They're from David.'

'David who, darling?' Tasha asked.

To be fair, Natalie had only mentioned David in conversation once, and a long time ago. Both women had been quite drunk, celebrating a big sale and the spoils of a fantastic year for the gallery. Tash had her new beau, Marcus—a lawyer of note and years younger—and Natalie was, well, the happiest she'd been for a long time. With the wine adding to her euphoria, Natalie had off-loaded the secret, confessing everything: her undying love for Matthew's brother, the coma he never recovered from, and running away with Matthew. She may have told Tasha she was pregnant. Maybe not—the alcohol had wiped all details of the evening away. In fact, Natalie had only remembered the conversation when, some months later, Tash mentioned David's name while the pair discussed love versus infatuation. To this day, Natalie was unsure how much a tiddly Tasha knew, or how close Natalie's alcohol-induced version of the story was to the truth.

'Listen to me,' Natalie said exasperatedly. 'I'm trying to tell you ... It's David. Matthew's brother.'

'*Your* David? The one you—'

'Yes, that one.' *She remembered!*

'But you told me he died?'

'He did.' Natalie's pulse hammered hard, her body throbbing in a staccato rhythm as the realisation set in. 'He was in a coma. No hope, the doctors said. His parents had to decide, and they went to Sydney to say goodbye.' Her mouth was suddenly sticky with the sour residue of too much red wine mixing with the tears she didn't know she was crying. 'When Matthew and I ran away, we agreed to leave the past behind us. But now ... My God, Tash! Matthew let me believe David was dead. Did he know all along? Did Matthew lie to me? Did he trick me into—' She groaned at the irony. While Natalie had thought she was securing her future by slipping into his bed to seal the deal, had Matthew been manipulating her?

No! Matthew wasn't capable of deception. The man was almost too honest, too blunt, and too content in his black and white world with his high, if not sometimes questionable moral perspective. She'd trusted him completely and thought she knew him.

'Darling, Nat, I don't know what to say.'

'Tell me how Matthew could do this, Tash. Tell me I'm confused and tired and so terrified about being on my own in this place that I'm having a nightmare. Tell me I'll wake up and know my call to you was part of the bad dream.'

Who was she kidding? Natalie's eyes were wide open to the truth. Matthew hadn't simply broken their pact by keeping the past alive. David *was* alive and her husband had kept it a secret from her. Not only that, but he'd kept in touch with his brother. *For years!* All those late nights hunched over his laptop, and the way he'd snap the lid shut when Natalie stopped by the study. She'd suspected late-night, online rendezvous—a love affair with a colleague—when all the while Matthew was connecting with his past. Their past.

'I'm not dreaming, Tash. David didn't die.'

'Nat, darling, is there someone there with you? Do you need me? I'll come.' Tasha sounded serious. In fact, she sounded breathless, like she was running.

Natalie was wired enough to run all the way back to Greenhill, but a lifetime ago she'd sworn to never return.

'I'm confused, Tash.'

'I'll jump on an early flight and come up. Okay? Hang on while I wake Marcus.'

'Don't, Tash. I'll deal with this. I shouldn't have called at this hour. I drank too much wine and overreacted. Sleep will help. Let me call you in the morning.'

'It is the morning, darling. Marcus, honey, all good. Crisis averted—for now. Back to sleep.'

'My apologies to Marcus. I love you, Tash.'

'I'll let you go now, darling, but only if you promise to stay in touch. I think you're right—you should sleep and call me again when you wake up. Call me anytime. Or I'll call you. Okay? Marcus, honey, you can switch off the light now. And Nat?'

'Yes?'

'What happened was … It was so very long ago. Best to let the memories go, darling.'

Twenty-nine years ago, to be exact, Natalie mused as she hung up the phone and turned back to the computer screen. Where might those years put David now, and why hadn't he sought out Natalie? If only the answers were as obvious as the emails. The folder marked *David* contained six—four from Matthew to his brother and two brief replies from David, all written within a two-year period. She re-read each one carefully, looking for clues as to David's whereabouts, but finding nothing. The emails were fifteen years old. He could be anywhere by now.

The tall grandfather clock in the hall chimed, frightening Natalie, the jerky movement of her index finger on the super-sensitive trackball accidentally launching another window to cover the email screen completely.

'Stupid machine,' she grumbled, pushing the laptop aside to power up her own PC—one she knew how to work. Launching the web browser she searched for the name David Hill. *Too many.* She refined her search, typing the word ARTIST, then trying gallery names and capital cities. Could it be that she and David had lived in the same city, attended the same galleries and openings but, like ill-fated lovers in a Hollywood movie, the pair missed each other by seconds?

Her frantic fingers flew over the familiar keyboard, trying different search criteria until, more frustrated, she looked back at Matthew's laptop screen to wonder. *Why so few files in the folder?* Had the emails stopped in favour of phone calls? Had the brothers spoken? Was Matthew's need to stay in contact the result of blood being thicker than water, or was there more to it than that? Was one of those supposed work trips actually a return to the Greenhill property to bring the family up to speed on his life. Had Matthew actually seen David? *Sometimes a secret can seem like an affair.*

At a certain point in their marriage, Matthew started obsessing over walking away from his inheritance. Maybe he'd tried getting back into the good books with his parents. Maybe... Oh what was the use? Natalie would never know. She lowered her head into both hands as the old clock struck three am, but there was no going to bed while her head was spinning with too much wine, too many possibilities, and way too many David Hills.

After investigating scores of web search results, she tried Facebook, only to see unfamiliar faces and too many generic profile pictures staring back.

'Why bother, Natalie? What are you going to do if you find him listed? Message him? Call him, maybe? And say what? Sorry for not believing enough in our love and your will to live. Sorry for running off prematurely. Sorry for marrying your brother. Sorry for forgetting you.'

Maybe David already knew everything about Natalie and the children. Maybe Matthew had talked to his brother about what he'd always suspected about Natalie's pregnancy but never asked her. By the time she saw a doctor in Sydney, Natalie was well and truly pregnant. The baby, however, could have been David's *or* Matthew's. Or the result of the one occasion with Albie—the mere thought of which made Natalie want to vomit. But any regrets had vanished once she saw Matthew cradling baby Sidney in his arms. That day, Natalie had her answer—the only one she could live with. What she hadn't understood at the time was how unbreakable the father-daughter bond would be, or how devastated Sid would be when Matthew died.

Sitting back in the office chair, Natalie contemplated a walk to the kitchen for a much-needed glass of water, then promptly poured another glass of wine. But no amount of alcohol could help her accept David had lived—*was living*. She turned to her husband's old laptop, flicking rapidly through the photos, hoping to see a picture of David. What did he look like almost three decades later? Knowing he was out there, somewhere, but Natalie might never find him—or have the right to walk back into his life after all this time—squeezed more tears from her eyes.

Then, for some reason, she thought of Albie, and all that poor boy had lost. During a second, brief telephone conversation with him, trying to avoid his questions with small talk, she had thought to enquire about the Marhkts.

'Don't know much,' Albie had told her. 'Since returning to Australia, I've tried contacting Ulf *and* Hilda. The phone is disconnected, and my last letter was returned to sender.'

'Returning, Albie? Where did you go?'

'I went back, Tilly,' he'd said with a joyful little spark to his voice. 'I went back to Malta to find her. I thought meeting my mother, my blood, would help me get over missing you, but being in a strange country made me more homesick for everything that might have been between us.'

'Oh, Albie, I—'

'Just hear me out, Tilly. I miss you. I miss us. I miss how we would tell each other everything. I'll never stop missing you. You once said we were the same—we were survivors—but I'm not. I'm alone and lonely.' A touch of sarcasm accompanied his next words. 'But you, Tilly! There's no holding you back. I see your picture in the social pages. Your dream was a gallery. You're happy and I'm happy for you. Truly, I am.'

'Then leave me alone, Albie,' she'd told him. 'Let me live my life without fear of—'

'Fear?' Albie's mood changed. 'What have you got to fear from me? I've never done anything wrong by anyone—ever.'

'Sorry, that's, um, not what I meant.'

'I'm trying to move on, Tilly. *I* want to be happy. I want to stop feeling like a stinking piece of shit that everyone avoids.'

'Don't say things like that. You're a good man.'

'How would *you* know? You don't. You can't.' She could hear the torment in his voice. 'Maybe, if we can meet, just once. It's been long enough.'

Long enough for what? she thought about asking, before telling Albie, 'Okay, we can meet. I'll be in touch about where and when.'

That was the day Tilly changed their home landline to private. If Albie was going to persist, at least she could restrict his calls to the gallery and keep their catch up from the family. That was when the emails started turning up at work, which she read and deleted immediately to avoid anyone seeing them. Most read the same way:

> *You've stopped returning my phone messages. Don't delete this email without first reading what I have to say. If you promise to see me one more time, I promise to never talk about what we did that night—to anyone, ever. Please don't make me regret trusting you.*

With one bottle of red on the desk now blurring into two, Natalie regretted not having had that much-needed glass of water. Instead, all she had was a monster hangover and as many questions as there were boxes waiting to be unpacked.

31

PACIFIC COAST HOSPITAL, 2015

'I'm the one in hospital, sis. How come you look like, to use Dad's saying, the Wreck of the Hesperus? Have you been partying without me?' Jake asked while chewing on a sandwich.

Sid dumped her bag on the chair. 'I see you're back to normal.' She walked over to Jake's hospital room window overlooking scrubland, where a small mob of wallabies grazed on a grassy corridor between two buildings. One animal was close enough for Sid to make out an upside-down joey in her pouch, its stick-skinny legs jutting out at odd angles. Mama wallaby was not eating, instead standing tall, ears pricked and alert to predators that might want to harm her baby. The remaining mob seemed oblivious, lazing on their sides, some propped nonchalantly on an elbow. 'I hear your test results are good and you're mostly in the clear, with just bruising and a leg wound to be assessed and redressed. I'm glad.'

'I'll be glad to get out of here and into a comfy bed. So, why are you looking so bleary-eyed?'

'I worked late tweaking a design job to keep my client happy. So glad I packed the Mac.'

'Reckon I can borrow your laptop when I get out of here, sis?'

'Maybe. Why?'

'I want to look up stuff.'

'What *stuff*?' Sid was focused on the faint reflection of her face staring back from the window. She was smiling, both at her brother and at the pouch-bound joey, half in and half out, desperately trying to reach the grass. Instinctively, Sidney placed a hand on her belly, her long sigh fogging the window and blurring the view. 'I can search for what you need.' She peeled her jacket off and draped it over the foot of the hospital bed.

'I'm kinda keen to do it myself, sis, but my fingers are too big and manly for a phone keyboard. I know how your Mac works.'

'So you *were* you on my computer the other night! I knew it. What were you looking up? Were you downloading? Did you—?'

'Yeah, yeah, okay, guilty as charged, Your Honour. Not sure the request requires cross-examination.'

'You realise I can check the browser history. So Jake, if you've been downloading porn, or—'

'Whoa there, sis! Since when have I been into that stuff? Like never.' Jake huffed. And when he folded his arms across his broad chest, brat-like, he winced. 'Okay, I admit, I touched the golden Apple Mac. Geez, you've got on your *Mum mood* today. All I did was check out this albinism thing of Pearl's. There's so much to know.'

Sid bit back a grin. Her young brother was suddenly keen to under-stand a woman? What happened to the Jake who mostly saw females as something he picked up on a Friday night and bonked anywhere half comfortable in the hope he made a good enough impression to get a second date. With Pearl unlike Jake's usual pub pickup, Sid guessed he didn't want to turn her off him by asking dumb questions about her genetic condition.

'Aw, that's really sweet of you, Jakey. Is my little brother falling in love?'

'Go ahead, have your fun, Sid. Then check out that browser history for porn. You'll find nothing but legitimate websites about albinism, except for the first search when I typed the word *albino*, resulting mostly in baby rhino and hippo stories.'

'Oh, Jake!' Sid guffawed.

'I soon discovered the correct term is *people with albinism*. Then your battery went dead. Speaking of dead … Have you and Mum killed each other yet?'

'Not yet. I managed to book one night in a highway motel.' Shoving her coat aside, she perched on the edge of the bed and explained about the upcoming car rally, her brother's ears pricking up at the thought of throb-bing exhausts beating an exhilarating pace through the mountains above Coffs Harbour. 'Forget it, Jake. You've had all the excitement on wheels you're having this trip. Me too. I'll be happy once tucked away in Water-colour Cove. Mum will be, too, I'm sure. *When* I tell her.'

'What's going on with you two?'

'What do you mean?' Sid played with a pulled thread in the hospital blanket.

'Sis, I might not be the smart one in the family, but I can see, and I can hear, and I sure heard you and Mum going at it when I dropped by to do my laundry one day. It was no ordinary argument, and it was *before* you found the letter. So, what gives?'

Sid released an exasperated sigh. 'It's true, Mum and I are going from bad to worse. Everything I do seems to displease her.' Sid gestured towards the window. 'You see that wallaby? The one with the pouch?'

'Are you changing the subject?'

'No, Jake, I'm telling you I'm pregnant.'

'Yeah, I already figured that out, remember? Are you having second thoughts?'

'No, but ...' Sid's gaze stayed on the wallaby and her baby. 'That's going to be me soon.'

'Ah, I assume you're not telling me you're having a joey, because that *would* be upsetting for Mum—and tricky to explain to my mates.'

'Can you be serious for one minute? I mean, soon a new life will need me more than anyone has—ever. Little Bump will depend on me for everything.'

'You'll be great, Sid.'

'Thanks, but I'll be on my own.'

'Hmm, so, there's definitely no getting back together with Damo?'

Sid shook her head. 'Never. Me wanting to keep the baby ended us.'

'What the—?' Jake winced in pain. 'Ouch! That hurt.' He put a hand on Sid's and squeezed. 'Sis, that Damo is a stupid dumb arse. I never liked the bloke. You were too good for him.'

Sid surprised herself by bursting into tears. As a family, they weren't overly demonstrative. They loved each other—Sid knew without a doubt —but showing weakness by crying, or even accepting sympathy, was something none of them did well, or easily. Not even at their father's funeral had they shared their grief by letting their tears fall freely. If Natalie had got a say, there wouldn't have been a service at all, but Dad's boss had insisted. Colleagues had come from as far away as Western Australia, joining Leo Pelakanigos to pay their respects. That day, strangers had sadly outnumbered family.

'Hey, sis, come on.' Jake shoved a hospital-issue tissue at her. 'What else is going on in that head of yours?'

'I've been thinking about Dad and how he missed out on being a grandfather, and now you and I have missed out on knowing our grandfather. That means Little Bump, here, also won't know a grandfather.'

'Well, you and Bump have me. I'll make up for Dad not being around. I'll be the best bloody uncle ever. Footy, skateboarding, surfing, you name it. I'm there for the kid.'

'I'm sure *she* will love that.'

'She? It's a girl?'

Sid laughed. 'Maybe. But boy or girl—*especially* if it's a girl—my child will have the choice of all those things, and he or she will take after Uncle Jake and be exceptional at sports.'

'*And* a master of the kitchen.'

'Goes without saying,' Sid returned. 'Jamie Oliver has nothing on you, little brother.'

'So, what's Mum's problem with you being pregnant? Does she think you're too young to be a mother?' Jake winked.

'Ha! Glad to see your wit is intact.' Sid stood and wandered back to the window before blowing her nose on the tissue. The impending darkness was changing everything, the grazing mama wallaby now standing extra tall. What dangers might the night bring to threaten her joey? Were wallabies on high alert 24/7? Would Sid be? How would she know what to look out for? Did humans instinctively know how to be a mother like animals seemed to? At least wallabies had safety in numbers.

'Mum's mad because I'm going to raise the baby without a father. According to her, I should make Damien marry me. Or any man, for that matter.'

'You're kidding me.'

'Nope!' Sid swung around to face her brother. 'She once suggested I try reconnecting with Brian Maldon. Do you remember him? According to Mum, he was "*always very smitten*" with me and possibly still would be so I should "*get in touch. See how things go*". Those were her actual words.'

'Seriously? Bogan Brian?' Jake sniggered. 'And Mum suggested you don't tell the guy you're pregnant until you've suckered him in?'

'The inference was there. Then she told me about the guy in number sixty-nine Wagtail Lane, up the road from the B & B. He was chatting to her because he'd noticed me on my morning run. He's also getting over a breakup, so naturally we have something in common to chat about over coffee. Like … *Never!* We most definitely have nothing in common. Have you seen Mr Sixty-Nine?'

'Flippin' fishcakes! Mr Sixty-Nine, hey? Go for it, I say.' When Sid didn't laugh, Jake fell quiet—briefly. 'Maybe Mum's suggesting any bloke would be lucky to have you, whatever your, ah, condition. And I agree with her, except for the sucking-a-guy-in-first thing. You know, there were other choices. Not that I would've ever suggested or expect you to —' Red-faced, Jake's voice faded.

'Hey Jakey, it's okay. I also thought about an abortion—for about five seconds—but I could no more terminate this pregnancy than I could trick a man into marriage. Abortion is a choice and an option, and sometimes necessary, but it's not for me, and neither is conning a man.'

'I can't believe never-do-wrong Natalie would've dared suggest something so … so out there.'

'Maybe it's a mob thing,' Sid said, her attention on the wallaby family retreating in collective bounds to the safety of the dense scrub. 'Maybe that's what Mum's on about. She's telling me I need a mob to look after me and my little joey bump.'

Otherwise, how would Sid know what to be alert for? Her own childhood had been so safe, and she'd felt so secure that there'd been no need to develop survival instincts. For all her faults, Natalie had been a fierce protector. But that didn't make her a good mother—not in Sid's book.

'I'll stick up for you with Mum,' Jake was saying.

'Thanks, but it's time I started standing up for myself. My baby means my choices,' Sid replied. 'Even if it means learning to survive without a mob.'

'I'll be your mob, sis.'

32

WATERCOLOUR COVE, 2015

A mob of wild horses could not have dragged Natalie back to this part of the country. Instead, the love of her children had brought her and deposited her overnight in the last available motel room. Having started the day by visiting Jake to check on his care and to deliver a shopping bag of the requested treats, Natalie was again on the move, headed for new accommodation somewhere south of the immediate Coffs Harbour area. Sid had raved about the place, and Watercolour Cove sounded pleasant enough. There'd been a new villa-type village named Waterway not far from where Natalie used to live, and she'd even contemplated the gated community lifestyle, albeit briefly. According to Sid, this Watercolour Cove place was a small community that offered accommodation. Perhaps staying a week in such a place might even change Natalie's mind about the many benefits of residential estates. *But how far out of town was it?*

Too far, she mused. Once the rally ended, she'd relocate into Coffs CBD and secure a suite in a nice beachside resort. And she'd book an adjoining room because, once discharged, Jake would be needing his mother on hand, but also his privacy, given there was a girl on the scene.

'Sid, darling, you *do* know the rally is back in Coffs Harbour,' Natalie announced. 'What's the hurry?' While Natalie was quietly enjoying the changing scenery, nothing was recognisable. Then again, she recalled little of the regional town of Coffs Harbour, only that the trip in Ulf's bouncy old ute, and on a neglected highway pitted with potholes, had taken forever. Not that she'd tagged along with Ulf very often, even though a young Natalie had longed to venture beyond Dinghy Bay. Earlier, when Sid had described today's destination *as a little south of Coffs*, Natalie had briefly wondered if they'd venture as far as Dinghy Bay—a town obviously still too small for inclusion on the tourist map she'd found in the motel room.

Sidney had barely stopped prattling excitedly—or perhaps nervously —about the *amazing* place they'd been staying at, and how much Natalie would love the *amazing* local gallery the tourists love. Then she chatted about how impressed her new boss had been with Sid's *amazing* knowledge and appreciation of art. Natalie only half-listened, lost in thought and briefly wondering why her beautiful, smart, *amazing* daughter was so excited about selling arts and crafts to tourists. Why take on a job at all when the trip was supposed to be a relaxing break after a shocking event?

'Everything okay out your window, Mum?' Sid asked a little pointedly, drawing Natalie's focus back.

Where were they and when had they turned off the highway? This drive was definitely *not* okay. In fact, Natalie swallowed the lump in her throat, the narrow, unkempt road was frighteningly familiar.

'Sid, this place we're staying at is further away from Jake than I'd hoped.'

'Not long to go, Mum. Besides, with the hospital staff deeming the drain in his leg no longer necessary, Jake might be released as early as tomorrow—no doubt glad to be rid of him!' Sid laughed. 'While you relax, I can nick back to Coffs and deliver him to you. Then, all three of us can spend time together.'

Another all-too-recognisable bend in the narrow back road, and an overwhelming urge to be sick, had Natalie gripping the door handle, her fight-or-flight instincts kicking into overdrive as her daughter slowed before a sharp left turn. How many times had Tilly's bike skidded into that very culvert?

'Stop the car. I said stop!' Not waiting for the Jeep to come to a complete standstill, Natalie flung the passenger-side door open.

'Mum! Wait! You can't get out here.'

'I need a minute.' Propped half in, half out of the car, Natalie tried to breathe, but instead recognised the wintery sea breeze on her face.

Leaning over to open the glove box, Sid extracted a small packet of precautionary tissues and said, 'The good news is there are no more bends. I also rang the caravan park before leaving Coffs. We can check you into the villa early. Or, if you can manage a few more bends—not far

—is the Greenhill plantation road. I was hoping to show you something special before heading into town. The road up is part of the Coffs Coast Art Trail and the view from the top is incredible.'

'No. I don't want to go up there.'

'Pearl will be there.'

'Pearl lives on the plantation?'

'No, she lives by the beach. Jake and I are—'

'But, Sidney, you said you were with your brother in Watercolour Cove? That *is* what you told me?' Natalie clarified.

'Well, yes and no. Pearl is living in a beach house, and Jake *dreams* of living in one. Like he's ever going to have the money to buy real estate—even an old shack—in this place. When you meet Pearl you'll know why the guy is so hooked.'

'No, Sidney. I don't want to.'

'Why don't you want to meet her, Mum? You'll love her, too. She makes this *amazing* tea blend with honey straight from the hive. I have some in my room. And I haven't even told you the best bit about Greenhill. Honestly, Mum, you'll be amazed.'

'Stop talking, Sidney. Of course, I want to meet the girl my son is infatuated with. But I am *not* going up that road and I won't be staying anywhere close. 'Take me back.'

'To Coffs Harbour? But I've paid in advance.' Sid sounded miffed. 'Granted, it's only a villa in the van park—no fancy ribbons—but the rooms are well-appointed and comfortable. I asked for the Gumnut Cabin specifically—from the veranda you can see the seawall. Please, Mum, stay the night, at least.'

'I'm confused Sidney. I thought Watercolour Cove was … Well, not this place.'

Now her daughter looked understandably perplexed. 'Before the name change it was called Dinghy Bay. But don't hold that against it. Please, Mum? I'm not sure where else--'

'Fine,' Natalie cut off her daughter. She desperately needed time alone. Take me straight to the villa.' Natalie huffed, her head jerking back against the headrest. 'I'll tuck in while you do what you must.'

'But the gallery is right around that corner and a few minutes up the hill, and I need to collect clothes for Jake to wear home.'

'For heaven's sake, Sidney, I've seen enough galleries in my time. I hardly think this town is the art and cultural hub of the mid-north coast.' Natalie's brain buzzed. *I can't be here. Not here!* 'You won't make it in the art world staying in a place like this. How would our work get any notice out here?'

'*Our* work?' Sid stared, her daughter's big brown eyes blinking in confusion. 'Mum, whose work are you talking about? What did you mean by—'

'Oh, Sidney, enough of your questions. *Please.*' Natalie huffed back into the passenger seat and slammed the door so hard that her daughter jumped, then burst into tears, her head dropping to her hands on the steering wheel.

'Sid, Sid, I'm sorry. Come on.' Natalie reached over, wanting to pull her daughter close, wanting to cuddle, like she'd wanted to comfort her children after their father died. However, she'd been too numb with shock to be any good to anyone. Shock again paralysed Natalie. 'I'm not sure what came over me, except I don't think my stomach can cope with any more twists and turns. Forgive me? Let's check in, shall we?'

Sid sniffed, nodded, and wiped both cheeks before steering back onto the roadway. When she veered left, away from the mountain towards the town, Natalie breathed deep and told herself Greenhill didn't matter. There was nothing there for her anymore and nothing mattered, other than surviving a few nights in this town. Everything will be fine, she told herself while alighting from the car, as long as you don't look back and glimpse the top of the mountain. She didn't want to see. *Never look back.*

<hr>

The words Watercolour Cove were plastered everywhere: on the caravan park signage, on the coloured flags flying on poles along the main street, and integrated into a painted mural on the old toilet block, which probably no longer smelled of old fishermen and fish guts. Dinghy Bay was no more. The place was changed, charming, and filled with colour.

Natalie whipped her sunglasses from her handbag hide her face. 'Pop the tailgate so I can get my suitcase. Then you can go. I'll check myself into a villa.'

'G'day!' A young man wandered across from the petrol bowser as Natalie attempted to remove her bag, heavy with coats for a Melbourne winter. 'Checkin' in?'

'Gumnut Cabin,' Sid said. 'It's paid for.'

'I'll take your bags over.'

'Thank you,' Natalie said, hoping the boy's hands were clean. 'See, Sid? All under control.'

'Can't I help you settle in?'

'There is no settling in, Sidney. It's two or three nights at the most. I'll take it from here. You do what you need to for Jake.'

'What about food? I'm starving. The Fishermen's Club does a—'

'Sidney, this isn't a holiday. Jake is in a hospital. I also don't need to remind you—' She stopped short. 'Forgive me, darling.' *If only you knew how truly special you are to me, and how desperate I am at this minute to protect you. To protect us.* Natalie touched her daughter's chin to raise it, to show her a smile. 'I've been worried about your brother, but that's no excuse for snapping. Tomorrow will be better.'

'I thought we might spend some time together tonight, Mum.'

'Of course, yes. You do what you must. I'm sure you'll want to shower. Then come back here. We'll catch up over a wine. I have two bottles in my bag from that winery near Tasha's, and I'm sure the office will have snacks.' The very patient check-in guy nodded and smiled. 'Then you need a good night's sleep, Sidney—in a bed for a change. You're looking a little peaked. Your condition requires you take care and rest.' Natalie smiled and dabbed a tear from Sid's cheek before tucking a loose strand of hair behind her daughter's ear. 'Everything will work out. We'll all be fine, just fine.' Mother and daughter hugged awkwardly before Natalie pulled back. 'Off you go.'

Natalie had waited momentarily, mentally tracking the Jeep's route along the same road Tilly had ridden her bike, at speed, with David in pursuit.

Intending to stay put in the room, which was quite lovely, Natalie couldn't relax. Besides, she needed to find pregnancy-friendly food— preferably not packaged and processed snacks. A bakery might have something fresh. Sidney will need to eat, even if Natalie couldn't.

Having attempted and failed to extract suitable clothing from her bag, she'd made do with a woollen cloche hat and scarf, only to find the sun warmer than anticipated. The first store to grab Natalie's attention was a volunteer-run arts and craft gift shop. *Oh dear!* she mused, imagining her daughter behind the counter. Once leased as the creepy old doctor's surgery, the space now housed cheesy, chintzy souvenirs, and had tourist information brochures on a wall by the door. While ample crocheted bears, linen dolls, macrame and driftwood creations, and wooden signs painted with words like *IMAGINE, DREAM, WISH, LOVE* all shared shelf space in the compact shop, it was the collection of original paintings that caught Natalie's eye. She appreciated both the amateur and more accomplished pieces hanging side by side. But what had drawn Natalie into the store was the Visitor Information brochure holder featuring an upmarket B & B.

'I'm so very sorry,' said the blustering older lady who grabbed the remaining flyers. 'I'm afraid those brochures are an old version. The B & B closed down.'

'I see.' A wave of sadness washed over Natalie at the thought of her own abandoned Brushstrokes in the Bush languishing empty, its future uncertain.

'We've hung onto these expecting—hoping—the place would re-open permanently one day,' the woman explained. 'We used to refer a lot of people there. But the young chap who runs the B & B has had his share of troubles. Nice enough fellow,' she added. 'And I'm heartbroken for his most recent loss, even though most folk around here might not say the same. You can't judge a boy by his father, can you?'

'The owner is young?'

'Isn't everyone at my age?' The lady snickered. 'Young-ish and flighty, but the lad tried to make a go of the B & B. The thing is, few people who are clever with their hands have a head for business. And I'm not saying anything I don't know. Those four oil-on-canvas works you admired are mine,' she said proudly. 'And I'm certainly no genius. Now, if you want a nice bush retreat to relax, there's always—'

'Thank you. I'm not looking to stay long. A night or two. I have a villa.'

'Can I give you local information then?'

Natalie was curious about the state of the Greenhill plantation. In particular, how Ted and Rose had coped after Matthew left, and how rundown the place was now. But she was pretty sure that wasn't the sort of local information the lady was offering. Natalie toyed with the idea of asking how long Greenhill had been on the market. The real estate sign sitting a little to the right of the gate hadn't gone unnoticed, but it would be difficult to see when driving. Perhaps Natalie could ask if the sign referred to the Marhkt's old property only or the entire Greenhill parcel. She could fake interest in new house-and-land development opportunities.

'If you like your art, and you appear to have excellent taste,' the woman was saying, 'you might drop by the other gallery in town.'

'There's more than one? Fabulous!' Natalie said, glad to know this store was not her daughter's idea of an *amazing* gallery.

'Yes, dear. The Rose Gallery. Not far, but not walkable, unless you're half mountain goat.'

Natalie forced a smile. '*Rose* Gallery?'

'Not as in flowers, not that I blame you for thinking so. It's named after the lady who lived on the Greenhill plantation.'

Natalie stifled a small gasp. 'There's a gallery up there?'

'Yes, Rose was behind the concept. Strong woman, that one. Gave the last years of her life to the local arts community, and in numerous ways. A very fine artist herself, and an extraordinarily generous teacher, she held classes for locals. Studying nudes was fun.' The woman's cheeks flushed bright red. 'Mind you, we were all a few years younger back then and able to choof up that hill. While people credit Rose's husband with the growth of our little town, that woman was the driving force behind the Hill family.'

'And she's ... alive?' Natalie asked.

With a sad shake of her head, the woman added. 'But a fitting farewell,' she said. 'I know we all go eventually, but poor Rose ... So much tragedy. How does any mother recover from losing a son? A tragic, tragic story. Terrible, terrible shame. Then all that fuss and kerfuffle afterwards ... Tragedy eventually takes its toll on the strongest of people.'

'Tragedies, yes,' Natalie mumbled, wondering if the woman heard the regret in her voice. She'd genuinely liked Rose.

'Are you here visiting family? You look familiar.' The old lady looked at her quizzically.

'Oh, just one of those faces, I suspect.' *Get out, Natalie,* she told herself while putting her sunglasses back on. 'I must get going and stretch the legs.'

'Then the seawall is a must—and if you'd like to buy a tourist art kit, I can ...'

The icy wind gust responsible for whipping the woman's words away was a stinging reality slap—a sudden awakening to remind Natalie where she was now and who she'd once been in this town decades ago. She certainly hadn't expected to be recognised. In her immaculately cut caramel-coloured trousers and jacket, she looked nothing like that barefoot young girl with the wild hair and fresh face who'd skipped school in favour of the beach, and who wreaked havoc around town while wearing Hilda's homemade dresses. This Natalie was never out in public without full make-up, hair straightened and sprayed in place, and a mirror to check for lipstick on her teeth. But with the old woman's curious squint rattling her, Natalie fussed with the bobbed, blonde fringe now long enough to tip her tinted eyebrows. Worried about standing out further in the cloche hat unsuited to a sunny seaside town, Natalie stopped outside a shop displaying caps and straw panamas. Natalie selected a simple sun visor hat: plain, white, adjustable.

With nostalgia drawing her to the foreshore, and to the conglomeration of rocks built to hold back an ocean, nothing could hold back Natalie's childhood recollections. As wave after wave of memories came crashing back, she saw her younger self huddled on her haunches, the hem of her dress tucked under the elastic of her knickers. On the incoming tide, she would clamber over the giant boulders to the ocean side of the seawall to save the helpless marine treasures sheltering there. Why did they not understand the high tide would wash them all into the ocean, exposing them to predators? Foolishly thinking they were hidden, the tiny crabs, molluscs, starfish and sea urchins instead found themselves at the mercy of a receding current, and forced to fend for themselves.

But such were the perils of a sea—and life—when the slightest turbulence dislocated that which had remained undisturbed for decades. *And such were the perils of coming home!* Natalie thought as she drew nearer the water. Was this unexpected homecoming meant to be? Was fate telling Natalie it was time to let the tide clear out all those memories she'd thought would stay safely hidden?

Quickly overshadowing any fatalistic musings was the seawall itself, with almost every boulder transformed into a work of art, the informal and colourful open-air gallery visually stunning. Signage erected by the council welcomed visitors to *"enjoy or join in"*, and advised Art Kits were available from the town gallery and information centre. Natalie smiled. To think she and David had been at the forefront of the rock-art concept, although their works had been mostly hidden from public view for fear of censure. Today, the half-kilometre of colour reached out to the horizon, and with some of the artistic endeavours remarkable in their detail, many appeared more spontaneous—a fusion of family fun sitting beside exuberant graffiti. Scattered among them were expressions of devotion, regret and remembrances, no doubt left behind by the loved and the brokenhearted.

On the drive down, Sidney had prattled excitedly about a series of seaside sculptures commissioned to mark the town's upcoming centenary. Upon Natalie's arrival at the seawall, she'd noticed only a ceremonial plaque being fitted—the type that would be unveiled in the presence of local media. Nearby, two men stood in deep conversation, one wearing a shirt and tie and the other with a grey ponytail and baggy clothes befitting the artist stereotype. Drawn to the rocks, however, the art installa-tion had initially escaped Natalie's notice, making her now wonder if their subtle presence—the way all three life-size effigies were fashioned from an imperceptible mirror-like material that melded into their surroundings—was perhaps the artist's intention. Perhaps 'lost' was the theme, given the first piece was a curvaceous female figure that could have remained unseen except for the colourful and currently chaotic community space the material's reflection threw back. Although concep-tually clever, Natalie felt uncomfortable about the artist's choice of medium. Why reflect what's behind a person? Was it about looking back? Or was the meaning deeper, more symbolic? Was the creator challenging observers to consider how we each fit into our surroundings? Or perhaps, and more importantly, how we impact our environment. Sid, the self-appointed recycle police, would like that.

The reverse side of the reflective sculpture was neither glass nor mirror, but a delicate mosaic frame surrounding a quotation: *'It's what you can't see in a mirror that matters most.'* Credit to the author was on an engraved plaque: *Stephen Grey.* Intrigued, Natalie moved to the next installation. Another mirror in the shape of a person—this time male—featured the quote: *'The world is a looking-glass and gives back to every man the reflection of his own face.'* *William Makepeace Thackeray.* While not familiar with the person, Natalie approved of both the sentiment and his name. To *make peace* with herself and her daughter was clearly on Natal-ie's mind. In fact, she'd make the first move by finding Sidney and hugging her, hoping they can start over.

As Natalie made to leave, something drew her to the final sculpture comprising not one but two smaller figures—the children hand in hand. Had the artist not been chatting, she might've asked if the boy and girl were linked to the adult effigies and, rather than the message being about the lost or invisible as first thought, it was about family: how we are born, how we grow, and how our perceptions change. Thought-provoking art had always excited Natalie because it conveyed so much more. Clever art not only communicates emotions and ideas, it sparks questions, adds clarity, tells stories, or challenges beliefs. This simple concept, designed to blend in rather than stand out, demonstrated the relationship between art and landscape, at the same time showing how a person might view the world around them. But making this exhibition an exceptionally clever choice for a community space was the interactive element that encour-aged movement on the part of the observer. The concept actually relied on the observer's perspective of their surroundings, with a shift in their position altering the image being reflected back.

'Incredible,' she uttered while testing out the theory. Standing to the left first, then far right, showed the mirror-like material was, in fact, reliant on the eclectic rock art of everyday people for its colour and movement. Undoubtedly, if she was to stand square on to the figures, another version of would present itself, and so she did. But the move did more than prove her theory. In fact, did she just scream? More cater-wauling came from nearer the seawall as a rush of larger than normal waves in quick succession rapped out another thunderous warning to walkers. The shower of saltwater delivered was the drenching kind that had children scream with delight and wanting more, while adults cursed the cold and wet. Natalie was safe enough from the water, but was she safe from the building tidal wave of memories as her mind desperately tried to make sense of the mosaic rock art being reflected back in the mirror? The design—a blue and orange heart-shape with two names at its centre—sat chest height across the two child-like effigies. *David and Tilly.*

Needing to slow her heart, Natalie closed her eyes and let her head and arms hang limp while she repeated a quick mindfulness phrase. But when she dared look again, her reflection sat alongside that of the artist, their hands seemingly touching in the exact spot the children's hands touched. Slowly and deliberately following the reflection, she stopped on his face, gasped and clutched a hand to her chest. It might be thirty-six years older, thinner, and tired looking, but it was *his* face staring back at Natalie from the mirror.

33

WATERCOLOUR COVE, 2015

*W**here are you, Mum?*

Sid wasn't worried as much as annoyed. Natalie had wanted to rest, and yet the villa had been empty when Sid arrived, ready for a catch-up. Now, having completed a search of the street, she was nearing the seawall when a collective gasp and a commotion caught her attention. Entangled in the swell of stickybeaks, sightseers and beachgoers was David, and while worrying enough it was the person at the centre of the commotion that panicked Sid.

'Mum?' Sid clasped her mother's hand between both hers and helped a young man in a wetsuit guide a disorientated Natalie to the nearest park bench. When the surfer requested space and privacy, most onlookers complied, parting like soldier crabs on the sand.

'Thank you for helping my mum. Did you see what happened?' Sid asked the boy.

As the surfer shook his head, salt water showered both Sid and her mother. 'Nope. I heard a strange sound and saw the lady grab her chest and sort of wobble.'

'And you?' Sid looked at David who clasped her mother's handbag. 'Did you see?'

'I, um, I'm not sure what I saw. One minute she's admiring one of my pieces, and the next I—'

Surfer boy butted in to ask, 'Do I call an ambulance?'

Her mother's wide-eyes said no.

'Maybe give us a minute,' Sid said. Natalie was conscious and seated upright and likely embarrassed by all the fuss. Squatting down, Sid said, 'Let me look at you, Mum. Do I call an ambulance, or not?' With a definite shake of her mother's head, Sid reassured the surfer. 'She's fine. She says thank you, everyone, for the concern. I'll take it from here.' With that, the remaining onlookers returned to their sightseeing.

Only David remained behind the park bench. 'I have a bottle of water in the car. I can get it.'

With no thought as to David's physical limitations, Sid stupidly said, 'That's great, thanks. Try to relax, Mum. Water is coming.'

'I'm not waiting for water, Sidney. Can you *please* do what I ask and take me away from this place?'

'But Mum, David is—'

'*Now*, Sidney.'

34

WATERCOLOUR COVE, 2015

Safely ensconced in the villa, Natalie seemed to bounce back to her old self, citing the wet cloth pressed to her forehead as key to her quick recovery. Sid was not so easily soothed. Sid was angry and embarrassed about having left before David returned with his water. But her mother's dizzy spell seemed legit and worrying. Thinking it might be about blood sugar levels, Sid nicked over to the garage and stocked up on semi-healthy snacks, including a small yoghurt tub each —banana for her, but vanilla for Natalie. Her mother hated bananas with a passion, never allowing them in the house. Discovering her mother's intense dislike for the fruit happened after Sid traded her pear for her best friend's banana, then mistakenly left it overnight in her school bag. Soft and smelly by then, both the banana and the school bag went into the garbage bin, with a replacement bag bought on the way to class.

'I've made tea, Mum. Sadly, not one of Pearl's restorative brews.' Sid handed her mother the mug before falling onto the very comfortable sofa. 'Hopefully you'll try one of hers soon. Something tells me we'll be seeing a bit of her.'

Mother and daughter were both soon asleep.

Waking to find darkness starting to settle over the town, Sid realised her window of opportunity was closing. Trekking the gallery road was scary enough in daylight hours. She didn't fancy trying it in full darkness. Instead, she offered to stay at the villa, on the sofa, in case she was needed.

'No, Sid. I don't need babysitting. You can go. I'd rather be alone.'

The stern dismissal hardly encouraged Sid to admit to her fears. The road was, after all, one she'd travelled several times before—and Natalie would likely point out the same. But the deciding factor came with her mother's parting instructions that Sid collect her promptly in the morning so she could get back to the hospital, in case they discharged Jake early.

The last section of dirt road—the steepest—was as harrowing in the dark as Sid had imagined, especially the final bend when the tyres lost purchase, slipping sideways. Fraught with anxiety, and with her heartbeat almost audible, the urge to cry came, but left as her mother's mantra echoed in her head: *Buck up, Sidney. Tears do no one any good. Only the tough and the fighters survive in this world.* And so Sid pushed on to the very top, finally propping at the fork in the road. As she sat in the dark, emotionally fraught, the car's engine ticking over while the heater on high blew warm air, a soft tap on the window startled her more than it should have. On the other side of the foggy glass was David's concerned expression.

The man knocked again. 'Are you okay, Sidney? Unlock the door.'

'Of course. Hang on.' *How embarrassing!*

With Little Bump mucking with her energy levels and her hormones, the simple act of pushing open the door and dangling her legs was an effort. 'I'm fine, but I want to apologise about our vanishing act at the seawall earlier today. Oh, hello, Pablo.' Sid slid out of the car and bent down to push the dog's paws off her legs.

'Apology accepted. Now let me ask after your brother and apologise for being irresponsible.'

'You?'

'Yes. I let an employee use machinery without proper training.'

'You're not to blame. Jake knows how to operate a quaddy safely.' She reached back into the car, stretching across to the passenger seat to grab her handbag. 'Also, my brother has been falling off things since he was a baby. The guy has rubber bones that never break. He falls over, gets up and ... Oh! I'm sorry, David. What a stupid and insensitive choice of words.' Her embarrassment burst into a sob before progressing into a blubbering mess. *Could this day get any worse?* 'Sorry, again. I'm a tad emotional. Hormones,' she added, glad the man could not see the blush invading her neck and face. 'But time to buck up, as Mum would say. Tears are for the weak.'

'And there's no unhappiness a hug can't heal. Leave the car and come with me and Pablo.'

Sid was about to refuse when he wrapped a reassuring arm around her shoulders and pulled tight. The action felt so paternal that it evoked memories of her father's comforting hugs. No longer concerned about being stoic, Sid fell into the man and let herself pretend for a few moments that David *was* her father.

Having let her cry the tears of a child long enough, David gently pulled away. 'I feel a stiff drink is in order.'

Sid sniffed and smiled cheekily. 'I feel like tea.'

'*Tea!*' He repeated the word as if it might magically appear. 'Tea is what helps you through the tough times?'

Sniffing again, Sid nodded and tried not to think about the snotty nose dribbles she was bound to have left over his track top. 'Yes. Herbal, preferably.'

'Then herbal tea it shall be. I'll find a special buck-me-up brew to do the job. Pearl's forever putting homemade blends in my kitchen, no doubt hoping to wean me off other options. Come on Pablo, boy, let's head home for tea.'

Letting David lead the way, Sid hoped a buck-me-up brew would soothe her stomach and stop her from throwing up. *Wouldn't that be the ultimate humiliation?*

'Thanks,' she said, stepping through the door David held open and feeling instantly warmed by the corner fireplace. Pablo rushed ahead, jumping onto the hearth rug and pawing at it before circling several times and curling into a furry ball.

'I'll get straight onto the tea,' he said.

Initially left by the door and feeling awkward, the fire invited Sid in but set her on a convoluted path through the maze of easels and small tables scattered across the wooden floor boards. Hovering in the kitchen door, the circa 1970s décor, including the black and white tiled linoleum flooring and a gas hot water unit on the wall above the sink, was a surprise. The worker's cottage she shared with Jake had a fabulously modern kitchen. Not that her brother had embraced the fit-out. Cooking seemed to be the last thing on her brother's mind. Cooking didn't seem high on David's priority, either. The well-used microwave, and the contents of the small bin in the corner, suggested packaged meals for one were common.

Leaning a shoulder against the doorframe, feet crossed at the ankles, thumbs shoved in the side pockets on her pants, Sid observed a man who seemed lost in a kitchen, opening cupboard after cupboard and again suggesting he rarely prepared food.

'Ah-ha! Always found in the last place we look,' he said, holding a small tea canister decorated with white ribbon. 'Pearl's latest brew.'

Without a paintbrush in them, his hands seemed to tremble, especially when they reached up to the top of the cupboard for the plain blue teapot that didn't look to have had too many wash-ups recently. Sid was questioning her decision to be alone in the man's cottage when the vessel slipped from his fingers and landed on a yellow plate on the bench. Sid jumped forward, quick enough to catch the sturdier teapot before it fell over the edge and onto the floor, but the butter-yellow plate was as slippery as its namesake, breaking into multiple pieces.

'My right hand can fail without warning,' he explained. 'But on the bright side, I have an endless supply of the tesserae I need for my mosaics.'

Having tugged at a drawer clearly swollen with age, David used the same free hand to push the jumble of utensils back and forth before proudly brandishing two mismatched teaspoons. 'Ta-dah!'

Why did the owner of a luxury B & B not have matching cutlery, opening drawers, and a kitchen with mod-cons? Unlike the fully equipped main house with its no-expense-spared equipment, this kitchen resembled a seventies sitcom film set.

'I rarely make tea at home.'

Sid smiled. 'I *was* wondering.'

'And never with an audience,' he added. 'Which is not a hint to leave. I actually felt the need for company tonight and your presence is perfect. It's my coordination that's wanting.'

'Then let me help.' When she made to move from her spot in the doorway, he thrust the hand still clasping two teaspoons in her direction.

'There's too little room for you, me *and* these.' A head flick indicated the two crutches: one under an arm, the other leaning against the counter, the open kitchen drawer preventing the stick from sliding to the floor. 'Doing things on one's own is character building. The more independent we are, the more emotionally strong and the better our problem-solving ability. What?' David asked. 'You have a thinking face on.'

Smiling, she chose not to share that her mother was the epitome of independence, but also a woman refusing to foster the same qualities in her pregnant daughter. Sid was enjoying this opportunity to quiz David too much to invite her mother in.

'I am thinking,' she told him. 'Do you mind if I ask you something?'

'Not if you don't mind me not answering.'

How odd! Sid mused. Then she said, 'Can I ask why have company if not to talk?'

He stopped what he was doing to look at her. 'Is that your question?'

'Yes, ahh … No.'

'Which is it, then? Yes or no?' He was smiling, playing with her, their shared laughter the relaxant Sid craved. A sense of humour always put her at ease.

'I wanted to ask why you don't live in the main house?'

He shrugged. 'Not partial to big spaces. Having things within reach makes life easier.' As if to prove his point, he made his way to the sink without the aid of crutches. 'All I need is a bed and my art paraphernalia and easels. Less clutter also equals less cleaning. Besides, that enormous house is old and cold and filled with memories I'd rather not be reminded about every day. Building a fancy B & B was Dad's idea. With him no longer around, I hire the seasonal workers and ignore the place as best I can.'

'And your mother is …?'

'Lost Mum a while ago,' he said, inspecting the inside of two mugs.

But not so long ago that the loss didn't show on his face, Sid decided.

'I think I have everything we need.' David filled the kettle with water, flicked the switch and turned to Sid. 'Now we watch the water boil. Much like watching paint dry. I assume you paint.'

Sid nodded, even though the words he spoke sounded more of a proclamation than a question. 'I used to when I was young. My mother taught me about composition, and about light and shadow, and how art should inspire and bring joy to others. She says images can be powerful and important, and those who are creative—be it with words or pictures—can use their work to make a difference, or to start conversations and connect people.'

'Those are your mother's words?' he asked.

'Yes. Mum's clever with her hands, whereas Dad, having a more literal mind, preferred playing with words. What that means is my brother and I were destined to either write a masterpiece or paint one. Jake cooks them.'

'And which did you choose, Sidney?'

'Neither. I'm a graphic designer, making my creative output mostly computer-generated. You probably don't see that as real art. And I don't think my mother considers what I do as powerful and important.'

'Any creative endeavour is art, even the old phone doodle.'

'A phone doodle?'

'Yes. John Angus Boyd was discovered after doodling with a black pen on a pad while talking on the telephone. His girlfriend was breaking up with him at the time. He called the piece *Dear John*. You see, different artistic endeavours suit different moods, and as you've probably figured out, I have lots of moods. Acrylic for lazy days, oils when I need to refocus, and working in clay tends to be therapeutic.'

'You mentioned mosaics earlier.'

'Hmm,' he hummed, grinning. 'There are no material shortages with me around, but I put my many breakages to good use and love the irregularity of the tesserae—the glass and ceramic, the china and tile—that comes together and forms the mosaic. Now ...' he said, inspecting the inside of the fridge.

But when he took a bottle of milk from the refrigerator, removed the lid, and sniffed, Sid blurted, 'Black for me.'

'Me too.' He glanced her way, and with another wry smile poured the milk down the sink.

This man was a surprise a minute, his interest in her humdrum existence, and his easy banter, not at all what she'd expected. Except for the sound of chunky milk hitting the sink and testing her stomach, Sid was genuinely relaxed and enjoying herself for the first time in ages.

'You mentioned acrylics and oils before, yet I see mostly watercolours,' she said. 'What makes them a favourite?'

'Well ...' He inspected his wet hands, scanned the bench tops, and then wiped both palms across his navy-blue top to leave streaky, elongated handprints. 'Water is its own medium, making watercolours delightfully deceptive.'

'Deceptive?' Sid pounced. 'When is deception ever a good thing?'

He cocked his head, his stare intense. 'Might *sensationally simple* be better than *delightfully deceptive*? Although a watercolour is anything *but* simple. I like they can look whimsical, like child play, while still requiring a certain discipline. Watercolours require a delicate balance of control and letting go.'

Sid harrumphed. 'That sounds difficult—in both artistic terms and in life.'

'Nothing worthwhile is ever easy, Sidney. Perhaps I'm drawn to the unpredictability of the medium because real life—mine, at least—has turned out to be as predictable as one can get.'

'To me, predictability sounds rather comforting.'

He cocked his head in a curious way. 'Whether you're an artist embracing the unpredictability of your medium, or trying to understand life's randomness, sometimes the less control, the better the result.'

'You mean we should go with the flow? That sounds like a watercolorist's mantra.'

'Indeed,' he agreed. 'I sure don't want to be someone who can't feel genuine contentment unless I have control over every aspect of my art and life. We never will, Sidney. We need to learn from life's fickleness and trust in the materials we're given.'

'Better than putting your trust in people,' Sid mumbled.

David stopped pouring hot water to study her. 'People are often a surprise, and not necessarily in good ways.'

'You can say that again.'

'Let me add,' David said, 'sometimes good people do bad things. Would you mind passing my sticks? Let's sit.' He pointed to the small square dining table and chairs pushed into the corner of the kitchen. 'Are you warm? I have plenty of firewood cut, thanks to your brother, which makes me feel worse that he's ended up in hospital.'

'Like I said, Jake and hospitals are not strangers.' Sid set their drinks on the table. 'And temperature-wise, I'm fine. But the constantly changing weather is mucking with my moods.'

'For me, this season has been good for watercolours. I can better maintain paper quality outside, which is where I prefer to work. It's the lure of the natural light, I think. When conditions are just right, extraordinary things happen. Pigment creeps over the paper, and colours come to life.'

And so do you, Sid mused as the man chatted.

'I apologise, Sid. I carry on and forget not everyone is as interested in art.' He took a sip of tea and grimaced. 'I'm not used to visitors and clearly not used to making tea. I'm dreadful at it.'

'I agree, this tea is quite awful.'

While they both laughed, then sat together in silent thought, Sid sensed an unexpected easiness, a camaraderie, a connection.

'I can't help wondering,' David said, looking serious again. 'What's so bad in your life that a beautiful young woman has such a restrained smile?'

Touching her mouth, as if her lips held the answer, Sid said, 'Thirty-five is hardly young.'

'Thirty-five?' he asked, with more surprise in his voice than Sid thought necessary. 'I suppose I'd know your age if I bothered with proper employment processes. Only the rate I go through employees, too much admin would leave me no time to paint.'

'Yup, thirty-five and still figuring out my life and where I fit.' Sid fingered the colourful table centrepiece—a mosaic dish. 'Does being skilled at mosaics mean you're good at taking broken things and putting them back together?'

He grinned over the rim of his mug. 'I suppose it does, but a wise person stops short of doing the same with people. There's less danger working with fragments of glass and ceramic and, as I said earlier, there's no shortage around here.'

As if on cue, one of his crutches slid along the table, snagged the mug's handle and spilled tea. Then, in his rush to stop another breakage, David knocked over a water glass.

'Blasted crutches!' He brushed one damp thigh, only to leave a smear of red blood on his faded blue jeans.

'I'll clean up.' Sid grabbed a dish towel from the sink to mop the spillage. 'That gash will need and good rinse before we dress it. Go! I've got this.'

Clean up completed, Sid added hot water to the pot, hoping to refresh and dilute the strong tea, and began opening cupboard doors in search of fresh cups. The top row of cupboards, stacked like the pre-packaged food section of the supermarket, confirmed Sid's suspicion about David's diet. The lower cupboards—which David would struggle to access—were mostly empty, apart from cleaning gear and a wooden tray pushed to the back. At first glance, the tray looked like one of her mother's. Only Natalie had mounted hers on the wall, like a prized work of art. Natalie's timber-look tray featured an outback landscape with red dirt, ghost gums, a calm river, and a blue dawn sky. It was quite remarkable, even to a young Sidney. Jake had made a similar tray in woodwork class, the work fetching five dollars at a garage sale, after which he'd bragged about being a professional artist. One day, her mother's tray went from the wall into the camphor chest Natalie had designated Sid's glory box. *Where was that box?* Sid wondered, making a mental note to dig the tray out when she got back to Brushstrokes. A tray should be used. Or at least cleaned.

Having wiped David's tray, and hearing the recognisable gait, Sid called out, 'It's all a bit damp in here. I'll carry the tea into the living room.'

The tray was perfect for transporting the tea, the pot, and the biscuits she'd spied in a canister on the countertop. 'I found biscuits,' she nattered while negotiating an easel. 'Hope that's okay. '

David's expression suggested 'no' as he looked at her with the same displeasure as when he'd caught Sid with the letter.

'Sorry!' Sid snatched up the canister, prepared to return the Tim Tams to their rightful place in the kitchen, when she saw David's stare still fixed on the tray.

'I bet you don't recognise it after a good clean. And you'll never guess, but my mother has a similar tray she treasured.'

David's head snapped up, his stare hard, interrogative, distrusting. 'Your mother has one?'

'Yes! Mum appreciates all artistic endeavours, no matter the medium. Even stone and rock art. That was her at the seawall today. I ... Oh, did you not notice? You're still bleeding.' A tiny river of red trickled down his hand and along his forearm. 'The wound must be deeper than I thought.'

'It'll stop soon enough.' He drew a tissue from his pocket.

'Bleeding stops sooner with a little pressure,' Sid suggested. 'Do you have a first aid box?'

'In the bathroom.' He pointed.

She rested David's arm palm up on his knee, then positioned the tissue and the first two fingers of his other hand over the cut. 'Press until I get back.'

'Look for a red bag,' he called after her. 'I've got half a hospital in that bathroom.'

Having located the kit and a towel, Sid returned via the kitchen where she filled a bowl with boiled water from the kettle, adding salt.

'Let's take a proper look.' Sliding a footstool over to sit on, she slipped the towel over his knee and dipped a wad of scrunched-up tissue into the mild saline solution. 'A little sting,' she said, but David seemed too preoccupied—that, or the cut hurt more than he let on.

Was now a good time to ask what happened to her boss to put him on crutches. If not a car crash, had it been a childhood accident? And why did he live alone in such an isolated, albeit beautiful part of the country, with only passing travellers for company? Neither spoke as she bathed the wound, but when she glanced up, he was staring—at her.

Go ahead, Sid, and ask. Say, 'What happened to you, David?' Either he'll answer or he'll throw you out for being nosy.

'Do you mind if I ask you something?'

David cocked his head. 'You *are* a curious one.'

'Jake reckons I interrogate. I don't mean to. I'm curious and so I ask.'

David shrugged. 'I stopped asking the questions I didn't want the answers to a long time ago.'

'Well, when I was a teenager, I drove Mum crazy asking her about when she was my age. We still drive each other crazy. I once overheard my aunty Tasha telling Mum we clashed because we were so alike. Not to look at, but our personality.'

'You have an aunty?'

Strange question, Sid thought, but she could hardly object to him asking. 'Not a real aunty. I've known Tasha most of my life. She's fun, like the naughty one in the family.'

'You don't take after your mother.'

Was that a question? Sid wondered. She answered to keep the conversation going. 'I once overheard Mum tell Aunty Tasha I'm so much like my father that it hurt.' Sid shrugged the memory away. 'Maybe that explains our relationship. I was a curious kid.'

'Curiosity killed the cat,' David said.

Sid grinned in return. 'And satisfaction brought it back again. I *was* a curious kid about my roots, and like most, I went through a was-I-adopted stage. The day I asked, Mum went ballistic. No idea why.'

'Sometimes the surface is all we're meant to see, Sidney. Accept and appreciate things as they appear. Digging around and exposing the roots will kill what was a perfectly happy plant. Best to let things be. We're protected that way. Think onions.'

'Onions?'

'An onion is an onion,' David told her. 'It's not beautiful, but nor is it repulsive. No further scrutiny is required. It's an onion—full stop.'

'Am I supposed to be following this analogy?'

'What I'm saying is this. If left alone, an onion won't hurt you. The risk of tears comes when you peel those layers away.'

Sid argued back, enjoying the debate. 'But you'll also never see what's at its heart.'

He contemplated her argument—briefly. 'So, you really don't agree that we're better off if we do not delve too deeply?'

'I really don't, David.' Her mother's recent refusal to answer Sid's questions about her grandfather came to mind. 'But, your onion analogy sounds like something Mum would say.'

'She must be a wise woman. Can I suggest a daughter would be just as wise to listen to her mother?'

Sid shoved the unused bits of gauze and other paraphernalia back into the red bag. 'If I'd listened to Mum, I wouldn't be here. Besides, you don't know her.' Sid applied a second dressing to the cut, just in case.

'Tell me about your father?' he asked.

Sid sighed and relaxed her shoulders. 'So easy to get along with. We were close. How about you? Do you have children?'

'You *do* ask too many questions.' David slid his chair back so he could stand, surprising Sidney when he made it to the sideboard by supporting himself on the backs of well-placed furniture. 'And in case you haven't noticed, I'm not really a tea drinker. I have red wine and scotch.'

'Ordinarily I'd join you, but I'm not drinking right now. One more Tim Tam can't hurt, though.' Sid reached across, nabbed a biscuit, and nibbled the corner like a mouse savouring a morsel of cheese.

'To answer your question,' David called over his shoulder. 'I do not have children, although I suspect you will do soon enough. Your hand,' he explained, nodding towards her stomach. 'Either you're pregnant, or the tea and Tim Tams are playing havoc with that belly you keep rubbing. I assume that's why I'm drinking alone.' He carried a bottle of scotch by the neck and eased himself back into the armchair before pouring a shot into the empty mug, downing the lot in one go.

'I wanted the job and, well, I haven't been showing much—until recently—even though I'm quite far along. Kind of hoping that means a small baby and an easy delivery.'

'I hope you don't mind me asking *you* something.'

Sid shrugged. 'Go ahead. I've got nothing to hide—*now*.'

'Are you happy to be pregnant?'

She eyed him for a moment. 'I'm getting used to the idea. It's taken a while to comprehend the enormity, unlike Jake when I told him. He can't wait. Jake will be one of those naughty and fun relatives.'

'He's young. Everything's new and exciting at his age.' David's mouth slipped into a smile, another good-sized shot of scotch kicking in. 'I remember being young and passionate.'

'My brother is also falling in love,' Sid added.

David's smile dropped away. 'I remember that, too.'

'Shall I pour you another shot?' she asked.

'You want to see me legless?' David's smile was brief. 'Sorry. Bad gag. Sometimes seeing the funny side helps you through the tough times.'

'There's a funny side?'

'Funny might be the wrong word, but there's always another side to everything in life.'

'I guess you've had tough times.'

'Too many to keep a tally.'

'Mind if I ask what happened to your legs?' Sid prepared herself for a brush-off—no less than she deserved for being a stickybeak.

'Most people want to know, but rarely ask outright,' he said. 'I like that you did, but I'm not sure … It's been a long time since I told the full story.'

'I'm a good listener. First, though …' Sid reached over and took the scotch away. 'I hope I can find everything I need to rustle up a toasted sandwich—and more tea.'

The alcohol had loosened both David's lips and his inhibitions. He even laughed—a lot—though there had been melancholy moments in his story, like when he spoke of the isolation and loneliness of living on the mountain when, as a young man, he'd wanted to live a fun life in the city.

'I watch your brother and feel envy. He also makes me laugh.'

'Yeah? Well, he makes me crazy,' Sid quipped.

Over copious cups of tea, the entire packet of Tim Tams, plus extra servings of cheese on toast, David described life on a banana plantation in the seventies and eighties, and how he'd fallen for a local girl. Sid learned the accident was no accident at all, but a one-punch fight that went horribly wrong when David lost his footing and slipped after taking the hit. Bleeding on his brain and swelling on his spine had forced doctors to induce a coma, warning his distraught parents of the risks and the inevitable and tragic outcome.

'That's what happens when a body tangles with a tree trunk after a few tumbles, at speed, down one of those hillsides. *And* why I'm so grateful Jake is okay,' he explained. 'For me, it was the same hillside, but different times. Everything was different. Things were touch and go for a long while, not that I knew the angst and decision making my parents endured. Eventually, I woke up and got into rehab, only to learn my brother had run off, and so had the girl I was sweet on. Can't blame her for not sticking around. I never saw either of them again.'

'I wouldn't *want* to see them, let alone forgive them.'

'Forgiving is easy, but it never erases the memory, or changes the past, sadly.'

Sid thought about how angry she'd been at Damien when he'd failed to live up to her expectations. All he'd done was admit to not loving her enough and not wanting children. He hadn't lied or cheated or run off with one of Sid's best friends.

'How can you not be angry at the people you loved leaving you behind?'

'According to Confucius, Sid, there are three methods by which we learn wisdom: *First, by reflection, which is noblest. Second, by imitation, which is easiest. And third, by experience, which is the most bitter,*' David said. 'Hurt fades over time and sometimes, as much as we might want to, we can't stay angry. I choose to forgive people, even when they don't deserve it.'

'I wish I was like you.'

'Why? Who do you need to forgive?'

'Damien.' She rubbed her stomach. 'How can any man not want to be involved in their baby's life, especially once they've held them? I still wonder if he'll feel differently when she's born.'

'You said *she*. You know the sex? The baby's a girl?'

Sid shrugged. 'No, I don't know, and I'm not sure I want to ask. But my G.P.'s receptionist is convinced girl babies don't show until the last minute.'

'And Damien is the father's name?'

'Yep! First he was my boss. Then I fell in love with him. I'm that cliché.'

'And *he* is the idiot,' David said. 'That is until he or she looks up at him and Damien changes his mind.'

'That's what worries the most. If he chooses to be in the baby's life, will I ever forget the hurt he caused me?'

'Forgiving is not forgetting, Sidney. It's choosing inner peace over pain.'

The pair fell silent, until Pablo rolled onto his back, all four legs pointing to the ceiling, mouth open, tongue hanging limp, a noise—like a quiet motor running—coming from his nose. 'Speaking of inner peace,' Sid said. 'I have to ask you.'

'Yes, what you hearing *is* Pablo snoring. You'll need a brass band to wake him.'

A big belly laugh erupted from inside Sid. It felt good. 'That's not what I'm curious about.'

'I didn't think so.' The man grinned. 'Ask away.'

'Okay, well, what made someone angry enough to punch you and leave you unconscious?'

'Easy answer,' he said without hesitation. 'What's the one thing two young men fight over, especially strapping lads living in a small town? It's not unusual to have multiple blokes vying for one girl. I was a cocky kid, and life was all about what *I* wanted. But I also thought she and I shared the same dreams—until that fight and punch landed me in the hospital and I discovered we didn't. I never saw her after that.'

'Maybe you dodged a bullet. She doesn't sound very nice.'

'As I said, sometimes good people do bad things. Her dreams were important. I can't blame anyone for chasing theirs, especially knowing about her life before we met.'

No wonder Sid and David were connecting. Wasn't the demise of her relationship all about Damien putting his dream to build the business before Sid and their baby? She'd blamed Damien for not being more truthful in the beginning, while Damien had accused Sid of trapping him into marriage. The real problem was that they never discussed the personal stuff. When they did talk, neither listened. The one thing Sidney knew, having experienced a mother who'd put a career before parenting, was that she would never, never, never blame her baby for the split with Damien.

Maybe meeting David was to be a lesson in healing. Sid needed that. Maybe, as bitter an experience as it might be, she might learn a little wisdom along the way.

'Sometimes our dreams have to change, and we must adapt to new ones,' David was saying.

Sid patted her belly again. 'This baby will test that theory.'

He took a swipe at the crutches leaning against the arm of his chair. 'These blasted things are my test. Every day they remind me.'

'Of course they would. And no wonder you were so concerned for Jake after his fall. But he's fine. Now Mum's in town, I'm the one who needs protecting.'

'Why don't you and your mother get on at the moment?'

Sid explained she and Jake had detoured here without telling anyone, but she left out the bit about the letter and her felonious grandfather.

'It was my idea to stop in Watercolour Cove. I had my reasons, but I didn't tell Jake at the time, and I was never planning to tell Mum. Jake's fall forced me to fess up and now ... Well, if I was in her bad books before, things just got a lot worse. But that's a whole other story.'

'Then I think maybe we're going to need more cheese sandwiches.'

35

WATERCOLOUR COVE, 2015

When the dawn light cast a spotlight on the stormy indigo sky outside the cottage window, Sid pulled the featherweight doona tight to cover her head. But she was now fully awake after such a sleep and hoping she hadn't sounded like Pablo who was still enjoying his snore-fest. The dog remained nestled snugly against Sid's belly, but it was time she stretched.

'Good morning!' David said cheerily. 'I didn't want to wake you both, but the room needs warming.' When the creak of a fireplace door and the scrunching of newspaper roused Pablo. Sid nudged the dog to the floor. It felt good to stretch and rub away the pins and needles in her legs.

'You obviously haven't heard the saying about letting sleeping dogs lie.'

'I slept like one of those logs, though,' Sid returned. 'How's the hand?'

David wiggled his fingers. 'You are an excellent nurse.'

He wore an old jumper, several sizes too big. The type made with love, Sid decided. The sheepskin boots looked warm, but water-stained, like the hem on his jeans. 'I think I'll keep the gate closed to visitors today. Assuming you shut it behind you last night?'

'Yes, I did, and a day off sounds good to me.' Sid straightened both legs, wincing a little where her trousers had cut into the back of her knees. Then she dragged the scrunched tails of her shirt down over her hips before discarding the doona.

'Coffee? More tea?' David asked.

'Water is fine. I'm all tea'd out.' She reached for a throw rug, the colourful crocheted type someone had spent hours making. Less cumbersome than a doona, she draped the blanket around her shoulders.

'I need coffee.'

'And I need to freshen up. Then perhaps over coffee we can talk more about your art,' she called back while en route to the bathroom. 'I'd like that.'

'Morning sickness?' he asked, his gaze on the belly she rubbed in soothing circles.

'Yup! Although mine is not confined to mornings and not going away.'

'Then I'll tell you about bananas,' David said, nudging the mosaic dish full of the fruit towards her.

Sid eyed the man, wondering where the gruff version was hiding. 'First onions, and now a banana lecture? Do tell.'

'More nutritional advice than lecture. And as stylish as that draped rug look is, I found you a jumper. It's warm and roomy.' He pointed to the one draped over the chair. 'As for the humble banana, they're rich in potassium and a natural remedy for many things, including morning sickness.'

Having donned the jumper, Sid began to peel the banana skin away one strip at a time. 'My dad would tell you bananas are the reason monkeys are so happy. He had a mountain of bad banana jokes.' Sid thought she'd get another laugh out of her audience. But, no. 'Dad came out with lots of funny things when we were young. We believed him, of course.' Sid bit gingerly into the soft, fleshy fruit, hoping the cure-all worked quickly. 'He could spout off a list of every vitamin and mineral in a single banana. Then again, he was the type of person who regularly obsessed over facts and figures. He saved newspaper clippings and made scrapbooks. Someone once suggested to Mum that he had a mild form of Asperger's. But I don't think he was on the spectrum.' She nibbled more banana. 'Poor Dad did drive Mum to distraction often. I remember this one argument. *But*,' she said teasingly, 'you probably aren't interested in long-ago tales from a very ordinary childhood.'

'What if I told you I was interested in *your* long-time-ago tales?' David countered.

'Touché!' Sid grinned. 'I guess I owe you a tale or two after last night.'

David gestured to the chair opposite, settling back in his own seat as though preparing for a long story. 'Well?' he grinned. 'You said "poor Dad". Go on.'

'I have to admit that Dad didn't relate so well to people, and he tended to take everything we said literally—like the day Mum ended a fight by telling him to get lost. Dad went stony faced and stopped arguing so he could discuss why she would want him to get lost.' Sid couldn't hold back another small laugh as she recalled her mother's exasperation. 'Dad looked at Mum and said, "I don't understand. Even if it were possible for a person to lose himself—or herself—I'm not sure why you would want me to. But I suppose, if a person hiking unconsciously strayed from their path, you might consider they got themselves lost." By then, Mum was so frustrated she told him to forget she had said anything. To which Dad, by now genuinely confused, said something like, "Again, my dear, can you not concede that it might be equally difficult for a person to *forget* on demand as it is to get *lost* on demand?" That was my poor, funny, loveable dad.' Sid almost teared up at the memory. Even David looked unusually contemplative. 'But good news! I believe the banana has worked.'

'Hmm, good.'

Was the man even listening? 'I must be boring you with my story.'

'No!' David insisted rather vehemently. 'Not at all. You were saying?'

'I was saying the banana is good. I gather there's more where that one came from?'

'Plenty, but nowhere near the commercial quantity from twenty or thirty years ago,' he added. 'What started as two banana businesses on this mountain became one. And as any small producer occupying primary real estate close to towns will tell you, their time is limited. Farming in this country is like playing roulette in a rollercoaster, and small producers, like Greenhill Bananas, are a dying breed because most of what Australians eat now is produced on broad-acre, highly mechanised farms.'

'So, the land on the other side of the fence Pearl warned me would have snakes was also all banana farm?'

'Hmm, yeh, I need to have the area slashed.' David again appeared distracted. Or was it sentimental?

Sid tried recalling detail from David's story about the girl next door. 'She lived there, didn't she? The girl.'

David nodded. 'Along with her brother—the one-punch wonder.'

'Her *brother* hit you?'

'Stepbrother, I guess you could say. Both adopted, with Albie more a labourer than a son to the Marhkts. Had they been better business people, they might've ended up with a property worth something to hand down to him. But Ulf, inherently lazy, sold to my father after Albie took off.

They wanted money, but I never understood why Dad offered to pay so much. The Marhkt land was not productive.'

'Now your family owns the entire hill?'

'You make it sound grand, but yes. My father was something of an entrepreneur. We were also in the right place at the right time when a cyclone wiped out the Queensland banana industry. With New South Wales bananas suddenly in demand, prices skyrocketed and our family profited from the two plantations. I recall the day Albie, having heard about the impact of the cyclone, came back home. He'd planned to make amends with Ulf and Hilda and help them cash in on the banana boom.'

'But they'd sold and gone?'

David nodded. 'The guy was devastated. I felt sorry for him. While he never talked about his life before he came to live here, I knew he was abandoned twice by people who were supposed to care for him the most—the Marhkts and his birth mother, who'd been single and without the resources and support to care for a baby on her own.'

'Is that right?' The ah-ha moment had Sid eyeing the man suspiciously. 'And you're telling me this Albie-and-his-mother story so I'll realise how hard life will be as a single parent—as if I'm not reminded every day already!'

The accusation seemed to shock David straight in his seat. 'Not at all. Like I said, I don't meddle or try to mend people. My story bears no relationship. Your choices are yours alone, Sidney. In fact, far from concerned, the more I get to know you, the more convinced I am you'll make a wonderful mother. You've made sacrifices already and only you know what's best for you and your baby. Albie's story was different. One of those hard luck ones, and it messed him up bad. He had a traumatic childhood and, no doubt, a tough life. I hardly recognised the guy when I saw him a few years ago. Always tall but beefy, he'd lost weight and grown from a pimply teenager into a gangly, gaunt grown-up—and way too wiry to throw a proper punch these days.'

'He punched you again?'

David laughed for the first time in a while. 'Reckon he thought about it for a moment.'

Sipping coffee, he seemed to drift further into that memory until a clanging and banging sound outside sent Pablo into a barking frenzy.

'Sounds like the predicted southerly is hitting early.' David stood and leaned into his crutches. 'I'll need to batten down a few hatches.'

'How can I help?'

'You can check the gallery shutters are closed tight. I'll meet you back here, if the wind doesn't blow me away first.'

36

THE GREENHILL BANANA PLANTATION,
THREE YEARS EARLIER

'Well, well, you never know what the summer wind's going to blow in these days,' David said from the front door, one arm stretched to hold the screen door open.

'You're looking well,' the man called back from the bottom of the veranda steps.

'No thanks to you.' While David couldn't make out the visitor's face, there'd been no mistaking the whiney voice, nor the big head hanging on rounded shoulders, like it was too heavy for him. 'Forgive me for cutting your visit short. I've got a birthday cake waiting for me—fifty candles heavy—and last I looked, you weren't on the guest list.'

'I'm wantin' to see your dad,' Albie said.

David steeled himself, desperate to look strong in front of the man he wanted to hate. 'Then you must be looking to have your block knocked off. Dad's not been a fan of yours since you punched me and left me for dead. I remembered that much when I eventually woke up unable to move.'

'It was one punch. You weren't supposed to fall.'

'Yeah, well, I did, and you know what they say. It's not the fall but the stop at the end that kills you. I got lucky. It took a long time, but I walked when they told me I never would. And I'm living here and painting. Life could be worse.'

'I'm sorry,' Albie said. 'What happened … the argument … It wasn't about you. Tilly made me so angry.'

'You're sorry? Well, me too, but while Mum and I have moved on, Dad's not as forgiving. I'd stay clear of my old man. He's thirty-odd years angrier.'

'And Matthew? Have you seen your brother or your old girlfriend?'

David shrugged. 'I haven't seen either of them since you put me in hospital. They weren't here when I got back. You'd know that.'

'Yeah, but I wondered if you knew where they were.'

'Albie, I think you need to get back in that car of yours and piss off. Whatever it is you're after, I can't help.'

'You could forgive me.'

David snorted a laugh. 'What?'

'I figured if you could forgive your brother, you might forgive me.'

'Forgive Matthew? For what? He didn't punch me and leave me for dead. He did nothing but get the hell off this mountain and make a life for himself. I don't blame him for that.'

'Yeah, but ...' Albie's forehead creased into a thousand questions.

'What?' David pushed. 'Why so curious about Matthew—and Tilly, for that matter?' Without waiting for Albie to answer, David flicked a dismissive hand. 'Bugger off, mate! There's nothing here for you.'

'Actually, there is—or was before your greedy father got his hands on my family property. I heard.'

'Not sure what you heard, mate. The sale was legit. Dad made the right offer at the right time. No one twisted Ulf's arm.'

'So where are they now? Where are Ulf and Hilda? The place is boarded up and a bloody mess.'

David shrugged. 'I don't know. It's been a long time. Hilda might've told Mum about their plans. All I know is the money they got from the sale set them up in a nice little estate a long way from here.'

'Albie Marhkt?' Rose now hovered in the doorway, looking smaller still beside her bulky son, her voice timorous. 'What on earth brings you here?'

Albie straightened. 'I've come home, Mrs Hill. I need information about my parents' whereabouts.'

'I can't help you.'

'David said you knew.'

Rose glanced at her son. 'No, Albie, I can't help. Hilda left only a forwarding address for mail. A post office box. But it was so long ago. I've had nothing to forward and no cause to even keep the information handy.'

'So, you remember nothing? Not even the name of the town they went to?'

'It was a small suburb on the Sunshine Coast. A new estate in the hills. I'm an old woman who forgets.'

'Yeah,' David interrupted. 'Like we want to forget you, Albie.'

'David!' Rose scolded her adult son as she'd done the two bickering boys decades ago. 'I'm so sorry, Albie. I recall Hilda saying she had no reason to think you would ever be in touch. Not for a moment did I think you'd come asking after so many years.'

'I don't believe you. There's more you're not telling me.'

'I am truly sorry,' Rose said with genuine remorse.

'We can't help, Albie,' David added, 'and you're not welcome here.'

'Is that so?' Albie stiffened, his hunched shoulders straightening enough to put the sun on his face. The man's complexion was beetroot red, his normally poppy eyes narrow and accusing. 'Thieves *and* liars.' He spat the words like they were bitter crumbs in his mouth. 'You deserve every bad thing that ever happened to you. And that includes your girl-friend running off with your brother.'

'Albie, you horrid creature!' Rose cried out, all empathy gone from her voice. 'I'm not sure what you came here for. If you're looking for your parents or looking for forgiveness, you are out of luck. You were a horrible little boy who made up stories and I see nothing's changed.'

David put an arm around his mother's shoulder, leaned down, and kissed the top of her head. 'Leave this to me, Mum. Best go check that birthday cake hasn't caught on fire.' He smiled at her. 'And make sure Pearl doesn't eat it all. I'll be right in.'

David turned his attention back to Albie. 'You know, mate, the only person running off back then was you when you abandoned me on that hillside. And maybe I *could've* forgiven you—if only you'd toughened up and owned up, or at least checked I was okay. But don't push your luck by spreading stories. You were always coming on to Tilly. Even when she said no, you still tried. It wasn't right. You were like her brother. Matthew and I treated you like a brother, too. But here you are, all these years later, still a bloody no-hoper weirdo. So bugger off, Albie. I'm not interested in your troubles or bullshit stories. I think I know my own brother.' David went to close the door but paused. 'And as far as I'm concerned, I'm glad Dad has the Marhkt's old property. He's at the pub right now, celebrating. Council has approved his plans to carve that place of yours up and sell off residential blocks. He'll make a killing. That's what sticking around and doing the hard work gets you, Albie. Something you wouldn't know anything about because you were always too busy whingeing and telling lies.'

'I never—'

'I'm not warning you again,' David said before slamming the door shut.

37

WATERCOLOUR COVE, 2015

The strong winds as good as blew Sid back along the path to the cottage, where David stood sheltered by an alcove.

'All battened down over there?' he called over the howling sounds.

'One casualty only.' Sid ducked through the doorway and under his arm, never more glad to see and feel the flames from a glowing fireplace. 'Sadly, Henry the hanging possum hit the deck. Snapped his ringtail clear off.' Sid shuddered with cold as she re-tied the ponytail to gather strands whipped loose by the wind. 'When Pearl warned me about lightning strike, she never mentioned cyclonic winds. When she blows up here, she really blows, and with little warning.'

'I suppose we're used to Mother Nature reminding us of who's boss. I've topped up the pot with hot water.'

Sid stopped by the fire to warm hers hands. 'I'm still tea'd out, but keen to pick up where we left your story. The Albie one. Only if you want to, of course,' she added.

'I have some regrets about the day he fronted here. His beef wasn't with me,' David said, returning to the armchair and securing his sticks alongside. 'He was angry at my father because he assumed by buying the adjoining property we'd disadvantage the Marhkts and denied *him* his inheritance. My own anger that day stopped me from seeing how desperately he'd needed someone to care. The way I ended things between us that day was a wasted opportunity. A little forgiveness on my part might have changed everything. If I hadn't slammed the door in his face he might not have tried to kill himself, and my father along with him.'

Sid slapped a hand over her mouth. 'Albie died?'

'No. He and Dad survived. But locals going about their business that day, including children, lost their lives. As is often the case, two versions of what happened circulated around town—Albie's and Dad's. Mum and I had no doubts—my father's side of the story was the truth. But with Albie doing a runner soon after, the town needed someone to pay. Our family suffered terribly—Mum more than anyone as she desperately tried to clear Dad's name, but townsfolk saw themselves as both judge and jury. Instead, Dad served time, dying in prison an innocent man and rejected by the townspeople he'd done so much for.'

Sid sat—silent, sad, and staring at David focused on his bandaged hand. She felt so sad that the man had been trapped on this mountain for years. Initially by his physical limitations, then his commitment to an aging mother. Had the pair hidden themselves away up here, shunned by an angry community?

With the only sound in the room the crackle of burning wood and the whistle of wind being forced into the old cottage's creaking crevices, Sid ask David, 'At any time did you think to clear your father and family name?'

Without looking up, he nodded. 'I tried. It was important to Mum. But with no proof to overturn his conviction, any efforts to clear his name would serve only to bring more anguish to locals who'd lost loved ones in the accident. After Mum passed, I wanted to do it for Dad. But he said to me, "What will dredging up hurtful historic events achieve other than more hurt?". So who *was* I clearing the family's reputation for? My brother had estranged himself and I had no children to carry on the Hill line. With Dad's health in decline, especially after losing the love of his life —the woman he'd loving called his Rose among roses until the very end— the Greenhill Plantation, and everything associated with us, would eventually cease to exist.'

Sid's thoughts travelled to the art room in the main house and to the inscription on the notebook. *To my Rose among Roses.* David's mother was the loving wife writing letters to her husband, and an unfinished letter had detailed early talks with council regarding commissioned sculptures on the foreshore to mark the town's centenary. Thinking back to the date on Rose's letter meant David's dad had passed away after his wife, making it sometime during the last three years.

The thud over Sid's temples started small, the scrawled words '*every day and forever'* running like ticker tape in her head. Had the author of the notebook's inscription signed his name?

Enough, Sidney! she silently scolded. *Time to cap that curiosity. You have the rest of winter to exercise your inquisitiveness.* As of right now, Sid's priority was an expectant mother. Natalie, usually out of bed by sunrise, would be contacting Sid any minute. On cue, her message app beeped.

'Go ahead,' David said, as if sensing her reluctance to respond. 'Say hi to Jake from me.'

Cupping the phone at her ear, she wandered to the far side of the room and retrieved the voice message.

'Wherever you are, I've given up waiting. FYI your brother was discharged early. And, Sidney, you'd better start being more responsible. Soon enough you'll have a child relying on you for love and support, and lifts home from the hospital, God forbid.'

Sid groaned on the inside and deleted the message, then turned back to David. 'Jake's fine, but it's time I left. Thanks for the lovely fire chat.'

'Before you go,' David said as Sid collected her bag. 'When you arrived earlier ...'

'You mean last night!' Sid said through a yawn.

'Yes, last night,' David corrected. 'You said you wanted to apologise for ... I believe you said your "vanishing act" by the foreshore.'

'I did?' Sid was not keen to go there now. She didn't want to spoil what had been an enjoyable and interesting evening by apologising for Natalie's rudeness. Besides, her baby brain was at bursting point. She smiled at David from the doorway. 'I have no idea. I really must go.'

Raising his injured hand to wave her off, David smiled. 'You're a good nurse and a good listener, Sidney. Thank you.'

Sid smiled, returned the wave, and closed the door behind her. *Not to mentioned a good liar and a disappointment to my mother.*

Having negotiated the storm detritus littering the path, Sid hoisted her body up and into the driver's seat of the car, her mother on her mind while she warmed the engine. For some fifteen minutes, Sid had let the car idle, knowing she needed to cut Natalie some slack. She was a mother worried about her son and a woman caught up in a police investigation after discovering a man hanging in the bathroom. Sid struggled to image the shock Natalie had endured. She had only checked the weird guy in when he'd turned up that day without a reservation.

38

THE BLUE MOUNTAINS, 2015

The man's fake accent was weird, like he was trying too hard to be something he was not. But as Brushstrokes in the Bush attracted the wacky artistic type, Sid thought no more of the strange guest, except that the gentleman was extremely well-groomed, which made him different to most of the B & B's clientele. What his appearance lacked was the usual traces of paint under fingernails, ground into cuticles, or dotted over spectacle frames and watch faces. Last week, a guest had checked in looking like a flock of Rainbow Lorikeets had splattered him with rainbow poop. Today's arrival had a unique style of weirdness.

'My name is, ah … It is *Al-ess-andro*! Al-ess-andro Al-ber-tini, born *in-a* Malta. It *is-a* good-a to-a *meet-a-you!*'

'Good to meet you, too,' Sid smiled, snatching her hand back from the sticky, over-enthusiastic handshake. 'You have a reservation?'

When the man presented a document resembling a birth certificate—a really old one, and too faded and folded to read—Sid slipped into a smile, then slid the piece of paper back across the check-in counter. 'We need only your credit card.'

'I have cash. Lots.'

'Oh? Well, happy days! We also take that.' Sid smiled at the odd little man, genuinely grateful to him for the mood-lifting interaction.

Eager to tell her mother about him when she arrived home, the woman had been so flustered about something-or-other, Sidney mentioned only that the loft room was now occupied. One man. One night.

The next morning, as a sleepy Sid stood behind the island bench, hot tea clenched between cold hands, her mum seemed unusually preoccupied with something in the day's newspaper. Nicknamed *The Missile* by Sid, the cling-wrapped weapon was launched daily at her bedroom wall by a P-plated paper boy with an apparent sleeping disorder and a noisy muffler.

Sid tip-toed across to the table, planning to read over her mother's shoulder, but she'd barely glimpsed the article's heading—*Royal Commission Witness Breaks Down*—when Natalie slapped the pages closed and checked the time.

'Time we got moving. We have rooms to prepare.'

'But, Mum, the guy in the loft apartment hasn't checked out yet.'

Natalie looked at her watch. 'But Mandy will be here to clean at eleven. You told the guest about checkout?'

Sid sighed. 'I told *him* what I tell everyone. I remind them of the no-smoking rule, point out the emergency evacuation plan, and check they know when to nick off. Mind you, the guy was odd.'

'Sid, darling, while I love having you here to help, I've told you before not to speak about guests in a derogatory manner. You never know who might hear.'

'But wait until you see him, Mum. Plus, he does a really bad accent. Not sure why a person would want to be something they clearly are not. And it was particularly weird when he glared at me—like really interrogated my face—and spoke in a phoney accent. Creepy!' Sid shuddered. 'But I got the feeling he knew you. He asked for you by name, so I figured you'd forgotten to put him in the reservations book. And as you keep the loft for special guests, I put him in there. I'll go knock on the door, give him a hurry on.'

'And what about the gallery, Sidney?' Natalie asked, her fingers still holding the pages of the newspaper, as though she was keeping her place until she could read in peace—without the cross-examination. 'While you're in the kitchen lambasting our money-paying guests, who is minding the gallery?'

'Mum, it's Tuesday. We don't open on Tuesdays. What's got your attention in that newspaper this morning?'

'Nothing at all. In fact, you'll be glad to hear I'm about to pop it in the appropriate recycle bin. Not sure why I have the thing delivered. If not for the guests, I'm sure I wouldn't bother. The news these days is all party politics and celebrity rubbish.' As she passed by the open laundry door where a trolley of fresh towels and sheets waited for Mandy, Natalie stopped. 'You folded the towels, Sidney?'

'I did.'

'But why? Surely you've been here long enough to know at Brush-strokes we *roll* and then we *ribbon*. We do *not* fold flat.'

'We're out of ribbon, Mum,' Sid said, wanting to add she knew, too well, how long she'd been back under her mother's roof—back to being a teenager, saving her pocket money and counting down to the day she would get her own place. 'I used the backup ribbon supply to prepare the room for last night's unexpected check-in. Maybe what we need is less ribbon and more signs in the rooms to stop thieving guests flogging anything that isn't pinned down.'

'Don't denigrate our guests, please.'

'Sorry. I should have said to stop the guests *souveniring* the ribbon. Is that better?' Sid now *sounded* like a teenager. 'Why adults take the stuff, I have no idea. And we could try using less ribbon for each room. They're only towels, not works of art.'

But Natalie liked to show off her considerable artistic talents any way she could, and the elaborate rolling and placement of thick, luxurious bath towel on the guest beds—along with matching washers and two bathmats—required lots of ribbon, and always of the wired variety because, not only was quality wired ribbon strong, it could be crimped and curled into the perfect bow.

'You know I like the ribbon on *rolled* towels.'

'Mum, that's the sort of silly single-mindedness you used to go crook on Dad about. One day of folding won't kill anyone.'

'Except that consistency and quality has been the secret to our success for the past six years. Consistency and quality is what our guests pay for.'

Sid wanted to laugh. Paying guests were hardly the norm at Brush-strokes. Thanks to her husband's life insurance, the company compensation payout for 9/11 victims, and sound investment advice, Natalie's operational strategy—her preference—was more often a philanthropic approach.

'Okay, so what do you want to do about the paying guest in the loft room?' Sid asked. 'I don't want to disturb him if he's up there using that expensive art paper you provide to write a thank you note for the wonderfully rolled and ribboned towels.'

'I'm ignoring you, Sidney. And if the gentleman isn't out shortly, I'll be giving him a hurry on. I'll see *you* when you get back from town.'

'Town? Why am I going into Leura?'

'Ribbon, Sidney! The towels don't decorate themselves.'

The Blue Mountains morning peak, which basically comprised those driving to the many train stations, and those heading down the mountains to the Penrith CBD and beyond, was well and truly over, making the short drive into the pretty township of Leura a breeze. Sid enjoyed the drive and the thinking time away from the claustrophobic conditions at Brushstrokes. She had a lot to think about, with more still as the months marched on. In no particular order, Sid needed to get over the hurt, get more freelancing jobs under her belt, then get herself set up in her own place. She'd need somewhere affordable to live, which meant anything close to the city was out of the question. The chosen district would need to be a good one for a baby—safe and tidy, with plenty of green space and a public pool not too far away. What was the best environment in which to raise a child? The high-rise life? The suburban sprawl?

Neither option enthused Sid. And as lovely and secluded as the Blue Mountains might be, being in such proximity to Brushstrokes 24/7 was out of the question. Not because they didn't love each other. The pair simply got on each other's nerves too easily. Maybe Tasha had been right. Maybe being too alike was the problem. If only Sid had taken after her father.

Knowing she took after Natalie hardly bolstered Sid's mood as she returned to the car with a handbag overflowing with reels of precious pink ribbon. More irksome than wired ribbon, however, were the several missed calls on the mobile phone she'd mistakenly left behind in the car. The first missed number was Brushstrokes, making Sid shake her head. *What now, Mum? Am I not back soon enough with the ribbon? Are the towels suffering from separation anxiety?*

Missed call two, three and four—all from her mother—ended Sid's flippant thoughts, while the constant engaged signal added an urgency to her return trip to Brushstrokes. Deliberately breaking several traffic laws en route, Sid hoped the old copper from the local station didn't spot her Jeep. Then she turned the car into Wagtail Lane and saw blue and red lights flashing. Her stomach roiled. When she saw an ambulance blocking the driveway, her heart took a dive.

'Mum!'

Confused and concerned for her mother's wellbeing, Sid didn't bother complying with the street's *Parallel Parking Only* sign. Instead, she mounted the kerb, ignored the police tape she inadvertently hooked around the passenger-side rear-view mirror, and ran towards the guesthouse.

'Sorry.' The officer guarding the front door extended an arm, barring her entry. So taken by surprise, Sid stumbled and almost fell. Thankfully, the policeman was strong—or skilled at catching dead weights—as he quickly steadied her. 'Is this your permanent residence, mam?'

'*Mam?* Um, no. Sometimes. At the moment. Yes!' Sid whipped her sunglasses off and squinted at the officer, searching out a name badge or a number to reference when she complains. *Oh, you are so like Natalie!* 'Look, officer, just tell me what's wrong. This is my mother's house. I was at the shops when she called. Look.' Sid had managed to locate her phone in the side pocket of her busy shoulder bag. 'Look at the screen. Look at the missed calls. All Mum. Tell me she's okay.'

Without glancing at the screen, the officer said, 'She's upset, so a policewoman is talking to her.'

'Talking about what?' Sid insisted while trying to shove her phone back into a bag stuffed with the wired ribbon she'd bought. 'Damn!' She cursed as one of the spools spilled out and rolled, leaving a pink trail over the porch.

The officer's gaze followed the spool on its wobbly journey down all the three steps—*bomp, bomp, bomp*—and when Sid made to retrieve the wayward ribbon, he said, 'You can leave that right there, Ms Hill.'

'Why?' She tried shaking his arm away. 'And stop calling me Ms Hill. It's Sidney.'

'Can I ask you to wait at your car?'

'No!'

With one eyebrow cocked, he said, 'Then perhaps you might like to move the vehicle off the footpath and behind the police tape.'

'Seriously?' Sid huffed as Officer Officious bent down and scooped up the ribbon by hooking a pen through the spool's centre. 'Look, Officer Whatever-your-name-is, what the hell's going on?'

'The ribbon …' he replied, stony-faced. 'It's wired?'

'Good grief, not you as well. What about the bloody ribbon?'

'It's yours?' he asked as Sid channelled her exasperation into punching out Jake's number on her phone.

'This is ridiculous.' Was she still asleep and having a bad dream? Was her mother's painful predilection for perfection and pink ribbon now giving her nightmares? And why the hell was her brother not answering his phone? 'I just bought the ribbon in Leura. This is my mother's establishment. She likes a special wired ribbon, but we'd run out. So, how about you tell me what's going on?'

'There's been an incident involving a guest.'

Sid's first thought was the creepy guy she'd checked in last night. 'The guy in the loft? Did he hurt Mum?'

'What makes you think a guest might do so?' the police officer asked. 'Do you know the man involved?'

'Shit, Sherlock, how about you stop with the freaking interrogation? If he's hurt my mother, I'll … I'll kill him.'

'Too late. The gentleman took care of that himself.'

Sid choked back the next smart alec comment, almost gagging as bile whooshed up and into her throat. 'Are you serious? You mean he … In our guest room? And Mum …?'

'Found him and phoned it in an hour ago.'

'Oh, no, poor Mum. I need to be with her.' The gush of genuine tears seemed to relax the officer's stance. 'Please.'

'I wish I *could* let you in, but my job is to keep the crime scene protected, and I'm kind of new. But maybe while you're moving your car I can check how things are going inside.'

'Fine, fine, I'll move the bloody car—if you tell me one thing first.' The officer gave no indication, verbal or otherwise, to suggest he would, but Sid asked anyway. 'How did the man … You know …?'

The officer replied softly, 'The gentleman hung himself. Pink ribbon.'

'If this gets into the papers …' Natalie's hands clasped her head as she shook it from side to side.

Sid wanted to suggest they might show a little more concern for the poor man and his family, but asked instead, 'What could be so terrible to make a person take his own life? And why choose our B & B?'

Clearly still shocked, Natalie seemed almost on the verge of tears. *Almost.* Sid had never seen her mother cry—not even at their father's memorial service.

Having broken every speed limit and traffic law to reach the Blue Mountains ASAP, Jake was whipping up food no one wanted and agreeing with Sidney that Natalie should not remain in the guesthouse once the police were done with their questioning.

'Where do I go? This is my home.'

'Visit Aunty Tash,' Jake suggested. 'She's always asking you down and you're always saying the guesthouse is too busy.'

Natalie scoffed. 'A busy guesthouse is now a thing of the past. Who would want to stay here after …?'

'Don't worry about that now, Mum,' Sid said. 'As shocking as a suicide is, I'm sure the media will have juicier stories. You'll see.'

39

WATERCOLOUR COVE, 2015

'Can I come in?' Pearl nudged open the villa's sliding screen door open with her knee.

'Yeah, sure,' Sid replied through a yawn. 'How are you?'

Pearl dumped two string shopping bags on the table. 'I'm okay, but what gives between your mum and the boss?'

'Who?' What was Pearl on about? And what time was it? Sid's brain fog was becoming such that she barely recalled returning to the villa to collect her mother, and instead finding the place empty. Given Natalie was keen to be at the hospital—and no doubt just as keen to lecture her reckless daughter on being more responsible—Sid had plonked herself on the sofa to wait. But with time alone to poke through the mental jigsaw pieces from last night's conversation with David, a picture had begun taking shape. Then Sid had clearly nodded off, because when she woke to the sound of Pearl's voice at the door, the wall clock showed 11.59 am. 'Have you seen Mum?'

'She left you a note,' Pearl pointed to the table.

Pearl asked one of her brothers to transport your brother back from the hospital early this morning. I like Pearl. She's reliable. I couldn't sit around all day waiting for you to get up off that sofa, so I've borrowed your car.

'My car?' Sid peered closer in case she'd misread. 'Mum took my car!'

'That's what I'm trying to tell you.' Pearl shook the second bag's contents out and unwrapped a white paper parcel. 'As the car was yours, I presumed the woman driving was your mum. It was a while ago. I was just leaving the gallery when I saw her talking to the boss.'

'You bloody ripper! Hi, sis.' Jake hobbled from his bedroom, obviously planning to milk his injury for a while longer. 'Thought my nose detected food.'

'Sit,' Pearl commanded. 'I'll bring your prawns on a plate.'

'Will you peel them for me, too, wench?'

'Keep that up and you'll wear them.'

'Thanks for collecting Jake for me this morning, Pearl.'

'My brother, Adrian, was coming off a night shift. Helps to have a cabbie in the family.'

'Thank Ado again for springing me out of the joint,' Jake said. 'Sid and I could've done with his jail-busting talents a few weeks ago.'

'Jake!' Sid fired a warning glance to remind him the subject of their grandfather was not common knowledge. At least she hoped he hadn't mentioned the matter to Pearl. 'How about you peel a prawn for me?'

Realising his near-slip, Jake sheepishly snapped off the prawn head and unfurled the brittle shell and legs from around the juicy, plump pink-and-white flesh. 'Hey, Pearl, my girl, did I hear you mention Mum and the boss?'

Pearl nodded, her deft peeling of more prawns constant. 'I didn't like to interrupt. The discussion looked pretty intense.'

'Damn!' Sid feared another apology would soon be in order. 'Poor man! She's bound to be making a fuss over Jake's accident. Next, she'll have the *WorkCover* department investigating Greenhill.'

'I hope not.' Concern wiped Pearl's usual smile away 'That'll make the *unofficial* part of the employment arrangement tricky for David.'

'Uh-oh!' Jake added. 'You need to get up there, Sid.'

'I would, only Mum has my car.' Sid scooted the note across to Jake's side of the table.

'Marilyn's available,' Pearl said. 'She's parked by the workshop over there. Tell Troy I sent you. I'll stay with Jake. Oh, and David texted me just now to say the gallery will close for a few days.'

'A few?' Sid queried.

'Yeah! He said you had family priorities.'

Sid felt terrible. The man she'd initially thought rude and arrogant was actually super-considerate, charming, and funny, and the thought of him now at the receiving end of a Natalie tirade, not to mention in trouble with *WorkCover*, had Sid seriously contemplating Pearl's car offer. She would drive up in the Kombi van to apologise for Natalie, and sooner rather than later.

'I will borrow Marilyn.'

'Good,' Pearl said. 'She hasn't had a run this week. Troy's been waiting for a new exhaust part.'

'Okay, then I'll freshen up and head off. Wish me luck,' Sid said, knowing she had the time it took to reach the Greenhill plantation to come up with a suitable one-size-fits-all apology to explain her mother to David.

Letting Marilyn's engine warm, Sid deliberated over the manual gearstick, the clutch pedal, the floor-mounted steering wheel, and the fact no front engine offered little front-on protection. Then she reminded herself she could do anything. She'd learned to drive on an old manual transmission—hill starts and all. She needed to take a breath and take it easy on a mountainous road now slick with rain. And as Jake would say: improvise, adapt, overcome.

Come on, Marilyn, you and I can do this.

40

GREENHILL, 2015

Natalie's drive up the hill was a trip back in time to when an excited Tilly had sat on the bench seat of the Marhkts' single-cab ute, staring out the window, eager for her first glimpse of the mountain, and asking Ulf to retell Hilda's story about the magic hill where a little girl's dream of a forever home could come true.

'Tell me again, please,' she'd asked in her sweetest voice.

Ulf had glanced momentarily at Tilly and smiled. 'I think enough for now. We'll be home soon and your mother's the storyteller in the family.'

Tilly's heart had fluttered with anticipation, the words *home* and *family* landing on her heart like butterflies as she stared wide-eyed at the *huge-est* hill she'd *ever* seen.

That's when she first saw David struggling to push his bike up the steep hill, a canvas satchel slung across one shoulder and paintbrushes poking out of both back pockets of his shorts.

Even hunched over the handlebars, Tilly could tell the boy was tall. On his head he wore a battered straw hat with a wide brim, and a thick line of sweat stained the back of his shirt. Even Tilly sweated. The Marhkt's old ute was a furnace, even with the windows down and the car's fans blowing full force.

Slowly passing the boy, Ulf drew the car to a stop and called back to him. 'Chuck the bike on the tray and get on in here, boy.' Ulf then put a hand to Tilly's thigh, yanking her legs apart until the fan-forced air blew the lightweight cotton of her dress up to her knickers, cooling the sweat there. In a panic, she pulled the hem down as far as she could, only to hear Ulf snigger. 'You'll have to move on over close to me if we're to let the lad in.' Still grinning, Ulf hooted out the window, 'Ooo-wee, get on in here, boy! She's a hot one.'

When the clatter of bike hitting the metal ute tray made Tilly startle, Ulf again placed a hand on her thigh. This time rubbing up and down. 'No need to be scared, lass. You're home now. I'll keep you safe.'

The passenger door opened, and Ulf put both hands on the steering wheel, waiting as the boy clambered into the car, the colourful bouquet of paintbrushes from his back pocket now clutched in one hand, along with his scrunched hat.

He looked at Tilly and smiled. 'You her?'

Tilly shrugged. 'What if I am?'

'This is Tilly,' Ulf said. 'Albie's new sister.'

'Lucky Albie!' David muttered, his face turned towards the side-view mirror and glimpsing her reflection.

'David's startin' high school next year,' Ulf announced. 'He does very clever things with those paintbrushes of his. Plans on being a famous artist one day, so Albie tells us.'

'I like to draw,' Tilly said, her competitive spirit stirring. 'But I had to leave my paints and paintbrushes behind.'

'I'll lend you some. I've got loads,' David said as Ulf drew to a stop where two sets of car tracks disappeared in opposite directions, but both under the same dark canopy of the biggest, greenest leaves Tilly had ever, ever seen. She guessed they were banana trees.

'You'll be right from here,' Ulf told him.

'No worries.' The boy jumped from the ute, grabbed his bike from the tray, and as they drove away he called out, 'I'll see you 'round.'

Scooting hard up to the passenger door—away from handy Ulf—Tilly mumbled, 'You sure will!'

⚓︎

Decades later, at the same fork, Natalie sat in her daughter's car, the motor at idle. With the gentle purr of a new engine barely audible, it was quite the contrast to Natalie's old heart beating wildly to pump blood through her veins and get oxygen to her lungs. A sudden hot flush only added to her angst and a sense of impending doom. *Damn menopause!*

What was she doing and why reminisce when the best parts of her life had been made away from this mountain? That winter's night back in '79 when she and Matthew had left Greenhill, they'd made a pact never to think about the past, to never look back. Natalie had tried hard to forget David—first to spare herself the pain, and later out of loyalty to Matthew—but she never stopped missing him. Unable to control where her mind went at night, he'd often come to her in dreams. And when she learned he was still alive, the nighttime fantasies became more vivid, and her feelings more intense than anything she'd felt for Matthew.

Being back on this mountain exacerbated those feelings of guilt, as if being here was akin to betraying her dead husband. But hadn't Matthew deceived her by breaking their pact and secretly keeping in touch with David? Now, shifting the car into gear and veering left towards the Greenhill property, it was Natalie's turn to connect with her past, as she'd done so many times in her dreams.

As the old residence came into view, Natalie pictured Rose and Ted on the veranda, the pair settled like royalty in their Darby & Joan settee and surveying the gardens. But the castle that young Tilly had once considered posh and imposing looked less impressive, and the yard a lot less formal. Unsure about what she'd expected to find, it wasn't *this*.

Greenhill—the version she remembered—was no more. In fact, the house and the gardens looked so different that Natalie could easily have persuaded herself she had no connection to this place. Maybe she should get out of there before she found herself sucked, like Alice through the Looking-Glass, into an imaginary world where everything could go terribly, terribly wrong.

With no one around to notice her arrival, the urge to head back down the mountain and straight to her children strengthened Natalie's grip on the steering wheel. There was no reason to stay—not one that made any sense after all this time. But midway through her three-point turn manoeuvre, she checked the rear-view mirror and ...

There he was—the man she'd never stopped thinking about. How could she when every day seeing Sidney reminded her?

The car lurched to a stop, jerking her sunglasses from the top of her head to her nose. Time might have stopped for Natalie at that moment, but the man didn't, instead making his way, awkwardly and on crutches, towards her car.

There was still time, she told herself. Time to turn over the engine, to engage the gears, to be gone, and to leave David none the wiser. He might recognise the car and quiz Sidney, but she'd simply tell him the truth. My mother borrowed my car. David couldn't see Natalie's face now and he clearly hadn't recognised her at the seawall yesterday. But then why would he? Natalie could not be more different to the wild young thing he'd promised to marry.

Unsure how, Natalie was suddenly standing outside the car, but with a firm hold on the open door. Was she trying to stop herself running from him or to him?

David also faltered—probably when he realised the driver wasn't Sidney. But any hesitation she thought she'd witnessed was short-lived, replaced by a determined stride.

'I did wonder ...' he said, stopping short of the car, his voice guarded. '... down there on the seawall.'

'Hello, David.' She removed her sunglasses.

'Hello?' He mocked. 'That's it? After all these years I get a *Hello*?'

'I, um, I'm not sure ... I'm struggling to think what else I might say.'

'Maybe something like, *I'm sorry I ran off and left you for dead.*'

His tone was laced with such sarcasm, Natalie flinched. This could not be further from the meeting in her dreams: the loving embrace, the warm whisper—tender words of forgiveness.

'I haven't returned by choice, David.' His expression triggered instant regret. 'Sorry, that came out wrong. What I meant to say was I'm here because—'

'Are you planning on hugging that car door all day?'

'What?' Her grip loosened.

'Maybe you're planning on getting back in and driving away? I also wondered about that just now.'

'*Should* I go?'

'Best you make a choice,' David said as he shifted on his crutches, preparing to walk away. He clicked his tongue to urge the small dog at his feet to follow.

Was that it? Was he telling her she wasn't welcome?

Damn the man!

'David?' she called after him, her voice unwavering. 'I was asking if you want me to stay.'

He stopped, steadied himself, and glanced over his shoulder to smile for the first time. 'If you'd asked that question thirty-five years ago, my answer today would be the same.' He took a few more steps before again pausing to look back. 'I was about to make tea. I'm acquiring a taste for the stuff, but in need of practice.' He continued towards the house. 'Should you decide to stay, I'll be in the kitchen.'

'Wait!' Natalie took two steps towards him. 'I won't leave here today without you knowing.'

David didn't turn around this time. 'Knowing what?' he called back.

'That I *didn't* have a choice all those years ago.'

Though clearly an effort, he turned to face Natalie. 'There's always a choice, Tilly. Do I call you Tilly, still?'

The pair simply stared at each other—three metres and three decades between them.

'I've missed Tilly,' Natalie said.

'I've missed her too.' And with that, he shuffled back around and headed towards the house.

Natalie followed behind until they both loitered on the wide veranda. 'Look, David, I can apologise over and over—for all the good that will do. No apology or words can take us back.'

'That much I know,' he said, 'even though for a long time I longed for nothing else but to turn back time.'

Natalie thought about those little pink pills she had wished could take her back to when she'd been five, ten, fifteen years old. If only such a panacea existed. While despising drug-taking—a hangover from her mother's life-destroying addictions—she'd take anything right now if it meant undoing the hurt she'd caused.

'We should talk,' Natalie said, wanting to purge herself of every wrongdoing and justify every selfish decision, David needed more. He needed to know the truth. 'There are so many things that need saying.'

'Then you'd best come into the kitchen.' He was on the move again, calling back over his shoulder. 'I'll make lots of tea.'

41

____

WATERCOLOUR COVE, 2015

'David, please understand. I thought you were dead.' The empty cup and saucer he handed Natalie clattered, betraying the tremble in her hands.

He nodded. 'The prognosis was certainly grim. I wasn't expected me to live and my parents were told to prepare for the worst. But I sure showed everyone.'

'I suppose you did.' Seeing the same defiant spark as the spirited young man who'd sneaked out at night to rendezvous made Natalie feel something she hadn't expected from their meeting—optimistic. 'Let me help with the tea.'

'No, thanks. I've been managing on my own for a long time, Tilly. Although, lately, tea for two seems to be more challenging than it should be.' Still, David seemed to negotiate the kitchen skillfully, a single crutch and a solid countertop supporting his every move.

The room was bigger than Natalie remembered, no longer the cosy country kitchen in which Rose had cooked her array of sweet treats— *always with banana.* But when David flipped the lid on a plastic container, sliding the biscuits towards Natalie, she shook her head.

'None for me, thank you. Your little friend looks keen for a treat, though.'

'Pablo! Bed!' David ordered, before turning back to his tea-making task and spilling water while filling the kettle.

'Can I help—'

David's palm flash cut the offer short, and for a few moments, while he gazed out the window at an abundant vegetable garden, Natalie endured an uncomfortable silence and too many second thoughts.

'You think I look awkward now?' he finally said. 'So much seemed impossible in the beginning.' With a dark grey sky outside, and lights inside illuminating the kitchen, the window's reflection allowed Natalie to observe David's expressions. 'Nights in the hospital were hardest,' he continued. 'The dark. The silence. I'd been so scared of dying. But more terrifying was the notion of living but losing control of everything. Did you know it took me two months to sit up?' He turned, briefly, to plug in the kettle and flick the switch. 'Guessing you didn't.'

Natalie wanted to respond, but for once in her life she couldn't think of anything to say. Despite her earlier optimism slipping away, she slid onto a stool at the breakfast counter and continued to watch him in the window until, eventually, he caught her out.

'Sorry, I'm being rude, standing here with my back to you. But I find reflections comforting. So much easier than looking at things square on.'

Did that go some way to explaining the mirrors at the seawall? Though tempted to ask, there were more pressing discussion topics.

'While flat on my back, and viewing the world around me from a mirror suspended over my bed, I did nothing *but* think. The trouble with mirrors, though, is that while staring at your reflection, one can think way too much—and usually about all the wrong things. Over time, that mirror actually taught me a lot about myself, and my resilience.'

'"*The world is a looking-glass and gives back to every man the reflection of his own face*",' she quoted.

'You know Thackeray?' he asked.

Natalie shook her head. 'Not until yesterday at the seawall. The choice of quote is powerful.'

'I had a lot of dark times in the early days, and while I got pretty low, it was never low enough to give up on life. I had loads of emotional support from Mum and Dad—Mum especially—and the nurses in that unit knew all the signs and what to do when depression hit. Sometimes all it took to bring me back was the smallest intervention, like the touch of a hand, an encouraging smile, caring eyes. The medical team made sure I didn't dwell on what was and feel sorry for myself. I was determined I'd walk again.'

'And you did.'

'It was slow going over the two years it took for the nerves to regenerate and give me back the partial use of my right hand.'

'So, you couldn't paint all that time?'

David clenched and stretched his right fist several times. 'I couldn't do lots of things, including, believe it or not, leave the hospital when the time finally came. I'd been marking off the days, so desperate to get out of there and get on with my life, but the thought of leaving the hospital routine and the nursing support behind terrified me. Luckily, those nurses also knew how to kick a butt out of the place, giving me both a new goal to shoot for and a farewell card that each of them signed—using their left hands. They helped me see life was going to be different, but I still had a future, even if that future meant being a lefty!' As if to prove a point, David managed a left-handed pour of hot water into the teapot. 'At the five-year mark, I sent those nurses the first lefty painting. It was a self-portrait,' he said, 'and I was standing. And here I am now. Here *we* are —older and wiser. At least I am.'

Exasperation catapulted Natalie off the stool, and she slapped her palms on the counter, startling the dog from his slumber. 'Oh, David, David, why did this happen to you—to us? Why wasn't I told the truth? I want to be angry at someone—anyone.'

'I know. Believe me, I do. But there's no use getting angry or getting even, and no getting back the life we might've had.' David stopped to reach into a jar, then tossed a treat to the tail-wagging dog at his feet. 'But Tilly, you weren't the only one left in the dark.'

Natalie stopped her pacing. 'How do you mean?'

'No one ever told me the details of how you and Matthew left, just that you both got on with your lives. I didn't realise at the time it was a life together.'

Shame and sadness stopped Natalie from looking David in the face. She walked over to the window, but couldn't look at her reflection either, not liking what stared back.

'Mum told me Matthew was having trouble dealing with Dad and with the guilt, and you were focused on your dreams and a future in the city. I guess it wasn't a lie. They just left out a few facts, no doubt thinking I wouldn't cope. Maybe they were right. I was young and struggling with so much. The telling of difficult truths needed the proper timing.'

'If they told you so little, how did you find out? *When* did you know?'

'A few years back when Albie fronted up and said a few odd things. His visit upset Mum so much that I didn't probe her for answers. But it was Albie's words and Mum's silence afterwards that prompted a mental mosaic. But the picture forming was too painful, so I decided to stop piecing it together. I did want to let all that I'd been ignoring become real.

Tilly?' David positioned himself against the counter as if to get comfortable, ready for a long story. 'What you probably never knew about was Matthew was intense jealousy.'

Natalie turned back from the window, giving David her full attention. 'I remember he teased you—mostly about your art and your dreams.'

'My talent wasn't the problem. Mum would be quick with an excuse for Matthew's behaviour. She'd say his strong sense of right and wrong made him behave in ways the rest of us didn't understand.' David's snort signalled his dissent, or perhaps it was amusement. 'That may have been the case sometimes. Only Matthew's idea of morally right was, at times, questionable. He and Dad constantly argued over what was and wasn't fair, and Dad's investing in my education, while forcing Matthew to stay working on the property, ate away at him. You see, Dad was all about succession. He wanted his legacy and hard work to live on down the line. For that reason, the son who produced that much-needed next generation would inherit Greenhill and a greater split of the money. Matthew had disputed the arrangement, claiming he was older and staying put. As such, he would have invested more of his life into working the plantation, giving him a natural right to a greater share. Jealousy made Matthew fancy the same freedoms as me, but he'd wanted Greenhill more. That's why he surprised me when he walked away without a word.' David paused. 'You, on the other hand … I understood why *you* left. At least I thought I did.'

Struggled to think and to stand at the same time, she slipped back onto the kitchen stool, keen to absorb the detail his story was unearthing and wondering how, after so much hurt, the two of them could be sitting here talking like thirty years ago was yesterday.

'When did you first know about Matthew leaving?'

'When I woke up in the hospital. I asked for you both about a hundred times. I imagined you in the waiting room, impatient and pushy and trying every trick in the book to get to me. I expected you *would* get to me, Tilly.' David stared at her as if she was supposed to respond in some way, but what could she possibly say or do? So, she sat there, silent and sad. 'After the hospital, I went into a city rehab facility. Mum stayed with me and wrote to Dad every day. You remember Rose loved her letters,' he said with fond memory.

'Your mum would be hunched over a table somewhere and writing to someone.'

'When Dad went to prison, she wrote every day.'

'Of course she would,' was all Natalie said.

'Mum wrote such beautiful words, which is why I kept Ted's and Rose's correspondence. My parent's connection was so strong and their love for each other unconditional I admit to living vicariously through them. But while storing their letters, I found an unfinished one from Mum to Matthew. In it she advised Dad was struggling on the property but insisting he could manage the place alone. But Rose was asking Matt to call Dad and ask if he could return home. In other words, grovel, come back, and all will be forgotten.'

'Rose wrote to Matthew in secret? How did she know where he was?'

Another snort. 'Matthew's inheritance obsession, of course. He wrote constantly, but only to Mum. I can show you. They are hardly what you'd call letters. More like detailed proposals. Pages of postulation in which he put forward the same succession case over and over—all very logical and convincing, and all to justify his case.'

'What case?'

'He was proposing a return home, as per Rose's request, on the proviso Mum and Dad recognised and documented his entitlement. If they couldn't accept that he was the eldest son, and therefore owed, he would point out that he was also, as things turned out, the only son with a child to carry on the Hill bloodline. I'd certainly never have kids. Are you okay, Tilly?' David filled a glass with tap water. 'Here, drink some. Should I stop talking?'

'Thanks. No,' Natalie managed, taking a sip. 'Go on.'

'Well, in another letter, my brother stated I was welcome to stay on at Greenhill and he'd look after me. But, as I wasn't physically capable of contributing to the business or property, I couldn't claim equal inheritance.'

'I see,' was all Natalie managed, although she didn't. Not really. She was finding David's story hard to believe. Matthew had been very black and white about a lot of things, but could he really have been so insensitive and blinkered to his brother's needs? Had he planned to split up and take Jake back with him?

'Dad was so furious at Mum for corresponding in secret that he wrote back to Matthew, mostly to tell him off and to confirm Greenhill would be left entirely to me to do with as I saw fit. If not for Mum, Dad would've cut him off completely. But Matthew, being Matthew, he refused to let the matter go. That's when he started writing to me. I seriously believe he thought I'd see his reasoning and support him. Before long, he was back negotiating with Dad.'

'Negotiating? What do you mean?'

A smirk crossed David's face. 'If not the full inheritance, Matthew would settle for a majority share in Greenhill—with conditions—and always with the addendum confirming I'd be well cared for, and so on. Back and forth, back and forth, until Dad finally stopped replying. I also stopped replying to Matt's emails.'

If anyone other than David had been telling Natalie this, she'd have trouble accepting it as the truth. How could all this have gone on behind her back? Had she been so caught up in her own world?

'After stewing for several more years, because that's what my brother did—he obsessed over things,' David explained needlessly. 'Matt still couldn't let go, nor did he give in. His next strategy was to rub salt into my wounds by bragging about life with his wife and two beautiful children. Knowing I'd never have any myself, he would email baby photos. His idea of one-upmanship., I guessed.'

Feeling nauseous, Natalie drained the water glass, her hand noticeably trembling.

David looked concerned. 'Let's take a break from all this talk.'

'No! I'm just a little over-tired. Maybe I need fresh air.'

'I hope you're not planning to run off just yet. I'm happy to see you here and back in this house.' David's smile, while small and guarded, injected hope. Hope that Natalie might find her way through this with no one else getting hurt, or any more pain than David had already suffered. 'Can I show you Rose Gallery?'

'Okay.' Anything to divert the conversation away from the children.

Part way along the dirt path that wound through the ornament-heavy garden, David's next admission sent yet another wave of nausea through Natalie.

'You know, Tilly, I would look at those photos my brother sent, trying to see Matthew in the kids' faces. When I couldn't, I told myself the subjects weren't real. I convinced myself Matthew had used pictures from bought photo frames. They were simply another strategy to prove his success in work and in life. But both pictures showed good-looking kids —babies really—both perfectly posed and smiling and way too good looking to be Matthew's offspring. Then again, nothing would've surprised me. Seems there's not only another side to every story but also two sides to every person, and my brother's sides were—'

'David, please!' Needing a moment to catch her breath, Natalie changed topics. 'Please, tell me that's our destination.' But of course it was.

Oh God, Natalie! How did you get here and what now?

'Yes, that's Rose Gallery, and there's shade and a place to sit. The sun still has quite a sting, despite the temperature.' David indicated two seating options. A red cedar bench by the gallery door, or the restored Darby and Joan settee.

Natalie opted for the bench. She had to sit or else fall.

'Do not pass out on me now,' he said, joining her there.

What would he do if she did? Could she fake a fall, like she'd fooled him all those times running back along the seawall to their bikes, when he'd stop, worry streaked across his brow, his hands, soft and sexy, exploring her arms and legs for cuts and bruises. Even though, by the third or fourth occasion he'd cottoned onto the ruse, Tilly had continued her game, lying about being hurt so he'd touch her. But they were now too old for games. *No more deception.* Besides, if she were to fake a dizzy spell, David's reliance on crutches would likely mean letting her fall. *No less than what you deserve, Natalie!*

They sat next to each other on what looked a lot like a church pew—perhaps fitting, given the confession Natalie could no longer avoid. With David twisting his body to watch her, his gaze boring into the side of her neck, Natalie stared straight ahead, out across the plantation and to the place where there'd once been a path to their cave. He was so close that Natalie could easily lean her body against his and rest her face on that broad shoulder. How desperately she needed to reach out, to touch, to connect.

What she *didn't* need was to look into his eyes—*Sidney's eyes.* But look she did, and something about David's face managed to do what no one and nothing had ever done to Natalie. She shed a river of tears. *He knows. Of course he knows.* And why wouldn't he? Natalie had seen him in Sidney every day of her life. Every time her little girl had pinned a finger painting to the fridge, every time her troubled teenager had got excited, every time a grown-up daughter had tried to impress her mother with her latest design job. How could Natalie ever leave the past behind when she saw David in everything her daughter did, every question she ever asked, every enthusiastic exclamation, every hopeful expression?

'Tilly?'

Natalie couldn't respond. She couldn't do anything but focus on David's bare feet. Wasn't he cold without shoes? Natalie wore boots and thick socks under the navy trousers, and she was very cold. Freezing, in fact, even when David's arm wrapped around her shoulder and the prickles of her jumper pushed through the thin undershirt as his hand rubbed up and down—prickling, provoking, pushing her buttons to the point of wanting to scream, *Stop, please just stop!*

No, don't stop!

'Oh, David, you weren't supposed to survive,' she blurted, tears raining down her cheeks. 'That's why Matthew and I had to move on without you. We agreed to never look back, to only move forward. We were making a life together *for* you because you wouldn't get that chance. Then, I was pregnant and my decisions had to be for my unborn child. I did what I did to protect both children, giving them the life I never had growing up.'

'That's the thing, Tilly.' David shifted awkwardly to face her square on. 'One of Matthew's emails asked me not to tell Rose or Ted he and I were keeping in touch. I didn't question why at the time. I didn't question at all. Not even why Matthew never mentioned his family, other than that one time when he sent a photo of his children. Even then, he'd referred to his wife as *the missus* and the children as *the kids*. Mostly his emails were enquiries about Greenhill. So, for a long time, I knew nothing for certain. Of course I thought about you a lot. I imagined your life—every conceivable scenario—but never *that*. Never Matthew. Then discovering Rose's hidden stash of Matthew letters and finding your name mentioned once or twice narrowed those scenarios down. Mum's story was simply that you were both gone, with no mention of leaving together or marriage. Then Albie showed up years later linking you and Matthew. When I saw the panic on Rose's face that day, I knew.'

'You must've hated me. Did you, David?'

'I won't lie. I hated the entire world for a long time. My early prognosis was so grim I genuinely wished I'd died.'

'But here you are.'

'And here you are, Tilly.'

They fell silent, eyes locked on each other, their shared gaze penetrating, searching, remembering.

'You and Matthew, eh?' David finally spoke, his lips curving into a wry smile, one eyebrow cocked. 'Talk about chalk and cheese.'

Natalie looked down at the strangled hands in her lap. 'I-I couldn't be on my own.'

'So you said. And I couldn't cope with any more of Matthew's emails. But there's no sense wishing he hadn't sent them, or that Albie hadn't shown up that day and dropped his bombshell. There's no changing the facts any more than we can change the past. We must accept things and move on.'

When he tried to lift her face to his, Natalie shrugged him away like a sulking child. 'When did you decide to stop corresponding with your brother?'

David clearly thought before answering. 'The day Matt attached that photo of his kids, suggesting our parents might like to know their grandchildren and amend their wills accordingly. I left any contact to Mum. And yet, to this day, the nostalgic nerd in me still carries these around.' David shifted to retrieve a wallet from the deep side pocket on the cargo-style pants. He exposed two small photos sitting under a mould-spotted plastic cover. 'Don't ask me why. Maybe deep down I wished they were real, and there was a living child to carry on the Hill name. Rose had wanted that more than anything, and I'd have given anything to let her have that. Also,' he said with a small smile. 'I would've made an awesome uncle.'

'Oh, David, they are wonderful children, and you could've been so much more.' Natalie watched his expression move through curiosity, confusion, and finally clarity.

'So, they *are* real.' It wasn't a question.

'The children in that picture are very real, David. I know this to be true because ...'

'Because they're *your* children.'

'Yes. A boy and a girl. Both photos are from their first birthdays.'

David looked at her, a softness invading his face and lighting his eyes. 'I can finally put real names to real faces?'

'Yes. That's my son, Jake.' She went to point, withdrawing her hand when she realised she was trembling too much. 'He's the youngest.' Adding proudly, 'Twenty-five now.'

'Jake.' David repeated the name, his eyes never moving from the wallet in his hands. 'And the older one—the girl—would be ...?'

Oh, God, was he making me say this aloud to punish me? You know, David. I know you do.

'Tilly? Will you tell me her name?'

Every regret, every emotion Natalie had held back for decades wanted to burst out, the ache of holding it back unbearable. 'David,' the truth trembled out of her. 'She is now a beautiful and independent woman and named after one of her father's favourite artists.'

After an agonising silence watching David finger-trace the child's pert nose and her smile, he finally spoke the name aloud. 'Sidney Nolan.'

Natalie nodded. 'She is why I couldn't stay and why I couldn't be on my own.' David's eyes, moist with tears and disbelief, quizzed Natalie. 'If not the Marhkts, then your parents would've forced either abortion or adoption on me. Do you know how many Braidenfield girls had babies taken away from them? That's after they'd been dumped on the doorstep —pregnant and a disgrace to their family. It was at a time when society and parents did terrible, terrible things to single mothers and their babies. Those who defied the home, taking their newborns, grew up living rough on the streets. Some with mothers who did whatever they … Oh God!' Natalie sobbed.

Natalie, who never cried, was a frightened five-year-old girl, gripping her only book—a fairytale—and bawling her eyes out in the back seat of an old station wagon, while wondering what her happy ever after would be.

42

WATERCOLOUR COVE, 2015

Natalie sat in a sliver of sunlight, needing time alone. Maybe David had wanted the same because, without a word, he'd walked away, disappearing inside the gallery, and leaving Natalie to cry and to dry her own tears. Knowing she didn't deserve his sympathy, nor his forgiveness —and expecting he might leave her to endure a well-deserved walk of shame back to the car—a tiny spark inside hoped otherwise.

That spark flickered with promise when David eventually reappeared. Carrying a loose-knit throw blanket, he sat beside Natalie, his proximity and the cover bringing warmth to a body benumbed.

'Thank you,' she said.

'For what?'

'For letting me speak and not sending me away.'

'Why would I? I never wanted you to leave in the first place?'

'Please know I loved you, David. I just didn't know how much at the time. I was so young and confused. I knew only that I couldn't stay. Had there been one scrap of a chance that I could've kept our child *before* your accident, that scrap would've been tossed to the chooks afterwards. There was no place for me in your family so I lost you. But I couldn't lose our baby.' Natalie paused to gather her thoughts and dab her cheeks with a wad of already wet tissues. 'I'm not proud of my choices, but I am proud of my determination to keep Sidney wrapped in love. Never would I beg on the streets or sleep rough. I refused to become my mother—single, alone, destitute and desperate enough to sell her body to strangers—and I couldn't trust Albie to keep my secret. So, when Matthew said they were taking you off life support, I—'

'Wait!' David interrupted. 'You told both Albie and Matthew you were pregnant with my baby?'

Did she just shake her head? Or did she nod? Was it time for the whole truth, including how she'd used Albie?

'Why not tell *me*, Tilly? Even if you'd only suspected. I would've helped you.'

'I wanted to, but we'd been arguing and you were so angry at the time. I guess I was too stubborn. Then you were in the hospital and I wasn't allowed to see you. Your family blamed me. I was so afraid and so … desperate.'

'Desperate enough to leave this place and live *our* dream with my brother.'

'*Desperate* to give the child a father, David. Your parents said you weren't expected to live.'

David's head cocked to the side. 'My parents or Matthew?'

Natalie thought back to the discussion that night. Some things were still so clear, even after all these years, like when Ted had looked up— cheeks wet with his grief—to speak those words: *Don't you understand, Tilly? David isn't there. We've lost our beautiful, spirited little boy. He's gone.* The click of Ted's fingers had sent a shock of despair and desperation through Tilly.

All these years later, with David's question messing with her memory, Natalie relived the shock. Had she been too young and too distraught to read the subtle nuance in Ted's words? David was *'not there'*, his spirt *'lost'* because of a coma there was no waking up from. If only she'd waited a while longer, but Matthew had said …

What? What did he say, exactly? Natalie tried to recall, but heard only Rose's words: *All that provocative strutting around the property, tempting all the boys and making them fight over you.*

Had Tilly meant to tempt Matthew in order to impress his younger brother? Did she enable Matthew's jealousy?

'I remember now, David,' Natalie said, her eyes wide with the memory. 'It *was* Matthew who told me. We bumped into each other at the seawall when I was upset after fighting with you. He said your parents would never let you be with me, and then he said something about there being winners and losers in life and that him and I were born losers. He'd even known that we were fighting, and he said our break up had put you back in your dad's good books. He said you had a place at a Melbourne university. Then he told me they were turning off your life support and—' Natalie slumped in the seat, wanting to shake herself silly, because she was. 'I'm an idiot!' She could barely look David in the eye. Matthew had well and truly tricked her.

How had a master manipulator like young Tilly not seen someone manipulating her?

'Tilly? What's with the shaking head? Talk to me.'

She shivered with cold but she wouldn't use David for warmth. She deserved to suffer. 'Even before your accident, Matthew was trying to come between us.'

David's nod was perhaps silent acceptance of something he'd known all along. Then he spoke. 'Matthew warned me once. He said if I wasn't quick enough, someone would come along and snatch you up. Never did I think he was talking about himself. I mean, the two of you had nothing in common. But Matthew had wanted you, Tilly, and a single coward punch to my head from Albie gave you to him. Suddenly, he could have everything. He could leave this place and give you what you wanted, confident Greenhill would eventually be his to hand down to the first-born grandchild of Ted and Rose Hill.'

After a long while staring at the sky, Natalie asked, 'So, you've known all along you didn't slip and fall? That it was Albie's punch?'

David nodded. 'My memory returned in bits and pieces and all out of context. By the time the puzzle was complete, Albie was gone. The bloke didn't mean to hurt me. Call it a lucky punch for him and a bloody unlucky landing for me.'

His snigger surprised Natalie. 'How can you laugh?'

Through a boyish grin, David said, 'Lately, I've found myself smiling more and oddly keen to connect with total strangers. I've even developed a fondness that both disquieted and delighted me in equal measure. Then you arrived, and I knew. I understood those feelings. But what I can't believe is that my parents knew about you and Matthew from the start and never said a word.'

'I suppose it was their way of protecting you.'

'Yes,' David nodded, 'and so fiercely that I fear they unintentionally encouraged Matthew's estrangement in order to keep him, and you, from Greenhill. I've found all manner of evidence over the years. It was Mum, mostly.'

'Rose?' Natalie turned to look at David, but his eyes were fixed on a distant memory somewhere. 'What evidence?'

'There were lots of letters *and* a bank account. Dad might have disowned Matthew, leaving him nothing, but Mum sent money regularly.'

The other bank account! Natalie remembered discovering thousands of dollars—all deposits—when tidying up her husband's financial affairs. While she'd been working day and night, keeping her job at Raphael's every way she knew how, her husband had been squirrelling away his mother's money.

'Your parents paid to keep their son from coming home because he was married—to me.'

'They wanted to help me to get over you. I tried to so a couple of times, all by myself and in all the wrong ways.' David pushed down on his thighs and rubbed, like he was pushing away the memories. 'I can only think they did what they considered best.'

'They loved you, as did I, David, and I never stopped thinking about you—about us and what might have been.' The confession felt good. 'When I found Matthew's old email files and realised you were alive, I wondered where you were and what you were doing with your life. But then I had to let you go again. I think I went back to imagining you'd died. I had to stop torturing myself with why you'd communicated with your brother, but not wanted to see me. Then, when I saw your reflection in the foreshore sculpture, I told myself to keep you, and this place, a memory.'

'So, you might have simply come up to Coffs Harbour for your son, then left again without seeing if I was still here?'

The intensity of his stare heated her to the core. Natalie breathed deep. 'No more lies, okay. The truth only. And the truth is, I'm not sure, David. First, I didn't know seeing Jake in a Coffs Harbour hospital would land me on Greenhill's doorstep. I knew only from those emails that you'd survived and were living with your mother. I figured the last place the two of you would stay is all the way up here. Then, when I drove into town with Sid and I saw a *For Sale* sign at the gate, I thought … Well, I guess I wasn't thinking clearly at all. Yes, getting Jake well and back home with me as fast as I could did cross my mind. As recently as yesterday, in fact.'

'You were leaving?'

'Yes.' Shame licked Natalie's cheeks, the warmth in her neck and face quickly making the blanket redundant. 'Ironic, I know.' She cast a small smile David's way. 'I was once so eager to live an exciting city life—to succeed—I was prepared to do anything. But yesterday, when I had the chance, I couldn't go without seeing you again—to know you are real and still here.' Her fingers touched his cheek. 'I had to see if you'd changed the way I've imagined all these years. But more than that, I had to hear your voice. Oh, David!' Natalie wiped a tear from her cheek and smiled. 'If not for my daughter's insatiable curiosity, I would never have come back to this town.'

'Sidney!' He smiled as he finally spoke her name, the lines on his face a map of love. 'I'm not sure why I didn't see something in her sooner. Or maybe I did.'

'What do you mean?'

David took Natalie's hand and held tight. 'That first time I saw Sid. She was sitting in a room, in a dim light and surrounded by drawings. Drawings of you.'

'Me? What kind of drawings? Where? I don't—'

'Shh!' David's finger shushed Natalie. 'Like her mother, Sidney is not short on words, opinions, nor questions. But I have a question of my own,' he said. 'What happens now—with Sidney?'

Natalie crashed back to earth, her reality kicking in. 'Nothing, David. Nothing can or will happen.'

That light in his eyes dulled. Today's reminiscing *was* a mistake, any thoughts of a happy ending nothing more than fanciful fiction and wishful thinking. Hers and David's story was more than a romantic reunion for two lost lovers. With serious consequences for so many, Natalie was keenly aware of the hurt any such confessions would cause.

With the car keys in her pocket now clenched in Natalie's hand, she looked towards the path and her getaway car at the end. If only she'd taken disappeared down the mountain. David would be left wondering only about the mystery driver. He would be none the wiser, the truth would stay buried, and Natalie's relationship with her daughter—fragile at the best of times—would not be under threat. One slip, one word, one look was all it would take for a curious, tenacious daughter to uncover the truth, just like the serendipitous discovery of a grandfather.

'I hope you can understand. It's been so long.'

'Sure has,' muttered a despondent David. 'Can you at least tell me where Matthew fits in all this? He's Jake's father?'

'Of course,' Natalie said, although embarrassed by her righteous tone.

'I gather you're still together?'

'Together? Oh, um ...' Natalie stiffened. So, David didn't know everything about his brother. 'I'm sorry to be only telling you this now. Matthew died in 2001.'

'Hmm, right,' he said wistfully. 'I wondered. How did he die?'

'New York. World Trade Centre Towers. He was there representing his company.'

David's eyebrows rose in a well-well-what-do-you-know way. 'He did okay, then? The no-hoper son went out there and made something of himself.'

'He did, David. I worked while Matthew studied for a degree in engineering. He then went on to …' Natalie checked herself. She was having trouble feeling loyalty for a man who'd lied throughout their entire married life. Matthew's past was not important. Protecting David from hurt was her priority. 'I can tell you as much or as little as you like about your brother's life. The choice is yours.'

David seemed to consider her offer. 'I need to think about that.'

'Of course, well, while you do, please consider this. Sid idolised Matthew. She was actually closer to him than to me, and I've seen how finding out about a grandfather she never knew of has affected her. She's not fragile but …'

'She's a curious girl.'

'Yes, one who knows her father as an only child, estranged from his parents. She took this trip with Jake to find Ted, only to learn he'd died. To be honest, I'd worry about more stress. You know she's pregnant?'

'I do.' David smiled some more, as though the thought of what that meant had only just dawned on him. 'And I agree. Telling her at this stage is not a good idea. But Tilly, you can't expect me to say or do nothing forever.'

'They know *Matthew's* version of his past, David. I'm asking you to help me keep the children's memories undisturbed until—'

'Undisturbed?' he interjected.

'I'm saying, the time for difficult truths needs to be right. *I* need time. Maybe after the baby. Tell me you won't say anything now.'

'Sure, okay, except …'

Natalie swallowed, fearing the worst. 'Except what?'

'Sid already knows the other side of the story.'

'What does that mean? How?'

'She's a good listener.'

'Sidney?'

He looked slightly bemused by her questioning tone. 'And she's inquisitive and asks questions. Lots of questions.'

'Huh! *That* I do know.'

'We got talking last night and, well, I just about told her my life story, including how I was in love with a local girl who ran away. I think I might have said with my brother. She asked about him and my accident. Did I mention she has well-honed interrogation skills?'

'Sid also has her father's compassion and understanding.'

David scoffed, his laugh sarcastic. 'Now I know you're not talking about Matthew.'

'David, whatever you think about your brother, he was a good father, and Sidney loved him. Please tell me you'll take time to let the ramifications of all this sink in before you act. Sidney is a smart girl, and I fear too smart for her own good.'

'I can be careful what I say, Tilly, and she may not realise you're the girl I told her about unless ...'

'Unless what?'

'Unless she sees me looking at you.'

'David, don't!' Natalie looked down at the hand on her lap clutching the keys so hard that her knuckles were white, and her palms were patterned with jagged red lines. 'I should go before the children wonder where I am.'

'How nice for you—having children to wonder.'

Natalie stood without looking at his face. But as she made to leave, she paused. 'I'll stay in town until the end of the week, after Jake goes back to the hospital for a fresh dressing.'

'Then what?'

'I don't know. Just tell me you agree about not saying anything. We can talk some more—if you want.'

'I do.'

She took his response as the answer to both questions, and left David on the seat. But when she looked back, his gaze was fixed on the children's photograph in his wallet. Tempted to rush back to the veranda and wrap her arms around his neck, she stayed her course. And thank goodness she did because the two of them had been so focused on the past, neither she nor David had noticed the present arrive.

'Mum?'

43

WATERCOLOUR COVE, 2015

'What are you *doing* up here, Mum?' Sid asked

Natalie was used to her daughter's reproaches, but not the hushed tone. Ordinarily, a lecture or demonstration followed—such as how to sort papers from non-recyclable plastics—but the urgency in Sid's whispered accusation worried Natalie. How much had she seen? How much did Natalie need to explain?

Foolishly, she'd thought her plan to take Sid's car a good one, as her daughter would have no way up the mountain.

Unless, of course, she managed to borrow a bohemian Kombi van!

'What are *you* doing here, Sidney?' Natalie demanded, reasoning that attack was the best form of defence. 'Why aren't you with your brother?'

'What am *I* doing?' Sid whisper shouted. 'I'm here because Pearl told me she saw my car arrive ages ago and a woman get out and start arguing with—'

'Hello, Sidney,' David called, announcing his approach from behind.

'Oh, um, hi. My mother—'

'Your mother came to view the gallery,' he said convincingly. 'And whatever Pearl thinks she saw, I'll remind her she should know the difference between an argument and a healthy debate about what is and isn't art. She's seen me have enough of them.' David cast a brief but reassuring glance in Natalie's direction. 'I suggest what Pearl saw was someone conveying their passion and artistic expression. Your mother is, in fact, coming back tomorrow so we can continue our discussion and tour of the gallery. Isn't that right, *Natalie*?'

Sidney was the depiction of complete scepticism and confusion, her eyelids the only thing moving as her gaze danced back and forth. Only once the bewilderment passed, the interrogation would begin, and Natalie would need to have the answers.

'I said isn't that right, Natalie?' David gently prompted.

'Oh, yes, I would dearly love to continue our, ah, debate tomorrow.' Inside, Natalie was groaning, aware Sid was too astute for her own good. The suspicion in her daughter's eyes was unmissable.

'But, David, Pearl told me you were closing the gallery for a few days.'

'Mmm, that's correct. Yes. In the circumstances, I thought it best. For your mother, I'll make an exception. It's the least I can do.'

'Terrific!' Natalie chirruped, keen to make her escape. 'Sid will look after her brother. And David, thank *you* so much for today. For *everything*.' Natalie took off at speed toward the car. 'Are you coming with me, Sid? Best you return the car.'

'You go ahead, Mum. I'll see you back at the villa.'

44

WATERCOLOUR COVE, 2015

Something about her mother's goodbye messed with the puzzle pieces in Sid's head. Usually the epitome of artistic sophistication when in gallery mode—and an out-spoken control freak in Mum mode—Natalie had been inexplicably cloddish and vague.

Sid turned to David, tilted her head to the side and raised both eyebrows. 'Welcome to my life!' she quipped. 'And I know you know what I mean because your face just now has *the look*.'

'And what look would that be?' David queried.

'One I've seen plenty of times. It's the *oh-no-now-here's-the-daughter, I-bet-the-apple-doesn't-fall-far-from-the-tree*. That look.'

Unsmiling, David said, 'I have no idea what one of those expressions might look like. Where's a mirror when I need one?'

'I'm just saying, I don't take after my mother. At least not in the attack pit bull way.'

'I'm not sure I follow, Sidney, but if you say so.'

When his gaze went to the Kombi van, Sid said, 'I guess you were expecting Pearl to get out?'

'Actually, I gave up expecting things a long time ago. That said, today is turning out to be quite out of the ordinary.'

'Sorry if Mum was out of place. She still thinks her kids need protecting. Nice paint job on the Kombi, by the way.'

'Murals on vehicles aren't my thing, and the job was far from the

"

career highlight of painting a public toilet block, but Pearl asked and she's been a good friend—a kind and generous spirit.'

'Yes, and lovely enough to loan me her car because mine was up here—*apparently*. With my mother—*apparently*.'

David scrunched his face, and with unmissable sarcasm said, 'So you *drove* up here to get your car?'

'No, I drove up to save you. I gathered good old Natalie was in full Jake Protection Mode and letting you know what she thinks about unsafe work practices—or something to that effect.'

'Or something,' he said, vaguely. 'Excuse me, Sidney. I need to get off these legs.'

'Oh, okay, sure.'

The man seemed to fumble with his walking sticks, the sudden clumsiness a contrast to his normal ease and confidence. Something had stirred him up.

'David, wait! I'm sorry.' Sid ran in front of him, thinking he'd stop, but the man forged ahead. 'Please,' she said again.

'Please what?' He stopped abruptly. 'What are you sorry for, Sidney?'

'I-I don't know. For whatever my mother said to make you this angry. What *did* she say?'

'Mothers get concerned. They question. You have a mother who loves you both.'

'Yes, but—'

'That's all.' David had regained his powerful stride, leaving Sid struggling to talk and walk backwards at the same time.

'Please, let me just say something.'

He stopped and stared Sid down. 'Go ahead, but be careful.'

Sid cocked her head. Not only was this riddle of a conversation a challenge to her full-to-bursting brain, how come the man was suddenly sounding like a father warning a wayward daughter? 'What do you mean by "careful"?'

'Unlike art, Sidney, words cannot be erased and painted over to make a fresh canvas. Words are more like toothpaste. Once they're out, there's no putting them back in. Remember that every time you go to speak.'

David strode walked away, leaving a gob-smacked Sidney shaking her head.

Well, that went well!

45

WATERCOLOUR COVE, 2015

'**B**rrrr! Shift your butt over, sis.' Jake flopped down on the cane sofa and wrapped an arm around Sid's shoulders, keen to share the blanket. 'It's cold enough out here to freeze the balls off a pool table.'

'But warmer than inside the villa with Mum tonight.'

'If it helps,' Jake said, 'she's gone to bed. You two really need to pull your heads in. Honestly, sis, cut her some slack and remember … You're going to be a mother soon enough. You don't want Karma biting you on the arse.'

'I know, I know, but something's not right, Jake. I can feel it.' Her words shocked her brother ramrod straight.

'Not right with the baby?'

'No, no, Bump is fine, but making themselves known.' Sid rubbed her stomach, flinching when the same sharp pain hit. 'I do have one hell of a headache and my back is pinching, but neither ailment concerns me as much as Mum's moods. When I found her with David at the gallery earlier, the pair of them acted like naughty school kids caught out behind the school shed. You know what I mean?'

'Flippin' fishcakes, Sid! I know what I got up to behind the shed and I do *not* want to be thinking *that* about my mother.'

'Be serious, Jake. You know Mum's not taken an interest in any man since Dad died and, well, David is a nice guy.'

Jake scoffed. 'Since when? You said he was … Let me see …' He began counting on his fingers. 'Rude, arrogant—'

'Yes, yes, but that was before.'

'Before what?'

'Before I spent the night with him.'

'You *what?*'

Sid snatched the blanket up before it fell to the floor. 'Relax, Jake, sit down. We sat up talking all night. After finding common ground, he was easy to connect with. We discussed his art, too. He has the same passion as Mum. Do you understand what I'm saying?'

'Nup! And I don't think I want to.'

'You remember what Dad was like with Mum's art and her gallery stuff? He didn't get it or her passion. People must *get* each other, or else there's no connection.'

'I *get* that.' Jake grinned. 'But what's this to do with Mum?'

'I don't know, except that David acted all guarded and awkward, and Mum was weird and kind of nervous and giddy. That was until she went back to being Mum.'

'You mean she went ballistic?'

'Interestingly, no. And if that's not strange enough, seeing her with a man got me thinking about how nice it would be if she were to connect with someone—like David.'

'Are you matchmaking our mother? Wow! You reckon you haven't pushed her buttons enough already?'

'But, Jake, if Mum had someone else in her life she might stop trying to control ours.'

'Hmm, good point, and I like your thinking, sis, but you're on your own. I treasure my life too much.'

'Wuss!' Sid giggled, drawing the blanket around her body after Jake slipped out and stood. 'Hey, little brother, maybe this trip wasn't about our grandfather, but fate. Do you believe in fate?'

'I'm learning to,' he said, surprising her.

Jake was surprising Sid in different ways. She remembered lying in her bed at Brushstrokes before the trip, hoping some good might come out of this expedition. At the very least, she might learn more about her father's side of the family. Not for a moment did she think Jake would fall in love, or that their mother, who hadn't been privy to Sid's plans and was like a fish out of water in a small town, would be making plans to see David again. Could this be the start of something, or was it simply a case of two like-minded adults meeting and sharing the same passion?

The gallery *was* closing for a while, and Sid sure could do with a sleep in. A lazy day alone might help ease the headache and body bloat that wasn't going away, while also allowing Sid the time and mental capacity to concentrate on the family puzzle that was, right now, like a mosaic in the making. To complete the picture, she'd need to find more pieces— more tesserae, as David called it—but without breaking anything in the process.

Rest, yes. That's what she'd do tomorrow. Sid would say she needed a lazy day and suggest Natalie take the Jeep, take David up on his offer of a personal gallery inspection, and take her time. Then Sid would let nature —or fate—take its course.

46

WATERCOLOUR COVE, 2015

Last night, Natalie had barely slept, too keen to pick up where she and David had left off yesterday—before Sid turned up in Pearl's car and surprised them both. The awkward parting had left so much unsaid.

Grateful Sid had decided to sleep in, Natalie could confidently drive up the Greenhill plantation road, hoping David hadn't had second thoughts overnight. Part way up the hill, she nosed the car onto the flattened area where forklifts had once darted about, stacking and shifting pallets loaded with banana boxes. Needing to breathe some oxygen into her lungs and clear her head, she climbed out of the car and, with a sense of nostalgia, peered inside the old shed. Her gaze shifted to the hillside behind—up to the rocky outcrop that pinpointed the secret cave—and then over to the right and along the road to where it forked. She thought about how many times she and Albie had trudged up and down that roadway each school day, until Ulf took Albie out of school and put him to work.

Poor Albie. He'd been thinner than spaghetti when Natalie last met with him in Sydney. He'd looked so unwell, the tremble in his hands almost stopped the flat white coffee getting to his lips without spilling.

⸻

'I don't have long,' Natalie told him, having first called out her coffee order to the barista.

'Me either. Thanks for seeing me.'

'What do you want, Albie?'

'I want to know. Is she mine?'

While on tenterhooks all week over this so-called reunion, Natalie was determined to maintain her composure. That was until Albie's question lit a fire under her, threatening to melt the semblance of cool. 'What are you talking about?'

The man gave up on the coffee, pushing the cup aside. 'Your daughter. I was a kid back then. I know better now. I was your backup plan. Right?'

'Oh, Albie, please don't do this now.' Her angry response, sparked by fear and a feeling of being violated and tricked into meeting, inflamed the situation. 'We're supposed to be enjoying a friendly catch-up. Don't start something—'

'I started nothing, Tilly. You did when you took me into your bed.'

Albie started sobbing, and people at an adjacent table stared. The Natalie of old might have walked away. Only remorse glued her to the chair. If her childhood with an addict for a mother had been hard, poor Albie's past had been ten times worse.

'Hey, come on. Buck up, Albie. Let's start over. Tell me. Did you ever find your mum?' Natalie hoped to steer his conversation and his interest away from Sidney. 'You once told me you tried.'

'No, I never did find her, but there's this bunch of people helping me, and others like me, to reconnect with family.'

'Others like you? What does that mean?'

'It's all a part of the royal commission into abuse. I'm testifying.'

'Albie, that's really brave of you.'

He shrugged. 'I don't call it brave. After I left Dinghy Bay, I tried to get help. Lots of people thought they were doing good. Some helped a bit. A couple of shrinks thought they could make a difference, but the sessions only brought all the memories back, forcing me to relive the things those priests did to me. I didn't want to remember the beatings in the shower block and the long nights spent lying in the dark, listening, praying and pretending to sleep when I heard someone coming. But when the government announced a royal commission into institutional child sexual abuse, I decided it was time to remember. I want to testify, Tilly. That's why I had to see you.'

'Why me? I don't understand.'

'I'll need to speak about all those things people did—and I'm scared. If I thought you were there, Tilly, I would feel brave. It would be like old times. I could always talk to you about that stuff. You used to say we were forever family. I need you to help me.'

'I'm not sure, Albie.'

'Just help me remember. Come with me. Be there in the room. Let me see a friend while I tell my side of the story to strangers. Then I can finally rest my mind. I need to let go and rest, Tilly.'

When Natalie had met Albie that day in the café, they'd said so many things—not all good. They'd also both unknowingly made a decision each. Natalie knew hers was right and the best thing to do. But when hurriedly saying goodbye to Albie, she hadn't known it would be for the last time.

Like she didn't know if her trip up to Greenhill this morning would be the last one. That would depend on David.

47

WATERCOLOUR COVE, 2015

'You came back,' David called as Natalie approached the door to the cottage. 'I wasn't sure you would. Come on in. I have the fire going.'

'We have more to talk about,' Natalie said. 'And I wanted to thank you for yesterday. How you dealt with Sidney, I mean.'

'Well, thanks, but that's only because I agree. Before anyone else knows anything, the two of us need time.'

Natalie sighed—relief most likely—while easing herself into the huge velveteen armchair, the scent of an artist's studio soothing her frayed nerves.

David sat opposite in a matching chair. 'I laid awake last night thinking about so much, and I'm curious. What did Sidney hope to achieve by trying to see Ted?'

'She's inquisitive—always has been. And now she's pregnant and—' Natalie faulted. 'Family is more important than ever, which is why, when the man she's lived with for seven years thought abortion was the best way forward, her heart broke. Discovering a grandfather has given her something to focus on other than her situation.'

David nodded. 'She told me about her baby's father.'

'Oh, and did she tell you we've been arguing since she moved back in?'

David's lips turned up at one corner. 'She suggested being back under the same roof hasn't been easy.'

'I see, well, in Sid-speak that means *I* haven't been easy on her. She's convinced being a single mother is the best thing for her child and, to that

244

end, has put herself firmly on the shelf, even though there's a lovely man who lives a few doors up and is quite keen. They chat each morning when Sid goes for her walk. He asks about the baby and how Sid's feeling. He's sweet. He's single. She could do a lot worse.'

David looked aghast. 'But if there's no love ...'

'Look where loving Damien got her. Sometimes we settle for the next best thing.'

David didn't respond, his silence a warning. She was speaking too freely, like they were contrary teenagers again—full of opinions that would be forgotten by morning. But the pair couldn't be any more different from those days. Tilly was a mother, while David was a father wanting to know his daughter. Naturally enough, his protective instincts would kick in.

'She craves independence,' he said. 'I relate to that.'

'And she's single-minded.' Natalie smiled. 'Which is why, when I asked her to not contact her grandfather, she did the opposite.'

'Sounds like her mother.' David winked.

'Speaking of Ted ...' Natalie switched back to the more comfortable topic. 'What brought such a tough man down? How did he die?'

'A stroke. No warning, no signs. At the time of the bus crash, he'd been strong and still wielding the whip with seasonal workers. You know how he was. Mum wrote letters just about every day, planning their retirement. He'd already served half his sentence. But the whole affair took time and the nastiness, the hate, and the hearing took a toll. His lawyer remained hopeful they'd clear his name. They lodged an appeal, but Dad died broken-hearted and disrespected by the town he loved. Ted deserved more. He was the one behind the town's name change, and getting Watercolour Cove on the state's Arts and Culture trail.'

'Really? I can't image tough Ted doing anything so arty.'

'He did it for me. Dad saw my wheelchair as an impediment and something that would stop me from doing the things I loved. He could never see past my disabilities to understand my chair actually liberated me. It was the one thing I could rely on to be there for as long as I needed it. You might have seen a couple of old wheelchairs about the place, enjoying a happy retirement.' David smiled. 'I planned to ditch them and walk again, but getting up on two feet took lots of hard work. In the meantime, Mum was trying to get me back into my art.'

'You'd stopped painting?'

'I went through different phases for the first few years, most of them morose. Dad wanted to do something for me. He'd say things like, "If you can't get to the art scene, son, I'll bring the arts to you." In a way, he and Mum did by reinventing Greenhill into a gallery and accommodation place. He was pushing for further rezoning when the crash happened.'

'Rezoning for what?'

'The plantation. He'd started whittling the property down and selling it off. He was planning to get into property development. It was that or diversify into blueberries, but there's already a biggest and best blueberry farm in those hills behind us, and Dad never liked to be second best. There's a lot of Greenhill land with impressive views. He saw residential development as a way of making money off the unused portion. At the same time, the development would mean better infrastructure and facilities for the town. And the town was ready. People agreed the council had ignored us long enough. Dad started by protecting the beach shacks in the dune area, listing them as heritage buildings so no one could knock them down. By then Merv was in jail.'

'They finally found the evidence to put him away?' Natalie had to smile, imagining Merv giving a judge the finger at sentencing.

'Yes. Unlike Dad, Merv was guilty as hell.'

'Can't believe he got away with it for so long.'

'He not only grew the stuff, but he also set up a drug lab in the beach shack. How the place never burned down with everything he had going on in there, I don't know.'

'How did they catch him out?'

'Someone reported kids sneaking around the shacks. Of course, the little thieves had nicked off long before the cops from Coffs attended. When the boys in blue checked Merv's premises for signs of break and enter, they got the surprise of their lives. When Merv moseyed home that night, the drug squad was waiting. The bloke needed money to pay for his defence, so he sold his beach properties to Dad. Pearl is renting one shack until I decide what to do with the place. Unfortunately, the whole drug incident alerted Crown Lands, who wanted to come in and take over the beach shacks and basically throw everyone out—the only road in is over government property. Ted successfully negotiated with them to allow each owner to buy a portion of the access road.'

'He really did a lot of good for the town.'

'Yes, until the car accident. The town turned on him—on us. There were angry letters, hurtful looks, and snide remarks when Mum ventured into the village. Then there was the gossip that went on behind our backs. That's when the seawall became a hate wall. Locals wrote awful things about him on those rocks. Mum was so devastated she rarely left the mountain.'

'But Ted wasn't to blame.' The conviction in Natalie's voice did not go unnoticed. David looked surprised.

He would never have imagined Natalie might know something he didn't about his father, or that she might, *might*, be able to clear Ted's name, finally putting to rest the rumours. But it was too soon to tell David anything. She hadn't heard from Tasha and Marcus on that score yet.

God bless Tasha for immediately recognising the gravity of the situation when Natalie had telephoned her last night for legal advice. Tasha already knew about Albie. The first thing Natalie had done when lobbing on her old friend's doorstep after the incident at Brushstrokes was to ask Marcus, Tasha's toy-boy lawyer, if admissions of guilt in suicide notes were legal grounds to amend another person's criminal record. And, second, what sort of trouble might Natalie find herself in for having withheld such evidence from the police investigation? In the days following the incident, Natalie had convinced herself she'd done nothing wrong by secreting the second letter away. It was, after all, addressed to her, but … *How stupid. How terribly, terribly stupid!*

'Tilly?' David was staring, his eyes brown and speckled with gold, just like Sid's. 'What's wrong? Why do I feel you know more about this?'

'I can tell you that Ted tried to track Matthew down recently,' she said. 'I received a letter from a solicitor he'd hired—the letter Sid found that started all this.'

'How recently?'

'About a month ago. Written on behalf of your father, the letter offered Matthew the property if he came back to Greenhill.'

'Really? Why the change of heart after all this time, I wonder? Not that I mind what Dad did with everything he worked so hard for,' David added. 'His estate left plenty of property to go around. Do you have the letter?'

Natalie shook her head. 'I'm sorry, but I threw the thing away. Please, understand,' she added, 'Matthew has been gone a long time. And I was sorrier still that Sid found the blasted thing in the bin and started asking questions.'

'And you chose to not tell her?' he asked.

'What happened was so long ago, David. The truth would only have affected her memories of Matthew. Instead, we fought, and I reminded her that Matthew had cut all ties with his parents for a reason. But Sid had to find her grandfather!'

'And that's how she ended up here?'

'I think the letter mentioned Watercolour Cove, but the name meant nothing to me. The content was shock enough, so I discard the thing. Perhaps if I'd been more careful disposing of it, we might not be here now.' She half expected David to ask how she felt about that. Unsure of her answer, she was glad he didn't, adding instead, 'I'm sorry about Rose. Your mum was so sweet.'

'And profoundly unhappy by the end. My accident changed everything. Matthew left, and she was never the same, though she always had her brave face on. Rose only ever wanted to be a good and loving mother, wife, and eventually, grandmother. In the end, with Dad gone, misery consumed her.'

'Poor Rose,' Natalie said. 'Her eldest son not only left his home and family, but he left with me. She would've known. They knew me. They hated me. They never wanted us together.'

'No, Tilly, they didn't hate you. That's what Matthew told you.'

'But they had plans for you, David. Rose had such expectations.'

'Yes, and that's why they wanted you and me to slow down. But, we were kids—reckless and selfish and convinced our parents had no clue about love. Now I'm older, I can see they were wise enough to know what might happen if they didn't slow us down.' David cocked his head, his smile getting her attention. 'Don't you reckon Sidney might have proved them right?'

Natalie didn't feel like smiling. 'But they also wanted better than me for you, and I knew you'd respect their opinion and find a way to make everyone happy. You would've agreed to stay, thinking I'd fall into step and into line with your parents. But I was so desperate to leave this place.'

'They wanted better for *us*,' David said, serious again. 'That's why Dad was so insistent I finish my education and get tertiary qualifications so, as a fallback, I could at least come home and *teach* art. He was always big on building opportunities to keep young people in town. I can hear him now: "Small towns have big hearts, and its people keep that heart beating. Lose the population to the big city and a town dies. Country schools will always need passionate teachers".'

'Oh, you sound so like him, David. I'm sorry he's gone.' It was true. Natalie was sorry for David and for Rose. Ted had been a good father. He'd worked hard all his life. But at a moment of anguish for the son he thought was dying, Ted had dared tell Tilly "*no*" and ignore her pleas.

Maybe Ted regretted his decision to deny Tilly access to David. Who knows? Had it been a mistake forced by grief? Probably. Natalie had made plenty of bad choices, thinking they'd been right. 'Your father was a prominent advocate for the town.'

'Yeah, which meant being blamed for the crash that killed local children was the cruellest of ironies.'

'And the Marhkts?' Natalie asked. 'What happened after Albie left home? When did he leave?'

David shrugged. 'I'm not sure. I was still in rehab. The Marhkts stuck it out for a while. Dad was always giving Ulf help and business tips. I remember Ted saying Ulf would soon give the banana game away. "Once a man loses his passion, failure is only a matter of time," he'd say. Another reason Dad was so insistent I keep painting. As for Albie. He fronted up here a few years back wanting to contact Dad in prison.'

'When was that?'

'A bit before Mum died. One of Dad's last letters to her mentioned Albie, but not what he'd wanted. Forgiveness, I suspect.'

'Forgiveness from your father? For what?' Natalie couldn't let on she already knew—not yet.

'For leaving Dad to take the rap. Dad wasn't alone in the car. The crash wasn't his fault.'

His word rocked Natalie. 'You've always known?'

'Dad's version of the story never changed throughout the trial. He might've been driving, but it was Albie who tried to kill them both by grabbing the wheel and steering Dad's car into the path of an oncoming bus.'

'But they found Ted guilty.'

'No proof to suggest things happened any differently. No one saw them get into the car together that night, and the traumatised driver and kids on the bus didn't notice Albie running from the scene. The town wanted blood, and then there was a story in the local paper that said Dad had been drinking at the club beforehand.'

'Your dad hardly ever drank. He always sprouted: "bananas are good for a hangover, but bananas are better without the hangover in the first place".'

'Yep! Old Ted had his one-a-week ritual at the club. That night, after his altercation with Mum and me, Albie—all fired up—waited for Dad in the car park. Dad gave him some fatherly advice and a clip over the ear and told him it was time to stop whining—or words to that effect. Dad was so over arguments about inheritances. But then he bought a slab of beer as a peace offering and Albie put a few away in the car park while they talked. Then Albie asked for a ride to the motel on the highway. Before Mum died, Albie wrote her a letter that said he was sorry he'd run off.'

'Couldn't she have used that letter to prove your dad's version of events?'

David shook his head. 'What Albie wrote was vague and hardly a confession—worth nothing on its own. Mum did write back, telling Albie she'd forgive him if he told the real story about that night. Albie never wrote again.'

Natalie sighed, long and loud. 'Yes, David, he did.'

'What do you mean? Are you still in touch? Do you know what happened to him? If the bloke ever dares cross my path again—'

'Albie's dead, David. He killed himself.'

David's anger gave way to surprise. 'You're kidding! So, you've kept in touch?'

'No, I didn't see him for years. Then, one day, he phoned me at the gallery. I'd not long opened up that day.'

'It was *yours*!' The lilt in his voice said he'd expected as much. 'You finally had your own gallery.'

Natalie continued without commenting. 'Anyway, Albie didn't say why he was phoning, insisting instead that we meet in person. I told him we could, just once. But once wasn't enough. Never was with Albie. When he phoned again, only a couple of years ago, I agreed to meet him for the last time. That's when he told me he was planning on telling the royal commission about his early years and the abuse. He wanted me to help and to be there on the day he testified.'

'And you attended?'

'At first I told him no, and to not even bother looking back. All that stuff was in the past. I told him I couldn't help. But then …' Natalie shook her head. 'I started reading the numerous newspaper reports. One showed his name among a list of people providing victim impact state-ments. He was in Sydney. He was doing it.'

'And you went along to the public hearing?' David must have seen the shame in her expression. 'It's okay. Albie was like a brother. You had to support him.'

'Yes, but I did too little too late. I didn't contact Albie to tell him, so he never knew I was at the back of the room. Even when he got up to testify, I stayed hidden. It was wrong of me. Testifying was so hard. I had some idea about what happened at the home he was dumped in. I thought I could imagine the rest. But the personal accounts and details were shocking.' Natalie squeezed her eyes shut. 'Such insidious, evil acts against any child is unfathomable. Albie broke down several times, and the papers wrote about him the next day. They even posted his picture, his face all scrunched in pain.'

'I never knew about Albie's past. You never said. I wouldn't have given him such a hard time.'

'We kept each other's secrets, David,' Natalie said. 'I can tell you he was a scared and gentle giant who was rejected throughout his life. He thought if he told people what had happened, they'd reject him all over again. So, he learned how to protect himself. I rejected him the night of your accident,' she said cautiously. 'I guess he snapped—'

'And I happened to be in his way.'

'Yes, but no, David. I was to blame. I did something so stupid. I hurt him. Not in the same way as everyone else.' Natalie told herself it was different. But was it really? In the end, did the *how* matter? She'd been mean and selfish. 'I hurt him again recently by not being brave enough, or thoughtful enough to recognise he'd needed me. Not long after the hearing, he came out to the B & B I run in the Blue Mountains. I guess he snapped again. I don't know. Sidney signed him. I never even knew he was there.' I failed him, she could have added.

Natalie could no longer make things right with Albie, but she could use his letter to help David clear his father's name.

48

WATERCOLOUR COVE, 2015

'Nat, darling, it's Tash. About your message, I … What's that noise? I can't hear you.'

Natalie cupped a hand around her mouth and the phone. 'Probably wind and beach waves.' She'd ventured over to the seawall after leaving David, needing space to breathe and to think because, if she was going to do this, then she had to get the wheels she'd put into motion moving faster.

'The beach?' Tasha gushed. 'Marcus, honey, Nat's at the beach.'

Natalie considered telling her best friend the truth. That she was standing in front of a mirror sculpture, staring at her reflection, her true self hidden behind a mask of tear-stained make-up, her bottle-blonde hair blown about in the breeze. But for once, Natalie's appearance was the least important thing.

'Marcus and I are sitting in front of a roaring fire and talking about your letter. As we speak, he's making subtle enquiries with a few trusted colleagues.'

'Please, tell Marcus thank you. I'm afraid I'm going to need all the advice he can give on the matter.'

'Darling, you sound tired. What else is wrong? Is it Jake?'

'No, the kids are fine.' She wandered from the seawall, back towards the villa to get out of the wind, and when passing an old fisherman, she instinctively waved. Stranger still, the man smiled and waved back. 'Oh

Tash, everything I've tried so desperately to forget is about to come crashing down on me.'

'Where's all this coming from, Nat? I'm sure things aren't that bad. You were always one for a little drama. But tell me how I can help.'

'There is another favour I need to ask.'

'Anything, darling.'

'First, tell Marcus the situation has changed. Edward Hill is dead.' Out of habit rather than necessity, Natalie checked the quiet street both ways before crossing.

'Dead?'

'Yes, so I need you to scan that letter I gave you and email both pages to me.'

'I'll do that straight away, but Nat …' Tasha hesitated. 'What exactly are you going to do with the letter? Nothing foolish, I hope. Implicating yourself is neither wise nor necessary, in my experience. But Marcus will be best to discuss the whys and wherefores with you directly, as soon as he's off his call.'

'Tash, to be honest, I don't know what I'm going to do with the information, except I promise you my decision will be the right one. I'm doing what's right, finally.'

'Surely, with Edward Hill dead, you don't need to *do* anything.'

'I might have thought so before I came back home, Tash.'

'Home?'

'Yes, any minute now I'll be on the veranda of a caravan park villa I'm currently sharing with Jake. The place looks across at the Dinghy Bay seawall.'

'You mean *that* Dinghy Bay?'

'There's only one. They've renamed the place Watercolour Cove, and it's quite wonderful. Sidney seems content. Jake is in love.'

'And you?' Tasha asked.

'I'm standing here asking myself the question: if I share that letter, who will I hurt the most?'

'And do you know the answer, darling?'

'Unfortunately, I do. Matthew once told me there are winners and losers in this world, Tash, and that I was a loser. I wasted so many years trying to prove he was wrong. In the end, I lose either way. If I share the letter, I'll hurt the very people I've tried to protect. The people I've always loved.'

'Darling, I wish I could help.'

'You can,' Natalie whispered, stopping short of the villa. 'Only time will tell if Matthew was right. Whether I win respect or lose everyone I love will come down to one thing. That letter you're about to email to me.'

49

WATERCOLOUR COVE, 2015

Albie started the letter with *Sorry Tilly*, each shaking stroke of his pen scratching against the fancy unlined notepaper. Then he mumbled, 'No.' This was his last chance. He didn't want to start the note to Tilly with an ordinary *sorry*, even though he was—sorry. Balling the notepaper and discarding it in the empty bin, he tried again.

Hello Tilly,

It's Albie. I've missed you. Although I'm guessing you never missed me.

Albie put down his pen and took a moment to look around the guest room with its raked ceiling rafters and the occasional cobweb tucked in a corner. He thought about what he wanted to tell Tilly in this letter, things he would prefer to say to her face. If only he wasn't so afraid his words— or his resolve—might fail him. He'd failed at just about everything his whole life.

'An apology was a start,' he muttered while looking at the sheet of fancy paper he'd taken from the desk drawer.

I need to tell you I'm sorry, Tilly. Sorry for so many things. Right now I'm sorry we won't get to say a proper goodbye. This wasn't my plan, I don't think, although I can't be sure. I came to see you and to see your daughter. I thought she might have been my daughter. When you never said, even when I asked, I've imagined it to be so all these years.

Albie cast his mind back to the check-in desk and to the pretty woman who'd introduced herself as Sidney Hill.

I see now that she can't be mine. I'd wanted to know for so long, but I was afraid of the answer. If you'd said 'no' I would lose hope. Instead, I pretended. Then I came here to see her for myself, once and for all. If she was mine, I wanted to reassure her that not being in her life did not stop me from loving her. Family is forever. Do you remember telling me that, Tilly? That was the night we spent together. The night with the blue moon.

Anger forced the pen nib through the delicate paper. Should he throw the letter away and start again?

'No. No time,' he said, taking a deep breath and starting on a fresh line.

You were lucky to get your forever family. I only wish I'd stayed a part of that. All my life I've wanted to belong to someone or have someone belong to me. People told me my mother loved me so much she sacrificed her own happiness to give me a future in a new country. But they lied to me, Tilly. People never stopped lying.

Not long ago, I found out people lied to my mother. Everything the authorities in Malta told her was a lie. When she tried to stop them, they still took me from her. They told her I'd be safe until she found either work or a husband who could support a family. Before anyone knew, the government had shipped me to the other side of the world, with no one to protect me.

When Ulf and Hilda took me in, I finally felt wanted and safe. Then you arrived, Tilly, and from that moment all I wanted was you. If only you'd wanted me. I mean really wanted me, not as second best to David Hill.

Albie paused to look outside the loft room. Darkness would soon tinge everything outside blue. Inside, the last shards of sunlight—the colour of good whisky—drenched the room. He reached out to his only friend—a half-empty scotch bottle—and resumed his scribblings.

I've never forgotten that time we made love. And afterwards I stayed watching you from outside. Then I saw David, and even though I could still smell you on me, you were telling him he was your forever family. I thought you wanted and understood me, and you saw a future—with me. So, I fought for you to prove I was a man ready and willing to protect you. I never meant to hurt David. He was supposed to fight back, but he slipped after that one dumb punch from me. I panicked and ran home.
Later, when I saw your grief, I wanted to comfort you and plan a life with you. Instead, you chose Matthew. You were getting off that mountain any way you could—just not with me. You rejected me. You left me behind. So I left the mountain not long after.

Albie wiped one cheek, but not before a tear dropped to the paper, the ink blurring. He half-filled the glass with scotch, sculling the liquid in one go.

When I finally returned, the gate was locked, the house empty, the packing sheds boarded up. There was no banana business, and Ulf and Hilda were gone. I asked Mrs Hill if they'd left a message for me. I asked if she knew where they were. She lied. Of course she did. People always lied to me, and the Hills were always looking to own the entire mountain. They as good as stole the property from me. So, I got mad. I was so angry, so hurt, so out of control. You used to tell me not to cry. You'd always say, 'Albie, first get angry, then get even! That's what I did. I got angry, like you said. Then I got even.

After two years sober, I started drinking. I went to the Fisho's Club and there, being all loud and boasting at the end of the bar, was Ted Hill. He was buying his mates from the council a round and bragging about getting approval to subdivide MY home. Later, I bought a bottle of scotch and waited in the car park for him. By the time he came out, I was too drunk to talk any sense, other than swear and call him names. One of Ted's quick backhanders across my head, like he used to do when we were mucking around in the packing shed as kids, was hard enough to knock me sober. Thinking back, I wonder if his whacking me over the head left me concussed. I recall him buying me a slab of beer and offering to take me back to my motel. After that ... It's all a bit of a blur.

I recall the crash. The sound of the impact sucked every ounce of air from my body. I couldn't breathe. Then, I heard it ... All the little kids on the bus. Nothing I did that night was planned. I just remember wanting to die, and taking Ted Hill with me would hurt David and his mother. They'd know what it felt like to have something taken away from them. If I couldn't live on the mountain, Ted Hill wouldn't either. So, I grabbed the wheel and drove us into that bus. When I realised I was still alive, the kids' screams took me straight back to the home where I'd screamed and screamed at night. But no one cared enough to rescue me. Instead, they did things that made me want to run. And so, that night, I ran, and I left Mr Hill for dead. To this day, the screams won't leave me alone.

Like I said, I never set out to hurt anyone that day, even though people have hurt me one way or another my whole life. I became blind with rage and booze and I hurt those children. Two of them died. I destroyed families, and I hated myself for running and for being silent all these years, so I'm fixing that by confessing to you now. Testifying at the royal commission changed me. Truth telling and talking about what happened to me as a child wouldn't bring the children back to their families, but maybe I could help protect vulnerable children from predators. What I never expected from giving evidence was to have people offering to help find my mother. But she'd already died years earlier, alone in a rented apartment, and later buried in an unmarked grave in Malta. I couldn't do much, but I could let her know I loved her by officially recording her death.

Then, when I found out Matthew was dead, I saw you as my last hope for happiness—my forever family with you and Sidney. But the very second your girl smiled at me from behind the desk I saw two things. First, I saw she was far too beautiful to be mine. Then ... I saw David.

Funny the way things turn out. You were right to not choose me. I never did make anything of myself. A loser like Albie Marhkt could never be good enough for the likes of you. But I'm not Albie Marhkt—I never was him. I'm Alessandro Albertini and I'm going home. My mother loved me, and she is waiting for me. Goodbye, Tilly.
Love always, Albie

50

WATERCOLOUR COVE, 2015

As promised, Tasha had attached the scanned document and emailed Natalie. The letter with its small handwriting now filled the phone screen, but Natalie knew the contents by heart. Over the years, she'd re-read the letter countless times, trying to imagine Albie's desperation on that bleak day on the eve of winter. While she'd been downstairs with her daughter and arguing about pink ribbon, a man had found the world so dark and depressing he'd left it by his own hand.

⎯⎯

Having dispatched her daughter to Leura to buy more ribbon, Natalie stood outside the loft apartment, her ear pressed to the solid timber door to listen for noises inside—the kind that indicated the guest was up and making moves to check out. But rather than running water, footfall, or the zipping of suitcases, Natalie heard only an eerie silence.

She rapped her knuckles on the door twice and waited.

Silence still.

Banging harder, she called out, 'Mr Albertini?'

Nothing. Perhaps he'd left when it was still dark outside, while Sid and Natalie had slept. Stranger things had happened over the years. One couple had checked out after only two hours, their departure loud and angry. They'd probably fought the entire trip home.

'I have a key, Mr Albertini. I'm opening the door.' At the same time,

Natalie delivered a final warning knock. The last thing she wanted was to confront a semi-naked stranger. 'Hello?'

The stench of stale booze hit her first. The room would need a good airing. Adding to Natalie's annoyance was the bath towel set strewn carelessly across the still-made bed. She always took such pride in presenting the towels perfectly rolled and ribboned. Naturally, the ribbon was missing.

'Another souvenir collector.' She'd grumbled the words before noticing the fancy notepaper from the desk compendium Natalie chose to supply each guest, even though Sidney considered compendiums old-fashioned and unnecessary.

'People email these days, Mum,' her daughter had said. 'You'd be better off providing free Wi-Fi.'

'Except that Brushstrokes guests like to draw,' Natalie had argued. 'An artist appreciates having a quality paper on hand.'

One of Brushstroke's early guests had given Natalie the compendium idea after he'd used a paper napkin to leave a tiny work of art on his breakfast tray. This morning, it seemed Mr-Late-Checkout-Albertini had also left a note of thanks—on the pillows. Humming smugly, and planning to wave the work under Sid's nose, Natalie threw open the curtains. Keen to get fresh air circulating, even though outside was bitterly cold and blustery, she unclipped the window latch and nudged the old sash window pane so high that the sturdy breeze scattered the thank-you note across the bed.

Tisking and tutting, Natalie gathered the pages. But rather than an art, handwriting filled the pages and, just like the morning's frost on the window, Natalie's gaze froze on the salutation:

Hello Tilly.

She hadn't read more than the first paragraph of the multi-page letter when her hands began shaking, the tremor travelling along every extremity to leave her weak. Plonking herself on the edge of the bed, she turned her attention to the second, brief note of only three lines. It began:

To Anyone Who Cares.

Unsure how long she'd stared at those three lines, Natalie refocused on the long letter, before shifting her focus again to the scuff marks on the varnished timber floor. Soon the boards would need sanding and polishing, she noted. Then she thought, vaguely, maybe rugs were a smarter option. Rugs provided warmth, and Natalie was suddenly colder than the gust of wind whipping through the window and making the curtain rings clatter. From the bathroom behind her came a creaking sound, like a door was opening. *Oh, no!*

'Mr Albertini?' Natalie said a little nervously. But when she turned around, moving towards the wide-open ensuite door, a burst of sun streamed through the highlight windows specifically designed to provide mountain vistas when a guest was reclined in the bath. Squinting against the brightness, her initial thought was that the guest, fully clothed except for his feet, was standing tiptoed on the edge of the claw-foot bathtub. *Getting a better look, perhaps? Or was he replacing a blown light bulb? Yes, that's it. I'll need a ladder,* she told herself.

Then, despite not seeing the face of the man hanging from the rafters above the bath, something told Natalie.

'Albie!'

As she clutched the door frame to save herself from falling, a carousel of memories swirled in her head. Suddenly, she and Albie were together in the park by the beach, and Tilly was spinning the wonky playground roundabout as if possessed. 'Faster, faster,' she's squealing. 'Come on, Albie, get on. Just jump, Albie!'

But it was too fast and too dangerous for him. Not Tilly, though. No matter how terrifying the ride, nothing scared Tilly.

Until now.

With her head still spinning, Natalie backed out of the bathroom with only two conscious thoughts: her daughter returning from Leura with ribbon, and her son's laundry ritual every Monday.

Is it Monday or Tuesday? Natalie tried to think, to clear a path to the coping part of her brain. Did she call an ambulance or the police? Did she try to cut him down? *No!* How she'd found him was evidence. *Evidence! What else might they find?* She scanned the guest room, spying a lone ball of scrunched-up paper in the middle of the otherwise empty basket by the desk. Without knowing why, she retrieved the rubbish, shoving the paper in her pocket before rushing from the room—one hand clasping the two letters while the other hand, clamped to her mouth, held back the bile rising in her throat.

Almost slipping on the loft stairwell, she regained her composure and walked purposefully to the kitchen, grabbed the phone from its charger on the counter. But her hand trembled so uncontrollably she could scarcely punch in the numbers.

Only when the operator answered did the scream inside Natalie release.

———

'Oh, sweet Albie,' Natalie whispered where she sat on the villa's veranda, toying with her mobile phone while re-reading the last line of his letter. 'Of course, your mother loved you. Mothers love their children—even my mother—but they make mistakes. We all do.'

Natalie had made a mistake that fateful day. She'd lied to the first police officer to arrive at the scene. But was it really a lie to say, 'No, officer, I've never heard the name Alessandro Albertini before?' Once spoken, any change in her story would've implicated her. As for withholding evidence, there'd been no choice. If anyone had read the letter he'd addressed to her, Natalie would … Well, she didn't know what she'd do.

Despite a deep sadness she'd felt for Albie over the following days, Natalie had managed to rein in her grief every time the police officer dropped by the B & B for 'another chat' regarding the deceased's identity. For those few seconds each time the officer had said, 'thank you for your time', Natalie had been tempted to confess. But she'd tell herself the contents of the letter had no bearing on the investigation. With the cause of death—suicide—not in dispute, the *why* made no difference to anyone else but Natalie.

'Until now!'

The realisation hit Natalie while staring at the scanned letter on her phone and recalling David's earlier words concerning his father. In the email Tash had sent was a comment from Marcus confirming Albie's handwritten words would most likely be enough to exonerate David's father of manslaughter. And that meant, while Ted might not have lived to see his name cleared, the man's legacy, and his rightful place in Watercolour Cove's history, could be corrected.

51

WATERCOLOUR COVE, 2015

Though keen to learn more about the one-on-one gallery tour with David, Sid had opted to observe from inside the villa, deciding time alone for mother and daughter was prudent. But all that changed when the woman who never cried looked visibly shaken.

Sid popped her head out the door. 'Mum? I was watching you just now and I—'

'You're spying on me?' Natalie slammed the phone's protective cover closed.

'No, I'm worried. Whatever you're reading, it looks like bad news. The world's not about to end, is it?'

Her mother didn't laugh. 'Did you want something, Sidney?'

'Well, since you asked … You've been so cross with me.' Joining her mother on the outdoor sofa, Sid lowered her voice so the couple in the neighbouring Banksia Cabin didn't hear. 'I wish you were happier and supportive of me bringing this baby up on my own. It is my choice to make.'

After a beat of silence, Natalie said, 'You kids today are lucky. You get to make choices.'

'Oh, here we go again with the usual *you-don't-know-how-lucky-you-are* speech.'

'When did you become so bitter, Sidney?'

'Ooh, I'd say it started somewhere around the time I lost my father.

Losing my partner recently, and probably any career hopes I might've had in the design business, hasn't helped. Nor has walking away from my home of seven years with virtually nothing and, at thirty-five years old, finding myself living with my mother. And let's not forget a man hangs himself in the room next to mine and I find out I have a grandfather, only to lose him in a matter of days. Then my daredevil brother ends up in hospital and somehow I'm to blame for it. But wait! There's more. There's the bit where my mother doesn't think I'm capable of raising a child without a partner.' Sid took a breath and pressed a hand to her belly to soothe the twinge—the second in as many minutes.

'I never said you weren't capable, Sidney. What worries me is this single-mindedness about doing it all on your own.'

'I'm not making decisions lightly. I'm terrified.' Needing to stretch her back, Sid shifted her butt to the edge of the sofa and drew her shoulders up and back several times. 'But I'm responsible for my situation, and you not having faith in me isn't helping.'

Natalie made a little scoffing sound. 'You hardly got *yourself* into this predicament alone.'

'I get that, but after seven years together I never expected Damien would react the way he did. If I hadn't been confident in our relationship I would've been more careful. I made the wrong choice, but I'd expected him to welcome the news.' Sid looked down at her belly.

'Choice?' her mother said. 'You chose to get pregnant?'

'No, Mum!' Sid slumped back against the chair and clamped both hands between her knees. 'I missed my pill a couple of nights and didn't tell Damien. But it wasn't the first time I'd forgotten or skipped a night. I know I was exhausted at the time. The business was taking so much out of us both. I mean, we hardly had time for sex, let alone the energy to walk to the bathroom for my pill. Before I knew it …' Sid's hands cupped the top and bottom of her belly, growing bigger by the day. 'Then, when I found out, I figured it was fate and Damien would feel the same as me. But he didn't and now I'm scared I won't know how to be a mother.'

'You're being ridiculous,' is all Natalie said.

'That's all you have to say? I'm being ridiculous?' Sid's frustration wouldn't allow her to stay seated, and she desperately needed to look her mother in the eye. 'Why aren't you comforting me or crying with me? Where's those reassuring hugs? Instead, you're composed and perfect, while I'm your *im*perfect daughter who's never been quite good enough, in your opinion. Yes, I made a mistake. So what? Everyone does. Well, everyone except you, it seems.' Sid couldn't stop the rush of tears, and she no longer cared about portraying strength when she felt anything but strong at that moment. 'I'm done trying to fit into other people's expectations of me. I've decided, as soon as Jake is okay, I'm going to Casino to see Bill and Kath.'

'Damien's parents?'

'Yes. Kath has asked me a dozen times to visit. I'm still like a daughter to them, and they feel like family.'

'I see.'

'No, you don't, Mum. Sometimes I'm not sure what you see when you look at me, but you don't see me, because if you did you would know how scared I am and how much I need my mother's hugs.'

Sid hadn't expected a grin to grace her mother's lips, but there it was—fleeting, slightly infuriating, but sincere and loving. As if to prove it, Natalie reached out and took Sid's hand.

'I do see you, my darling girl,' her mother said, her voice unexpectedly soft. 'You will never understand how much I see in you.'

'Then *make* me understand, Mum.'

Natalie looked contemplative, making Sid hopeful, but she'd been hopeful on past occasions and usually been disappointed.

Releasing Sidney's hand, Natalie let out a long, defeated sigh and fell back against the chair. 'Despite what I might have said in the past, the one thing I am most proud of is you, and I'm scared for you because ...' She sighed again. 'Because I wasn't married when I fell pregnant.'

'Wow!' Sid barely contained her grin. 'A single mother. And you're only telling me this now? I'm *shocked*!'

'Sarcasm is uncalled for, Sid.'

'Sorry, Mum, but I don't understand. Are you saying the story you told everyone about me being premature was a cover-up? Not that being illegitimate matters to me—not in the slightest—but how can you be so against me getting pregnant and being a single parent?'

Natalie didn't speak for some time, and for a moment mother and daughter looked everywhere but at each other.

'I said we *conceived* out of wedlock, Sid. I was married when I had you. And that cocky smile of yours will end up on the other side of your face when things get tough and you realise you're not superwoman and invincible. My mother—your grandmother—wasn't married, as you know, so I saw first-hand what happens when things go wrong. History would not repeat itself when I fell pregnant. I didn't want a hard life for you then, or now.'

'About Grandma …' Sid queried. 'You never told me anything about her other than she never married. And anyway, the times and attitudes have changed. They don't take babies from unmarried mothers, or put them in institutions.' Sid hesitated, but quickly decided this opportunity wasn't likely to come up often. 'Mum, I want to ask you something. You've said, after Grandma died, you were in a home and in foster care. So, I'm wondering … Well, it's just I've noticed your preoccupation with news reports of the royal commission on child sexual abuse.'

'Is this going somewhere, Sidney?'

'Were you mistreated in the girls' home you grew up in, or by the people who took you in?'

Natalie flapped her hand as if flicking away a pesky fly. 'No, never.'

'I just thought … Maybe you'd had a bad experience, and you worry about me not being married and my child ending up in some kind of dodgy foster care if anything were to happen to me.'

'Nothing's going to happen to you, Sid.'

'Hopefully not, but we can't predict how our lives will pan out. So, for that reason, and with Little Bump's future in mind … You *will* raise my baby if something happens to me, Mum?'

'Stop this talk now. Nothing is going to happen to you, Sid.'

'Nothing was supposed to happen to Dad on a business trip to New York, either. The fittest man I knew died because he had breakfast in the wrong café on the wrong day. Things happen to good people all the time. Look at Jake—he could easily have killed himself on that quad bike. Hospitals can make mistakes and women do die in childbirth.'

'And if you're anything like me, and with that little bump, you'll have an easy birth. Then you'll have a growing and endlessly inquisitive child who pesters *you* for answers. I believe it's called karma.' Natalie smiled, the ice cracking a little more.

'But, Mum, we're all born with an expiration date.'

'Yes and yours is a long way in the future. Now, where's that indomitable daughter of mine who's going to make me a grandmother? In fact, *that* is something I would like to discuss right now.' She took Sid's hand in hers, squeezed and smiled. 'Please, do not encourage the child to call me Granny. And before you suggest an alternative, both Grandma or Nanna Natalie are just as bad.'

Sid chuckled. 'Agreed. You're way too young to be a granny. How about *Glam-ma*? You're still attractive. In fact, maybe when you get back to Brushstrokes *you* should try your luck with Mr Coffee Invitation up the street. You might find the perfect mate.'

'I'm fine without one, thank you very much.'

'Well, me too,' Sid said with a little too much enthusiasm. 'You and I can be there for each other though, can't we?'

'Of course. Always.' Natalie patted Sid's knee with some finality, suggesting the conversation was over. 'You know, thirty-five years ago, I remember promising myself I'd be the perfect mother. Maybe I can start now and do things better.'

Wow! Who was this woman claiming to be less than perfect? Little Bump was already making a big difference in all their lives.

'How about I get us both a cuppa and that leftover cake—if Jake didn't find it first?' Sid hoped a hot drink might further thaw her mother. Besides, sitting in the cold night air was not ideal. Even Little Bump was complaining.

Sid still had questions—lots of them—but did she dare ask tonight and risk ending the rare and rather wonderful mother-daughter moment? Switching the kettle on, she took two mugs from the cup stand on the counter and glanced in the kitchen window at her mother's reflection. The woman was looking at her phone again, the soft glow of the screen illuminating a worried expression. Tempted to ask what was so damn interesting, was it worth pushing this evening?

Sid had come to Watercolour Cove hoping to find out something— anything, really—about her father's family. She'd always been curious about her grandparents on both sides, but Matthew and Natalie were never willing to talk about them in detail. Now Sid was having a child of her own, family history seemed more pressing. In particular those ques- tions around genetics and health. Sid had never heard of Asperger's in association with her father until after he died, and even then it had been Tasha, and not Natalie, who'd told her. Sid had doubted her dad was on the spectrum. It had, after all, only been Tasha's opinion of a man she didn't know well. But what if autism was somewhere in her genes? What might that mean for Sid's children? And Jake's, for that matter.

While slicing the remaining morsel of cake into two pieces and pondering what else there might be to know about her father's medical history—or his family's—a sudden thought unsettled Sid. Was Natalie's interest in the royal commission because their father was the one who'd suffered from abuse? Childhood trauma might go some way to explain her dad's often peculiar ways. Did domestic violence force him to leave his home and cut off all contact? Had his father been a violent alcoholic? Sid fought through the brain fog doctors had said would end soon, her increasingly confused state taking her mind to strange places, like the possibility of David's dad and *her* grandfather being incarcerated together.

'Mum!' Sid squealed and slammed the knife down as blood oozed from the cut on her finger. 'I need help.'

'Heavens! Not with that dirty thing!' Natalie whipped the tea towel away and turned on the cold-water tap, guiding Sid's hand directly under the flow. 'Put your other hand here. Apply some pressure while I find a sticky plaster.' Reaching for her handbag, Natalie fossicked inside until finding a black purse with a zipper. She spread the contents over the counter to pick through the miscellaneous bits and pieces: sticky plasters, alcohol wipes, a tiny tube of antiseptic, and more.

'I can't believe you still have that little kit.'

'Old habits,' her mother replied. 'Do you forget how many times I patched up your brother? You also kept me busy.'

How easily Sid had forgotten those times. On one occasion, her mum had sat up all night while six-yer-old Sid wheezed and coughed. Years later, she'd held back a tipsy Sid's hair over the toilet bowl. Soon, mother and daughter will be holding her hand while Sid gives birth.

'Thanks, Mum.'

Natalie shot a curious smile her way. 'I haven't fixed you yet.'

'I'm not referring to the first aid.'

The pair locked eyes, smiling for a split second before Natalie returned to the task at hand. Having washed, dried and stemmed the bleeding, on went the sticky strip. If only Sid could stem the gush of ques-tions and her gut feeling that David's father and Sid's grandfather somehow fitted into the same picture. Did an unknown connection go some way to explain why David and Natalie had looked so comfortable with each other the other day? David had talked about his brother leaving home and stealing the love of his life.

Who was the love of his life? Sid mused as her mother re-packed the paraphernalia into the little black purse.

'I was thinking just now, Mum,' she ventured, inspecting the plaster while Natalie transferred the cake to a small plate. 'I get there are things about your past—and Dad's—you'd rather not talk about. But sometimes I feel like I didn't know my father.'

Natalie made a dramatic *tsking* sound and took over pouring the tea. 'What on earth would make you say such a thing?'

'Maybe I'm only just realising I wanted to meet my grandfather so I'd feel closer to Dad. Or I might get to know him through his father.'

Natalie paused for drama, sighed for effect and then silently ushered the mug of tea across the counter, saying, 'Your need to connect should not have surprised me. I'm sorry I made a fuss about you trying. You've always been curious.'

'David told me curiosity killed the cat, so I told him that was something you always said to me. Then he suggested you were a wise woman and I should listen to you.'

Rather than laugh at the loving jab, her mother again tsked and tutted. 'You talked about our family so casually to a stranger? I'm stunned.'

'It's called conversation, Mum. We chatted for most of the night about nothing specific. I enjoyed getting to know him. He quite lovely once you get to know him. And while getting him to drop his guard took me a long time and lots of tea, the other day I sensed something between you two—and after not very long at all. You do have things in common. Maybe you and he—'

'Let's change the subject,' Natalie said.

'Why?' Sid dared. 'Me trying to fix my mother up makes a change from my mother fixing me up.'

'Touché!' Natalie turned away, and for a moment Sid wondered if she was about to walk away. Instead, she stopped behind a chair, patting the back cushion. 'Come here and sit.' As Sid complied, her mum gathered Sid's hair to start braiding. 'If you want to talk, I'll tell you the whole truth about your grandmother—what sort of person she was and how I ended up in a home for girls. It's time you knew everything about those days, including why I might seem a little intolerant, and why I try hard to stay strong and keep the past in the past.'

***

Sid had sat quietly and listened, not interrupting until Natalie spoke about living rough for the first five years of her life.

'I can't believe I'm only learning these devastating details now. But I understand you've been guarding yourself.'

'The truth is, Sidney, I've avoided the subject to protect *you*. I didn't know my father, or even who he was, and I barely remember my mother. Whenever I tried recalling her, only one image came to mind—me screaming as the police dragged me from the car. I never saw my mother after that night. That's why I don't dwell on my childhood.'

'But don't you see how it makes everything you've achieved so much more impressive?'

Releasing a deep, slow sigh, Natalie said, 'Except for the bad choices I've made along the way.'

'From the sound of it, my grandmother made worse ones!'

'Yes, and if I could go back in time, I'd do many things differently. That's why I'm adamant about you being sure of your options—all of them. But, unlike me, you don't need to fear being unsupported. You'll always have Jake and me, and your baby will be loved. I know that as certain as I know your brother will never settle down and have a career, and that I'll be doing his laundry every Monday until the day I die.' Natalie laughed. '*And* if there's a Westinghouse washer in the afterlife, I'm sure he'll find a way to get his dirty clothes to me there as well.'

'Don't make me laugh, Mum. I don't think Little Bump likes frivolity— *or* me sitting down for long periods. In fact, I'm sure he or she—Ouch!' As pain squeezed her uterus, Sid lurched forward, staring down at the wet stain between her thighs. 'No, no, no! What's happening to me, Mum?'

'Keep calm, Sidney, it's likely your waters breaking.'

'No! It's too soon.'

'Jake?' Natalie almost screamed the name to compete with the television blaring from his room where he watched with Pearl. 'I need you. Now!'

The hospital bed sheets were white, except for where her daughter's blood stained them. Sid was almost as pale, clearly exhausted and terrified. The strap around her belly held the baby monitor in place, and the sound of her tiny baby's consistent heartbeat was at least reassuring.

'You're fine, Sid. You're scared because you're having a baby. I understand that fear. I was terrified.'

'I can't imagine anything terrifying you, Mum.'

'I've had to become strong, Sid. I wasn't always, and it's meant doing things I'm not proud of, but I'd do them again in a heartbeat because they were for us. I would do anything for my family—for you and Jake. I love you, Sidney. I've always loved you, and for so many reasons.'

'If I ever disappointed you, Mum, I'm sorry.'

'Oh, Sid, Sid, you don't disappoint me. You never could and you certainly never have.'

'When I was young, the way you would look at me ... I saw sadness in your eyes, Mum. Then I'd see—'

'Love,' Natalie interjected as Sid fought through another painful job in her belly. 'What you saw was my love for you. And when you and I are on the other side of this birth, we'll talk some more, and you'll understand. But let's wait till I have you both home and settled.'

Sid tried shaking her head. 'Home? With you? But, Mum, I, um—'

'Relax, darling. It's just to begin with, while you adapt to motherhood. When you're ready, we'll get you settled in a place of your own. And I promise to not interfere.'

'Well, that's lovely but I'm not rejecting your help, Mum. My hesitation was about Brushstrokes. After what happened there, I'm not sure I want—'

'Ha! There you go.' Natalie rammed both hands on her hips. 'We're already agreeing. When I was in Melbourne, Tasha talked me into selling up, even though I was already considering a move. She's since suggested a broker, and she's making it her personal mission to find a rental for me. Of course, I told Tash I have you and Little Bump to think about for now, so make it a three-bedder.'

'You did?'

'Yes, so maybe give some thought to where you might want to live. Tash is hoping I'll eventually move to Melbourne, but Melbourne is cold, as is the Blue Mountains in winter, and I'm getting too old for the cold.'

'Mum, where you live is up to you. Wherever that is, we'll happily stay for a while. But then Little Bump and I will need to find a home and, can you believe, I'm fast falling in love with the idea of life in the country, or by the beach.'

'You won't stay in the city?'

'Not if I can establish enough contacts. My work will let me live anywhere. Better here and working from home than a job in the city with Little Bump in childcare.'

'Here? As in Coffs Harbour?'

'Or Watercolour Cove. Why not?' Sid said. 'Jake won't be going anywhere fast. Little Bump and I can then visit Grandma in the big city. Other times, Grandma can come to us. It'll be like a holiday each time.'

'Stop with the Grandma thing. I sound like a little old lady.' Mother and daughter laughed until another pain sliced through Sidney. 'I'll get the nurse and something to help make you more comfortable. Then I'd better get back to the waiting room and fill Jake in on your progress.' Natalie made to leave, then stopped. She turned back and took her daughter's hand. 'Until you find your feet, I'll take care of you. We'll talk, and I'll even answer all those blasted questions you've got whirling around in your head as we speak.'

'How do you know what's in my head?'

Natalie stopped in the doorway long enough to say, 'Because I know you, Sid. I'm your mother and a mother knows everything.'

'Okay, then maybe you can tell me everything will be okay, because I think I'm about to have my baby—*right now*!'

52

PACIFIC COAST HOSPITAL, 2015

'You kids are certainly making sure I see plenty of this hospital.' Natalie fell into a waiting room chair.

'Can I get you something to drink, Mrs Hill?'

'Oh, Pearl, please. I'm sure I told you to call me Natalie. I'm feeling old enough.'

'Grandmothers *are* old,' Jake piped up.

'And Nanna Natalies are eternally youthful,' Pearl offered, casting Natalie a smile of solidarity. 'Name your poison.'

'A lemonade would be lovely.'

With Pearl now out of earshot, Jake asked, 'Do you like her, Mum?'

Natalie nodded. 'Very much.'

'Me too.' Her son grinned. 'So, how's Sid really doing? What was the problem?'

Jake's eager enquiry made Natalie smile. 'Your remarkable sister did a wonderful job in difficult circumstances. Part of the baby's placenta came away. They call it a placental abruption, and that caused the bleeding.'

'So, that's why they cut her open?'

Natalie nodded. 'With the placenta detached from the wall of the uterus, the risk of starving the baby of oxygen meant there was no choice but to deliver her by Caesarean. The Caesarean was best for both the baby and Sid. '

'Phew!' he sighed. 'Okay, so now *please, please, please* tell me the kid looks like Sid.'

'She does, Jake. She's beautiful and perfect. Sid was able to hold her briefly and bond. While she did, I counted all ten toes and fingers. The baby is fragile, coming far too soon, and your sister's rightfully scared, but she's determined.'

'She's Sid! What else would she be?' Jake joked. 'When can I see Little Bump?'

'Right now, *Grace* requires special care.'

'Grace?'

'Sid's named her after Grace Cossington Smith.'

Jake scrunched his face and scratched his head. 'Who? And tell me this Grace Cossing-whoever is not another long-lost relative, like our grandfather.'

'Grace Cossington Smith pioneered modernist painting in Australia. An extraordinary talent, she was instrumental in introducing Post-Impressionism to our country and—'

'Hey, whoa!' Jake interjected. 'Maybe stick to the need-to-know details, Mum. A yes or no would've been fine.'

'Will do from now on, Jake,' Natalie smiled. 'For now, your sister needs rest. With her team keeping a close eye on her, there's nothing we can do except get a good night's sleep ourselves and be back here bright and early. She'll need our support. How about you get the car, Jake? I want to let Sid know we're leaving.'

<hr>

'Sid, honey, are you awake?'

Her daughter looked so small and pale, her skin almost grey. There were tubes attached to drips and catheters, and monitors beeped relentlessly. Blood from bags dripped into her veins, and an intensive care nurse watched the monitors from the corner of the room.

'Grace?' Sid muttered through parched and pale lips.

Natalie stroked her daughter's forehead, wiping the hair away from her eyes. 'Your little girl is getting more beautiful by the minute.'

'Can I see her again?'

'In time, darling. The doctor has prescribed rest. A good night's sleep will see you and Grace stronger. You'll be needing all your strength.'

'I know, I know.' Sid was fighting to stay alert. 'I don't have a husband to help me.'

'No, but you do have me. And you have Jake—and the way that boy is headed, I think you're right about us having Pearl in our lives.'

Sid managed a small smile. 'Poor Pearl. I didn't warn her about Jake being the family clown.'

'Well, I dare say there's your godparent problem solved.'

Sid half-laughed, half-coughed—her pain palpable. 'If anything will force me to get well, it's seeing Jake change a baby nappy.'

'You, darling, are getting well for Grace. She needs you to get strong.'

'In the meantime, Mum, I have you to lean on. You're my problem solved.'

'Me? I think that is a discussion for another time.'

'No way,' Sid coughed again. 'You're not changing the subject. I need you to promise me you'll look after Grace if anything happens.'

'Nothing is going to happen, Sid. I could tell you the hardest part is over, but of course that's not true. And, my darling, you'll have the next eighteen, or more, years to say I was right. But if an answer now will help you rest easy, then of course I'll take care of Grace—and you, for as long as you need me. And I hope you need me for a very long time. Family is forever, and ours just got bigger by one.'

'Before you go, Mum. I wanted to ask. Am I doing the wrong thing by taking Damien at his word? I'm not interested in making us a family, but I can't help wondering if he was to see the baby, he might change his mind about his involvement in her life. Am I right to make that decision for him?'

'Believe me, darling Sidney, you'll be wrong and make mistakes during your lifetime. Look at me. I did.'

As weak as she was, her daughter's face managed to show her amusement. 'Never thought I'd hear those words from your lips.'

'Well, get used to hearing things that may surprise you.' Natalie collected her coat and bag from the chair, preparing to leave. 'For now, get some sleep.'

'I will, Mum, but I want to talk more than you know. I love you,' Sid whispered as Natalie leaned down and planted a kiss on her daughter's forehead.

'I love you, too, Sidney. Thank you for being my wonderful, wilful, sagacious daughter who doesn't take no for an answer. You have no idea what you and this trip with Jake has brought into my life—our life.'

Sid's sleepy eyes widened a tad. 'Seriously? You have to tell me.'

Natalie squeezed her daughter's hand. 'As soon as you're well enough, we'll talk. There are things I should've told you before. Now *sleep!*'

53

WATERCOLOUR COVE, 2015

Pearl had called by the villa earlier, bringing fish and chips for three, but the exhausted trio had hardly touched the food. Even Jake had seemed too preoccupied about his sister to bother eating. Natalie couldn't wait to see Sidney laughing when she heard *that*.

Now sitting in silence on the sofa beside her love-struck son, Natalie considered the effect Pearl was having on Jake. A delightful country girl, and clearly infatuated, she and Jake had not only taken ten minutes to say goodbye, but within minutes they were texting each other, Jake hunched over his phone and chuckling at her replies.

When the cabin's small brass bell jingled, Jake responded as if expecting to find Pearl on the other side.

'Ahh, g'day!' Her son sounded confused.

'On the mend, Jake? Sorry I haven't been down to check on your progress.'

'No worries, mate. I'm sweet, and back on deck whenever you want me. If you're here to see Pearl, you just missed her.'

'Yes, we caught up just now and she updated me on your sister. Your mum around?'

'I'm here, David. Sorry, I meant to call.' Natalie looked across at her son still holding the door and scratching his head, his confusion obvious. 'Jake, honey, perhaps you might take a walk?'

'Actually, Natalie,' David said, 'I was going to suggest you and I do the seawall.'

'Oh, okay. Let me grab my coat. Jake, if you hear anything at all, I have my phone.'

———

'So,' David began as soon as they were off the cabin's porch, 'Pearl says things were a bit touch and go.'

'Yes, but Sid's okay. She is strong and determined.'

David huffed a laugh. 'Then she clearly takes after her mother.'

'She's you!' Natalie smiled and slipped one arm through David's, while her free hand pulled her coat tighter. 'It's hard to believe I'm back here. The seawall's changed.'

'Hasn't everything?' David was quick to return. 'Tell me, Tilly, do you remember my lessons about the rule of reflection?'

'I recall you saying if an object leans to the left, its reflection will also lean to the left. You also said everything has a reflection, there's always another side to every story.'

'That's right, and I need to know the other side of *your* story, Tilly. Oh, sorry, I can't seem to stop using that name.'

Natalie waved off both the apology and his curiosity. 'I told you earlier I don't mind. I've missed Tilly. But so much has happened in my life. I'm not the young girl you remember.' Natalie slowed as if walking and talking were suddenly too taxing. 'And what's important is not the story of *my* life. There's someone else's story you need to hear and, David, I'm the only one left to tell it.'

'Is this about Matthew?'

'No. It's clear Matthew is not the man I thought I knew. He was a good father, but we were never a family. He and I were too different.'

'I know what you mean. He and I were brothers, but nothing alike. To him, I was a spoilt, pain-in-the-butt skiving off while he worked. Sure never thought he'd leave Greenhill.'

'David, there's so much you should know. Not about Matthew, but about your dad and Albie.'

It was David's turn to stop. 'And you can tell me, Tilly?'

'I can do better. I can show you. Right here. Right now.' *Before I change my mind,* she told herself while fishing the mobile phone from the pocket of her coat. 'But can we sit first? I fear another dizzy spell and I really need to be clear-headed for this.'

Natalie stopped at a park bench set between two light bollards and waited for David to position himself, although unsure whether sitting was even possible for her in such a heightened state of agitation. She instead rocked back and forth on her heels and wrapped her coat so firmly there was no choice but for the truth to squeeze out of her.

'Albie left two letters behind,' she announced. 'Please, bear with me if I skip some detail for now. I need to get this out in one go.'

'And I need you to sit before you fall. Come on.' David patted the wooden planks beside him until Natalie submitted. 'Two letters, you said?'

'Yes. One was a brief *To Anyone Who Cares* type note, which I gave to the police. The other one Albie wrote to me. I guess he hoped I'd find it—and him. Both notes were—'

'*You* found him, Tilly?'

She starred into the bright light of the nearby bollard, hoping to burn away the image. Then, breathing in deep, she nodded 'Yes. I'll never forget the moment I realised it was him and … To think he'd been so troubled right there, in my house.' Natalie shivered, not from the cold but from the memory, and aware she had contributed to his despair. 'We make choices, and I've done things I'm not proud of, David. Running off with Matthew was wrong, and denying Rose a grandchild was selfish. But Sid is not me. She doesn't take after me. That girl's done nothing wrong by anyone.'

'You've raised a strong and independent woman. Take pride in that achievement.'

'I do. But I'll be more proud when I can fix things. I started the other night by telling her the truth about my mother, and I felt better having admitted to everything aloud. I can only hope telling Sidney the whole truth—about everything that followed at Greenhill—will strengthen our connection. The thought of losing her, the thought of not having either of my children in my life, would I fear …' Natalie scoffed, berating herself for such insensitivity. 'Oh, David, I know that sounds hypocritical. I've kept you from knowing your daughter. But what I did to Rose by taking her son away was …'

'Hey, hey, shhh,' David soothed. 'Some things won't be undone. They just are, Tilly. We overcome and find ways around the grief and the disappointment. And we recover so we don't ruin good tomorrows thinking about bad yesterdays. We move on and start over with a fresh canvas.'

'Or,' Natalie added, 'we try to fix the fixable when the opportunity arises. And that time is now.' As she opened her phone to show him the scanned letter, a bitter wind gust whipped hair in front of her eyes. She fumbled, almost dropping the phone. 'Impossible damn things!'

'Take a breath,' David said, draping one arm across her shoulders. 'What's got you so rattled?'

'The thought that I might lose the people I love the most. But I can't keep what Albie wrote in his confession to myself. In fact, as we speak, a lawyer is checking the contents. In particular, Albie's explanation of the bus accident. My hope is the letter will go towards clearing your dad's name.'

Initially stunned, David seemed to deflate in front of her eyes. 'Albie confessed in a letter? He *was* in the car, like Dad had said all along? And you have proof of this?'

'I promise all will soon be clear, David. I wanted you to read the note for yourself.' Natalie's fingers enlarged the PDF document to show only the confession part. Then, handing him the phone, she hoped David didn't scroll down and read the rest of the letter. If he *did* try, she wondered if she'd stop him. It was one thing to share Albie's admission, but was Natalie prepared for the consequences of full disclosure, including the disappointment on David's face? 'Read this bit here.' She pointed at the screen.

The crash, all the little kids on the bus ... It was me. I didn't plan, and I didn't think. I only remember wanting to die. And taking Ted Hill with me would hurt David and his mother. So I grabbed the wheel and drove us into that bus. I realised I was still alive when I heard children screaming for help.

'There's your proof,' Till told him, her hand outstretched to retrieve the phone. 'Albie caused the crash.'

David made no move to give the device back, instead staring vaguely into the dark. 'What else does Albie admit to in the letter? Remorse for ruining my life? Does he apologise for breaking my mother's heart?' The vitriol in David's words shut Natalie down. What she had feared was unfolding. She was hurting people with the truth.

'David, I won't stop you reading the rest. You deserve to know everything. But I'm terrified of what you'll think of me if you do. Can't we start over without looking back at those bad yesterdays?'

David looked from Natalie to the phone in his hand and back to Natalie again. 'We're too old and we've been through too much to be keeping secrets.'

As shame fell over Natalie like a fog, she stood and walked towards the seawall, the winter wind ineffective on a body numb with regret. Shivering while staring into the blackness, she roused warming recollections of Grace—and then Sidney. Her wonderful, wise, wilful and infuriatingly loveable daughter had done so much more than bring a new life into the world. Sidney had brought Natalie back, and now she was bringing closure for David, regardless of the personal consequences.

'It's the right thing,' she whispered into the wind after glancing back to see David's expression, illuminated by the phone screen, a mix of puzzlement and pain as he scrolled.

As David's hand squeezed her shoulder from behind, Natalie steeled herself, closed her eyes, drew breath, and waited to be berated.

'Thank you,' he said in her ear. 'Please, take your phone back. I slipped it in my coat pocket—the left one.'

Too ashamed to look him in the eye, she simply said, 'I'll understand if you want to leave.'

'I will go, but not before you look at me.' He waited for her to turn around but, unlike their daughter, Natalie was not brave enough to look him in the eye. 'Almost,' he said. 'But Tilly, there's something *you now* need to know about *me*. When I say words like *look at me*, you actually need to look—*at me*. I can do a lot, despite these blasted sticks, but some things are inherently difficult,' he explained. 'Especially and most frustratingly, those romantic things like pressing my finger to your chin to lift your face to mine. No. Can. Do. Similarly, reaching out and pulling you into me is likely to see us both hit the deck. Oh, and running over the sand towards each other—in slow motion, or at any other speed—is just not going to happen with me. Not while I have these things.' He jiggled the crutches he relied on most times. 'So, work with me, Tilly. When I say I need you to look at me, please take me at my word and look up.'

She appreciated the attempted humour and, even though she acquiesced to the request, the pair still stood like adversaries.

'I'm sorry,' she cried. 'I was too young to realise the repercussions of that one mistake would last a lifetime. Despite agreeing with Matthew to never look back, I mourned you and never forgot you, David. I've made the worst mistakes and hurt people who loved me, but when I say I'm sorry, I mean it more than you know.'

David stepped back, putting distance between them, his voice tiring. 'It's been too many years and we're too old for sorries.'

'That may be, but it's not too late to have your father's records reflect the facts. Please, hear me out. And if you never want to see me again, I'll understand.' Knowing a happy ever after for her was unlikely, for once this wasn't about her happiness. This truth was for David.

'Okay, then come back to the seat,' David said. 'I prefer to sit.' Following him, she sat while he leaned both crutches to one side, lowering himself. 'I appreciate your intentions, Tilly, but I've never needed proof Dad was telling the truth. And there's this to consider,' he added. 'Earlier, you hesitated at the thought of me reading the full content of Albie's letter. Should you go on and use this confession to clear Dad's name, can you imagine how you'll feel when the entire letter goes on public record? I appreciate the sentiment, but the truth will make no difference to Ted or to my memories. The letter might, however, impact the relationship you have with your children. I don't want that.'

'David, for once in my life, I'm not putting my needs first. As of now, Ted is a great-grandfather. And one day his great-grandchild will want to know about her heritage. I'm going to document my mother's story because I want the truth to be part of who we are as a family. I've already told Sidney everything—the bad and the ugly. Albie taught me the importance of saying what needs to be said, and that it's never too late to tell your side of the story. We must make this right for our grandchild, David. *I* must get this right. Sharing Albie's letter with you will help clear my conscience, but then Sid will have my absolute attention. I want her and Grace back home and in familiar surroundings. I want them to feel loved and protected. Most of all I want them to know about us. That's assuming you don't mind me telling her.'

'That I'm her father, you mean?'

'And how I never stopped loving you.'

After thirty-five years of denying her feelings, she'd finally spoken those words aloud. But any relief was short-lived when David's body tensed and edged away. But rather than distancing himself, as she'd first thought, the move allowed David to stretch an arm across her shoulders. Then he pulled her body into him and kissed her head. But rather than warm and comfort her, a chill rattled Natalie.

'I don't recall it ever snow in Dinghy Bay, but it's got suddenly very cold.' She *was* cold, freezing in fact, her head reeling as she fell—in love with David again, and with her life. 'David? Tomorrow, after visiting Grace, I'm going to sit with Sidney. Then slowly and carefully, I'll tell my daughter—*our* daughter—the truth. Will you be there with me?'

'Let anyone try to stop me from being there with you, Tilly.'

54

―――――

PACIFIC COAST HOSPITAL, 2015

An alarm pinged, startling Sid fully awake, although she struggled to understand the noise, or even where she was. Within seconds she saw the kind eyes and comforting smile of a nurse she recognised. The nurse's face hovered over Sid's in the semi-darkness, her lips moving.

Is she speaking to me? Sid caught only the low drone of indecipherable words, playing like a talking doll with dying batteries.

Something was wrong.

Sid was cold and wet—colder still when the nurse yanked away the bedsheet, letting it flap flag-like.

Truce, Mum? Sid asked as the linen, stained blood red, billowed like a parachute before fluttering down to settle over her body.

Good! She let her eyes close. *I'll feel warm again soon.*

55

PACIFIC COAST HOSPITAL, 2015

Forty-eight hours ago, her daughter had accused Natalie of being cold and hard. And while standing with her back to the waiting room, watching her grieving son in the window's reflection, she almost fitted the description. When the waiting room door opened, she watched David's reflection close in behind her.

'You're here.' That cold, hard exterior disintegrated and she collapsed against him to sob, almost knocking him over. 'We lost her, David. Sidney's gone.'

'Pearl messaged me,' he told her. 'What went wrong?'

'Postpartum haemorrhage. She started bleeding in the night. They couldn't stop it, and they couldn't replace the blood fast enough. She went into haemorrhagic shock. She's gone. Sid's gone.'

Too numb with her own disbelief and grief, Natalie hadn't noticed Pearl arrive. But there she was, cradling Jake's head in her lap, stroking his hair and wiping his face like he was a baby, and like Natalie had done when the boy had screamed uncontrollably for weeks after losing his father. Natalie had been lost for what to do or say back then, too. Whatever Pearl whispered in Jake's ear made him look up and attempt a smile. He kissed her on the mouth, then she kissed him on both cheeks, his forehead and his lips again, lifting his face, nudging his body, coercing him out of the chair and shoving a wad of tissues into his hand. She smiled brokenly in Natalie's direction and led Jake outside just as a nurse came forward.

'I'm sorry to interrupt. I have jewellery belonging to Sidney.' The nurse extended her hand containing a beige envelope. 'I'm so sorry for your loss. Let me know if there's anything else I can do for you, Mrs Hill. Of course, when you want, I can take you to see Sidney. She's ready.'

Natalie wanted to scream.

Ready for what? Motherhood? A long life? The truth?

'Perhaps give us a minute,' David said, taking the envelope.

The nurse nodded, her eyes moist. 'I'm at the end of the hall,' she told them. 'I can take you from there.'

'Do you want me to come with you, Tilly?' David asked.

Natalie couldn't speak. She couldn't move or shake her head. She couldn't feel anything at all.

'You *do* want to see her,' he whispered. 'Believe me, you do.'

'A mother should not have to say goodbye to her child like this, David, and lifeless is not how I want to remember my spirited daughter. She can't hear me or see me? What will she know?'

'Saying goodbye is for you, Tilly.'

'That's the thing. Goodbye is hard. I couldn't even say goodbye to you.'

'So you ran.'

'Yes, and if I'd run when I was five years old, I wouldn't have sat beside my dead mother for three days pleading with her to wake up. Three days, David. You can't imagine how awful and how confusing that was for a child. That ordeal, the feelings of helplessness and desperation, has never left me. Then, finding Albie ...' Natalie's head shook a silent denial. 'Why can't I remember Sidney the way she was before—sassy, spirited, strong, smiling?'

'Because one day you'll wish you had said goodbye,' David said without hesitation. 'Come on. I'll take you. We can say goodbye to our daughter together.'

David held Natalie as she sobbed through the sad and silent farewell. He held her, without speaking, just a hand stroking her head, and eventually calming her. And he'd been right. Seeing her beautiful daughter, saying a last goodbye, had brought Natalie sense of serenity.

'If that was my daughter lying there I don't think I could bring myself to walk out of this room,' Natalie said. 'But that's not her. Sidney is in here, always.' She clamped both hands over her heart. 'Thank you for making me, David, but I think I'm ready to go now.'

Once in the corridor, Natalie dabbed her face dry, took David's elbow to guide him, and said, 'Speaking of sassy, spirited and strong ... You need to meet someone.'

Looking in on little Grace, her body so tiny that the web of wires and tubes keeping her alive seemed enormous, it seemed incomprehensible that something so fragile would survive when someone strong, like Sidney, had not.

'Perfect, isn't she, David?'

'She's a fighter.'

'Oh, I hope so. I want her to be.'

When the nurse subtly suggested it was time they left the neonatal ward, Natalie and David walked in perfect unison, stopping outside the hospital's foyer, where Natalie took out her phone.

'Are you calling Jake?'

'No, I'm looking for Sid's old work number. I have it somewhere.'

'Why?' David sounded surprised.

'To tell Damien, of course.'

'But why would you, Tilly?'

Just as shocked, Natalie replied, 'The man is Grace's father. Sid would want him to know.'

'That's not the way I heard it,' David said. 'Sid told me he'd refused to be listed as the father on the birth certificate.'

'Cross words said in anger,' she suggested. 'Sid loved Damien and, yes, he broke her heart, but who's to know what he said and what she heard? For all we know he's had time to reflect and he's wishing he'd handled things differently. Regret is something I understand. He needs a chance to speak for himself. Cutting Damien out is something the old Natalie might have done, David, but you of all people should see how a wrong choice can last a lifetime and destroy lives. I accepted without question what Matthew told me about you not waking from your coma, and his lie kept you from your daughter. I won't keep another father from knowing his child. I'll let Damien choose.'

'But, Tilly, do you understand what might happen if he changes his mind and wants the baby? Don't use Sidney's life to correct your mistakes. If you're going to ignore her wishes, at least wait a few days.'

'David, I think I know my daughter better than you do.' Her words, like a slap, could not be taken back. David may have even flinched a little.

'Please understand, if I don't do it now, I *will* change my mind. All my life I've made decisions that were right for me, and damn anybody else. That changes today. Now, I'd like to make the call in private.'

'Fine! I'll leave you to do what you must.' He leaned in to kiss her forehead. 'There's a vending machine inside. I'll get us some cold water.'

'Well?' David asked, returning with both track pant pockets bulging. He took a bottle of water from the left-side and handed it to Natalie before leading her to a brick wall where they sat under the giant shade sail covering the hospital's forecourt. 'You got through to Damien?'

'I did,' Natalie said. 'First, he wanted to let me know he'd had to step out of a meeting to take the call. Can you believe that? Then he said he knew she'd gone to hospital, because Sid had called Kath and Bill.' Natalie removed the screw-top lid, hoping the water would remove the bitter taste left after her communication with Damien. 'I didn't know until recently that Sid remained close to his parents. She was apparently the daughter they never had. I'd best make them my next call.'

'I can understand how they might have connected. Sidney is easy to love.' David smiled. 'Tell me what else Damien said.'

'First, he said he was sorry. Then he said he'd *text* me later.' Natalie almost spat water. '*Text* me? And what was he sorry for? Having to rush back into his precious business meeting? Why, why didn't I listen to you? And how is that you know Sidney better than I do?'

'Because ...' This smile was bittersweet. 'She's my daughter.'

56

THE BLUE MOUNTAINS, 2015

Unlike her devil-may-care departure decades earlier, saying goodbye to Greenhill and Watercolour Cove on this occasion had meant leaving behind everyone Natalie loved, including baby Grace, still under the care of the hospital's neonatal team. But Brushstrokes in the Bush would not pack and sell itself, and she needed to make a new home—a life for two. So much had changed—including Natalie. Her daughter was gone and her son no longer needed his mother's hugs to get him through the tough times.

Loss and grief might tear some families apart, but the fortunate ones bond, stronger than ever, and Natalie was very fortunate and grateful. The many trips back and forth between Coffs Harbour and the Blue Mountains, many with Jake sitting cocky behind the wheel of his sister's Jeep, had been another eye-opener. For hours, she'd happily listened to her son's ramblings, hearing about his ambitions, passions, and dreams. Where had Natalie been? Her baby boy was all grown up. He'd mellowed, matured, and become more responsible. He had Pearl, and she was making him do his own laundry.

In the weeks following Sid's farewell, mother and son had also cried together, laughed long and loudly, and found courage in each other—that combined strength getting them through the funeral. David attended,

Tasha and Marcus too, while Bill and Kath packed the motorhome and travelled from Casino to Coffs Harbour. They arrived without their son, which was a good thing, given Natalie might have rammed Damien's phone where it hurt for the promised text message the creep never did send. Not a single communication. Nothing. Only after the funeral did Natalie write a long and carefully scripted letter to his parents, thanking them for loving Sidney, but also slipping in subtle hints about their son's lack of interest in the baby. She may have used the words *financial abandonment* and mentioned Damien was yet to divide whatever joint assets Sid was entitled to after seven years of living together and supporting Damien's business venture.

Kath and Bill were wonderful, hands-on grandparents and Natalie welcomed their support and input. While the older couple shared Natalie's grief over Sid, and to some extent her anger over Damien's behaviour, Bill and Kath were loving parents who would eventually forgive their son for his transgressions. Natalie understood. To accept and forgive is sometimes the only way forward because it's simply unbearable to go on without having that person in your life. But the couple would always be grandparents to Grace, and Natalie let them know they were always welcome in her life.

Another good decision had been allowing Tash and Jake to organise the funeral service, agreeing with Natalie that Sid would not want a fuss, nor the tragic come-back-and-cry-over-sandwiches tradition. As for where to lay Sid to rest … That call was, in Jake's words, a no-brainer. Sidney had talked often about the strong sense of connection she felt to Watercolour Cove, and to the people there. If only she'd come to understand why. A few more weeks, a few days, even a few more hours, and Natalie could have explained.

If only you'd lived long enough for me to tell you the truth.

'Our girl only loved long enough to be disappointed in me,' Natalie had said as she and David shed tears over the small brass plaque marking a life taken too soon. 'I don't want to make the same mistake with Grace—or with Jake.'

'You won't,' David had reassured her.

But Jake was changing. Her carousing son had settled down and secured full-time work for the first time in his life. With a nudge from Pearl, he'd applied for some sort of road worker apprenticeship. A construction company, contracted to improve the Pacific Highway, was offering regional people two-years paid work. The arrangement would also earn him study credits towards a certificate at TAFE, and a pathway into road engineering.

'I never knew you wanted to take after your father,' Natalie had said recently. 'As a toddler, it was all about owning your own fishing boat.'

'Yeah, but that was only so I didn't have some boss telling me what to do,' he replied. 'Much rather be cooking fish than catching it. A little café of my own is the ultimate dream—one day.'

Natalie tried her best not to look surprised. She should have known that about her son. Or was Sid right and Natalie had been too busy dragging the children through *her* dreams to notice their changing aspirations?

'You're an excellent cook. I've sure missed my Monday night seafood treat. Are you sure about this road work job?'

'For now,' he replied. 'Pearl and I agree that when life throws you curve balls, you duck and change direction—and dreams. Improvise, adapt, overcome is what I said to Sid when she'd needed a pep talk.'

'You gave your sister a pep talk?'

'We talked heaps during our time at Greenhill. She said if I was serious about owning a café, I'd better start saving. You and Dad helped each other and he started on a road crew. Dad did all right, too. You and he made sure us kids got a good start to life. The rest is up to me. I'm done skiving off. Time to knuckle down, as Dad would say.'

Bravo! Natalie wanted to shout. She knew Jake had it in him. Some people simply took longer to realise their true potential.

'I'm not afraid of hard work, Mum, and my café dream isn't going away. I'm letting it simmer.'

Her son fell quiet—something Natalie had been getting used to since telling Jake that David was his father's brother.

'So, an uncle, eh?' he'd said in his usual Jake style. 'Well, flip me a fishcake! Reckon Sid would have approved. She and David really connected. He's a pretty cool dude.'

'I'm glad you think so.' Natalie smiled.

David had agreed there was no reason to hide that fact from her son, but he'd also insisted people in general didn't need to know the whole truth. With Sid gone, the small but significant fact that David was her birth father could stay out of the public records.

'Out of *public* records—yes.' Natalie had reluctantly concurred with David over the telephone one night—one of many calls each week. 'Tasha's husband has seen to that the best he can. But I won't keep the truth from family. One day a curious, sagacious young woman called Grace might dig around the family tree and ask lots of questions.'

'She will if she takes after her mother,' David had countered affectionately.

'It would be wrong not to make things right,' Natalie had said. 'You once accused me of using Sidney's life to correct my mistakes. I agree my actions hurt many people, and I've learned the hardest lesson. I never wanted to delve into my family's past, mostly because I was ashamed of my roots, but life is no longer just about me. Times have changed. I have Grace to think about, and Grace needs to know everything. She needs to know who she is so she can make her own life choices. Hopefully, the right ones.'

On that score, Natalie had continued to hound Damien regarding the birth registration. Sid deliberately chose the words *Father Unknown* for the hospital admission paperwork, but Natalie had wanted to do right by Kath and Bill, who doted on Grace. With all Damien's reply texts shared, saved, and filed, and with Bill and Kath's blessings, Natalie finally applied for adoption. While Grace's birth certificate did not name a father, it saddened Natalie to see a young man refusing to acknowledge his daughter, and a son estranging himself from parents because they refused to stay out of Grace's life.

As the weeks and months passed, Natalie found reasons to smile again. She visited Grace at the hospital every day, chatted with David over the phone and a coffee and an occasional meal, ticked another thing off her to-do list, and silently cheered the changes in her son.

'Sidney, you'd be so proud of your brother,' Natalie told the stars each night. For the first time in her life, she hoped heaven existed. Her daughter would be there and asking a lot of questions. 'And, my darling girl, when Grace grows up and starts asking more questions, she will learn the truth from me.'

But that was the future. First, Natalie had to rid herself of the past.

The following January, when the gardens at Brushstrokes looked their finest, good old Tash flew up from Melbourne to help Natalie prepare the

B & B for auction day, which was just as well as Natalie had her hands full with Grace.

Since bringing her granddaughter home, and because Brushstrokes had too many bad memories, she'd moved what she needed into the smaller *Dharug House* for a fresh start. Selling the B & B and most things in situ, bar Natalie's most precious belongings and her artworks, was an unusual sales challenge. Thankfully, Tash knew of a real estate stylist and a business broker who, together, would ensure the best price at auction. Although the business was no longer a going concern, according to the broker, a shrewd buyer would see beyond the B & B's grim history, recognise the potential for income and the walk-in-walk-out inclusions, and snap up both properties well before auction night. Natalie just had to say goodbye to Brushstrokes in the Bush—her dream. But she'd never been without a dream that wasn't totally doable and in her control. She'd discovered the hard way how to make a home and to be a wife and mother while nurturing her love of art to provide an income.

'I've let go of so much, Tash,' Natalie said as her friend poured champagne into two glasses. 'Grace's love is the tether I'm happy to have. I just hope I do right by her.'

'Come on, pull it together, sweetie. Focus on the To-do list we put together. There are decisions to be made. "Buck up", I believe is the line you'd give the kids.'

'I don't have it in me to smile right now, Tash. Ask me tomorrow.'

'I understand, but sweetie, you've just brokered a deal on the B & B well over your expectations. That's Grace's future right there in all those zeros.' Tash plonked her butt on the kitchen seat opposite, tossed one end of the scarf over a shoulder and raised her glass. 'An extra ninety thousand dollars on top of your reserve price is not bad. The broker just needs your go-ahead. Then you can set yourself up anywhere. Maybe even open another gallery. In the meantime, my home in Melbourne is there for you both.'

'Grace and I will be fine. I actually have my eye on a small flat in Leura. We'll call that home for now. What's in your hand?' Natalie asked her friend who, at the first sign of a hot flush had peeled her lightweight over-shirt off her shoulders and plucked an envelope from the pocket to fan her face.

'Oh, this? I forgot. It was in the mailbox. Take it.'

Natalie ripped at the paper envelope. 'I recognised the handwriting. Oh, my!'

'What?' Tash asked.

'It's from Damien's mother, Kath. They're setting up a trust fund for Grace with the proceeds of his Melbourne apartment and the share portfolio he and Sidney had together.'

'Seriously? Let me see.' Tasha leaned in, dropped her half-glasses from her head to her nose and tugged at Natalie's hand holding the letter. 'Kath says they'll be in touch. And they send hugs to little Grace.'

As if on cue, a tiny squawk sounded from the baby monitor on the kitchen counter.

'Oh, let me,' Tash said. 'I need to get my cuteness fill before I fly home next week—assuming you haven't changed your mind in the last five minutes. I'm coming Gracie!'

Natalie stayed put, staring at the contract documents strewn across the same kitchen table where she and Sid had argued about recycling habits, wired ribbon, and Damien. Sid had wanted her partner to be accepted and liked, and with no paternity claim, Natalie kind of did. Grace would be raised by family who loved her, just as Sidney had wanted, telling her mother on the night her waters broke.

There was something else Sidney had said that night, and it required a trip to Watercolour Cove, and soon. Natalie didn't mind the drive. She looked forward to going back each time, especially her catch up with Jake. She wanted to see him happy, and to know the girl who had won her son's heart.

That's what parents do.

57

WATERCOLOUR COVE, 2015

Jake had offered to collect Natalie from the Coffs Harbour Airport, but she preferred the seven-hour drive. Just her, the highway, and Little Bump safe and snug in her brand-new, top-of-the-line safety capsule. But more than alone time, Natalie could rehearse what she needed to say to David. So many lives changed last winter because Sid wanted to know her estranged grandfather and tell him about his son. The mission exposed so many secrets and lies, and now, after six months with Grace in her care, Natalie was going to right another wrong and tell another truth.

But at the bottom of the mountain, Natalie did not pass through the Greenhill gates.

Tilly did, while making a pact with herself to unashamedly embrace her past and never forget.

Tilly was starting over.

She had a baby to love.

Her name was Grace.

'Hi-ya!' Pearl waved and called as she walked from the main house towards Tilly and her car. 'If you're looking for Jake, he's at work. A roster change has him onsite for seven days straight this week. Then he'll be home to cook a special Jake dinner.'

'Music to my ears.' Tilly smiled, returning Pearl's huge, warm hug. 'But today I'm looking for—'

'Me, I hope. Thanks, Pearl,' David said. 'You can head off. I'll head across and lock up the gallery.'

'Cool. Catch-ya both later.'

'She used to hang around a lot,' David said while delivering a welcome kiss to Tilly's cheek. 'But ever since Jake moved into her place at the beach, I can't keep her up here much at all. That's young love, I guess. Let me get Grace and I'll make tea for two. Would you like tea?'

'Maybe water,' she replied, watching anxiously as he struggled to manoeuvre the car capsule through the back door.

Keen to help—to take charge—Tilly refrained. One thing baby Grace had already taught her was how to ask for and accept help when it was staring her in the face. And he was—staring—waiting for her to tackle the one-clip-wonder pram that was meant to turn the safety capsule into a pusher with one quick flick of the wrist. Cursing under her breath, Tilly hoped to master the manoeuvre *before* Grace outgrew the overly complicated contraption.

'Let me drive,' David said after single-handedly snapping the capsule into place and laying one crutch horizontally across the pram's fold-out sunshade.

His progress back to the house was slow, but Tilly didn't mind. She could watch the two of them gooing and grinning together all day.

Having navigated the well-worn accessibility ramp, he and the pram stopped in the shade where David shooed the inquisitive Pablo away. 'Are you sure you don't want tea?'

'Only water,' she replied, smiling. 'But let me get it and the tea. You can rest here with Grace.'

'Don't,' David snapped. 'I don't need people doing things for me, especially you, Tilly. I'm sorry if that sounds bloody-minded, but I've looked after myself for a long time.'

'And you shouldn't have been alone. For that, and so much more, I'm sorry.'

'I thought we agreed to stop apologising. What happened is in the past and I've fetched and fixed all manner of things for years. But I admit, I would never have known how strong or how determined I could be if I hadn't spent months staring at my reflection in that mirror suspended over my hospital bed. I'll ask if I need help.'

As David made to leave, Tilly said, 'Let me explain. I wasn't trying to take over or ...' She dropped into the closest seat, exhausted in every way.

'This isn't how I planned today. Please, give me time to adjust. Every trip to this place comes with a memory and ... David, it's only been six months and I'm trying not to make more mistakes.'

For a while, neither spoke, instead staring down at a gurgling baby Grace who squealed excitedly when a Magpie landed on the veranda railing.

'How about we all go inside and get those drinks?'

'You've made changes in here,' Tilly noted. What had previously presented as a museum more than a home, with its accumulation of furniture and artworks from three generations—was now light-filled and less cluttered, making pram pushing easier, too.

'The place as it was hardly suited inquisitive little visitors, and this one will be walking in no time. But by putting my house in order I'm also getting on with the dream. Our dream, Tilly. Your Brushstrokes inspired me.'

'You're creating an artist's retreat?'

'Over the years, Mum and I made a couple of attempts, but my heart wasn't in it and then Mum was gone. But I figured with you having sold Brushstrokes, I might cash in on your clientele.'

'Ha!' Tilly scoffed. 'Half my clientele didn't pay, which Sidney was forever harking on about. Your mum had a good head for business, Little Bump. Oh, yes she did,' Tilly cooed.

'It's no wonder Damien's business got such a good start, with Sidney to do all the work,' David added. 'I see he's floated the company now. That can only be a good thing for Grace's future. Speaking of Grace ... I'm happy to see her—and you, of course, and anytime. I'm actually happier than I ever expected to be at this stage in my life. I might not have any family left, but you've helped me understand my brother, and by sharing the truth about Dad's crash, you've provided closure.'

'I'm glad, David, but you *do* have family. You have a granddaughter, and you can be as much a part of her life as you wish.'

'You have no idea how much I want that, Tills. I was going to ask about visiting Sydney more regularly. Have you found somewhere you like?'

'Tasha found me a place near her in Melbourne. She wants me for another start-up gallery.'

'Melbourne?' David said, dolefully. 'So, you came here to say goodbye?'

'I told her no. The city is too exhausting. When Grace is older, maybe.

For now, our rental in Leura is perfect. There's a lovely sense of small town in that community, which I know Sid wanted for Grace.'

'Have you considered this town? You can't get more small-town community than Watercolour Cove. Jake's settled in and you're now driving back and forth so often. Let me finish,' he said, a hand causing Tilly to hold on to her excuses. 'You left Greenhill once because you wanted the city lifestyle. You had a dream, Tilly. I get that. But you don't want the city anymore, and I need a business partner who knows how to get this artist-retreat idea off the ground.'

'I'd be thrilled to help, David, and happy to invest once the house sale and other financial matters are sorted and—'

'I don't need your money,' David interjected. 'If you're looking for a good investment, talk to your son about renovating the Hill-family shack on the cove. He and Pearl have been dreaming about turning it into a café. Dad always planned for Matthew to have it as part of his inheritance, and Jake is his son. Besides,' David shrugged, 'he and Pearl are already arguing over a name. Pearl likes *The Watercolour Café*. Jake, of course, is keen on *Flippin' Fishcakes*.' Tilly and David both laughed. 'You should see Pearl swanning around, planning a grand opening, and deciding who they'll invite. Reminds me a little of someone I used to know.'

'Pearl's a lot smarter than me. And I never swanned, David.'

'You *so* did.'

There was no holding back Tilly's grin, something that happened a lot these days despite an underlying sadness she couldn't shake and didn't want to—not yet.

A buzzer sounded. 'That's a gallery customer,' David said. 'Make yourself at home, make tea, drink water. I won't be long.'

With Grace sleeping, Tilly wandered into the adjoining lounge room, straightening the crooked frames and the sculptures sitting skew-whiff on antique sideboards and shelves. So much of Rose remained, but so much potential. Already, her mind was decorating the numerous bedrooms she passed. At the furthest door was a sign written in black felt pen on paper.

No Entry! Naturally, Tilly opened the door.

'Oh, my!' She slumped onto the only uncluttered chair to survey the stockpile of painting and drawings.

'It seems Hill women have a habit of ignoring directives.' David's smile was fleeting, as though remembering something sad. 'You know, I saw her for the first time sitting right there on that very chair you're in. And she looked very much like you now. At home!'

'What are all these drawing about?' Tilly asked, keen to deflect rather than dwell on her daughter's hands having rested on the same studded leather arms.

'Most are works of a man wallowing in self-pity and clinging to what was. Unable to chuck them away, I instead locked them away. At least I thought the door was locked.' He smiled small at her. 'Sid was the first to let me know it wasn't. I'll have to get someone to check the damn thing actually locks.'

'Or perhaps, David, the room is sending you a message that it's time you cleaned up and prepared for what will be. Our Grace will soon need a big-girl room, and with the shutters open ...' To prove her point, Tilly adjusted the louvres on all three windows and flung open the adjacent French doors. 'There's a gorgeous view. Rather than a locksmith, how about you get a landscaper to build a small courtyard right outside here? A safe enclosure for Grace to enjoy. I'd worry about her getting too close to the plantation.'

David had joined Tilly at the window. 'I like the sound of that, and having you come and stay every now and then.'

'Of course! Grace will want to visit her Poppy. In fact ...' She turned her ear to the door. 'I can hear her agreeing—or it's a wet nappy. And a nappy change waits for no man.'

After attending to Grace—both of them together—all three were settled on the veranda and enjoying the late afternoon bird activity, when Tilly asked, 'How do you know a retreat idea will work this time?'

'Easy answer,' he said. 'In the past, I didn't have a business partner who knew the ropes.'

'So, what you actually want is my business acumen?'

'For starters,' he said with a wink. 'I also want Grace to feel like Green-hill is home. After all, one day it will hers to do with whatever she wants.'

Tilly sighed, choosing her words carefully. 'Dear David, if life has taught me anything, it's to decide slowly and choose wisely. With Grace my number-one priority, and growing fast, I plan to savour every moment and respond to her every need. But come winter, when she's turned one, I'll know more—about what's best for me but, more impor-tantly, what's best for Grace. How about I promise to have an answer for you by spring?'

58

GREENHILL—FOUR YEARS LATER

'Hip, hip, hooray, hooray!' Jake chanted. 'Little Bump is *how* old today?'

'You know I'm *five*, Uncle Jakey.' Grace squealed as her uncle swung her in dizzying circles, around and around. '*Weeeeee!* More! More! More!'

'Maybe later, Gracie,' Pearl said, intercepting mid-swing to set her feet on the ground. 'Uncle Jakey looks like he needs to throw up.'

'Uncle Jakey also needs to get into the kitchen and prepare the you-know-what,' Tilly instructed. 'You'll find five candles in the top drawer.'

'What's a you-know-what, Nan Tilly?'

Nan Tilly! She smiled, remembering baby Grace's struggle to get her mouth around *Nanna Natalie*.

'Why does Uncle Jakey always wear those funny pants with all the little black and white squares when he's cooking? And where is Poppy? And—'

'Grace, Grace, all those questions! You're sounding more like your mother every day, young lady. Shall we all go to *Salty Morsels Café* for dinner tonight?'

'Yaaaay!' Grace cheered after spying David. 'Poppy! We're eating dinner at Uncle Jake's place.' As the girl ran, arms reaching out for a hug, Tilly was close behind, ready to intervene, as always. It wouldn't be the first time a cuddle toppled poor Poppy. 'If you sit at a outside table I can play on the beach.'

'Gentle, sweetheart. You know we must be careful not to knock poor Pops off his feet.'

'Stop fussing, woman. I'm knocked off my feet every morning I wake and realise what a fortunate man I am.' David tapped Grace on the nose. 'If not for your mum and all her questions I may never have found you. Or you,' he added in a whisper while kissing Tilly on the cheek.

'And if not for Gracie, I would never have come home to Greenhill.'

'Hey, Miss Five,' Pearl appeared on the veranda, a bright yellow gift bag swinging from her index finger. 'You missed a present. The card reads *To Grace from Nan Tilly.*'

'I was saving that gift until later, but bring it over, Pearl. We'll do it now.'

Grace met Pearl halfway, jumping and grabbing for the small parcel just out of her reach. And again, Tilly was close by.

'Come, sit on my lap and we'll unwrap it together. Start here,' she suggested as chubby fingers frantically fought for purchase on the paper. 'This belonged to your mum. I gave it to her when she turned twenty-one.'

'But I'm only five.'

'I know. We'll help you keep it safe.'

The family crowded around as the final bit of wrapping fell away from the artwork depicting two towering ghost gums and an early-morning sun casting shadow and reflection over a tranquil river.

Grace pointed at the signature she'd seen many times. Only last week her granddaughter had impressed her playgroup friends by signing her finger painting, like her Nan Tilly always did. 'Did you paint it, Nan Tilly?'

'Yes. A very, very long time ago. Your clever Poppy taught me about the importance of perception, and one day, Nan Tilly and Poppy will explain to you all about the rule of reflection. But for now, let's eat cake.'

'A *swuggle* first,' Gracie said.

'Did someone say *swuggle?*' David hooked his arm around Grace, lifting her off Tilly's lap with ease. 'Hold on tight around my neck. Ready?'

'*Swuggle!*' they squealed in unison.

The combination swing, hug and cuddle was her Pop's party trick, and while it came at considerable physical effort, David loved every second.

'Look at me, Nan Tilly,' Grace called between squeals. 'Spin me. Spin me.'

'No spinning,' Tilly told her granddaughter. 'Poppy's yet to master spinning manoeuvres.'

'Maybe by that twenty-first birthday, sweetheart,' David joked.

With both feet back on the ground, Grace looked up at David, her eyes sparkling. 'What's a man-u-vahs, Poppy? When's my twenty-first?'

'Hey, enough with the curious cat act.'

'What's a curious cat act?'

Jake came to the rescue, snatching his niece into the air. 'Hey, Little Bump, Uncle Jakey can spin you *alllllllllll* the way inside while Pearl hangs your birthday painting on the wall in your room. Come on, squirt. Then Pearl and me will hit the frog and toad and head to the café.'

'What's a frog and toad, Uncle Jakey? What's a squirt?'

'Oh, David,' Tilly leaned into him as she watched the trio go. 'All those questions and more will one day require answers.'

Smiling, the pair sat in silence, listening to the tapping sound of a hammer hitting a picture hook into the wall of her granddaughter's room, and hearing Gracie's constant quizzing.

But, as always, there comes a time when the sadness of every celebration hit home, and the what-ifs always hit Tilly hard in the heart.

'I can wish every second of every day that our Sid was here, and that we all got our happy ever after. But I've known since running out on you that day that I'd never deserve one. Was losing Sid my punishment? I wonder sometimes. If so, did the lesson need to be so cruel on Grace? I know *if-onlys* are a wasted thought, but … If only it wasn't Sidney, and it didn't hurt so much.'

'You're not a bad person,' David said.

'I was—once. But to survive, I had to be. Thankfully, Grace is giving me a second chance. I get to raise another child. I get to be a better mother. I'll do everything right this time.'

'And I'll be right here watching and supporting you.'

'There'll be no more secrets, David, that's for sure. Grace will know who she is and where she came from. And she'll know about me, too. No more hiding. I won't feel shame for what I did to survive a rough start or to raise my family. Everything I did, I did for the children because I didn't know any other way. I had to keep them safe and give them the best life possible. There's no pill, no potion, and no process to turn back time. But I know for certain that when the time's right, our Grace *will* know the other side of the story.'

Winter was never Tilly's favourite season on the mountain—three months of drab days, bitter winds, uninspiring skies, and a lacklustre sea. While her melancholy made the season more bleak, Tilly wallowed in the warmth of her family's love and their winter traditions, like little Grace's birthday party and Pearl's late-night picnic every solstice—now an annual culinary event at *Salty Morsels Café*.

Tilly had a winter tradition of her own, which she met with mixed emotions each year by waiting until they were on the other side of the season, when the spring blooms that speckled the lawn cemetery with perfumed colour could gentle the unbearable heartbreak she endured every day. Never once, in five years, had the first day of spring let Tilly down, providing sunny skies to thaw her winter-weary bones, and balmy breezes to stir the scent of freshly mown lawn and uplift her spirits.

Today was no exception and, as always, Tilly held on tight—often a little too tight—to her granddaughter's hand as they negotiated the gravel path the pair knew well. In her other hand, she held a basket of flowers.

'Now, Nan Tilly?' Grace asked, waiting for the nod of approval before racing ahead, always first to reach her mother's memorial plaque.

Tilly somehow managed a brave face while placing her own flower selection next to Gracie's. Then, sitting together on the grass, Tilly would tell Grace a Sidney story.

Today, and as always, she tugged a tearful Grace away, telling her, 'It's time for Grandma and Grandpa Hill's flowers. Here you go.' Tilly took two more small bunches from the basket—jonquils and freesia stems that now grew wild on the mountain.

Once standing at the headstones for her great-grandparents, Ted and Rose, Grace—having inherited Sidney's inquisitive nature—would insist on another story. Anticipating lots of questions each year, Tilly had readied herself with a repository of truth to share bit by bit.

'One more, Nan Tilly.' Grace reached into the basket for the flowers specially picked and always kept till last.

As more tears threatened, Tilly kept herself in check, relinquishing the last floral arrangement. It's not that she didn't cry in front of her grand-daughter—Tilly had shed many a sad and happy tear—but by reining in the profound misery she felt each winter, Tilly hoped Grace would grow up to appreciate missing someone is not all sadness, but a celebration of life and love and family.

'Uncle Albie is our family, too.'

'Yes, he is family, sweetheart. He was a good person who needed love.'

The night Albie died, he'd penned two goodbye notes. As her lawyer friend had suggested it would, the confession he'd addressed to Tilly did prompt the overturning of Edward Hill's conviction. But the other note— addressed *To Anyone Who Cares*—plagued Tilly. Three short sentences over three lines:

I am Alessandro Albertini.
I am from Malta.
I have no family.

While Tilly had thought she'd locked the memory of that misty Blue Mountains morning in an impenetrable vault, sealed forever, Sid's funeral had jimmied the door wide open and raised questions. What happened to Albie's body after he was taken away? Had the people left him in a cold and dark morgue somewhere, waiting to be buried? Albie had hated the cold and the dark.

Tilly had to know and, if possible, set things right.

Tasha's husband quickly ascertained that Albie's remains, once approved for release by the coroner's office years before, had been handed over to the funeral home contracted by the state to conduct burials for persons with no next of kin. They'd written:

Further to your request for information regarding the state-funded funeral and cremated remains of the late: Unclaimed Male, Date of Death 01/06/2015. They will remain in the ashes room of the state-contracted funeral firm of Starlight Funerals, to be scattered after twelve months if unclaimed, as per policy.

'Policy?' Tilly had repeated to Marcus over the phone. 'Unclaimed?'

'Unlike *unknowns*, who are unidentified, *unclaimed* means there is no known next of kin. The funeral home will keep the ashes for one year. After this time, if not collected, the policy document requires ashes to be scattered within the gardens of the funeral home. I'm afraid that's what happens with state-funded funerals.'

Just like that! A human boxed, a life obliterated, a future scattered—all because a government policy stated:

We provide only a properly made, conventionally shaped and suitably lined coffin. No headstone, no service, no extras.

The policy disallowed anything that attracted additional fees, such as church services, funeral notices, a coffin of choice. The policy might as well have stated:

Definitely no kindness from strangers. We cater only to the wealthy and the privileged. The paupers, the impoverished, the unloved and the forgotten are unimportant.

———

And so, the Coffs Harbour funeral home received a request. They were to arrange a dignified, bells-and-whistles service at the small Watercolour Cove Lawn Cemetery for a Mr Alessandro Albertini from Malta.

There were to be lots of flowers and a headstone that read:

By three methods we may learn wisdom:
First, by reflection, which is noblest.
Second, by imitation, which is easiest.
Third, by experience, which is the most bitter.
Alessandro Albertini ~ Born 1958 ~ Died 2015
Much-loved son of Constance and brother to Tilly.
Forever friend, forever family.

MORE FULL-LENGTH FICTION

HOUSE FOR ALL SEASONS

A Calingarry Crossing novel (& 2013 #5 bestselling debut novel).

Four women, four lives unravelled. The truth will bind them forever.

Bequeathed a century-old house, four estranged friends return to their hometown, Calingarry Crossing, where each must stay for a season at the Dandelion House to fulfil the wishes of their benefactor, Gypsy. But coming home to the country stirs shameful memories of the past for all four, including the tragic end-of-school muck-up-day accident twenty years earlier.

Sara—a breast cancer survivor afraid to fall in love;

Poppy—an ambitious journo still craving her father's approval;

Amber—spoilt and addicted to pills and cosmetic procedures;

Caitlin—a doctor frustrated by her flat-lining life.

At Dandelion House, the women will discover something about themselves as well as a secret tying all four to each other and to the house forever.

For more info: **books2read.com/House-For-All-Seasons**

(First published by Simon & Schuster, *House for all Seasons* is the 1st Calingarry Crossing novel)

SIMMERING SEASON

(The 2nd Calingarry Crossing novel)

A country hotel, an unexpected house guest, and a school reunion. Maggie's perfect storm is about to lift the lid off a lifetime of secrets.

Dan Ireland, a work-weary police crash investigator still hell-bent on punishing himself for his misspent youth, has ample reason for not going home to Calingarry Crossing for the school reunion, but one very good reason why he should—Maggie Lindeman.

Maggie is back in Calingarry Crossing trying to sell the family pub, while also dealing with a restless seventeen-year-old son, a father with dementia, a fame-obsessed musician husband back in the city, and a dwindling bank account.

The last thing she needs is a surprise house guest for the summer.

Fiona Bailey-Blair, daughter of an old friend and spoilt with everything but the truth, whips up a maelstrom of gossip when she blows into town in search of answers.

This storm season, as Maggie's past and present converge with the unexpected, she'll discover … *there's no keeping a lid on some secrets.*

(First published by Simon & Schuster, *Simmering Season* is the 2nd Calingarry Crossing novel)

For more info: **books2read.com/Simmering-Season**

Also available in audio with bonus song track: Aurora/Ulverscroft

HOUSE OF WISHES

(The 3rd and final Calingarry Crossing novel)

Three wishes, three mothers, three generations:

Dandelion House is ready to reveal its secrets.

Dandelion House, 1974

Two teenage girls—strangers—make a pact to keep a secret.

Calingarry Crossing, 2014

For forty years, Beth and her mum have been everything to each other, but Beth is blindsided when her mother dies, and her last wish is to have her ashes spread in a small-town cemetery.

On the outskirts of Calingarry Crossing, when Beth comes across a place called Dandelion House Retreat, her first thought is how appealing the name sounds. With her stage career waning, and struggling to see a future without her mum, her marriage, and her child, she hopes it's a place where she can begin to heal.

After meeting Tom, a local cattleman, Beth is intrigued by his stories of the cursed, century-old river house and its reclusive owner, Gypsy. The more Beth learns, however, the more she questions her mother's wishes.

When meeting Beth leads Tom to uncover a disturbing connection to the old house, he must decide if the truth will help a grieving daughter or hurt her more.

Or should Dandelion House keep its last, long-held secret?

For more info: **books2read.com/House-of-wishes**

Also available in audio: Download or ask your library.

SEASON OF SHADOW AND LIGHT

Sometime this season … the secret keeper must tell, the betrayed must trust, the hurt must heal.

When it seems everything Paige trusts is beginning to betray her, she leaves her husband at home and sets off on a road trip with six-year-old Matilda and Nana Alice in tow.

Stranded amid rising floodwaters, on a detour taking them to the tiny town of Coolabah Tree Gully, Paige discovers the greatest betrayal of all happened there twenty years earlier.

Someone knows that truth can wash away the darkest shadows, but …

…are some secrets best kept for the sake of others?

A PLACE TO REMEMBER

A portrait, an obsession, a curious daughter, and an affair to remember.

Running away for the second time in her life, twenty-seven-year-old Ava believes the cook's job at a country B&B is perfect until she meets the owner's son, John Tate. The young fifth-generation grazier is a beguiling blend of both man and boy, and a terrible flirt. With their connection immediate and intense, they begin a clandestine affair right under the noses of John's formidable parents.

Thirty years later, Ava returns to Candlebark Creek with Tina, a daughter determined to meet her mother's lost love for herself. While struggling to find her own place in the world, Tina discovers an urban myth about a love-struck man, a forgotten engagement ring, and a dinner reservation back in the eighties. Now she must decide if revealing the truth will hurt more than it heals.

For more info: **books2read.com/APlaceToRemember**

Also available in audio: Download or ask your library.

THE TIDES THAT LIE

The tide was the perfect accomplice.

The tide lied.

On her sixteenth birthday, Layla Scott uncovered an unimaginably cruel secret, and over the years tried too many times to stop the hurt. Now her sister is in the last place Layla wants to be, remembering someone Layla wants to forget, and dangerously close to the painful truth.

Loss, grief and guilt have kept Chelsea clinging to her childhood home, alienating her husband and kids. She's now alone in the house nobody wants to live in but her and surrounded by memories of a beloved father the sea swept away three decades earlier. Chelsea hopes to confront her past trauma by returning to Sandbar Campground, but her fears only intensify when her estranged sister shows up.

Can Layla, along with local surfing fanatic, Thaddeus Poulle, help Chelsea see she's holding too tight to all the wrong things and …

… the sea always gives up its secrets.

For more information: **https://books2read.com/The-Tides-That-Lie**

Also available in audio: Download or ask your library.

PRAISE FOR JENN'S NOVELS

Click through to more reviews on Goodreads
House for all Seasons (Calingarry Crossing Collection)

"The author has created a living, breathing small town, peopled with wonderful people - an amazing achievement."

— GREG BARRON, AUTHOR

"Captivating."

— WOMEN'S WEEKLY, MARCH 2013

Simmering Season (Calingarry Crossing Collection)

"A tangled wed of loyalties, guilt, and secrets. A great read."

— NEWCASTLE HERALD

Season of Shadow and Light

"McLeod delivers a story packed with pathos, Aussie wit and a great sense of place… an irresistible tale."

— ROWENA HOLLOWAY, AUTHOR

The Other Side of the Season

"Jenn's writing is evocative, gorgeously descriptive and transports you to the places she writes about."

— MICHELLE, BEAUTY & LACE BOOK CLUB

A Place to Remember

"I read 'The Thorn Birds' about forty years ago and still remember it. Similarly, I think the emotion and poignancy of this story will stay with me too."

— JANE HUNT (UK)

House of Wishes (Calingarry Crossing Collection - final)

"...a clever story. I was shocked as the truths emerged - absolutely did not see them coming. Absolute page turner. And TEARS! OMG!

Kathryn Ledson, Author

ABOUT THE AUTHOR
AND OTHER JENN J. MCLEOD TITLES

Five times published with Simon & Schuster and the UK's Head of Zeus, *House for all Seasons* (a companion story to House of Wishes) was 2013's **#5 top-selling debut fiction novel**. In her home on wheels, a purple and white caravan she calls Myrtle the Turtle, Australia's nomadic novelist is slowly ticking things off her bucket list while exploring rural landscapes and finding inspiration for more contemporary stories about friendship and family—all with a backdrop of country life. (Marie Miller image)

JENN'S OTHER TITLES

House for all Seasons
Simmering Season
Season of Shadow and Light
The Other Side of the Season
A Place to Remember
House of Wishes
The Tides That Lie
All eBooks or visit www.jennjmcleod.com